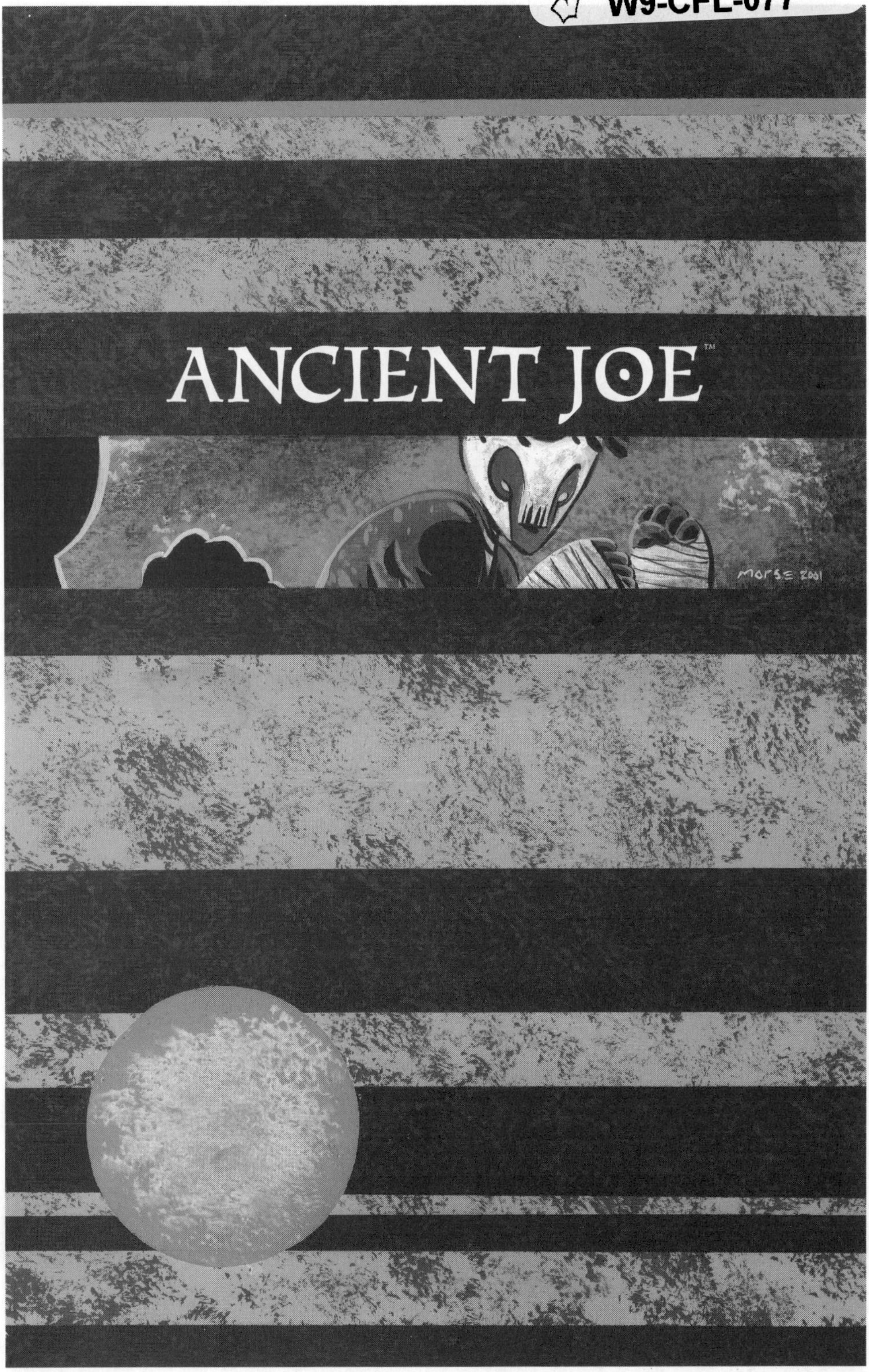
ANCIENT JOE™
morse 2001

Editor *DIANA SCHUTZ*

Designers *C. SCOTT MORSE & CARY GRAZZINI*

Publisher *MIKE RICHARDSON*

ANCIENT JOE: el bizarron

Text and illustrations © 1998, 2000, 2001, 2002 C. Scott Morse. All other
material, unless otherwise specified, © 2002 Dark Horse Comics, Inc. Ancient
Joe and all other prominently featured characters are trademarks of C. Scott
Morse. All rights reserved. No portion of this publication may be reproduced
or transmitted, in any form or by any means, without the express written
permission of the copyright holders. Names, characters, places, and incidents
featured in this publication either are the product of the author's imagination
or are used fictitiously. Any resemblance to actual persons (living or dead),
events, institutions, or locales, without satiric intent, is coincidental. Dark
Horse Maverick is a trademark of Dark Horse Comics, Inc. Dark Horse
Comics® and the Dark Horse logo are trademarks of Dark Horse Comics,
Inc., registered in various categories and countries. All rights reserved.

Published by
Dark Horse Comics, Inc.
10956 SE Main Street
Milwaukie, Oregon 97222

First edition: August 2002
ISBN 1-56971-795-8

1 3 5 7 9 10 8 6 4 2
Printed in Canada

This volume collects the Ancient Joe story from the comic book *Loud Cannoli*,
published by Crazyfish, issues 1-3 of the Dark Horse comic-book
series *Ancient Joe*, and the Ancient Joe stories published by Dark Horse in
*Scatterbrain*, *Dark Horse Maverick 2000*, and *Dark Horse Extra*.

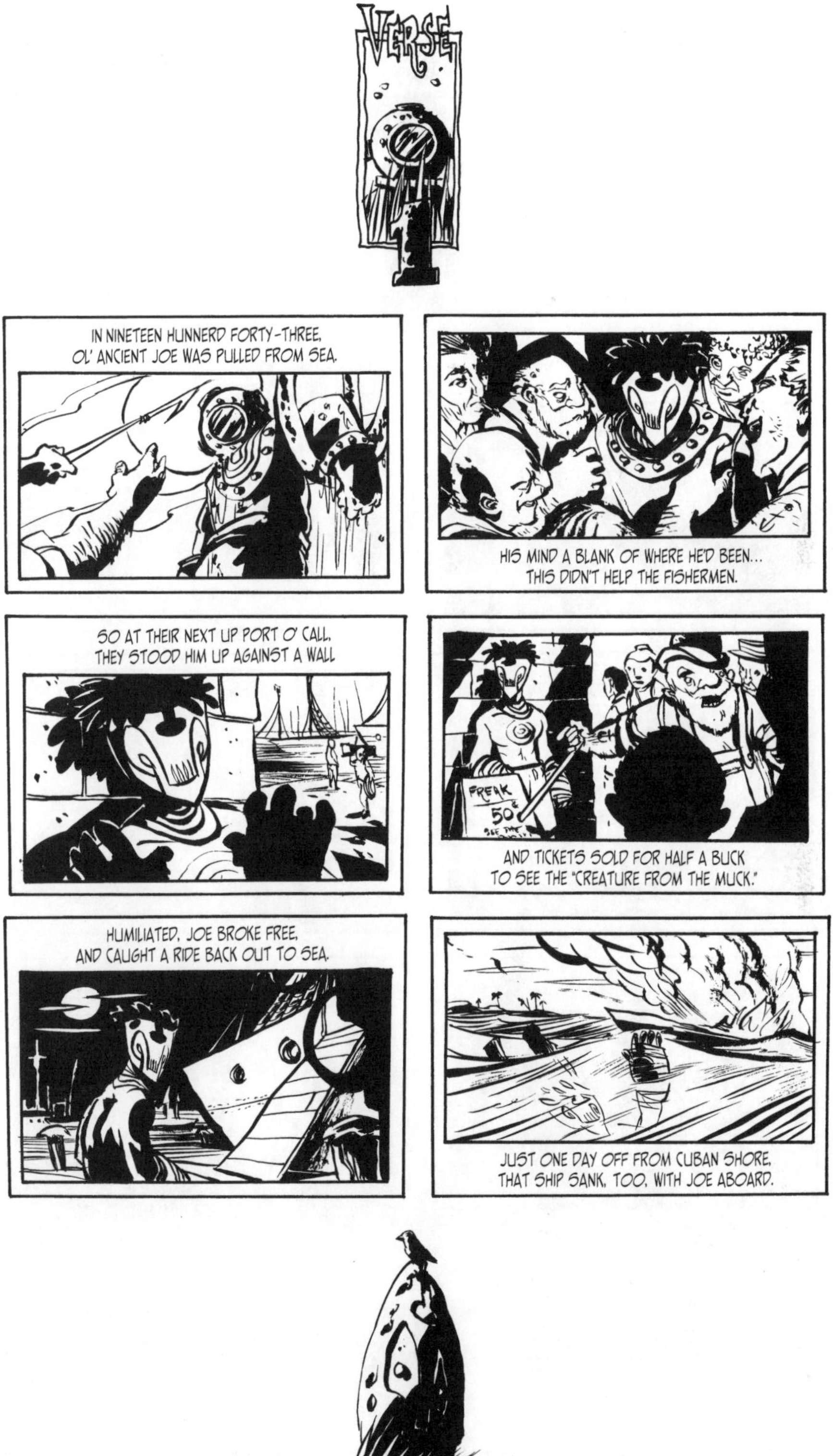
VERSE 1
IN NINETEEN HUNNERD FORTY-THREE,
OL' ANCIENT JOE WAS PULLED FROM SEA.
HIS MIND A BLANK OF WHERE HE'D BEEN...
THIS DIDN'T HELP THE FISHERMEN.
SO AT THEIR NEXT UP PORT O' CALL,
THEY STOOD HIM UP AGAINST A WALL
FREAK
50¢
AND TICKETS SOLD FOR HALF A BUCK
TO SEE THE "CREATURE FROM THE MUCK."
HUMILIATED, JOE BROKE FREE,
AND CAUGHT A RIDE BACK OUT TO SEA.
JUST ONE DAY OFF FROM CUBAN SHORE,
THAT SHIP SANK, TOO, WITH JOE ABOARD.

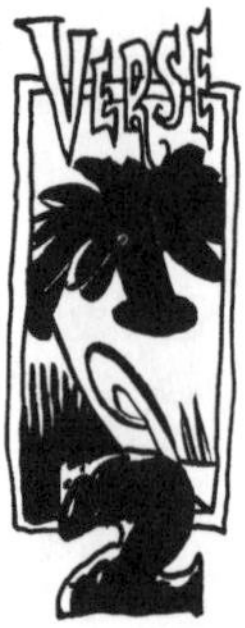
VERSE

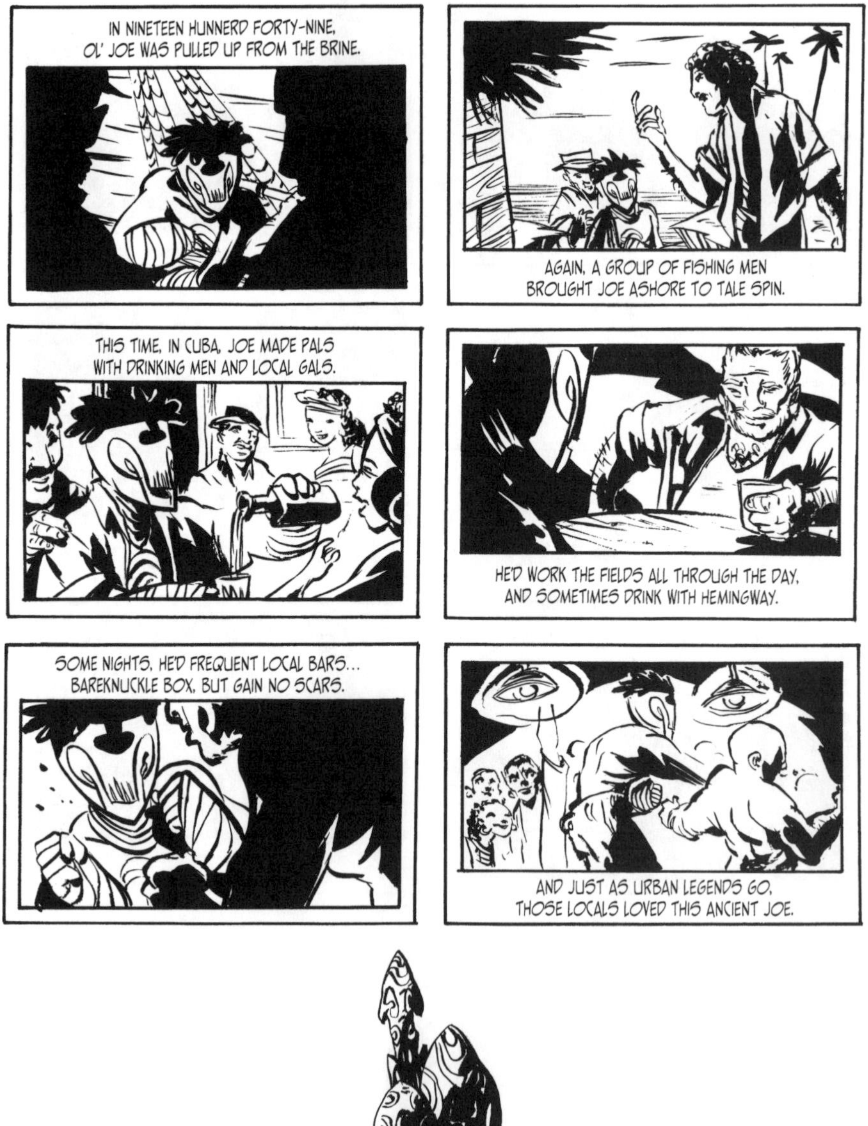
IN NINETEEN HUNNERD FORTY-NINE,
OL' JOE WAS PULLED UP FROM THE BRINE.
AGAIN, A GROUP OF FISHING MEN
BROUGHT JOE ASHORE TO TALE SPIN.
THIS TIME, IN CUBA, JOE MADE PALS
WITH DRINKING MEN AND LOCAL GALS.
HE'D WORK THE FIELDS ALL THROUGH THE DAY,
AND SOMETIMES DRINK WITH HEMINGWAY.
SOME NIGHTS, HE'D FREQUENT LOCAL BARS...
BAREKNUCKLE BOX, BUT GAIN NO SCARS.
AND JUST AS URBAN LEGENDS GO,
THOSE LOCALS LOVED THIS ANCIENT JOE.

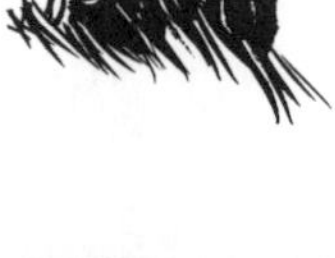

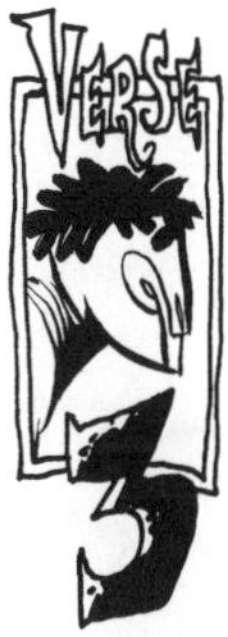
VERSE
3

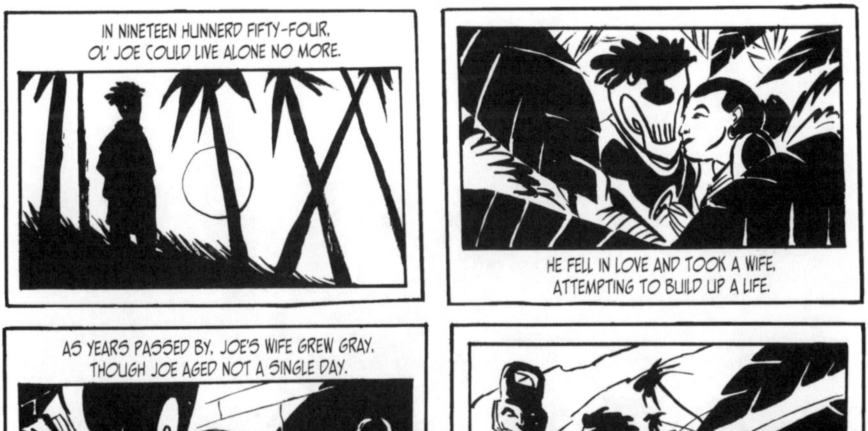
IN NINETEEN HUNNERD FIFTY-FOUR,
OL' JOE COULD LIVE ALONE NO MORE.
HE FELL IN LOVE AND TOOK A WIFE,
ATTEMPTING TO BUILD UP A LIFE.
AS YEARS PASSED BY, JOE'S WIFE GREW GRAY,
THOUGH JOE AGED NOT A SINGLE DAY.
SO ANCIENT JOE OUTLIVED HIS WIFE,
AS LEGEND GREW AROUND HIS LIFE.
HIS LOCAL FRIENDS JUST SMILE AND NOD
WHEN ASKED IF ANCIENT JOE'S A GOD.
A GOD? MYTH? MAN? OH, WHO CAN KNOW?
WELL, NOT A SOUL BUT ANCIENT JOE...

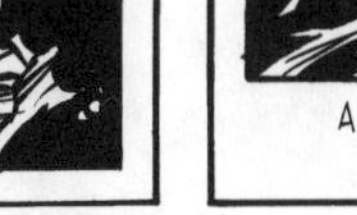

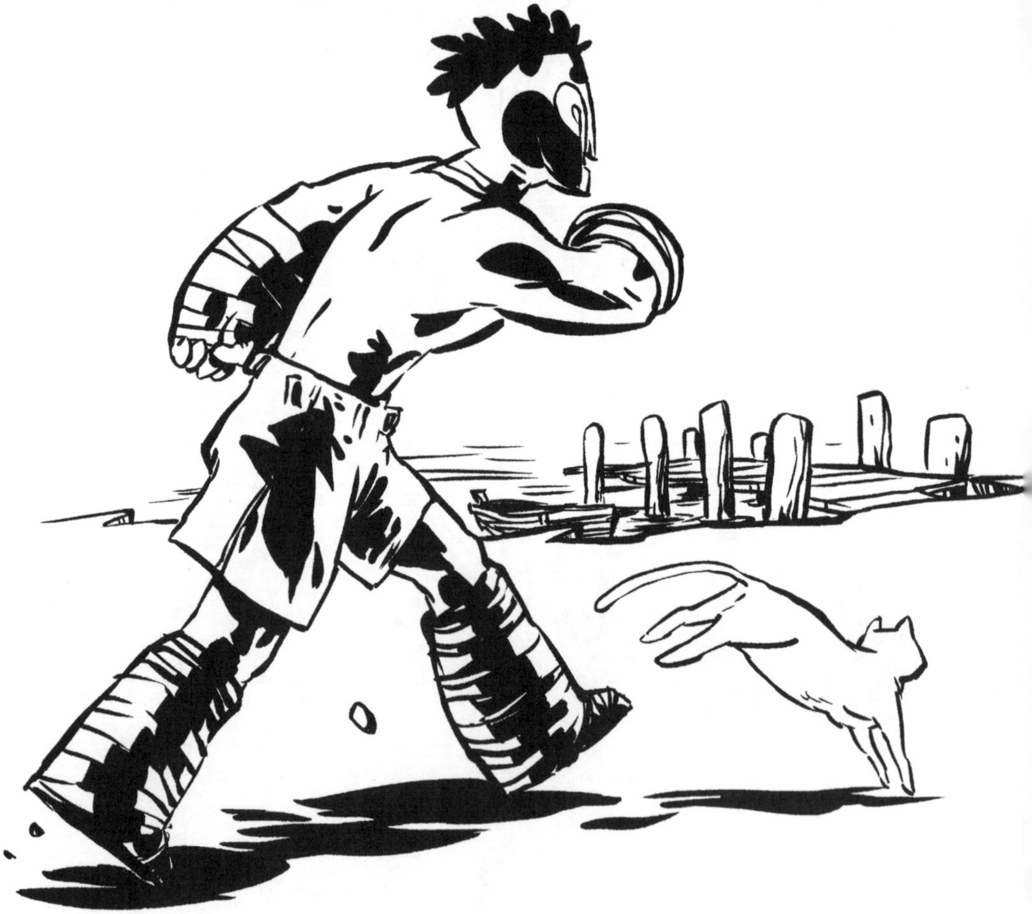

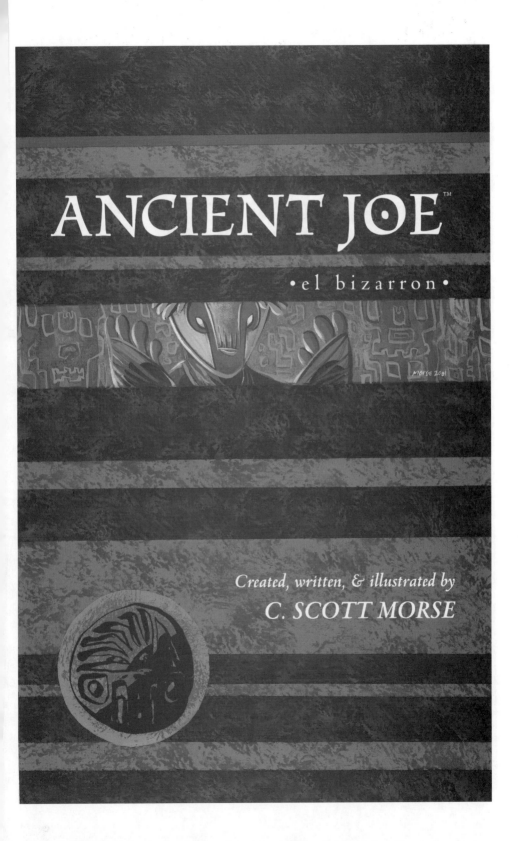

# ANCIENT JOE™

## •el bizarron•

Created, written, & illustrated by
## C. SCOTT MORSE

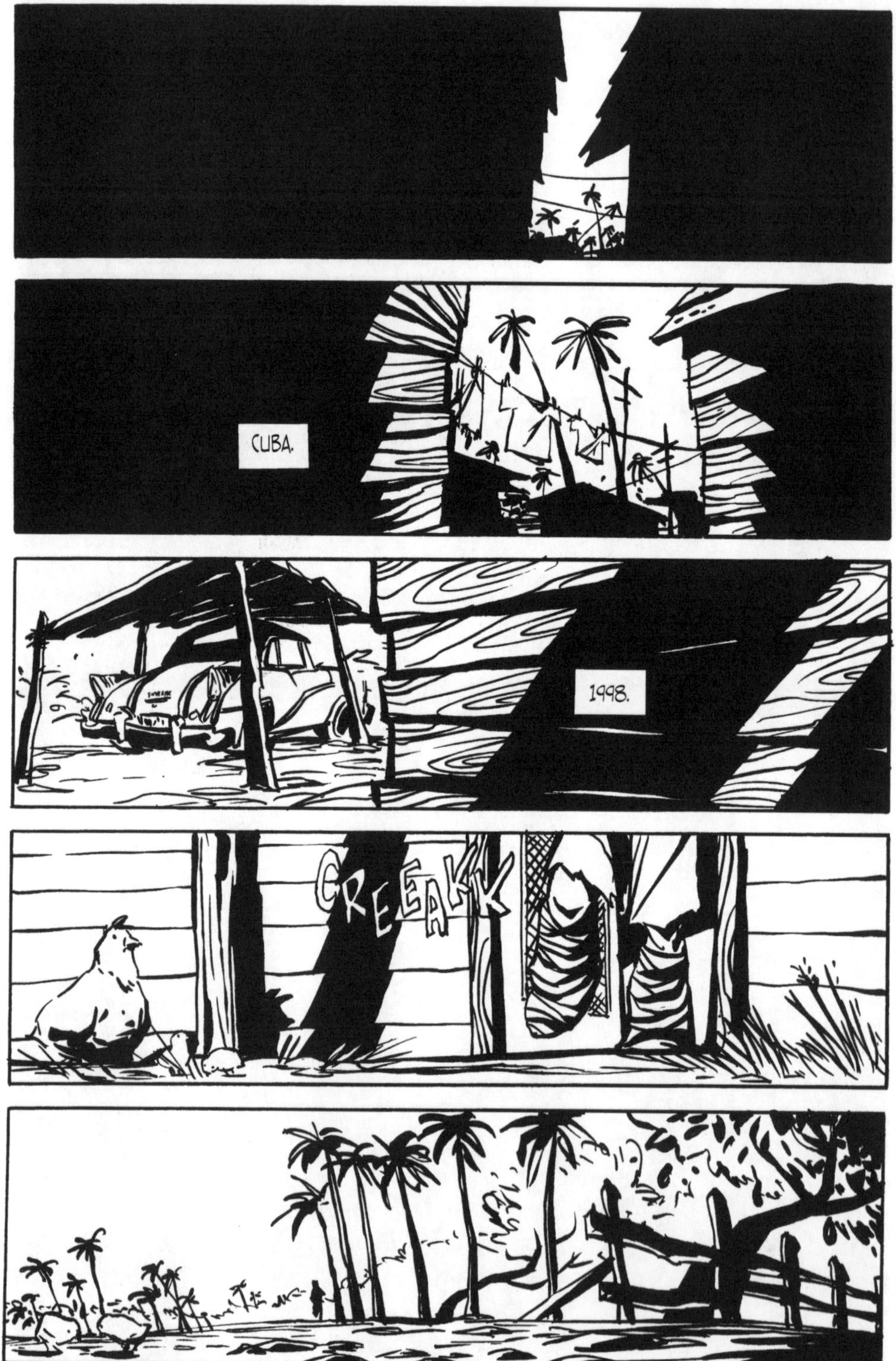
CUBA.
1998.
CREEAKK

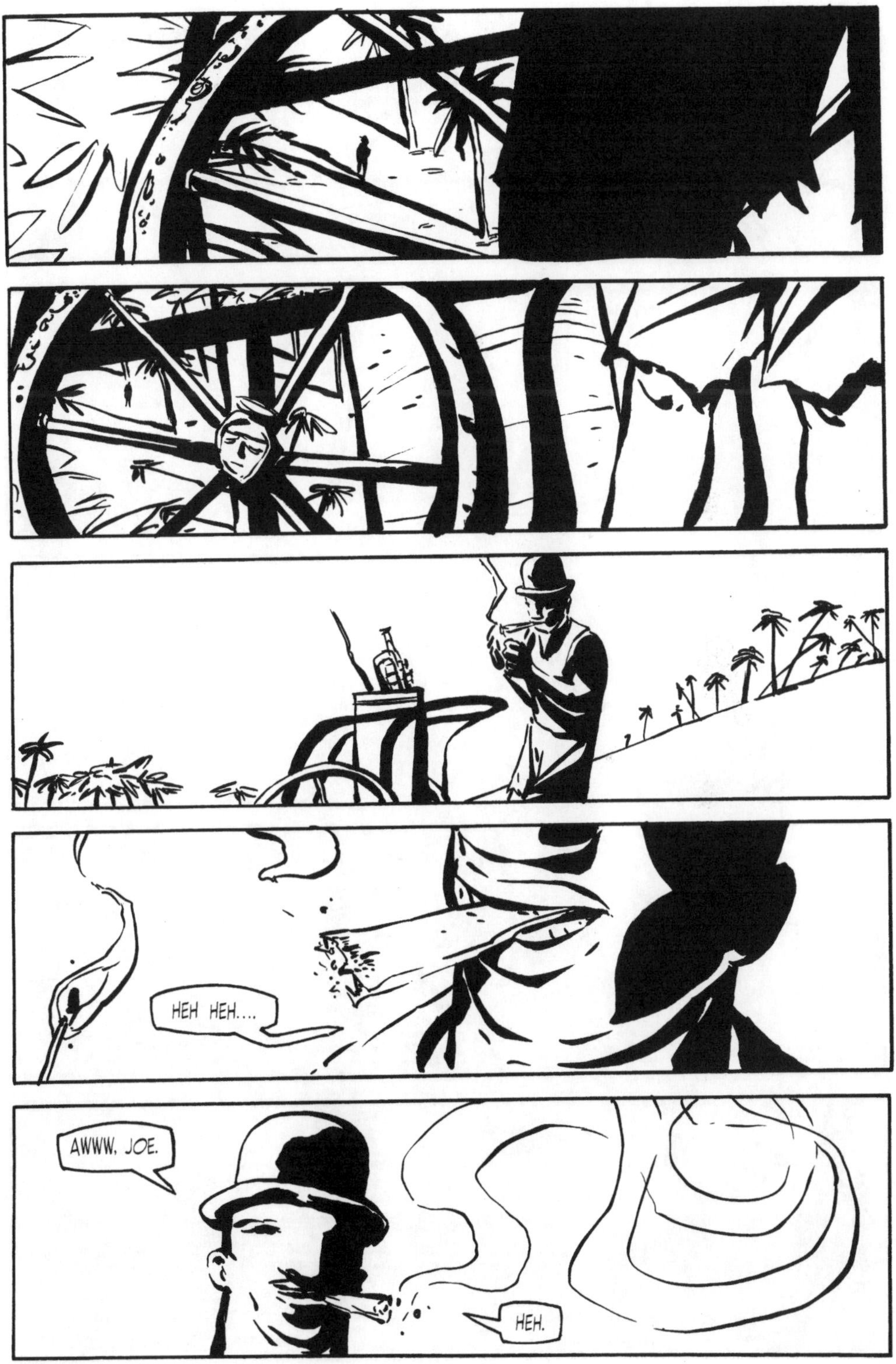
HEH HEH....
AWWW, JOE.
HEH.

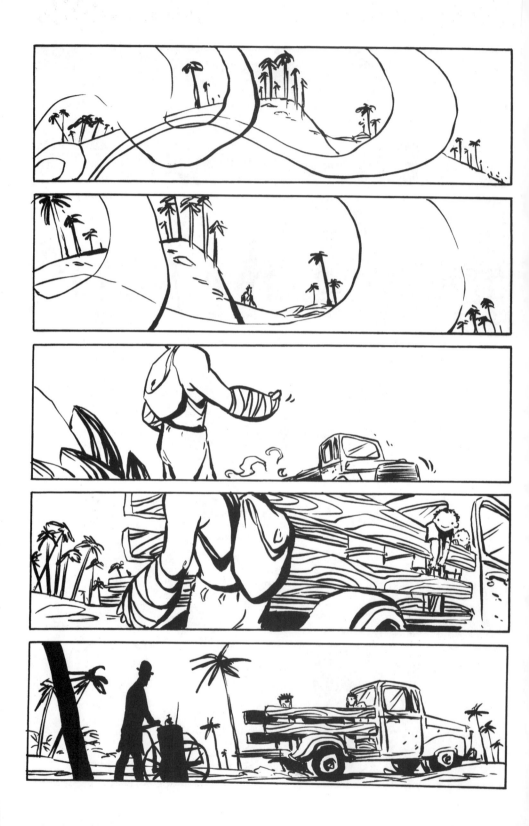

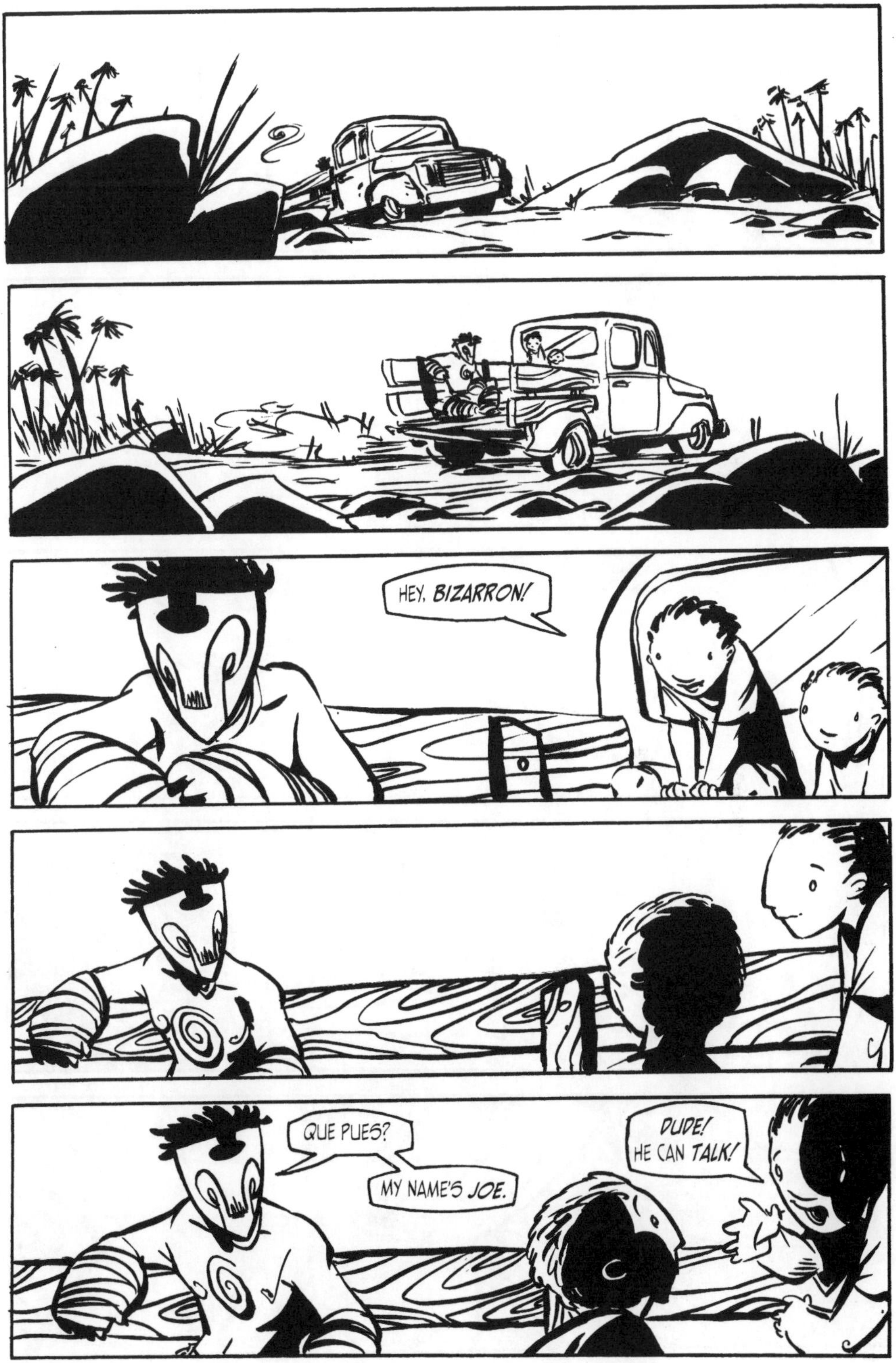
HEY, BIZARRON!
QUE PUES?
MY NAME'S JOE.
DUDE! HE CAN TALK!

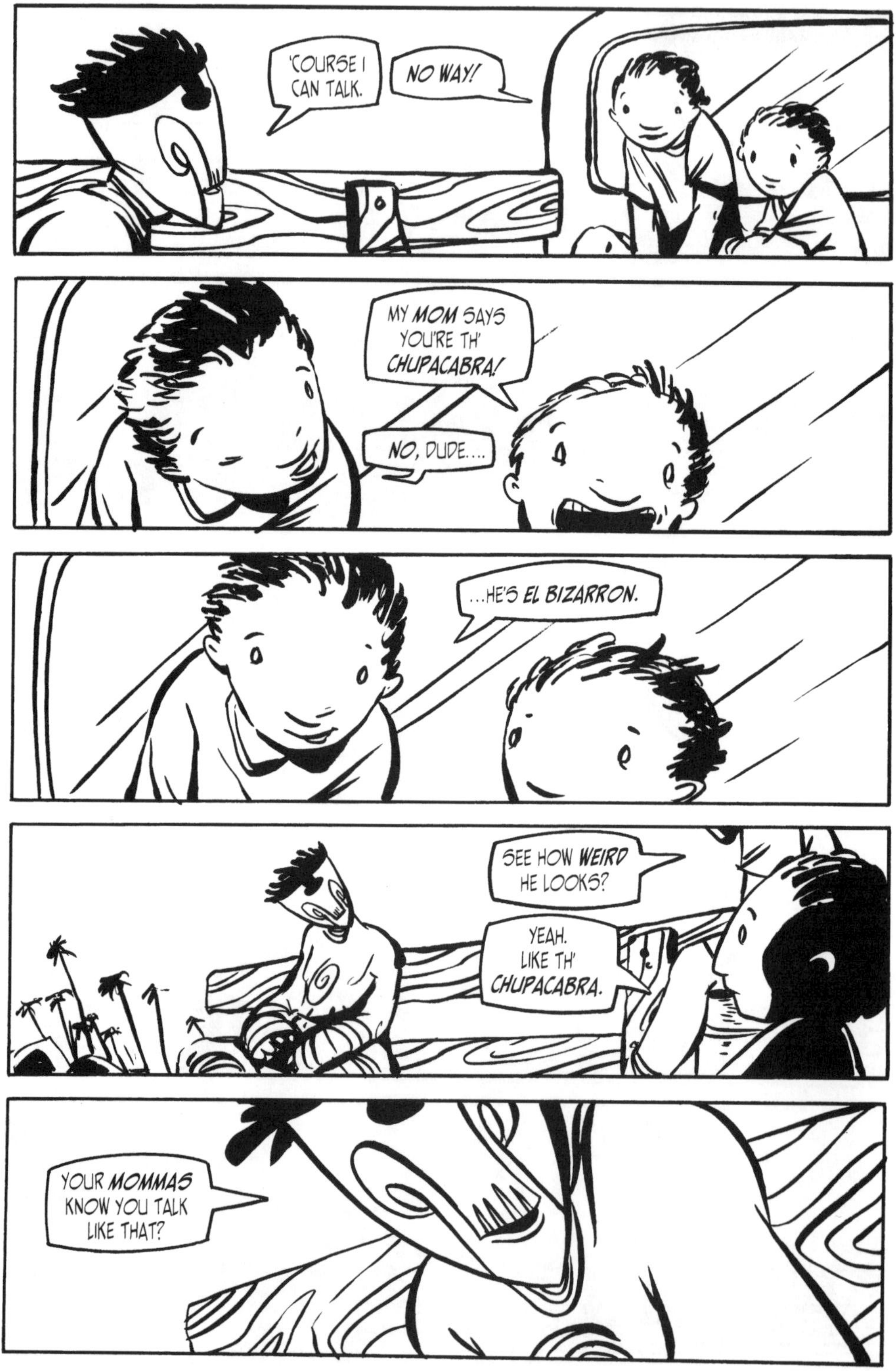
'COURSE I CAN TALK.
NO WAY!
MY MOM SAYS YOU'RE TH' CHUPACABRA!
NO, DUDE....
...HE'S EL BIZARRON.
SEE HOW WEIRD HE LOOKS?
YEAH. LIKE TH' CHUPACABRA.
YOUR MOMMAS KNOW YOU TALK LIKE THAT?

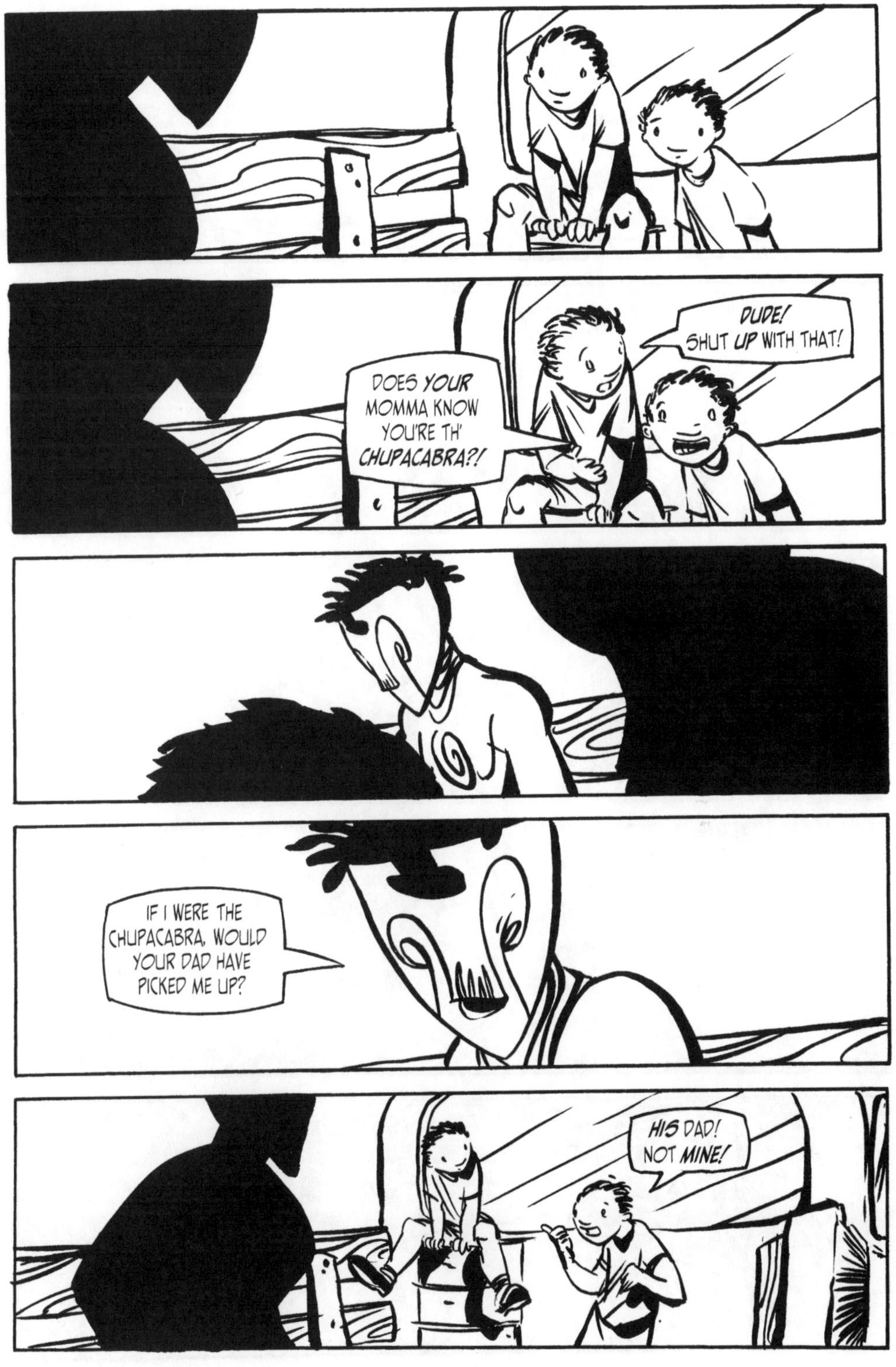
DOES YOUR MOMMA KNOW YOU'RE TH' CHUPACABRA?!
DUDE! SHUT UP WITH THAT!
IF I WERE THE CHUPACABRA, WOULD YOUR DAD HAVE PICKED ME UP?
HIS DAD! NOT MINE!

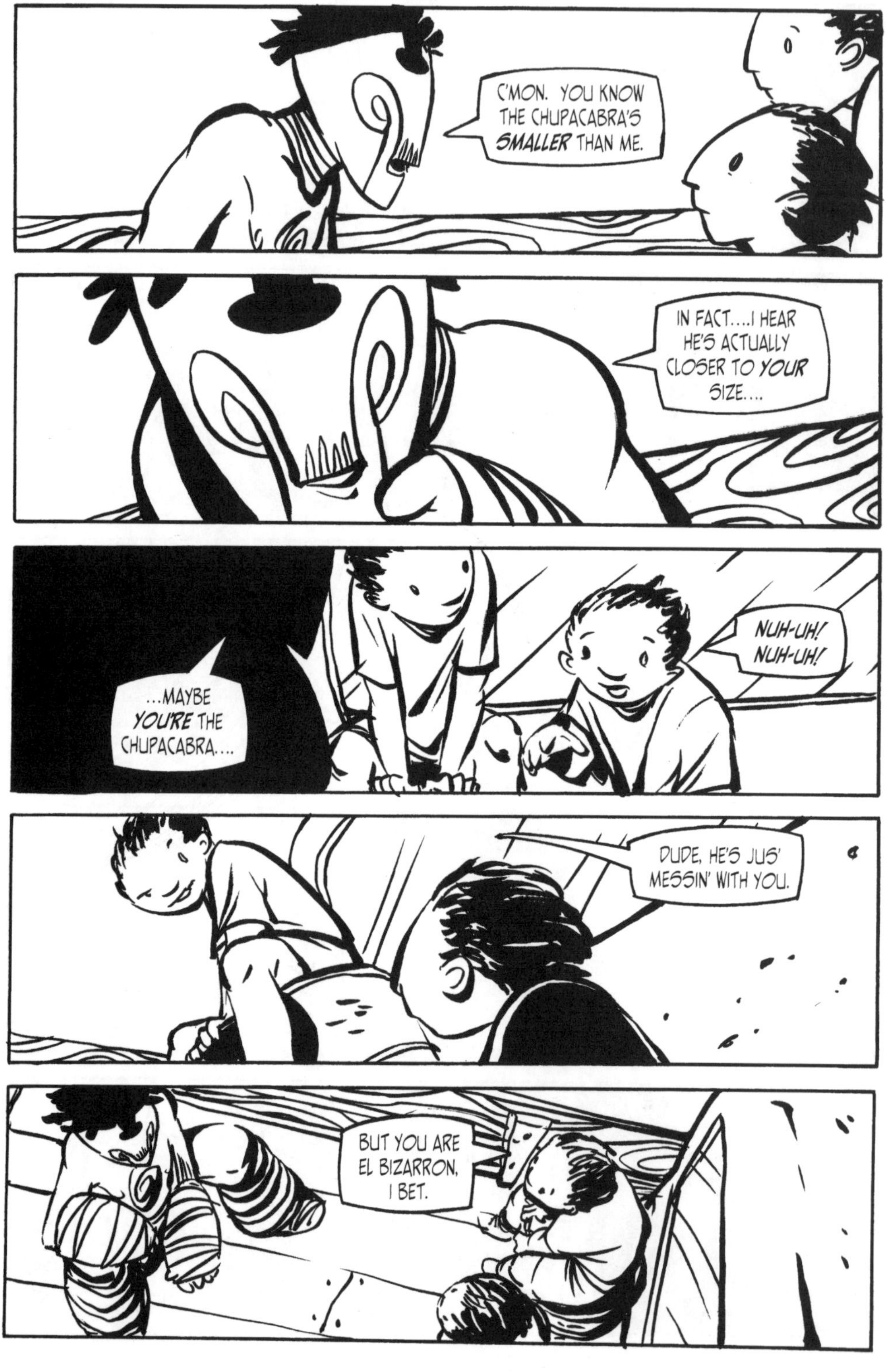
C'MON. YOU KNOW THE CHUPACABRA'S *SMALLER* THAN ME.
IN FACT....I HEAR HE'S ACTUALLY CLOSER TO *YOUR* SIZE....
...MAYBE *YOU'RE* THE CHUPACABRA....
*NUH-UH! NUH-UH!*
DUDE, HE'S JUS' MESSIN' WITH YOU.
BUT YOU ARE EL BIZARRON, I BET.

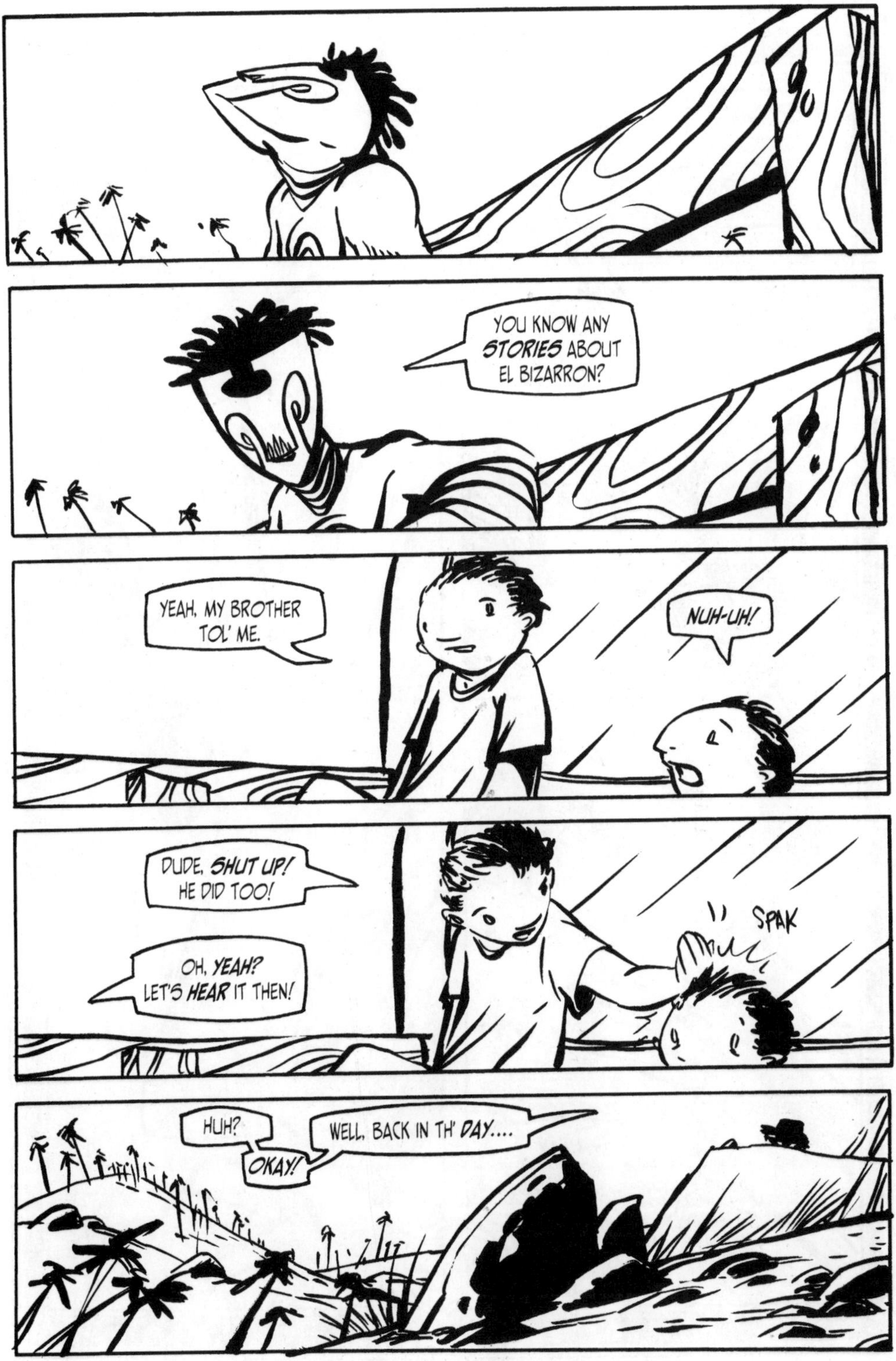
YOU KNOW ANY STORIES ABOUT EL BIZARRON?
YEAH, MY BROTHER TOL' ME.
NUH-UH!
DUDE, SHUT UP! HE DID TOO!
SPAK
OH, YEAH? LET'S HEAR IT THEN!
HUH?
OKAY!
WELL, BACK IN TH' DAY....

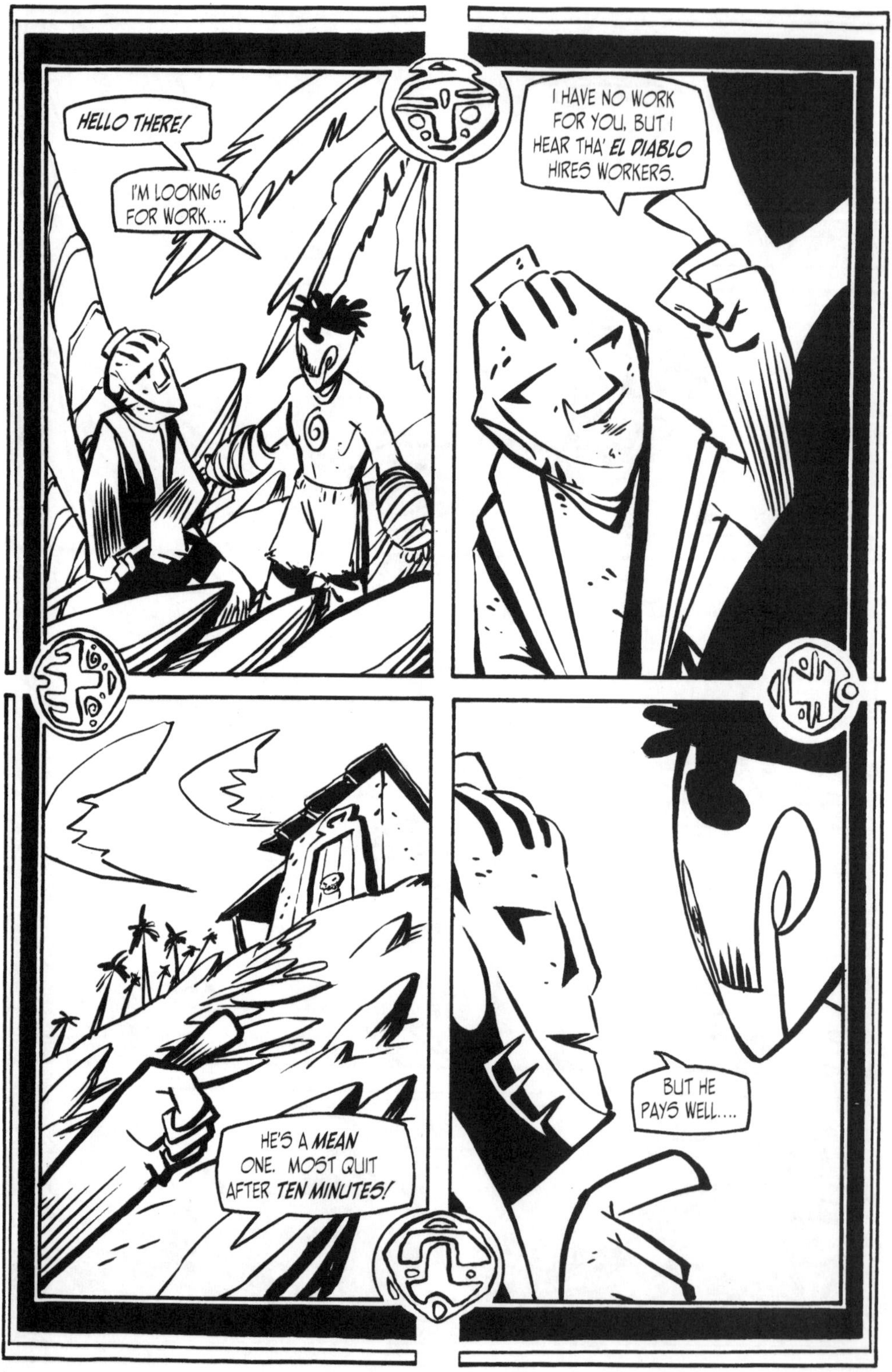
HELLO THERE!
I'M LOOKING FOR WORK....
I HAVE NO WORK FOR YOU, BUT I HEAR THA' EL DIABLO HIRES WORKERS.
HE'S A MEAN ONE. MOST QUIT AFTER TEN MINUTES!
BUT HE PAYS WELL....

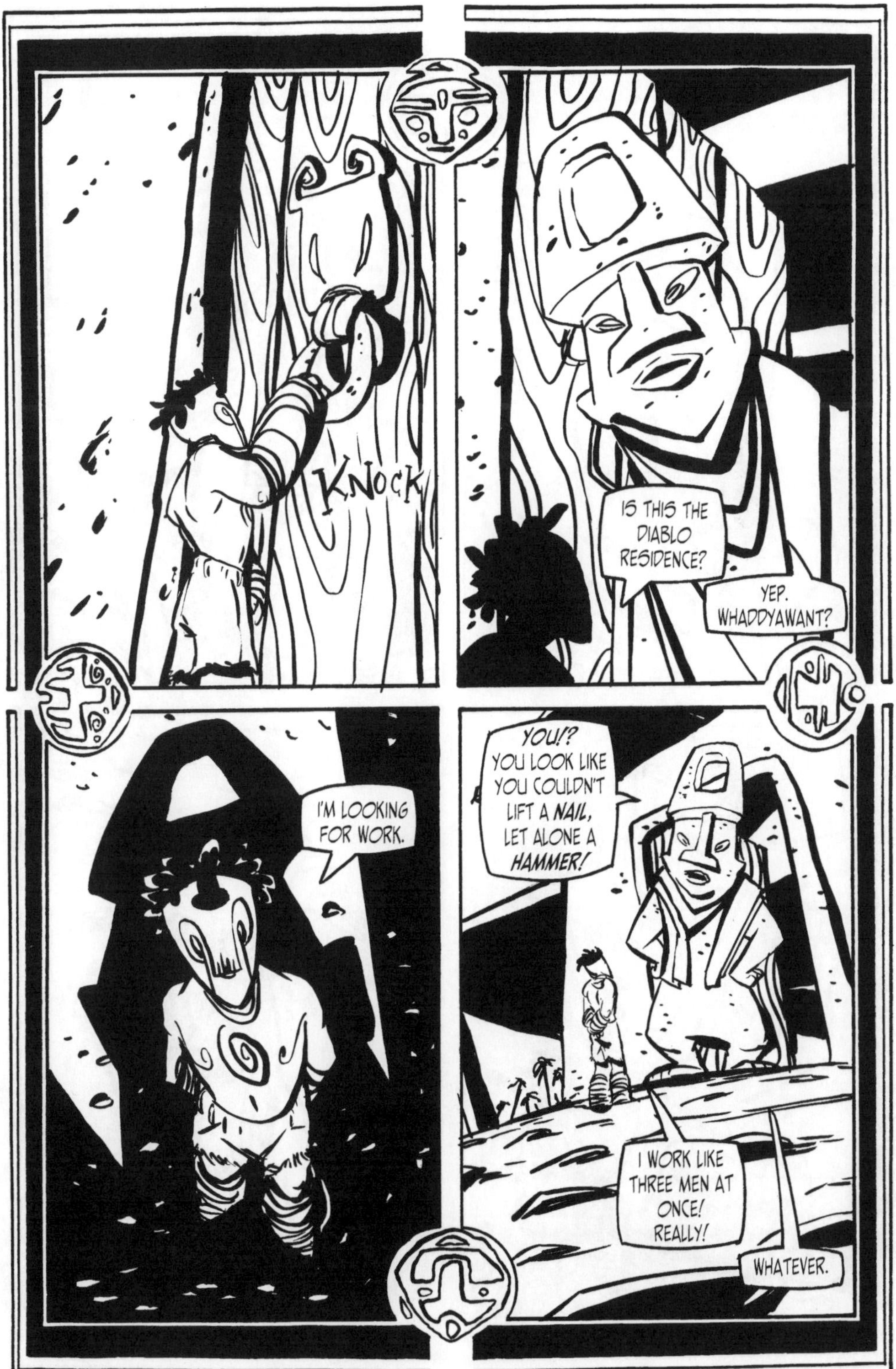
KNOCK
IS THIS THE DIABLO RESIDENCE?
YEP. WHADDYAWANT?
I'M LOOKING FOR WORK.
YOU!? YOU LOOK LIKE YOU COULDN'T LIFT A *NAIL*, LET ALONE A *HAMMER!*
I WORK LIKE THREE MEN AT ONCE! REALLY!
WHATEVER.

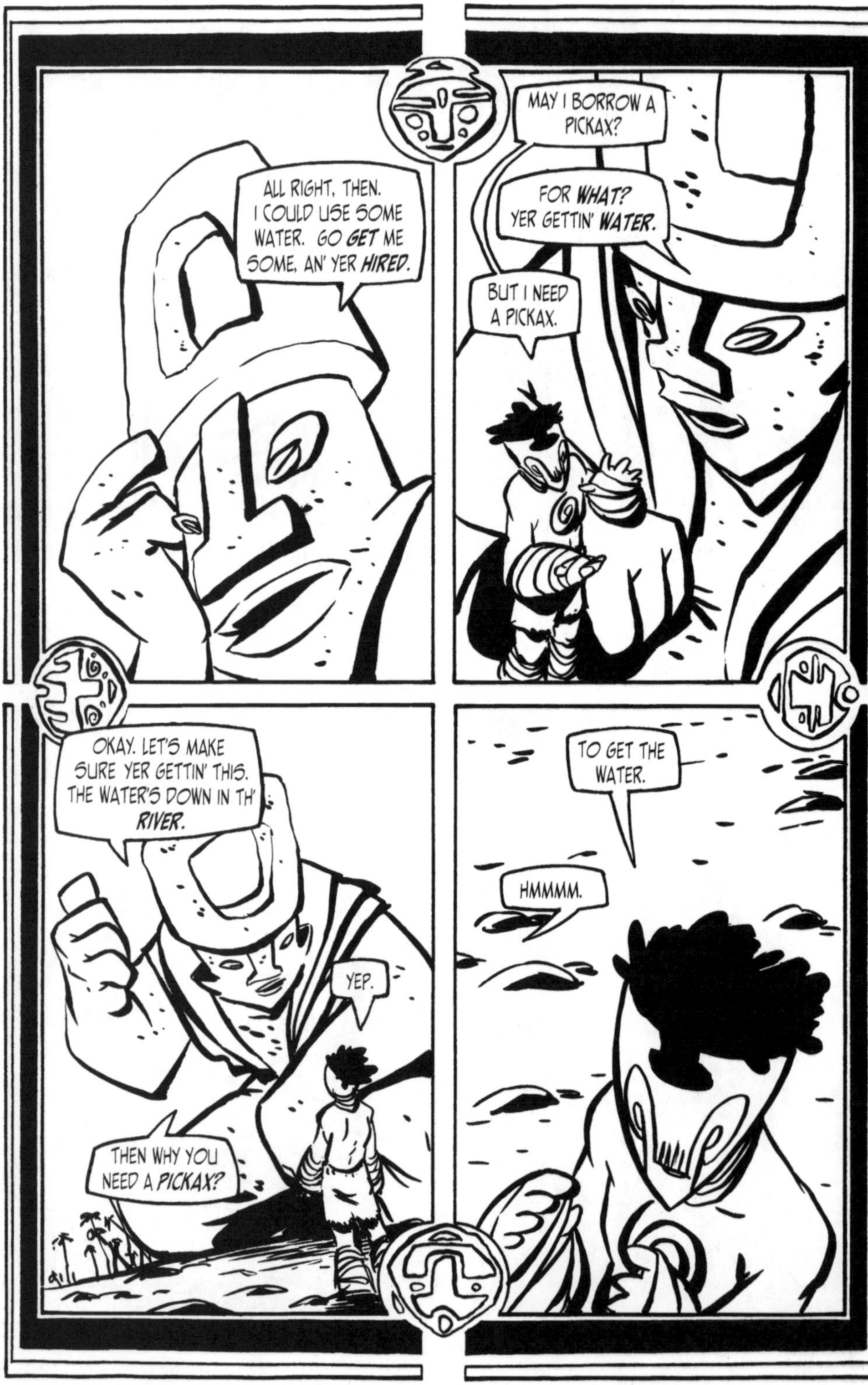
ALL RIGHT, THEN. I COULD USE SOME WATER. GO GET ME SOME, AN' YER HIRED.
MAY I BORROW A PICKAX?
FOR WHAT? YER GETTIN' WATER.
BUT I NEED A PICKAX.
OKAY. LET'S MAKE SURE YER GETTIN' THIS. THE WATER'S DOWN IN TH' RIVER.
YEP.
THEN WHY YOU NEED A PICKAX?
TO GET THE WATER.
HMMMM.

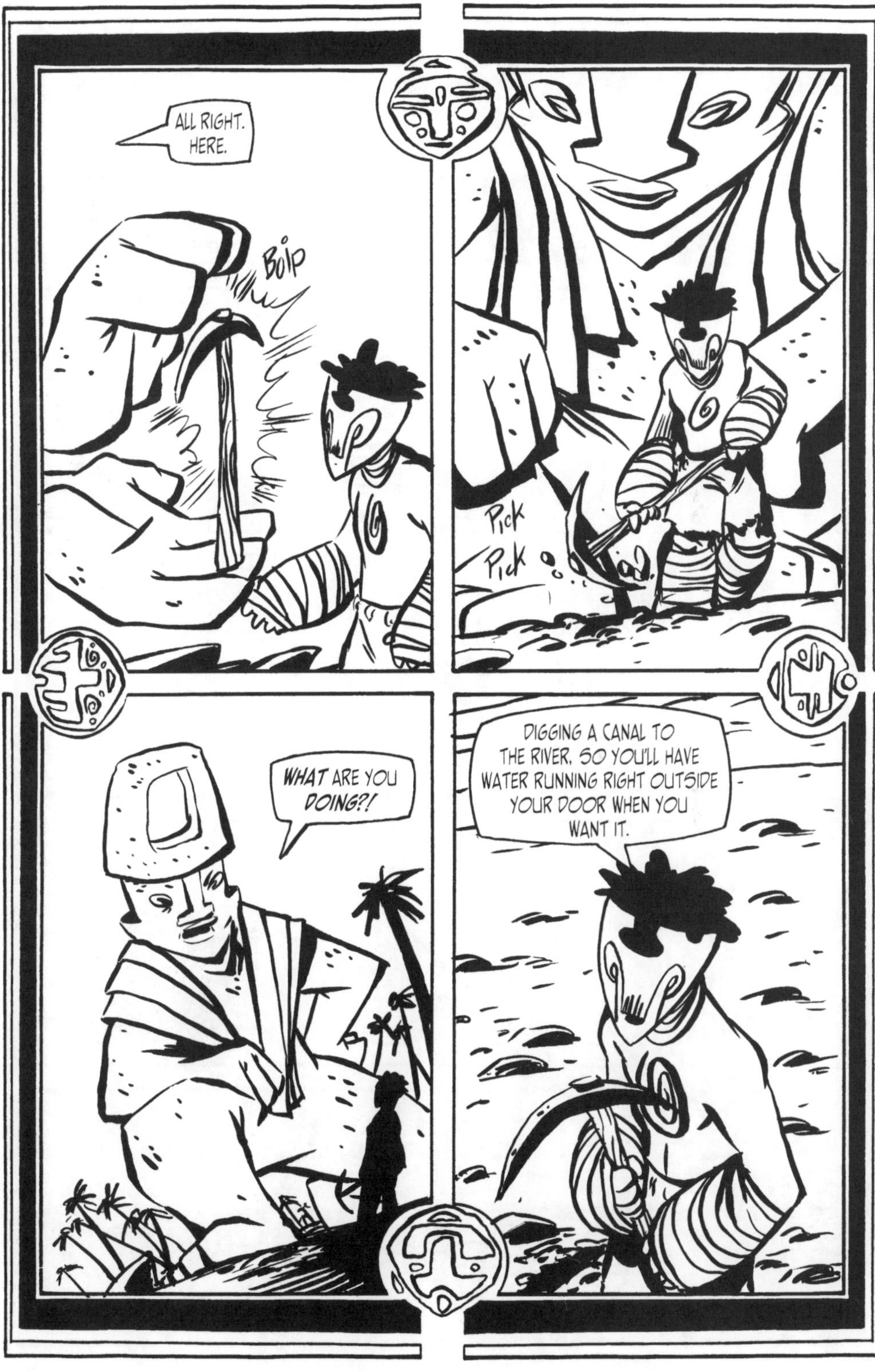
ALL RIGHT. HERE.
Boip
Pick
Pick
WHAT ARE YOU DOING?!
DIGGING A CANAL TO THE RIVER, SO YOU'LL HAVE WATER RUNNING RIGHT OUTSIDE YOUR DOOR WHEN YOU WANT IT.

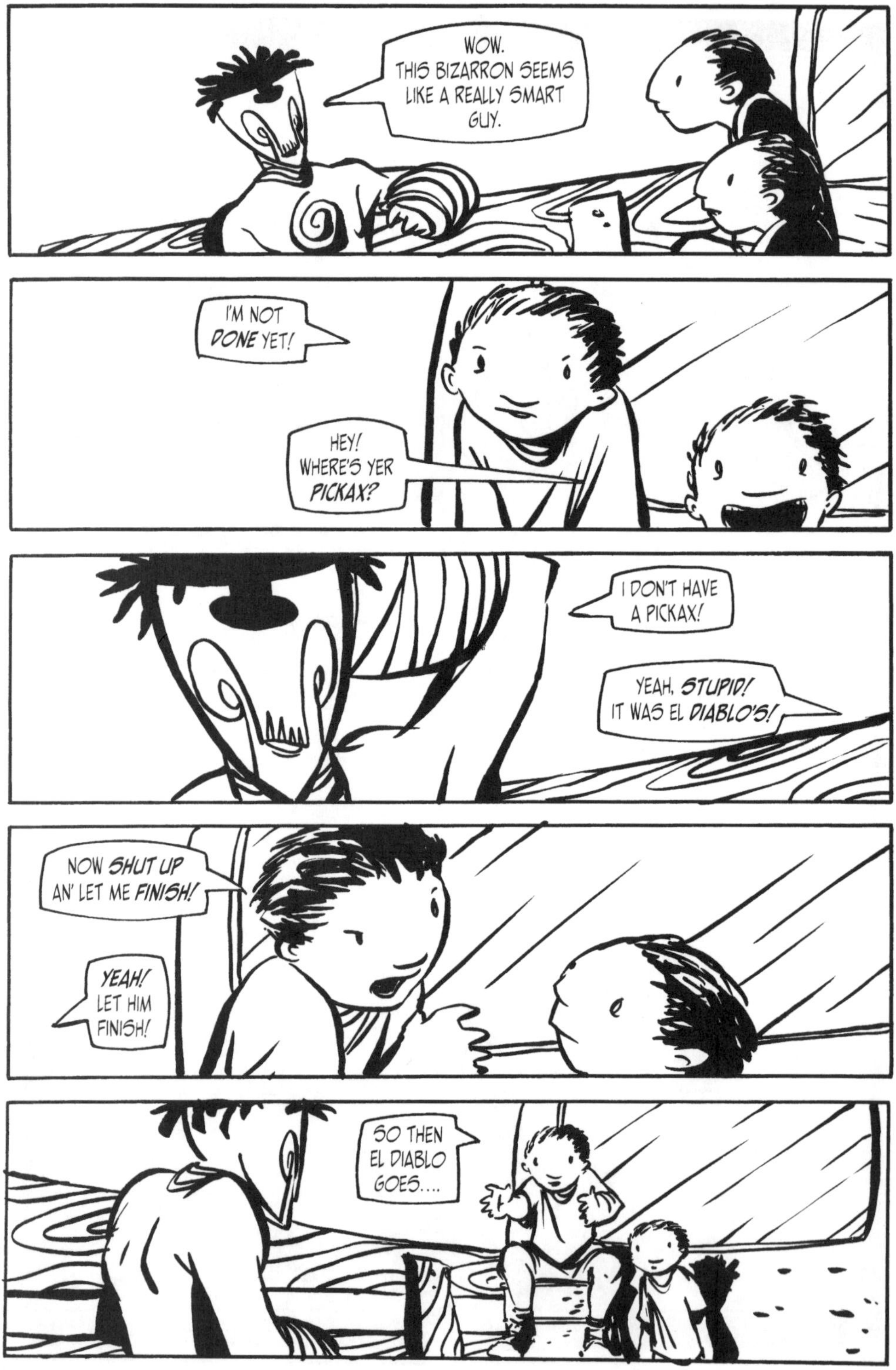
WOW. THIS BIZARRON SEEMS LIKE A REALLY SMART GUY.
I'M NOT DONE YET!
HEY! WHERE'S YER PICKAX?
I DON'T HAVE A PICKAX!
YEAH, STUPID! IT WAS EL DIABLO'S!
NOW SHUT UP AN' LET ME FINISH!
YEAH! LET HIM FINISH!
SO THEN EL DIABLO GOES....

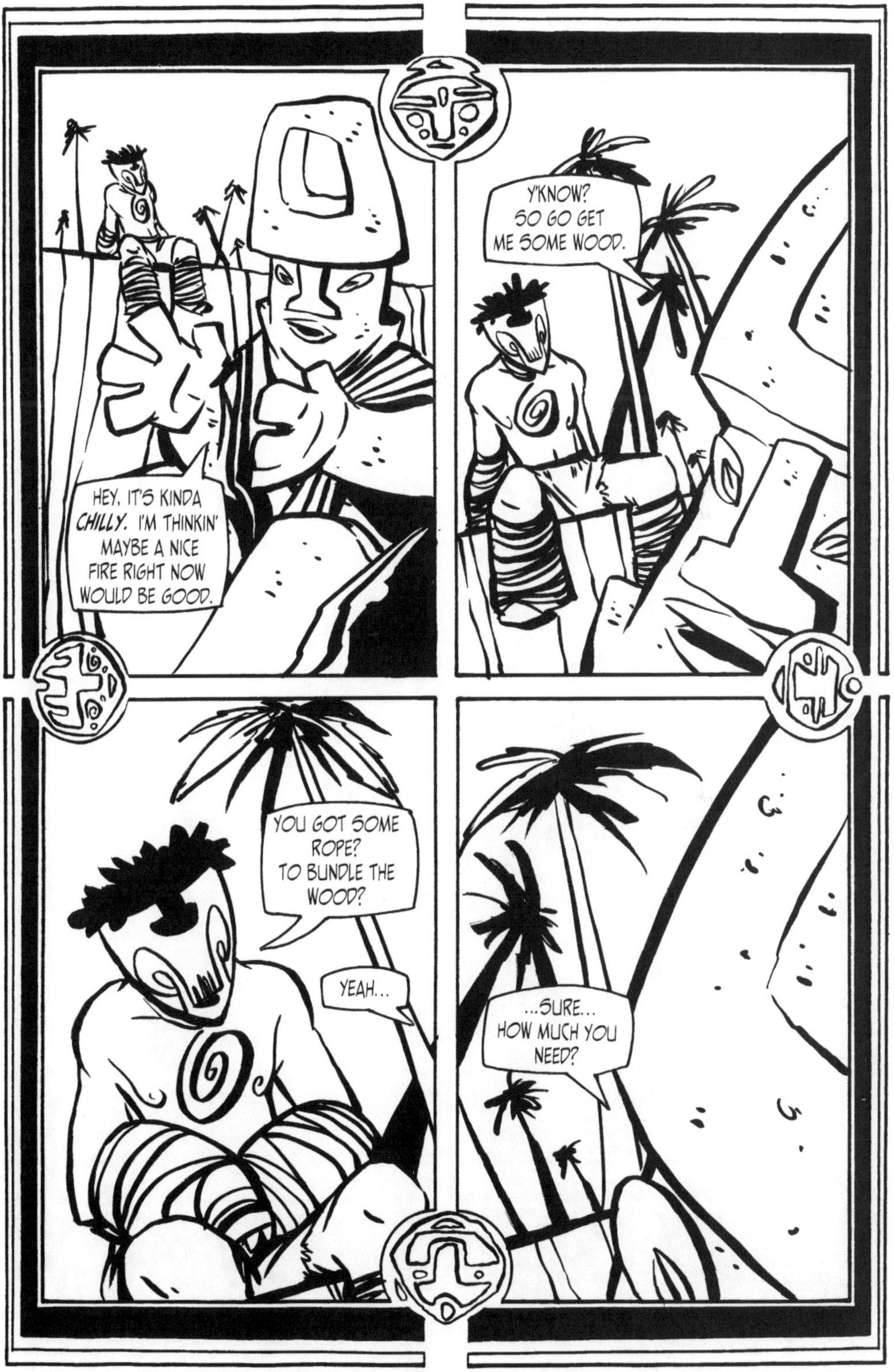
HEY, IT'S KINDA CHILLY. I'M THINKIN' MAYBE A NICE FIRE RIGHT NOW WOULD BE GOOD.
Y'KNOW? SO GO GET ME SOME WOOD.
YOU GOT SOME ROPE? TO BUNDLE THE WOOD?
YEAH...
...SURE... HOW MUCH YOU NEED?

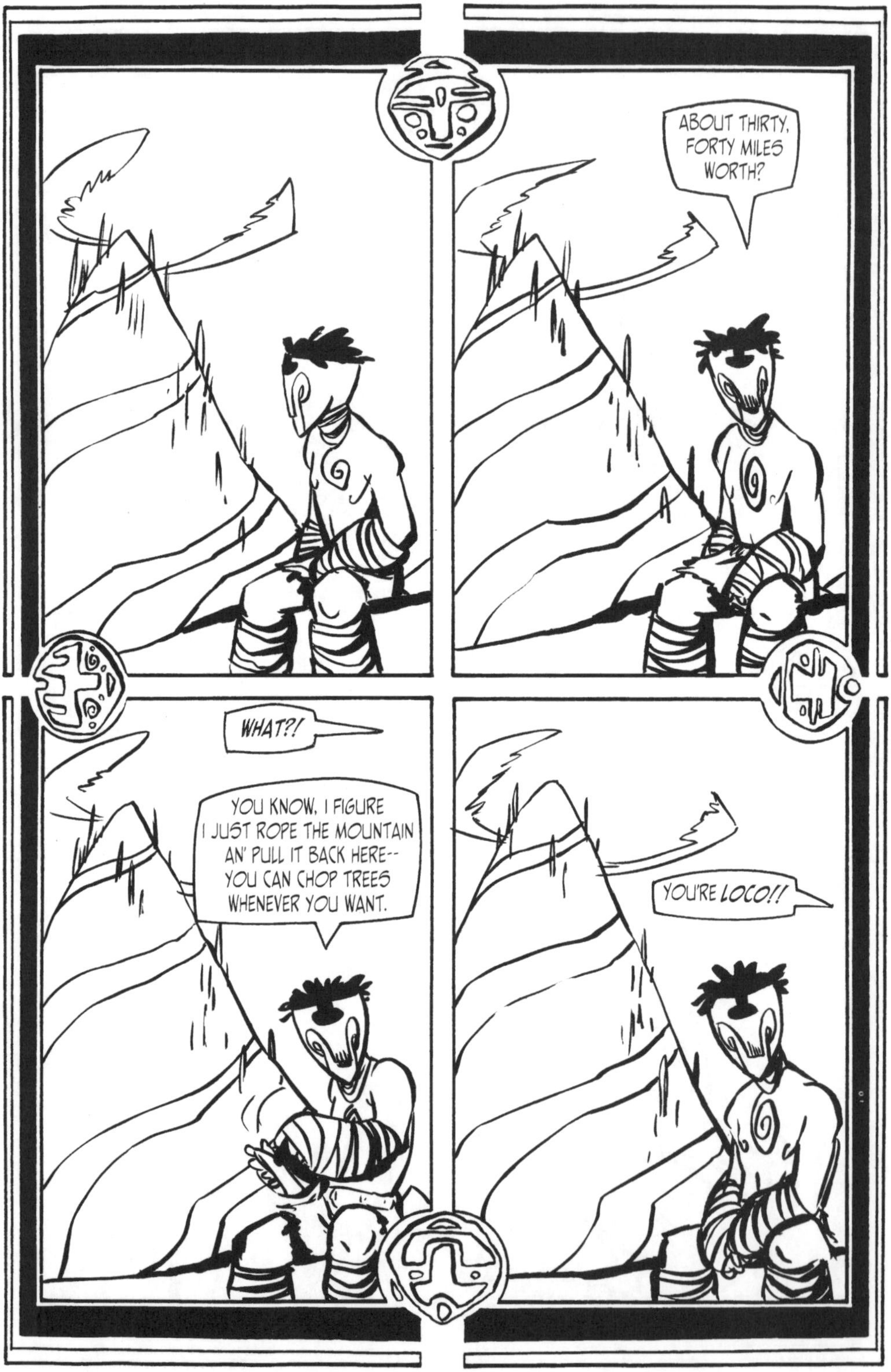
ABOUT THIRTY, FORTY MILES WORTH?
WHAT?!
YOU KNOW, I FIGURE I JUST ROPE THE MOUNTAIN AN' PULL IT BACK HERE-- YOU CAN CHOP TREES WHENEVER YOU WANT.
YOU'RE *LOCO!!*

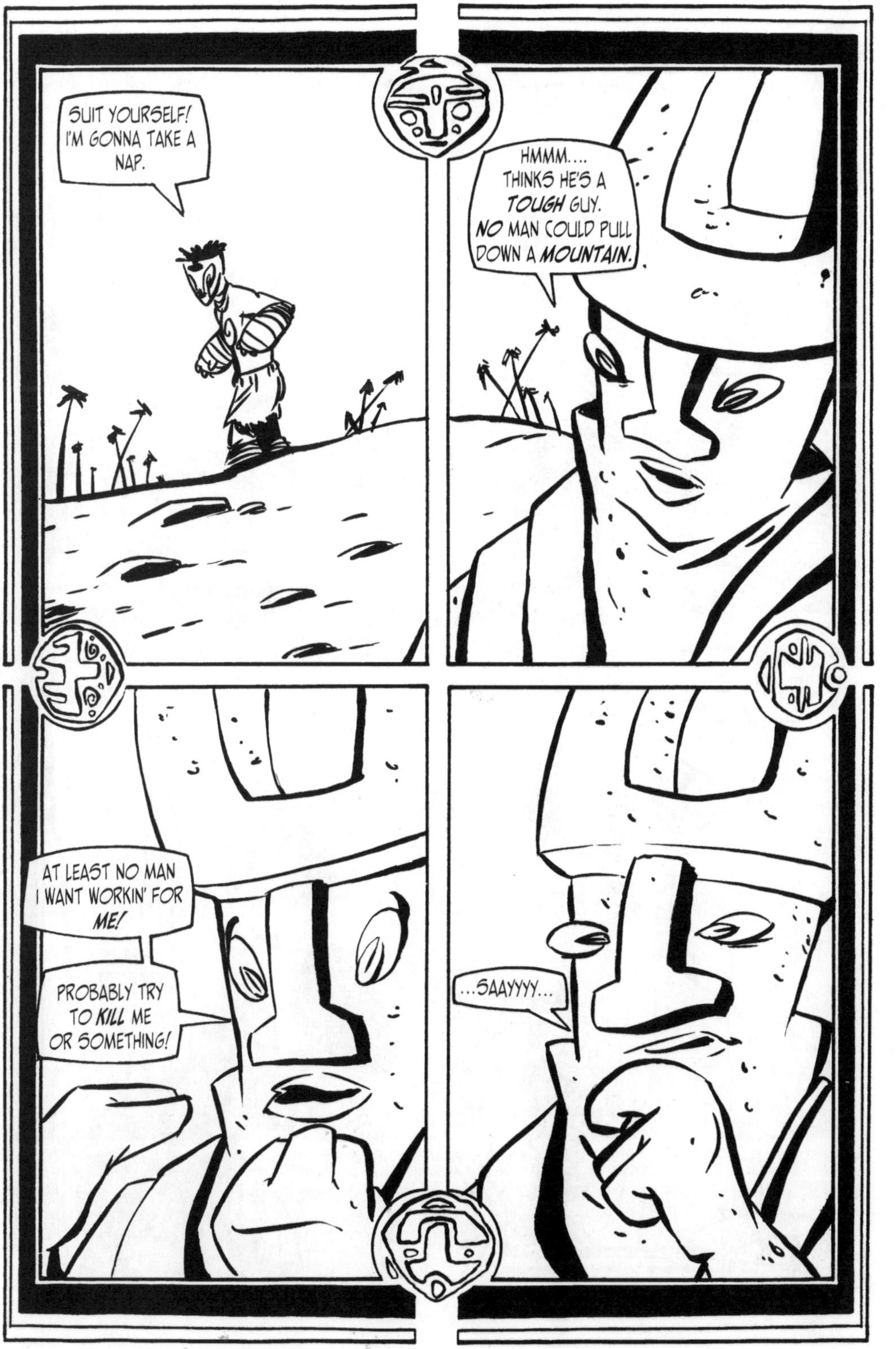
SUIT YOURSELF! I'M GONNA TAKE A NAP.
HMMM.... THINKS HE'S A TOUGH GUY. NO MAN COULD PULL DOWN A MOUNTAIN.
AT LEAST NO MAN I WANT WORKIN' FOR ME!
PROBABLY TRY TO KILL ME OR SOMETHING!
...SAAYYYY...

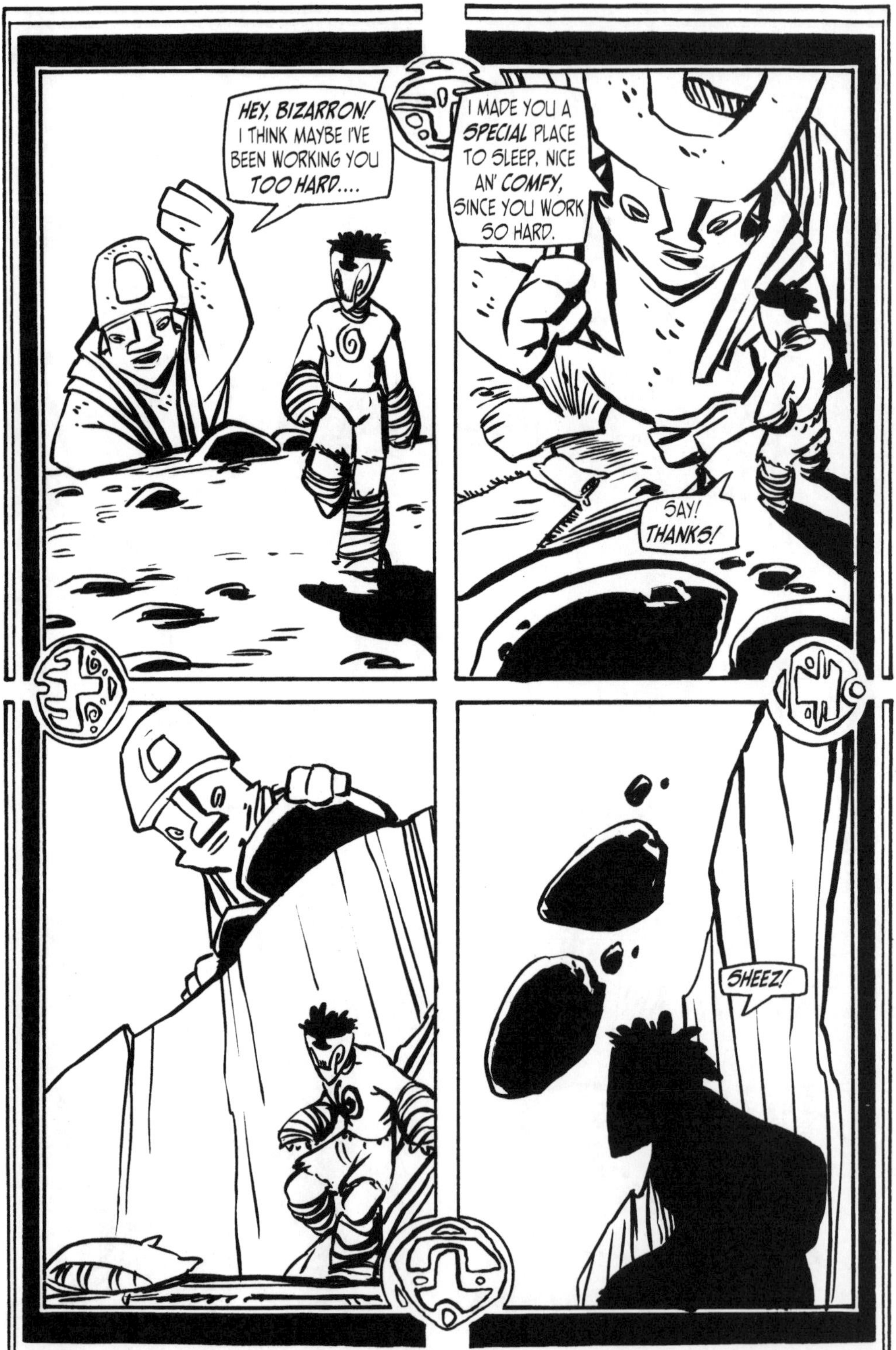
HEY, BIZARRON! I THINK MAYBE I'VE BEEN WORKING YOU TOO HARD....
I MADE YOU A SPECIAL PLACE TO SLEEP, NICE AN' COMFY, SINCE YOU WORK SO HARD.
SAY! THANKS!
SHEEZ!

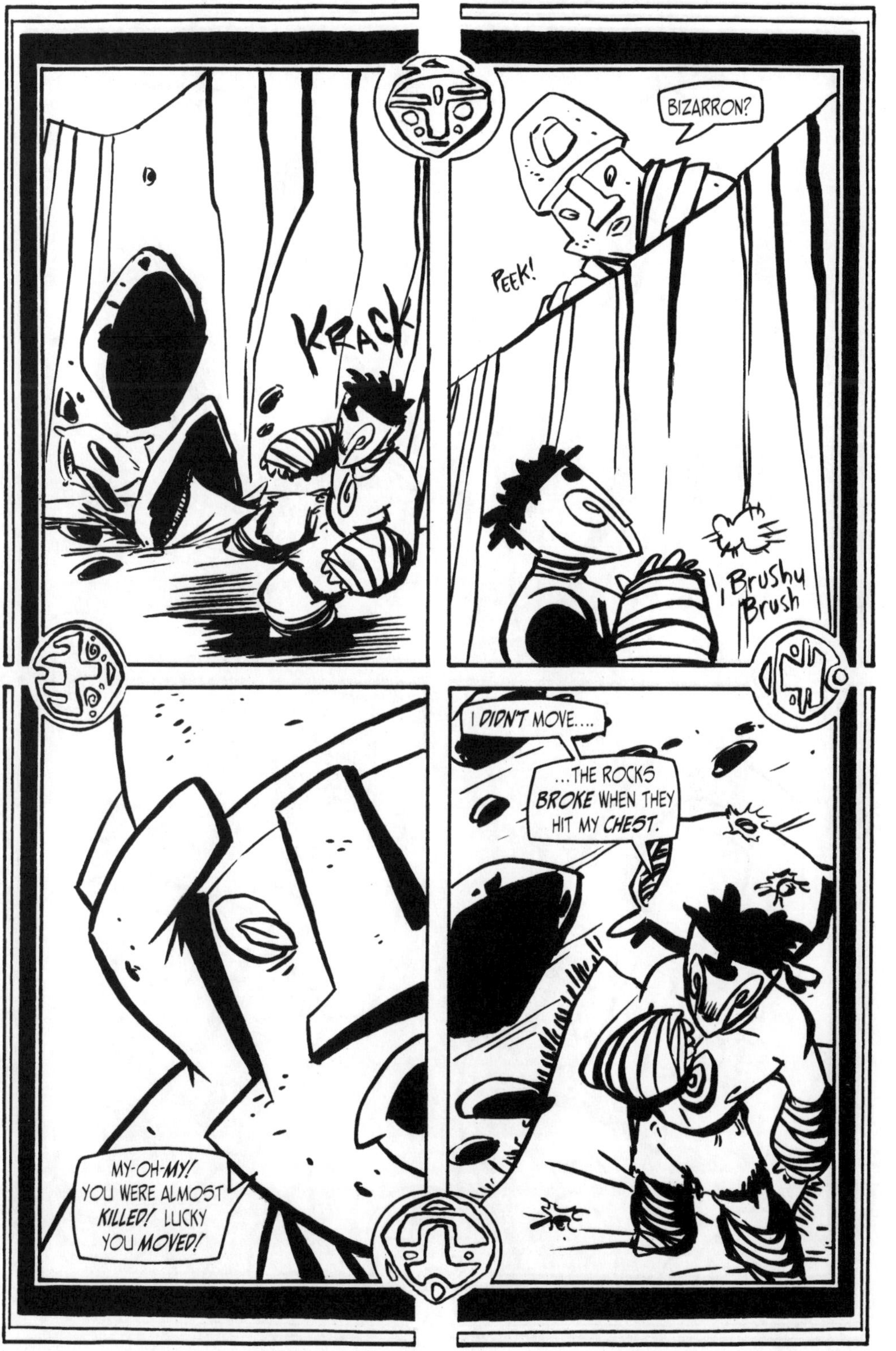
KRACK
BIZARRON?
PEEK!
Brushy Brush
MY-OH-MY! YOU WERE ALMOST KILLED! LUCKY YOU MOVED!
I DIDN'T MOVE....
...THE ROCKS BROKE WHEN THEY HIT MY CHEST.

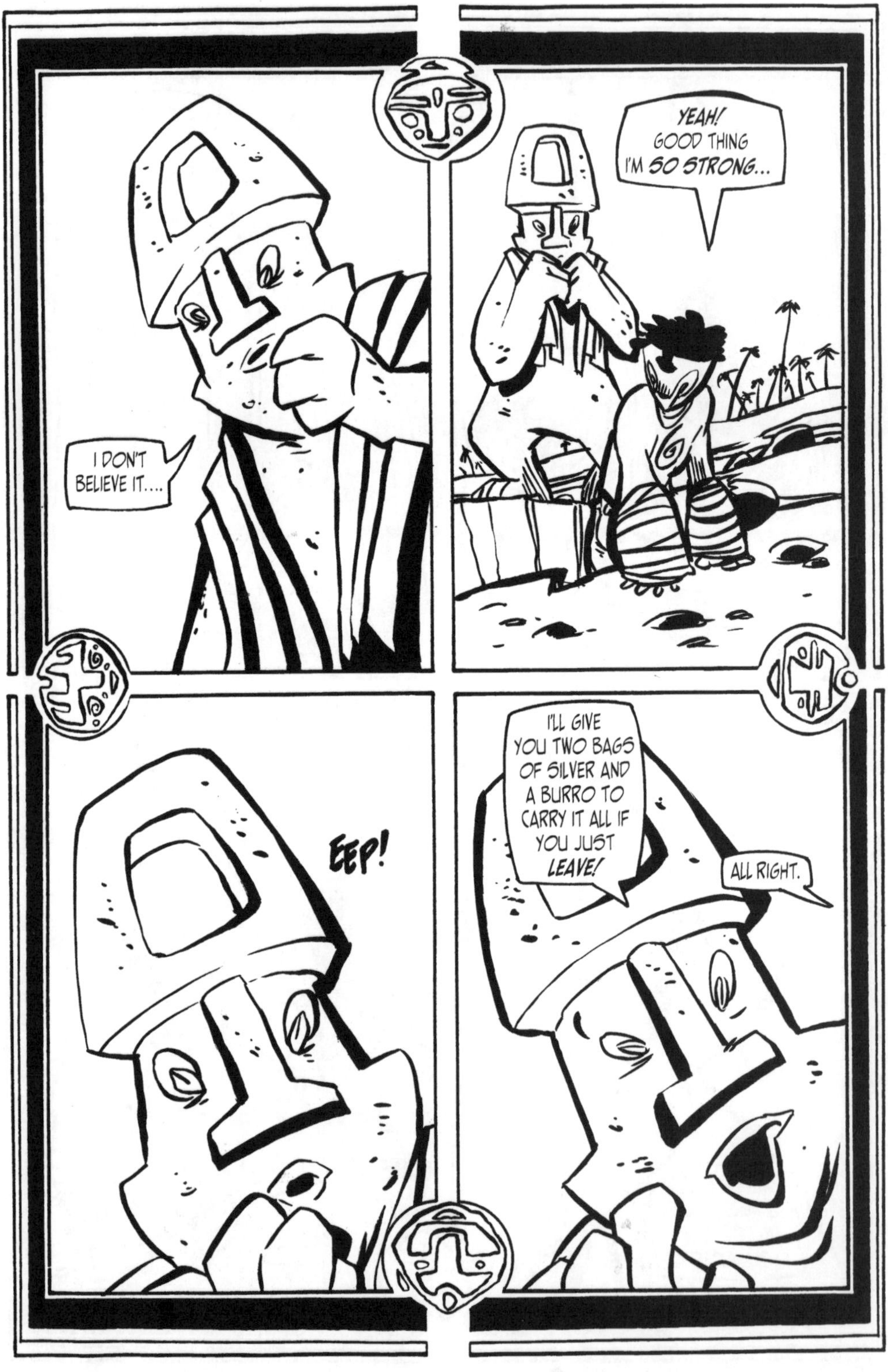
I DON'T BELIEVE IT....
YEAH! GOOD THING I'M SO STRONG...
EEP!
I'LL GIVE YOU TWO BAGS OF SILVER AND A BURRO TO CARRY IT ALL IF YOU JUST LEAVE!
ALL RIGHT.

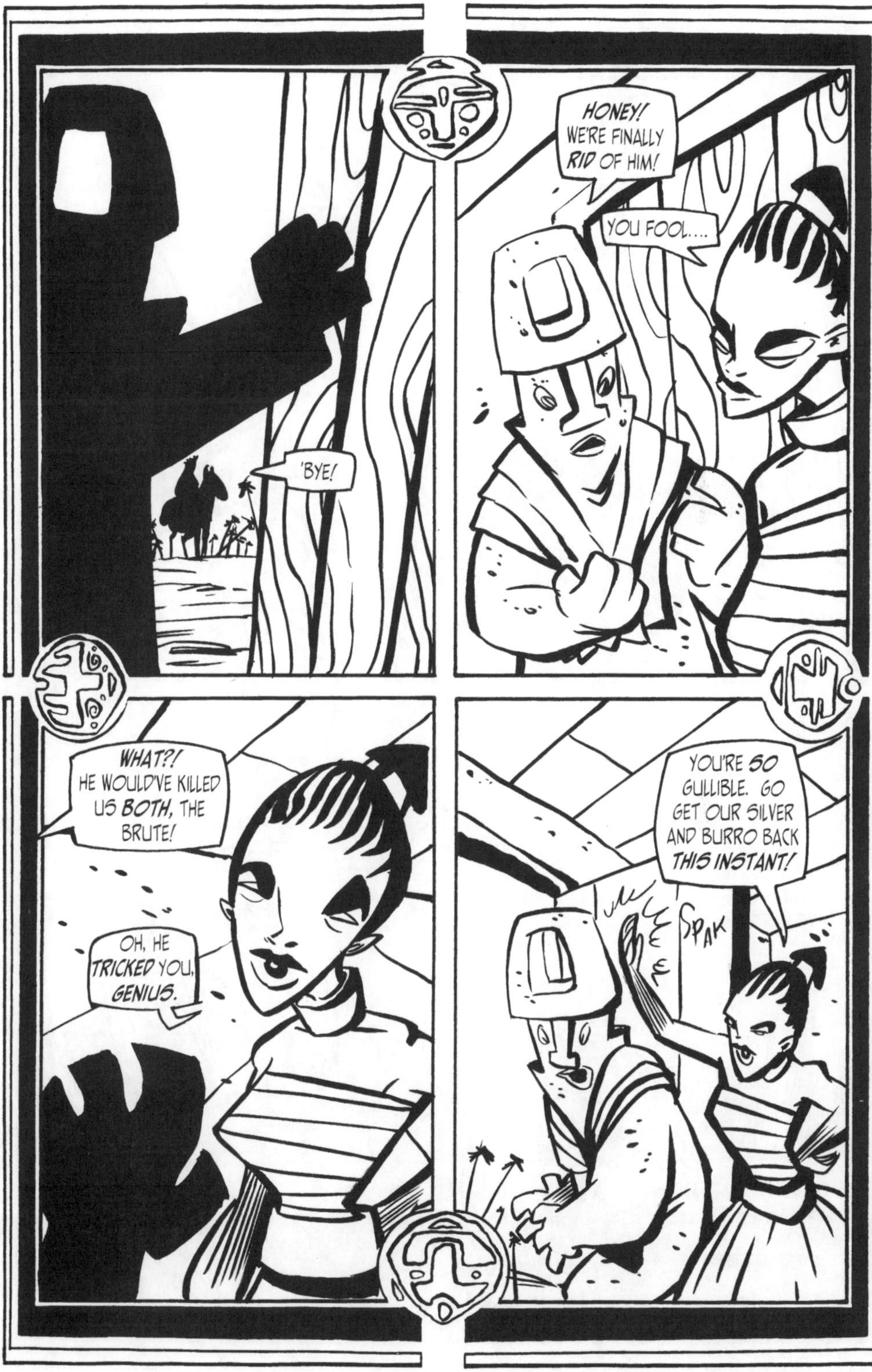
'BYE!
HONEY! WE'RE FINALLY RID OF HIM!
YOU FOOL....
WHAT?! HE WOULD'VE KILLED US BOTH, THE BRUTE!
OH, HE TRICKED YOU, GENIUS.
YOU'RE SO GULLIBLE. GO GET OUR SILVER AND BURRO BACK THIS INSTANT!
SPAK

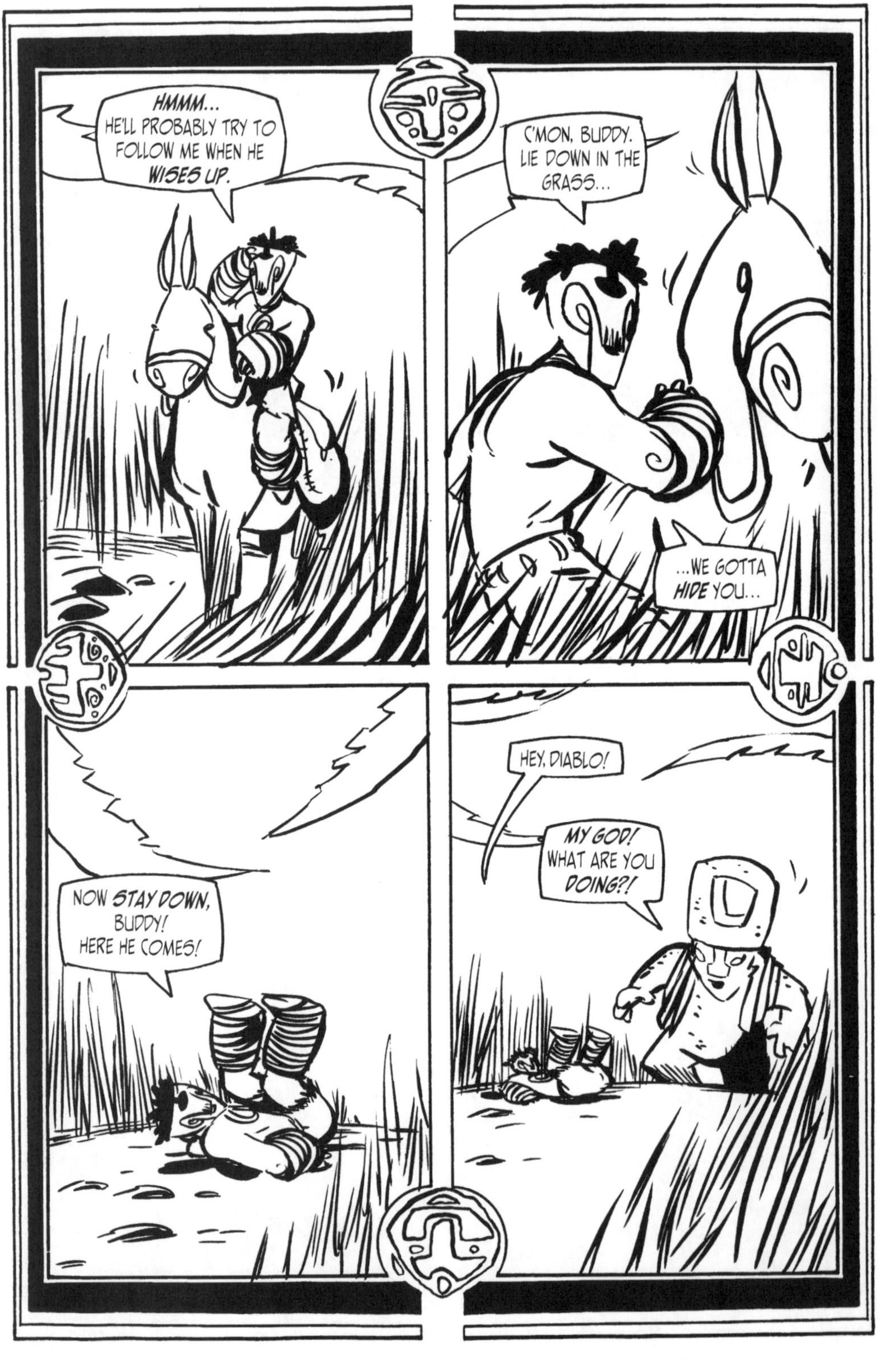
HMMM...
HE'LL PROBABLY TRY TO FOLLOW ME WHEN HE WISES UP.
C'MON, BUDDY. LIE DOWN IN THE GRASS...
...WE GOTTA HIDE YOU...
NOW STAY DOWN, BUDDY! HERE HE COMES!
HEY, DIABLO!
MY GOD! WHAT ARE YOU DOING?!

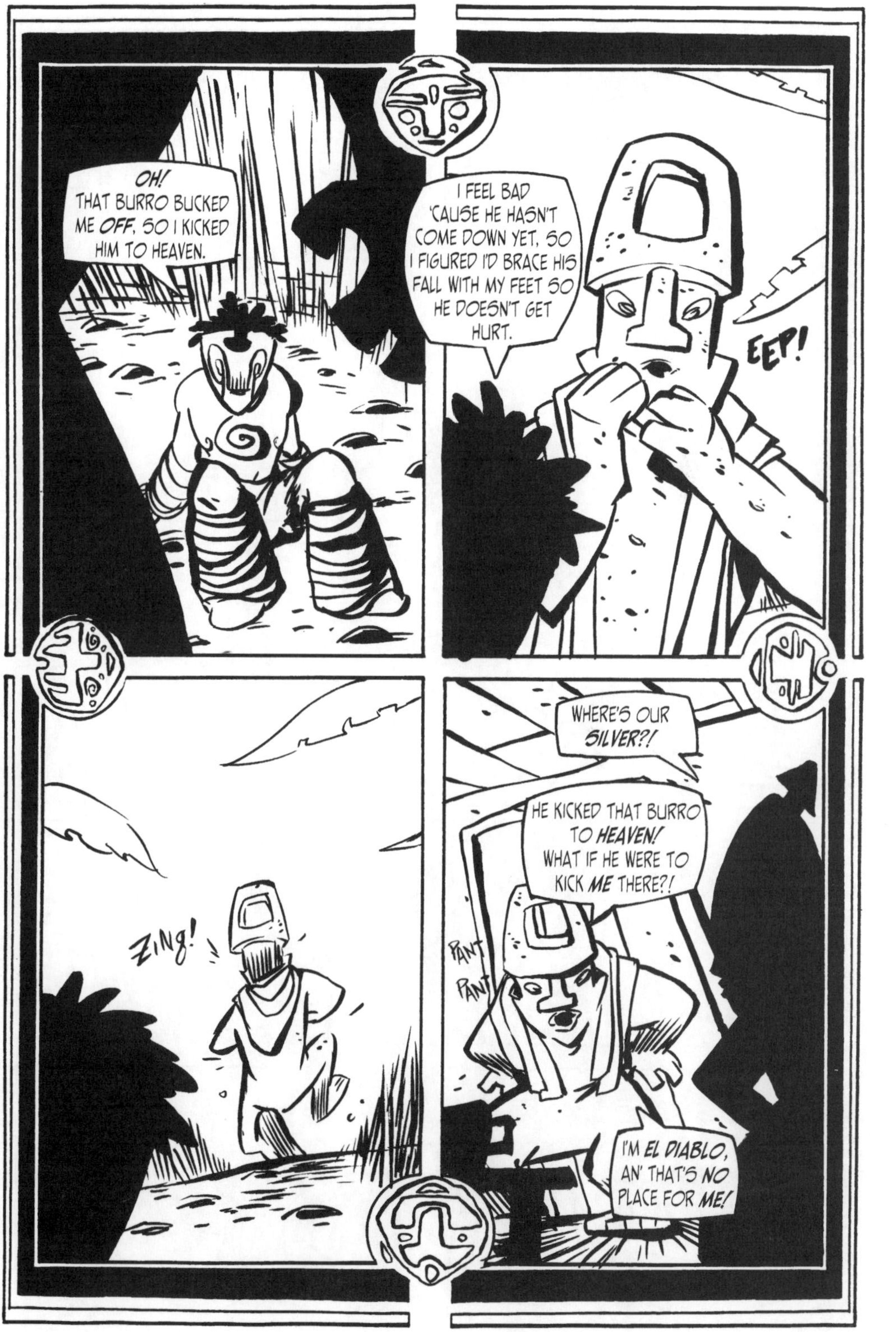
OH! THAT BURRO BUCKED ME OFF, SO I KICKED HIM TO HEAVEN.
I FEEL BAD 'CAUSE HE HASN'T COME DOWN YET, SO I FIGURED I'D BRACE HIS FALL WITH MY FEET SO HE DOESN'T GET HURT.
EEP!
ZING!
WHERE'S OUR SILVER?!
HE KICKED THAT BURRO TO HEAVEN! WHAT IF HE WERE TO KICK ME THERE?!
PANT PANT
I'M EL DIABLO, AN' THAT'S NO PLACE FOR ME!

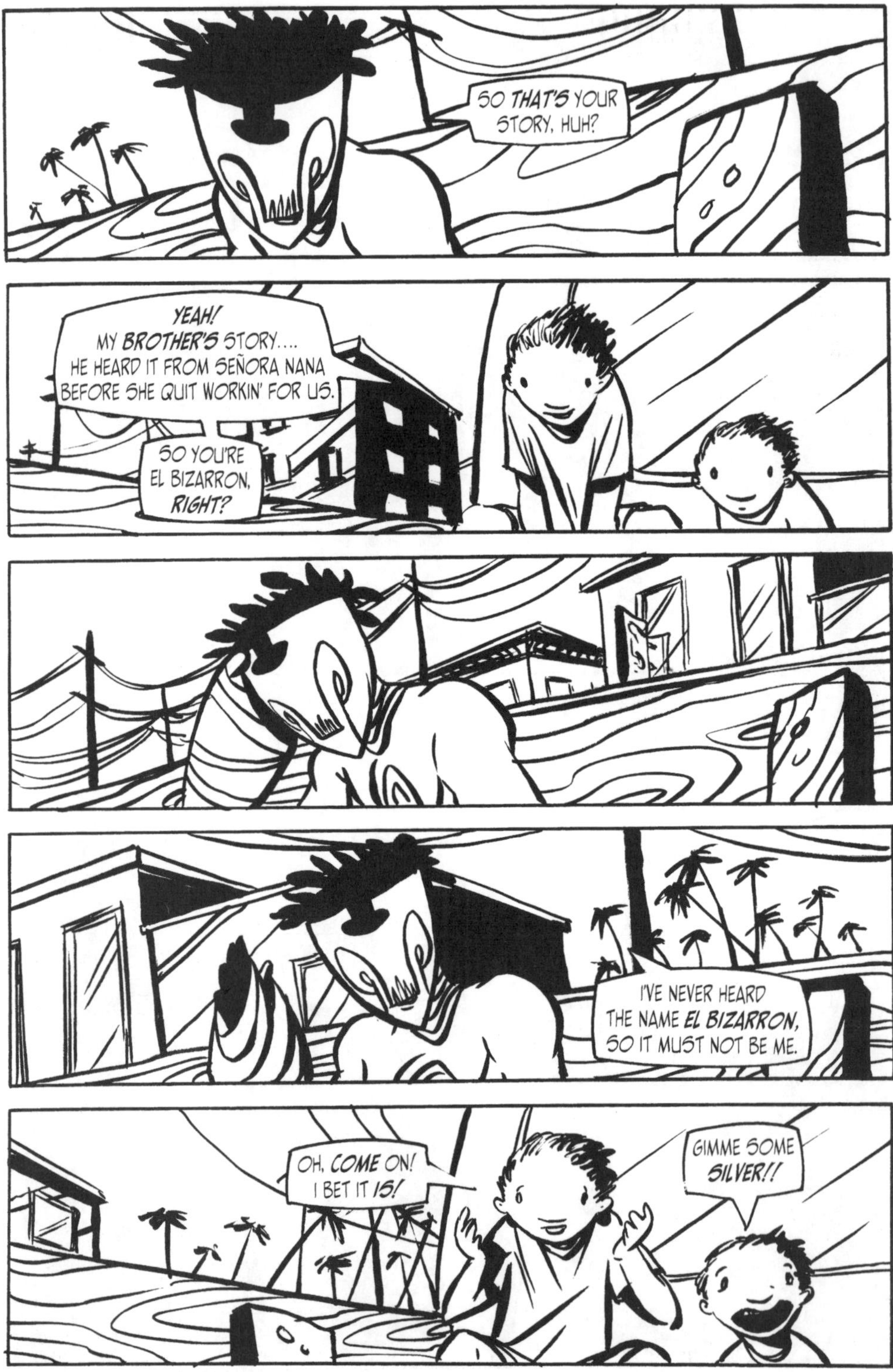
SO *THAT'S* YOUR STORY, HUH?
*YEAH!* MY *BROTHER'S* STORY.... HE HEARD IT FROM SEÑORA NANA BEFORE SHE QUIT WORKIN' FOR US.
SO YOU'RE EL BIZARRON, *RIGHT?*
I'VE NEVER HEARD THE NAME *EL BIZARRON,* SO IT MUST NOT BE ME.
OH, *COME* ON! I BET IT *IS!*
GIMME SOME *SILVER!!*

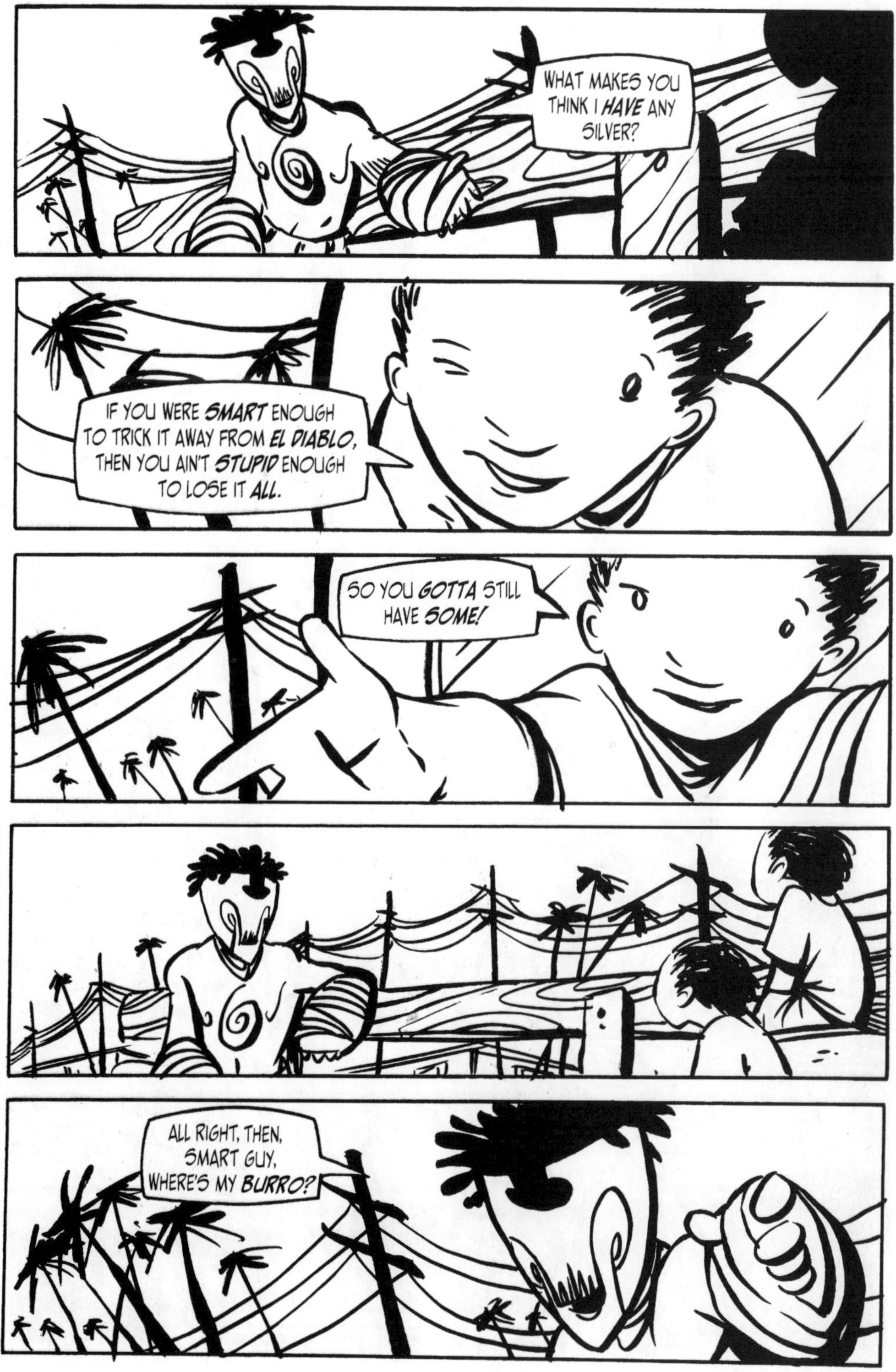
WHAT MAKES YOU THINK I *HAVE* ANY SILVER?
IF YOU WERE *SMART* ENOUGH TO TRICK IT AWAY FROM *EL DIABLO*, THEN YOU AIN'T *STUPID* ENOUGH TO LOSE IT *ALL*.
SO YOU *GOTTA* STILL HAVE *SOME!*
ALL RIGHT, THEN, SMART GUY, WHERE'S MY *BURRO?*

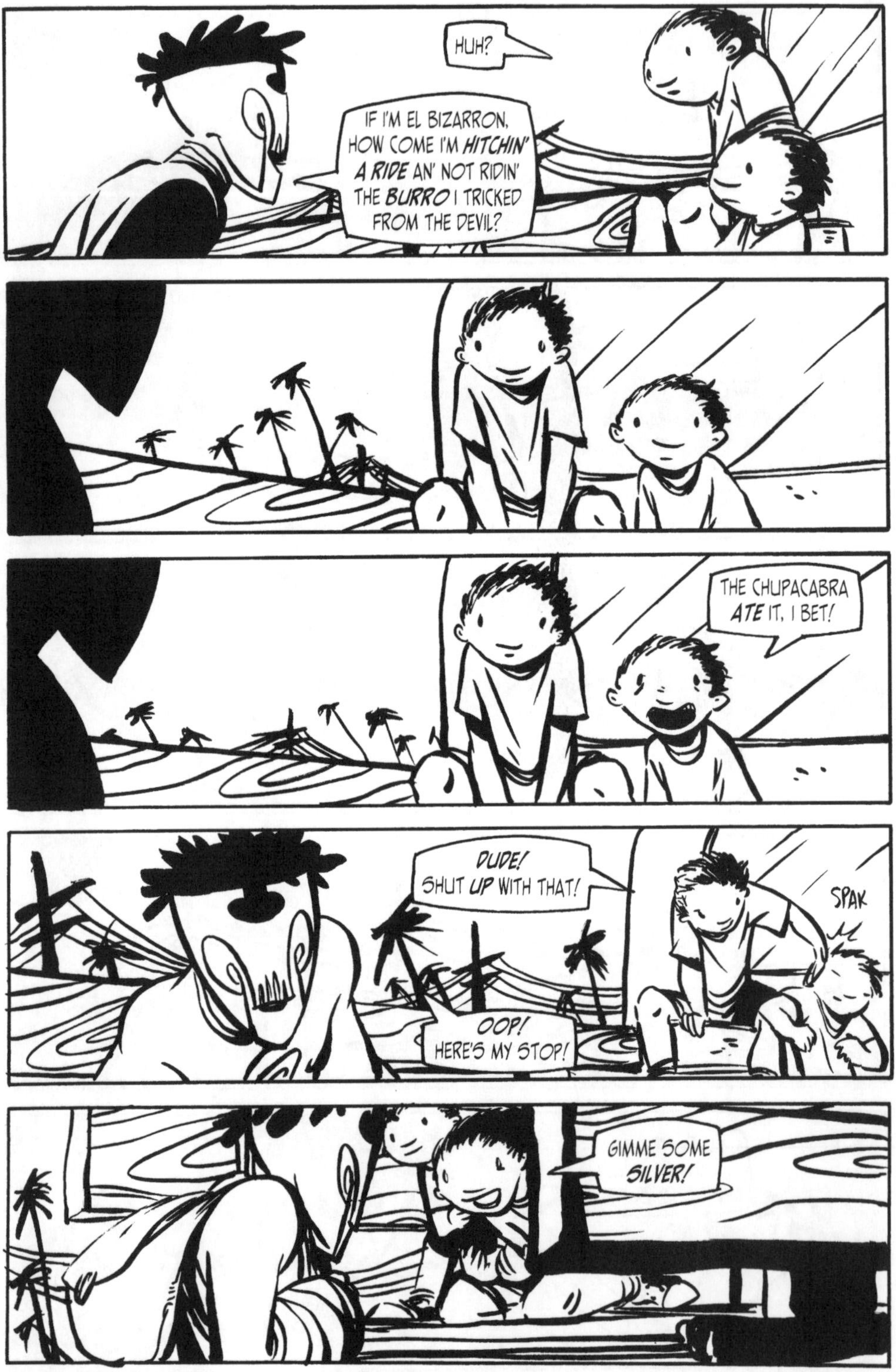
HUH?
IF I'M EL BIZARRON, HOW COME I'M HITCHIN' A RIDE AN' NOT RIDIN' THE BURRO I TRICKED FROM THE DEVIL?
THE CHUPACABRA ATE IT, I BET!
DUDE! SHUT UP WITH THAT!
SPAK
OOP! HERE'S MY STOP!
GIMME SOME SILVER!

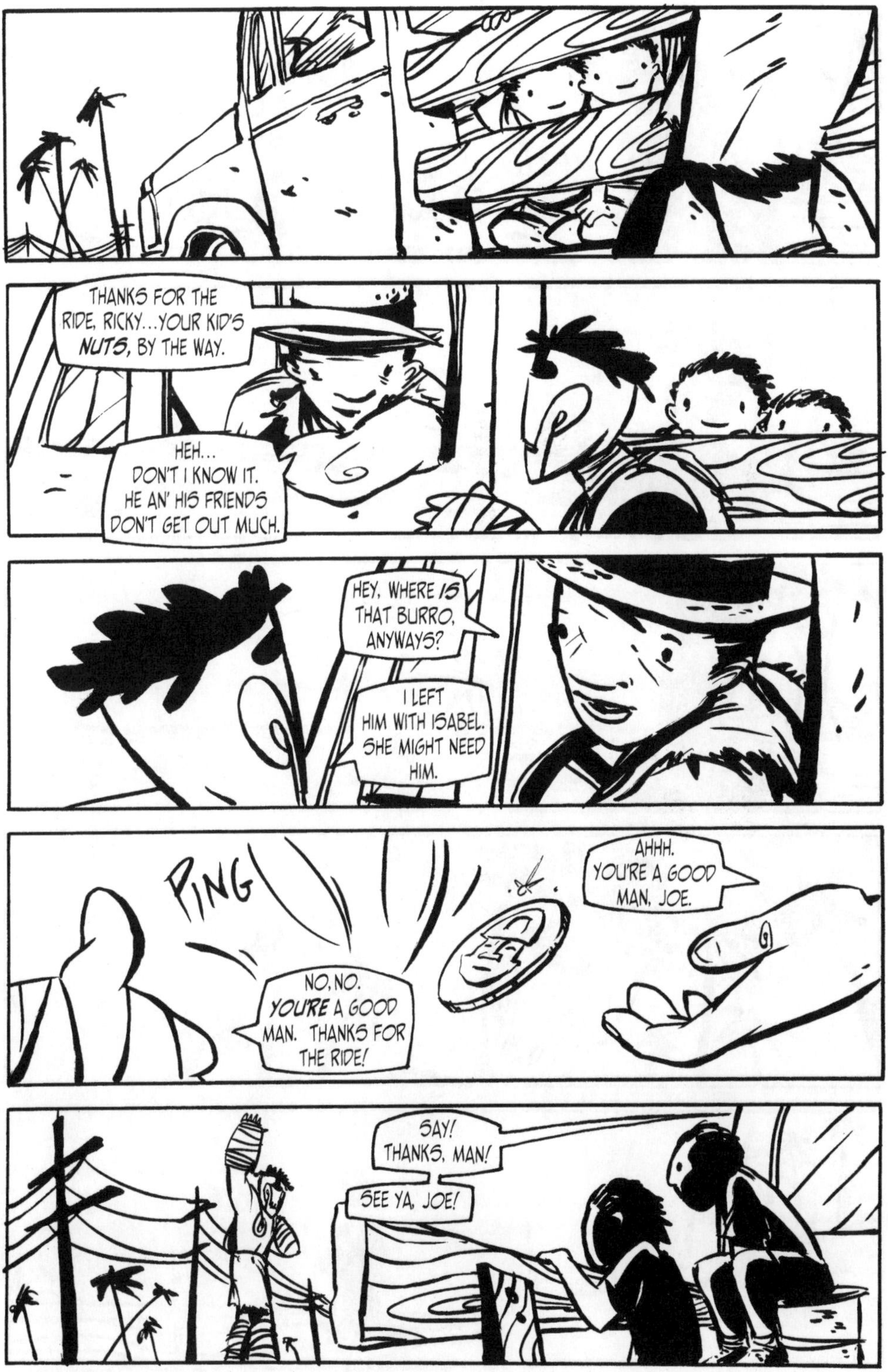
THANKS FOR THE RIDE, RICKY...YOUR KID'S NUTS, BY THE WAY.
HEH... DON'T I KNOW IT. HE AN' HIS FRIENDS DON'T GET OUT MUCH.
HEY, WHERE IS THAT BURRO, ANYWAYS?
I LEFT HIM WITH ISABEL. SHE MIGHT NEED HIM.
PING
AHHH. YOU'RE A GOOD MAN, JOE.
NO, NO. YOU'RE A GOOD MAN. THANKS FOR THE RIDE!
SAY! THANKS, MAN!
SEE YA, JOE!

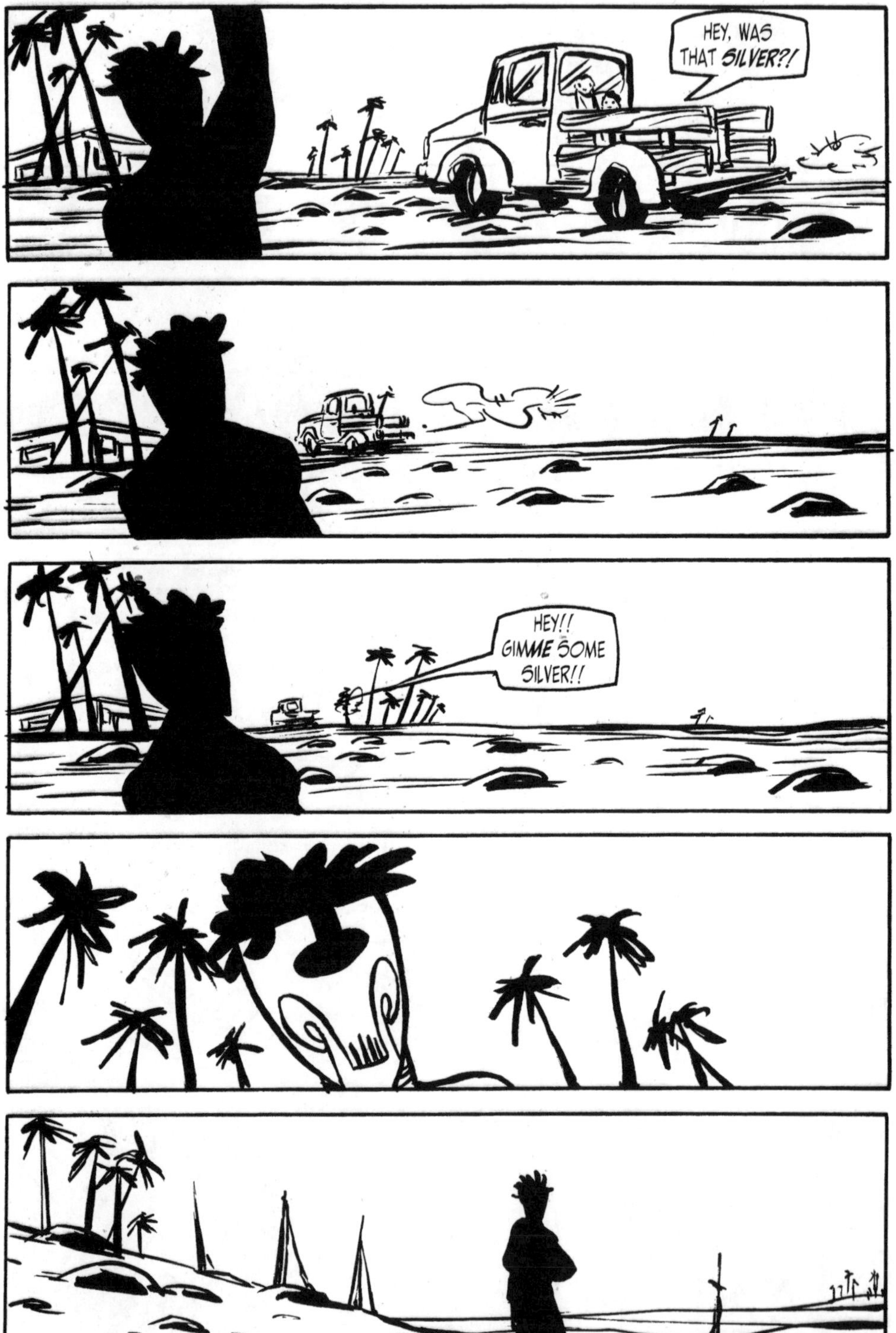
HEY, WAS THAT SILVER?!
HEY!! GIMME SOME SILVER!!

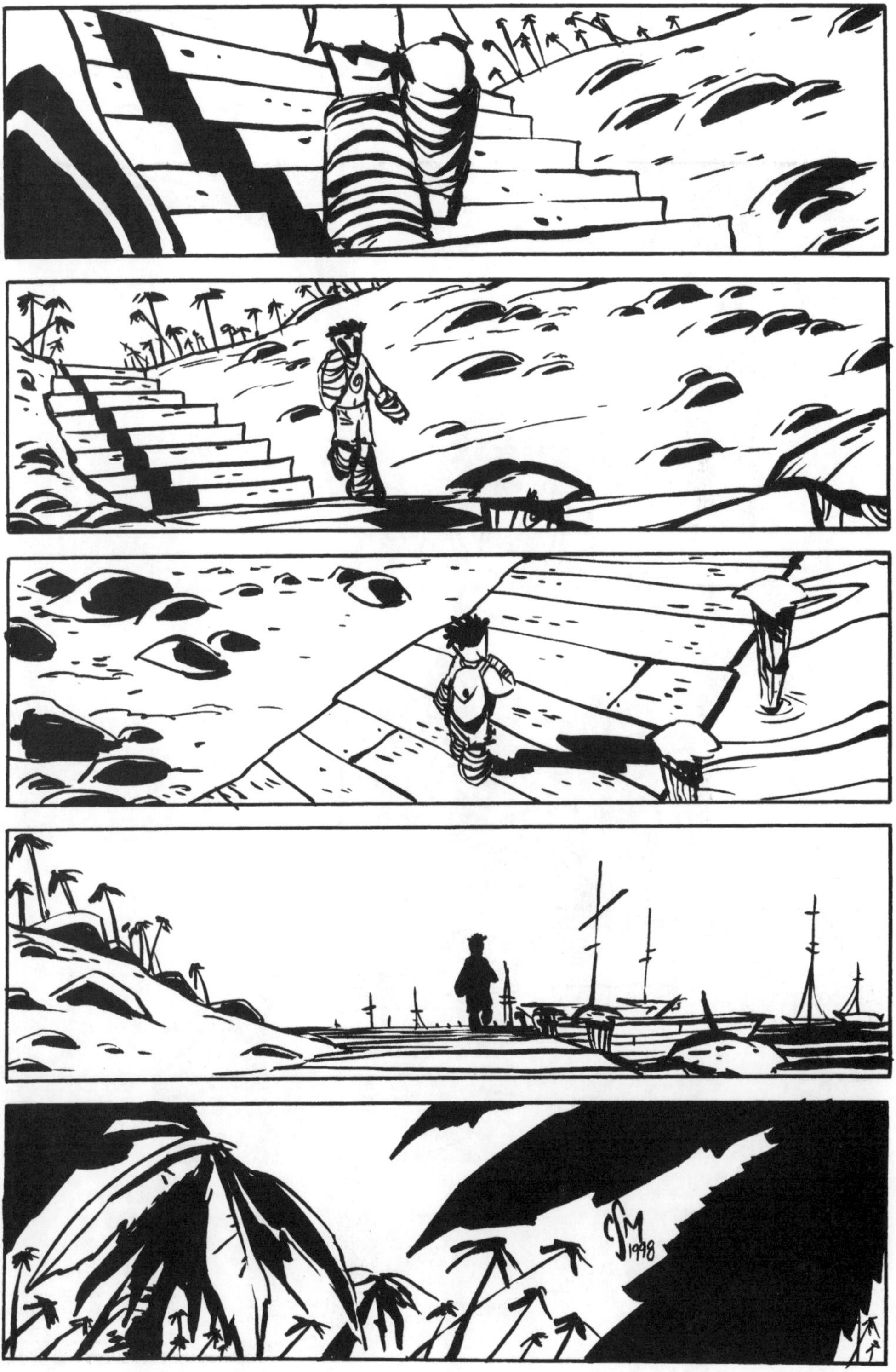
1998

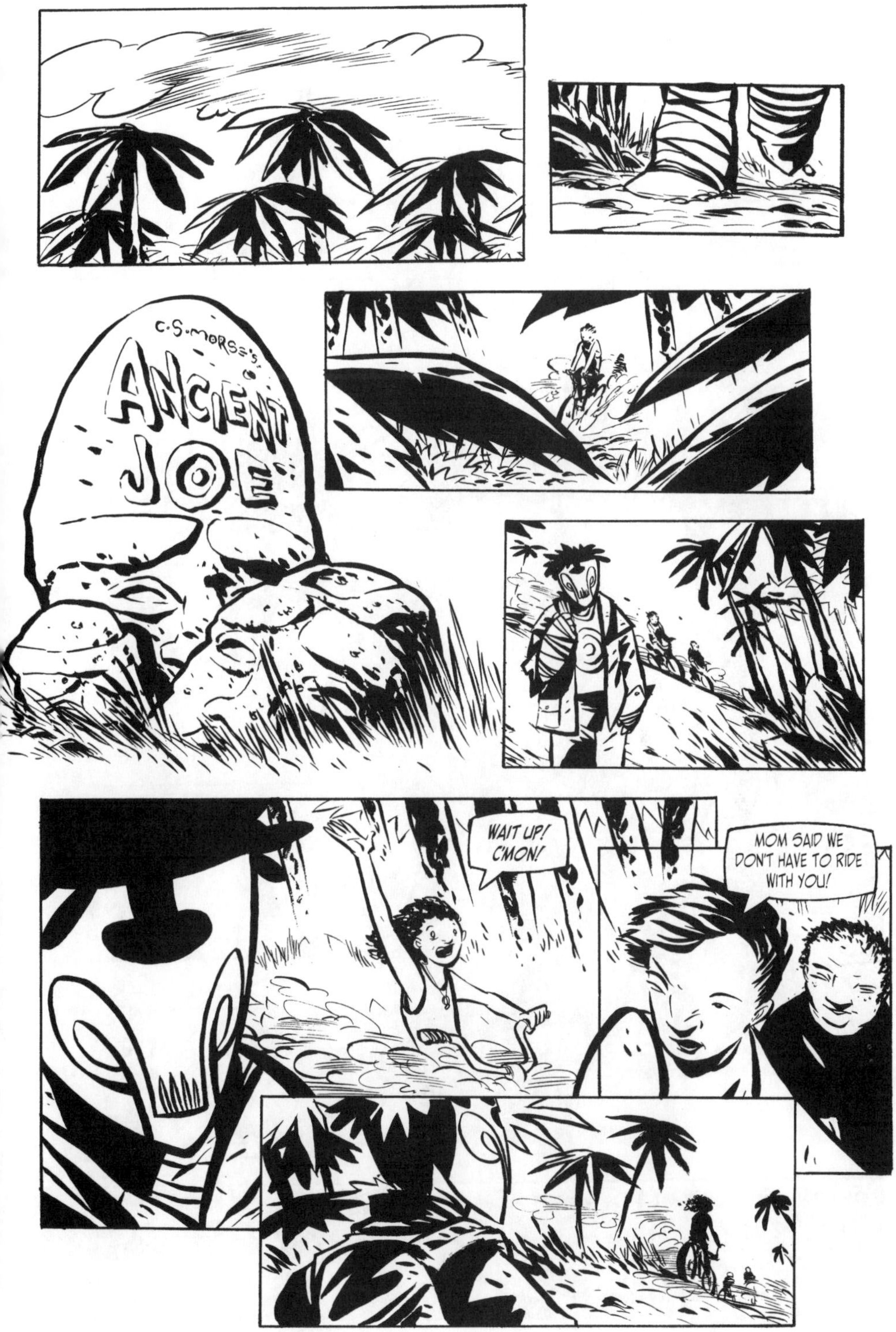
C.S. MORSE'S
ANCIENT JOE
WAIT UP! C'MON!
MOM SAID WE DON'T HAVE TO RIDE WITH YOU!

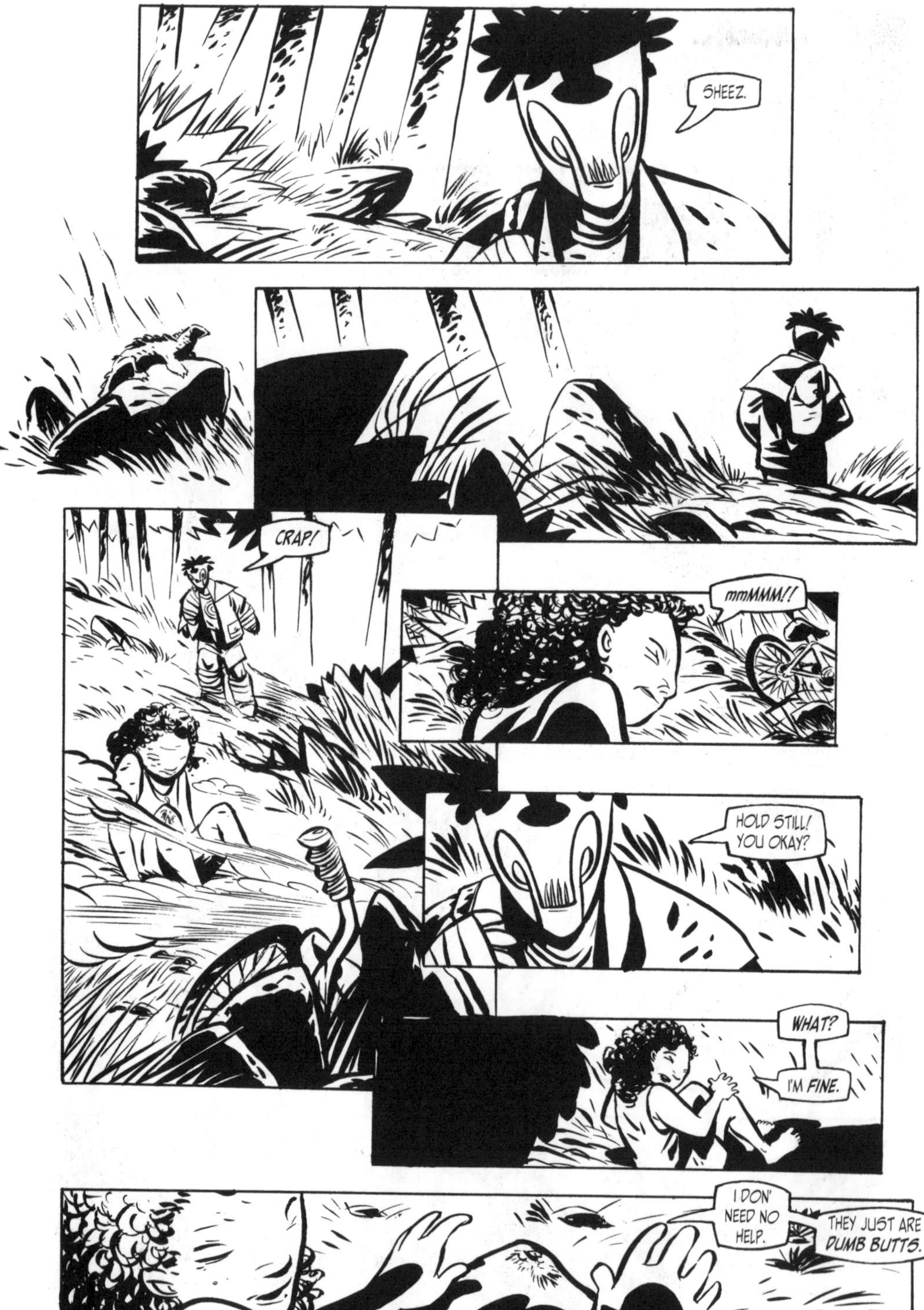
SHEEZ.
CRAP!
mmMMM!!
HOLD STILL! YOU OKAY?
WHAT?
I'M FINE.
I DON' NEED NO HELP.
THEY JUST ARE DUMB BUTTS.

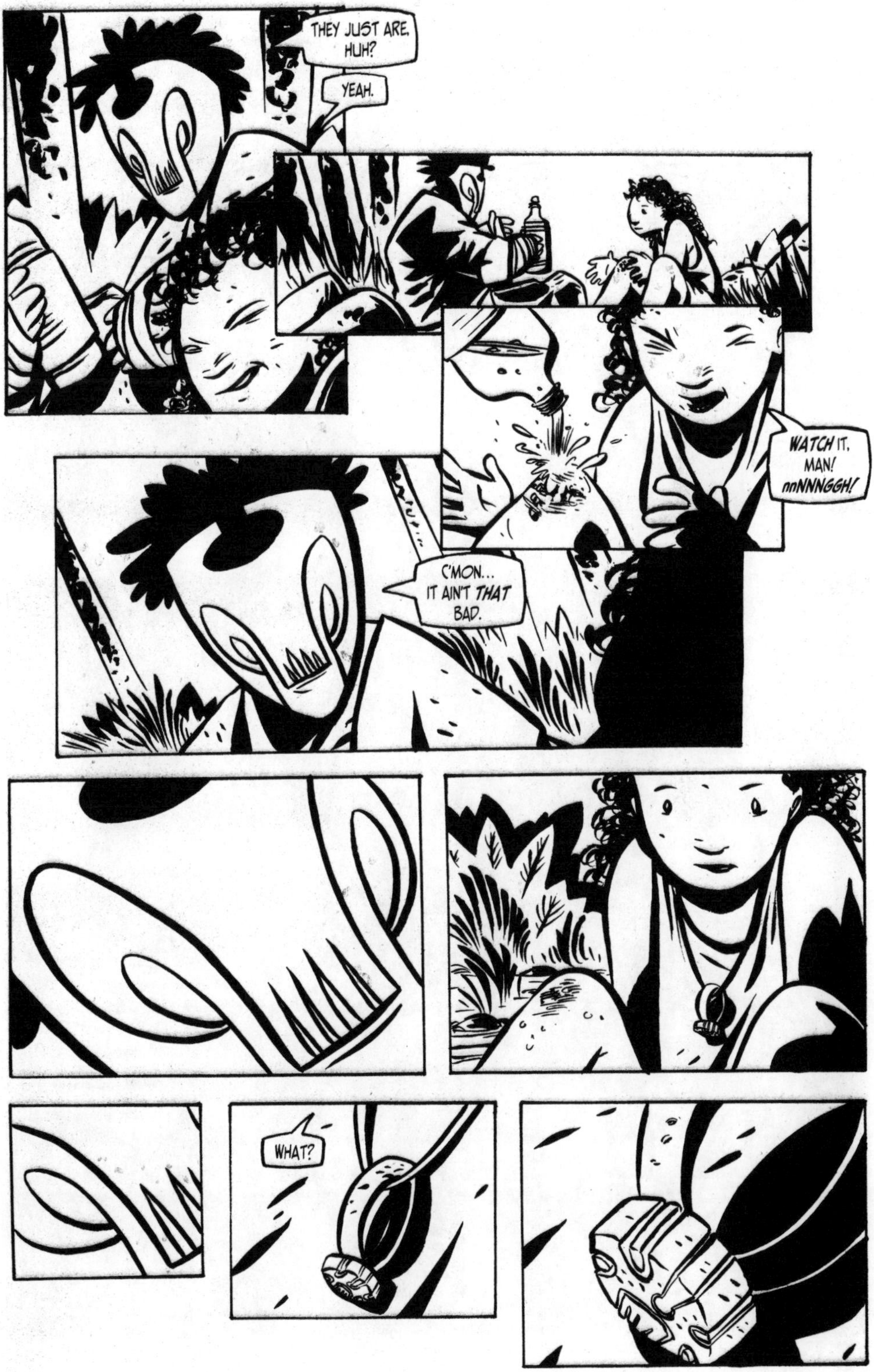
THEY JUST ARE, HUH?
YEAH.
WATCH IT, MAN! nnNNNGGH!
C'MON... IT AIN'T THAT BAD.
WHAT?

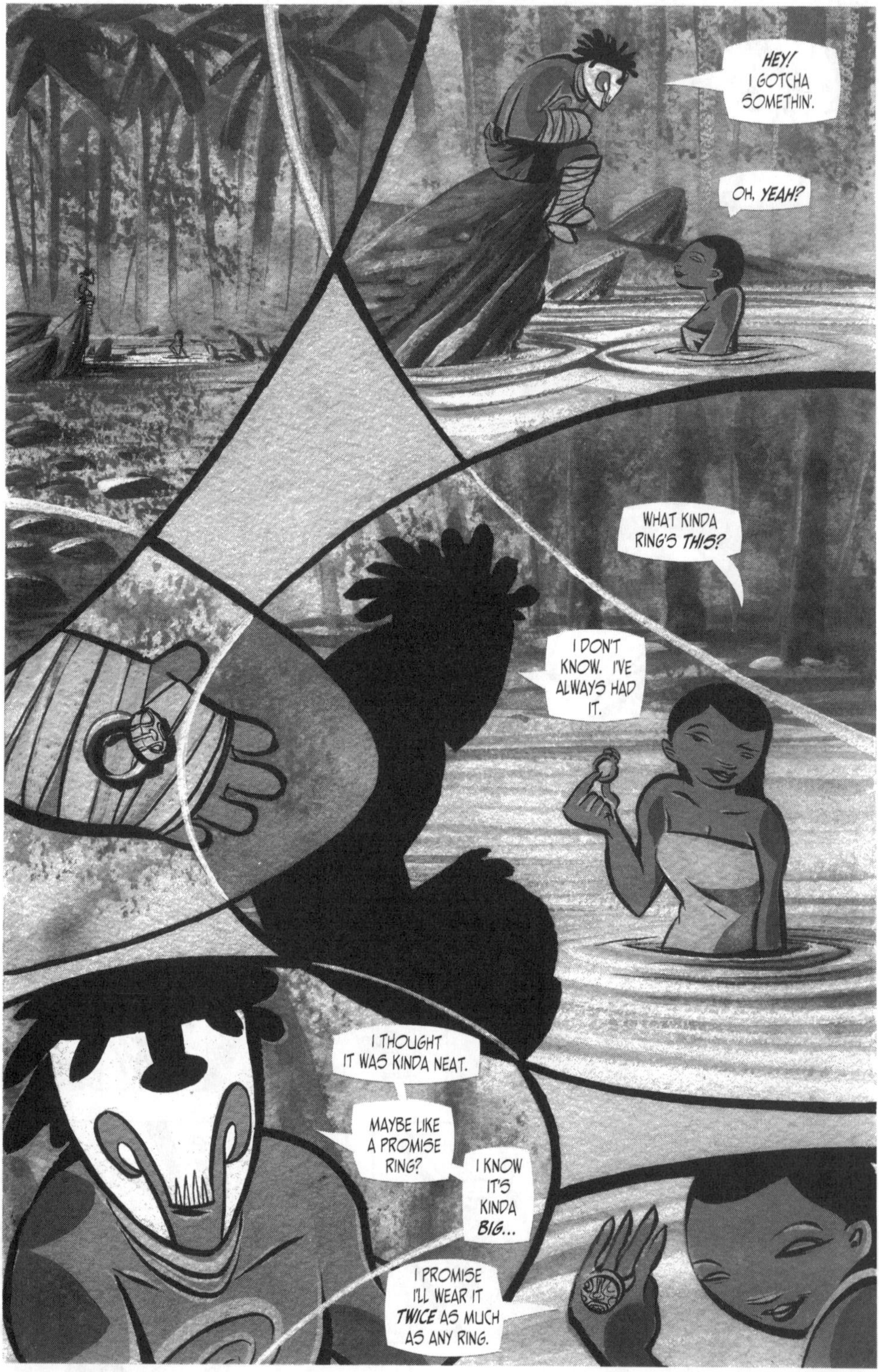
HEY! I GOTCHA SOMETHIN'.
OH, YEAH?
WHAT KINDA RING'S THIS?
I DON'T KNOW. I'VE ALWAYS HAD IT.
I THOUGHT IT WAS KINDA NEAT.
MAYBE LIKE A PROMISE RING?
I KNOW IT'S KINDA BIG...
I PROMISE I'LL WEAR IT TWICE AS MUCH AS ANY RING.

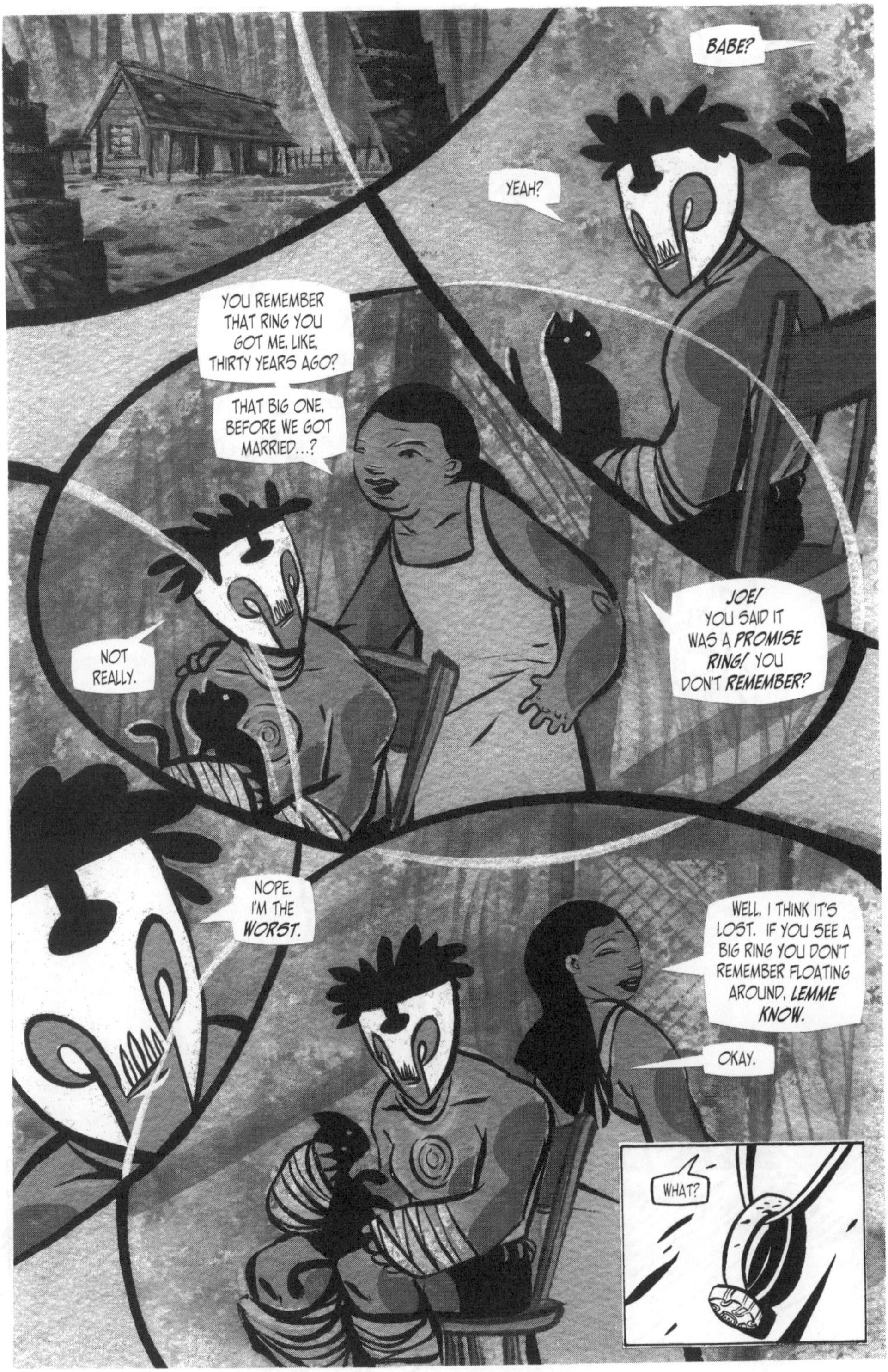
BABE?
YEAH?
YOU REMEMBER THAT RING YOU GOT ME, LIKE, THIRTY YEARS AGO?
THAT BIG ONE, BEFORE WE GOT MARRIED...?
NOT REALLY.
JOE! YOU SAID IT WAS A PROMISE RING! YOU DON'T REMEMBER?
NOPE. I'M THE WORST.
WELL, I THINK IT'S LOST. IF YOU SEE A BIG RING YOU DON'T REMEMBER FLOATING AROUND, LEMME KNOW.
OKAY.
WHAT?

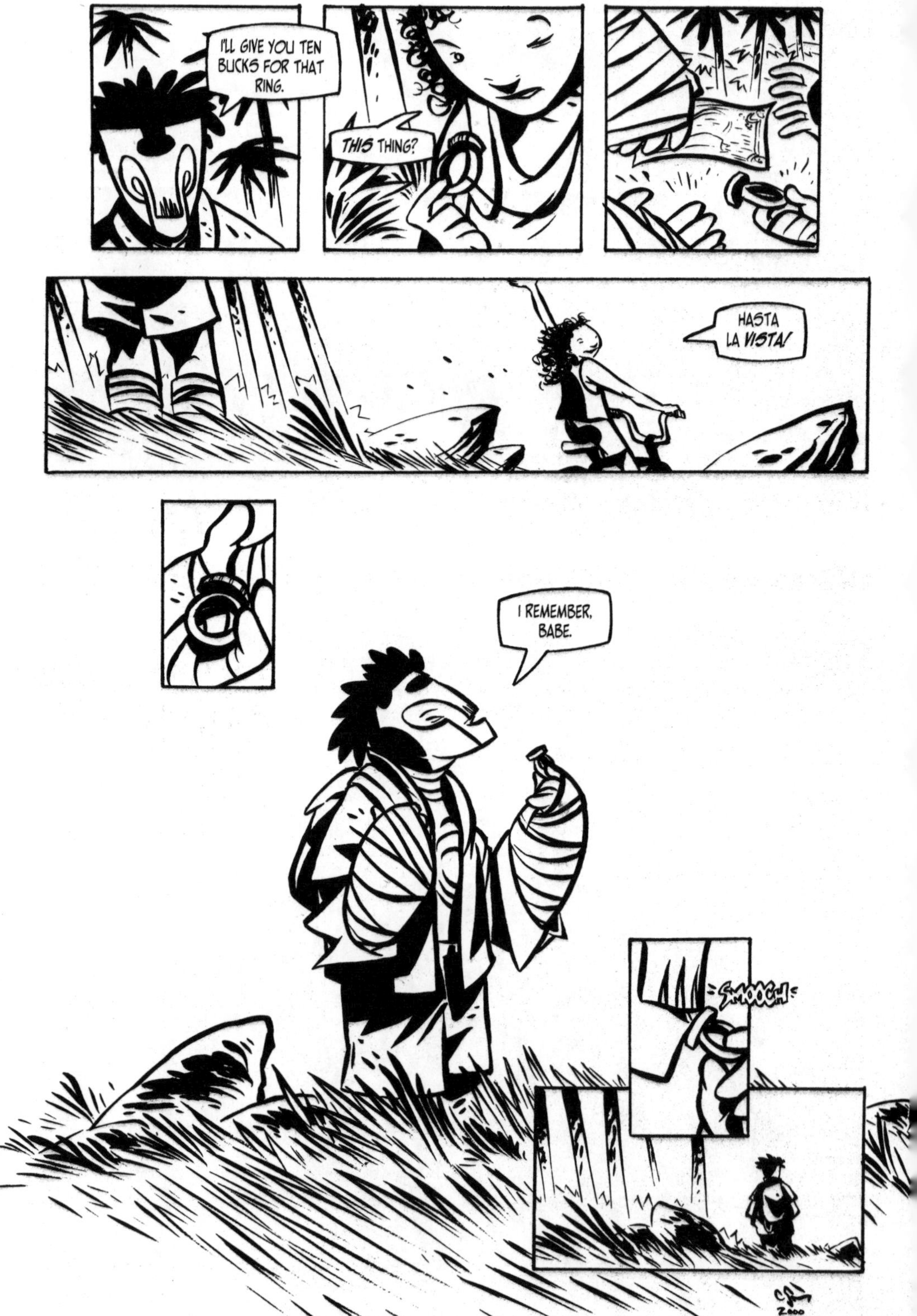
I'LL GIVE YOU TEN BUCKS FOR THAT RING.
THIS THING?
HASTA LA VISTA!
I REMEMBER, BABE.
SMOOCH

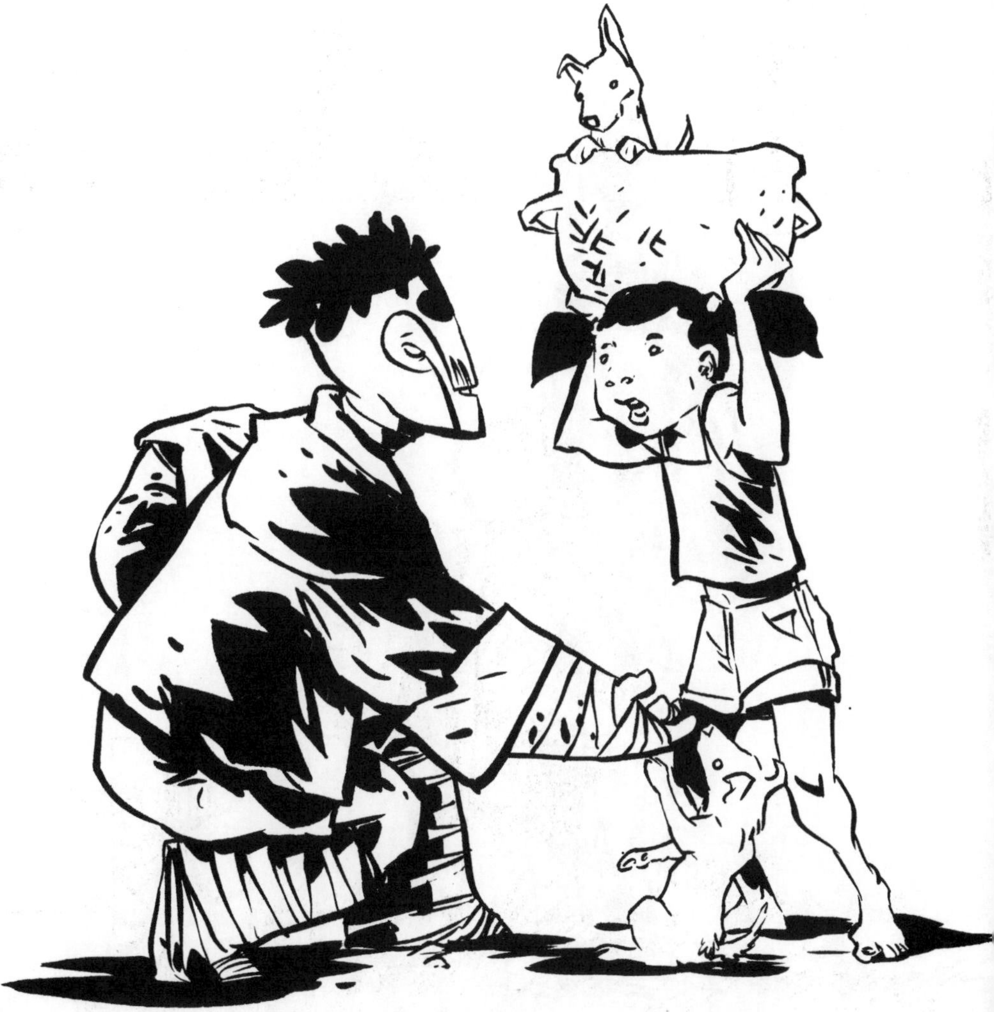

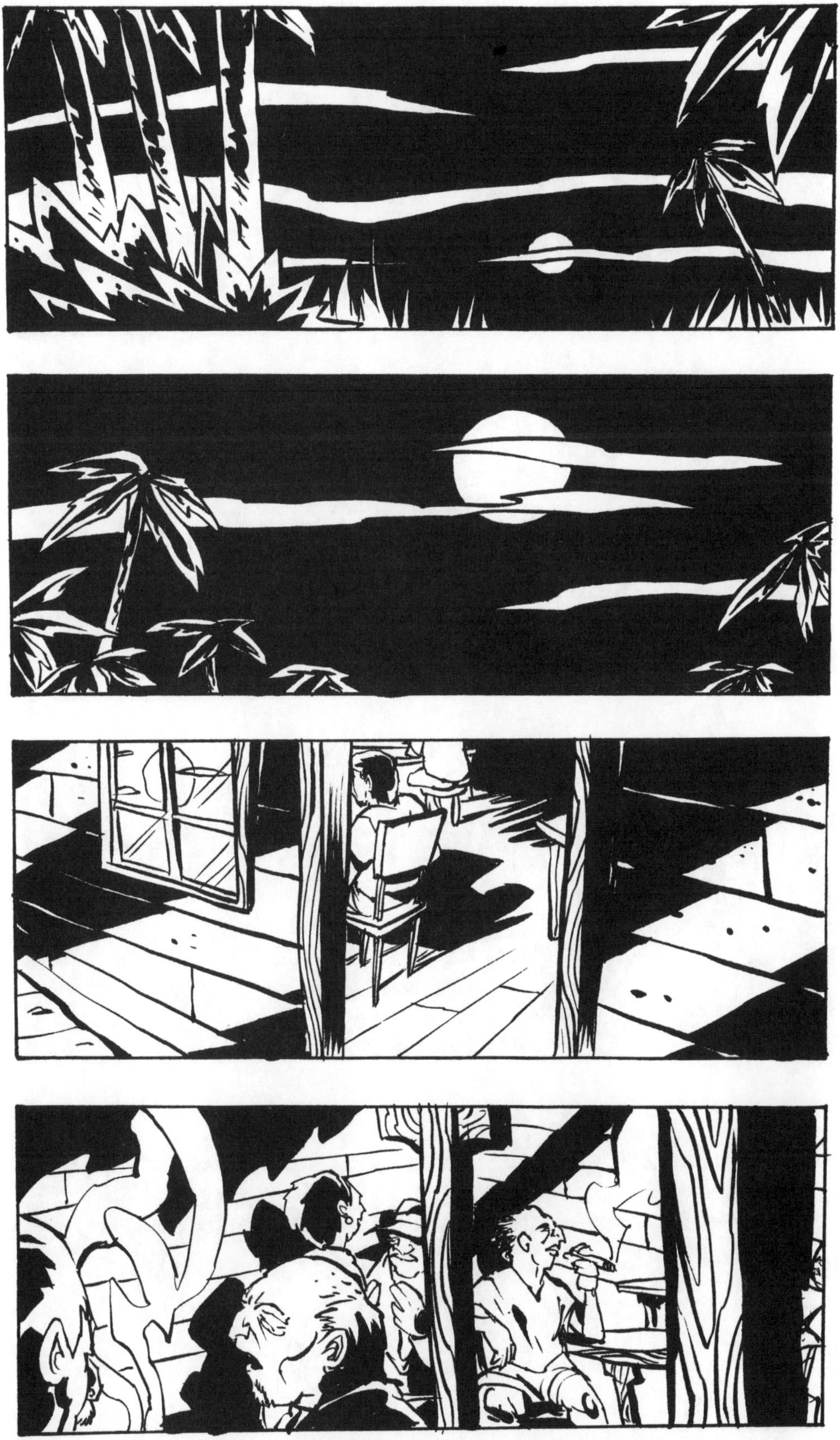

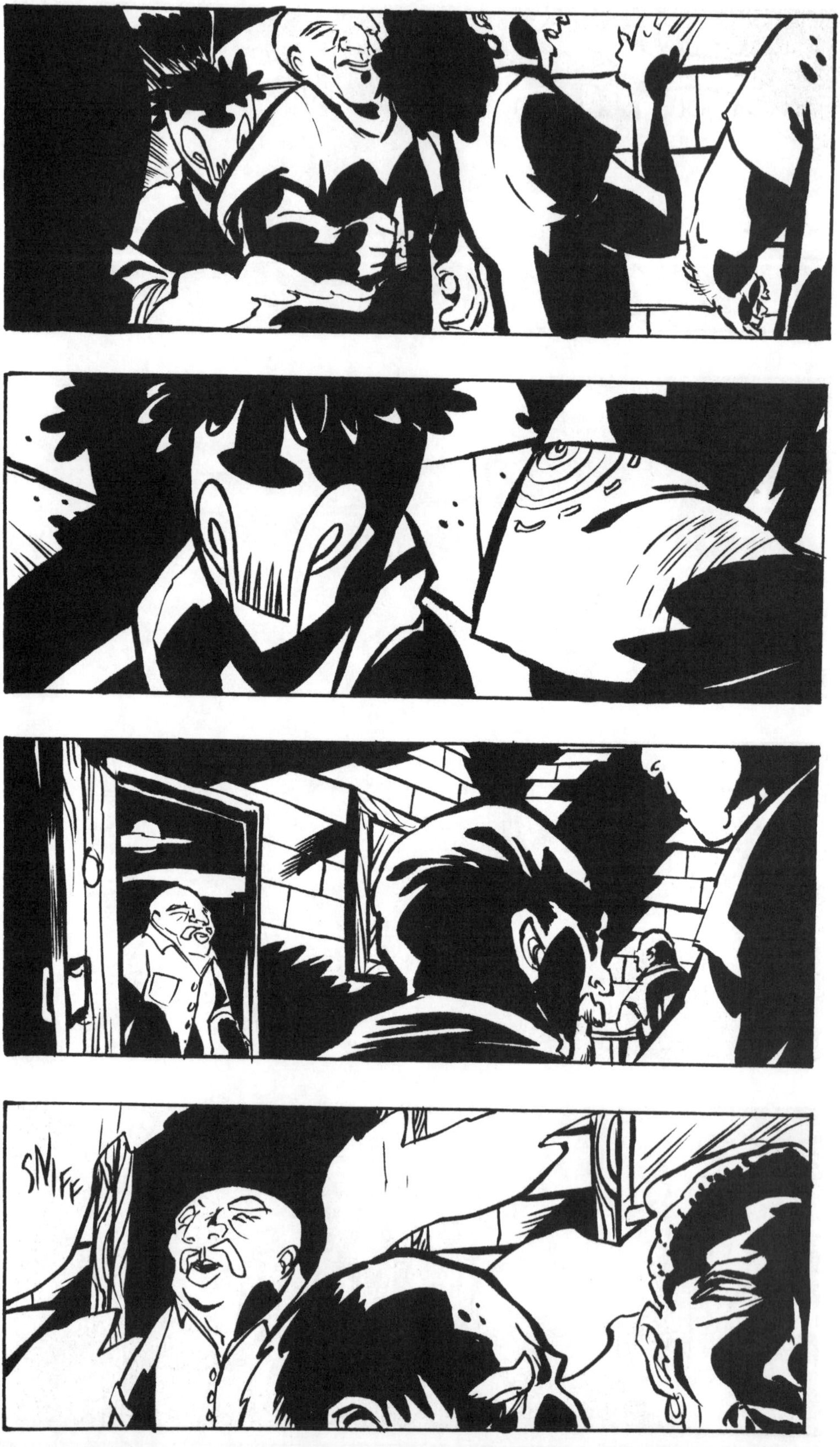
SNIFF

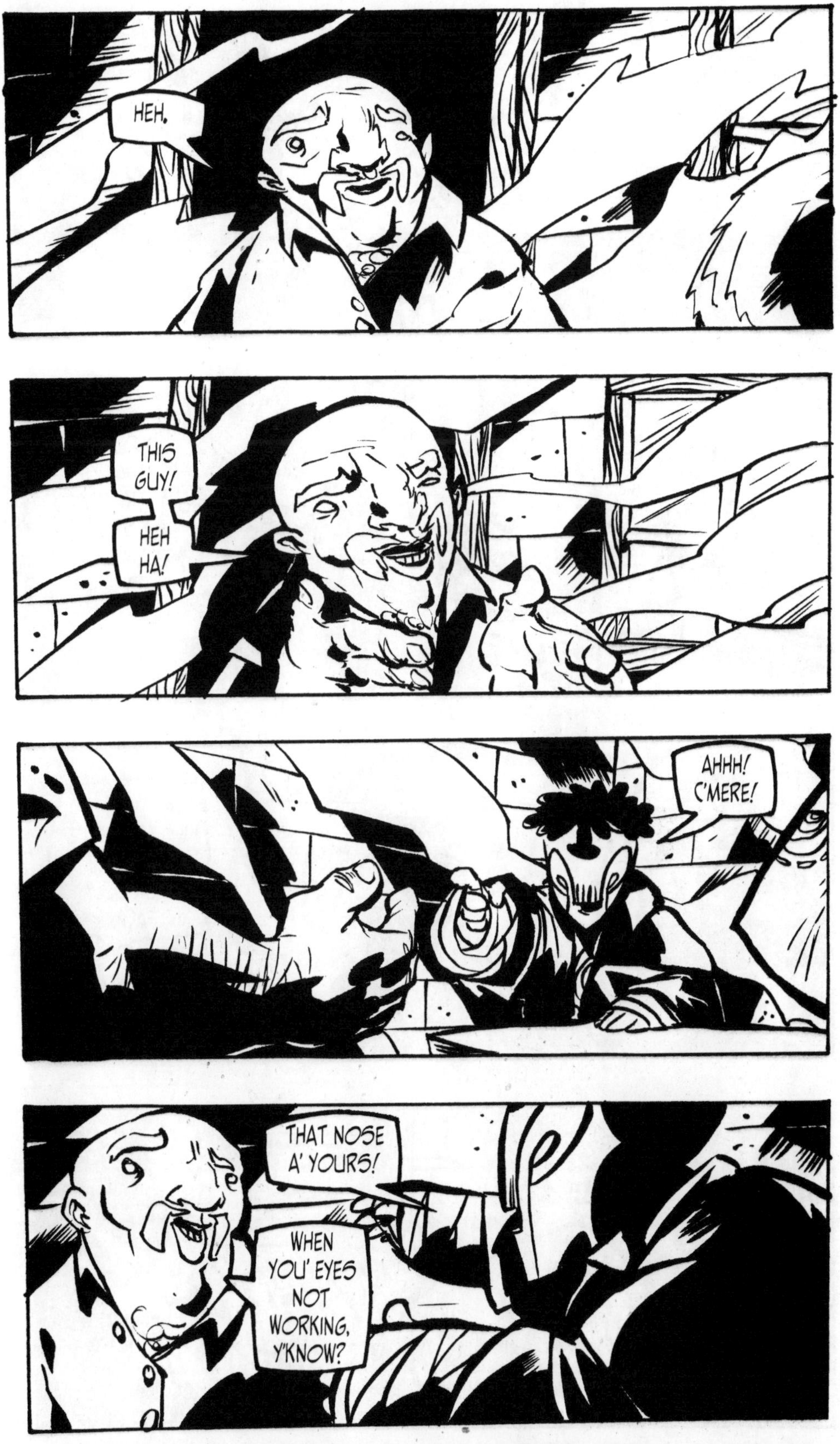
HEH.
THIS GUY!
HEH HA!
AHHH! C'MERE!
THAT NOSE A' YOURS!
WHEN YOU' EYES NOT WORKING, Y'KNOW?

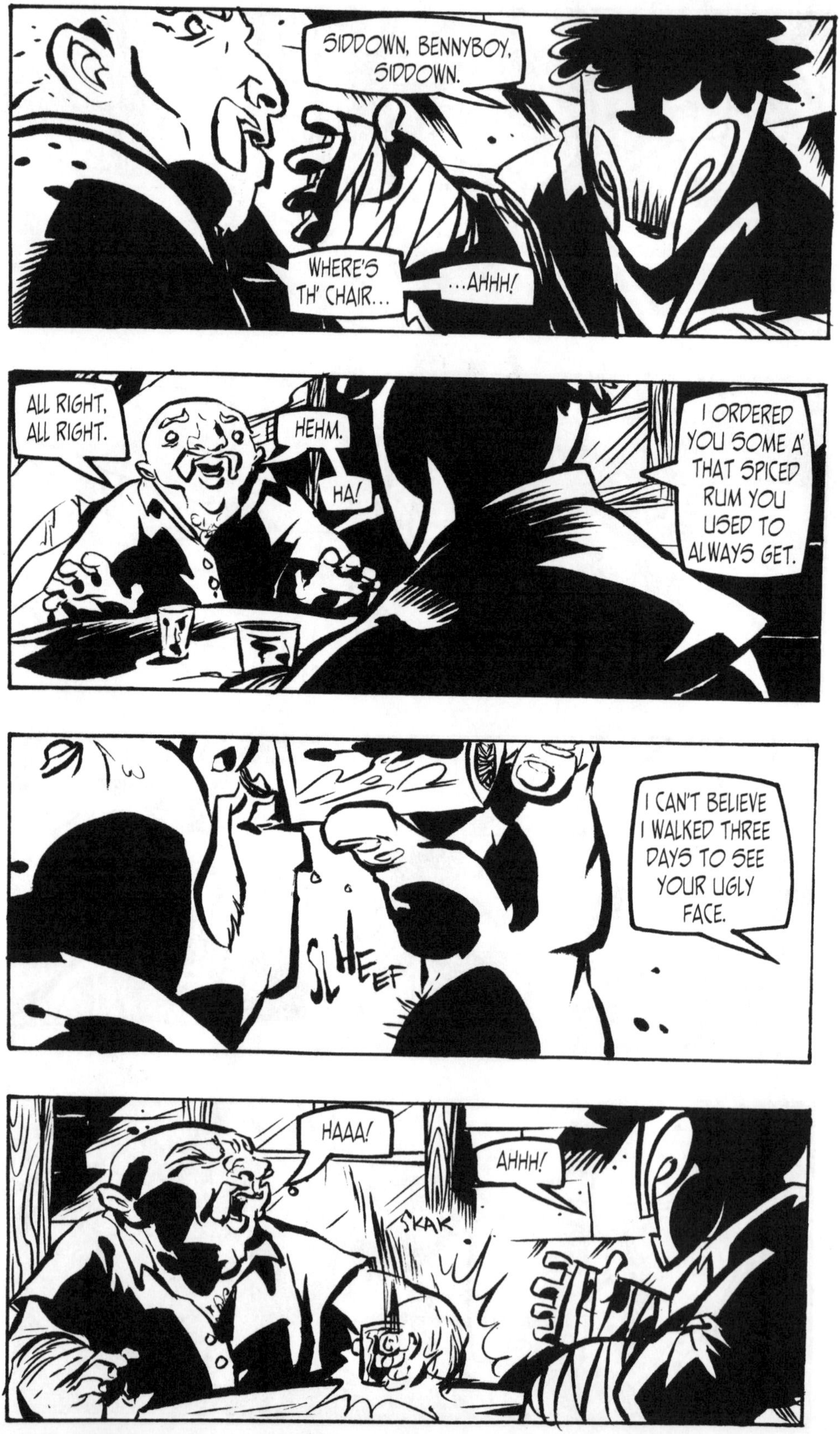
SIDDOWN, BENNYBOY, SIDDOWN.
WHERE'S TH' CHAIR...
...AHHH!
ALL RIGHT, ALL RIGHT.
HEHM.
HA!
I ORDERED YOU SOME A' THAT SPICED RUM YOU USED TO ALWAYS GET.
I CAN'T BELIEVE I WALKED THREE DAYS TO SEE YOUR UGLY FACE.
SLHEEF
HAAA!
AHHH!
SKAK

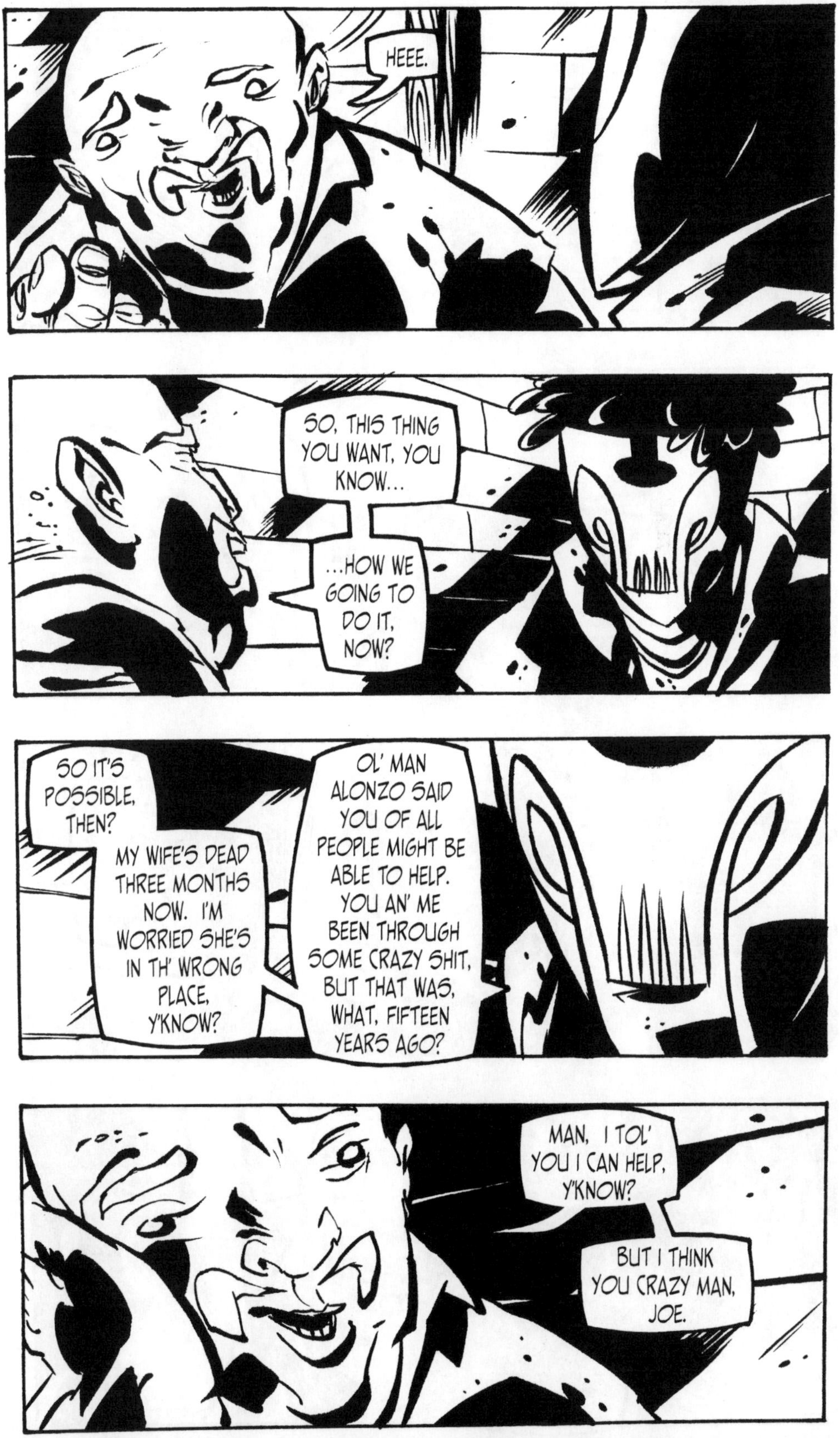
HEEE.
SO, THIS THING YOU WANT, YOU KNOW...
...HOW WE GOING TO DO IT, NOW?
SO IT'S POSSIBLE, THEN?
MY WIFE'S DEAD THREE MONTHS NOW. I'M WORRIED SHE'S IN TH' WRONG PLACE, Y'KNOW?
OL' MAN ALONZO SAID YOU OF ALL PEOPLE MIGHT BE ABLE TO HELP. YOU AN' ME BEEN THROUGH SOME CRAZY SHIT, BUT THAT WAS, WHAT, FIFTEEN YEARS AGO?
MAN, I TOL' YOU I CAN HELP, Y'KNOW?
BUT I THINK YOU CRAZY MAN, JOE.

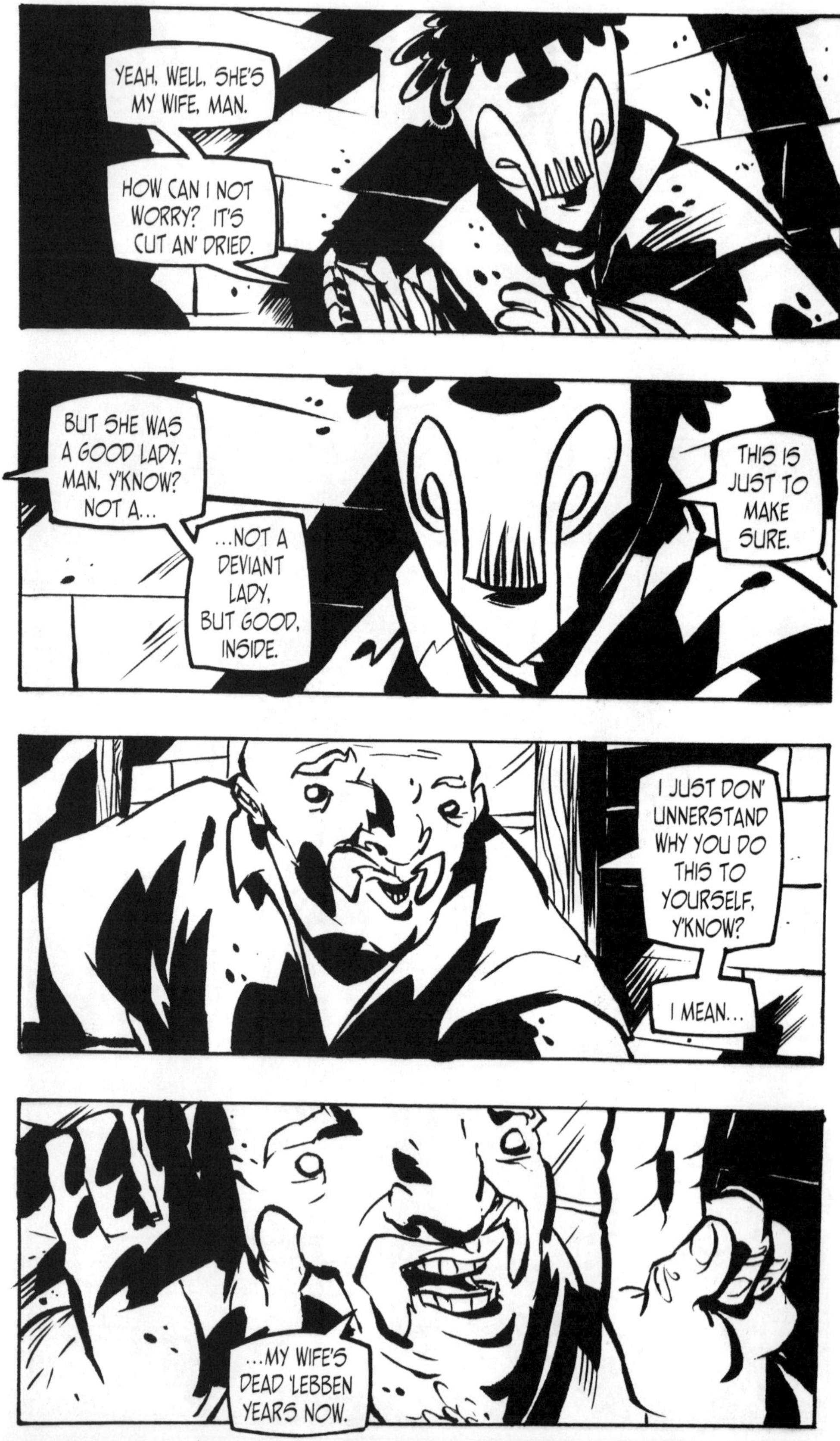
YEAH, WELL, SHE'S MY WIFE, MAN.
HOW CAN I NOT WORRY? IT'S CUT AN' DRIED.
BUT SHE WAS A GOOD LADY, MAN, Y'KNOW? NOT A...
...NOT A DEVIANT LADY, BUT GOOD, INSIDE.
THIS IS JUST TO MAKE SURE.
I JUST DON' UNNERSTAND WHY YOU DO THIS TO YOURSELF, Y'KNOW?
I MEAN...
...MY WIFE'S DEAD 'LEBBEN YEARS NOW.

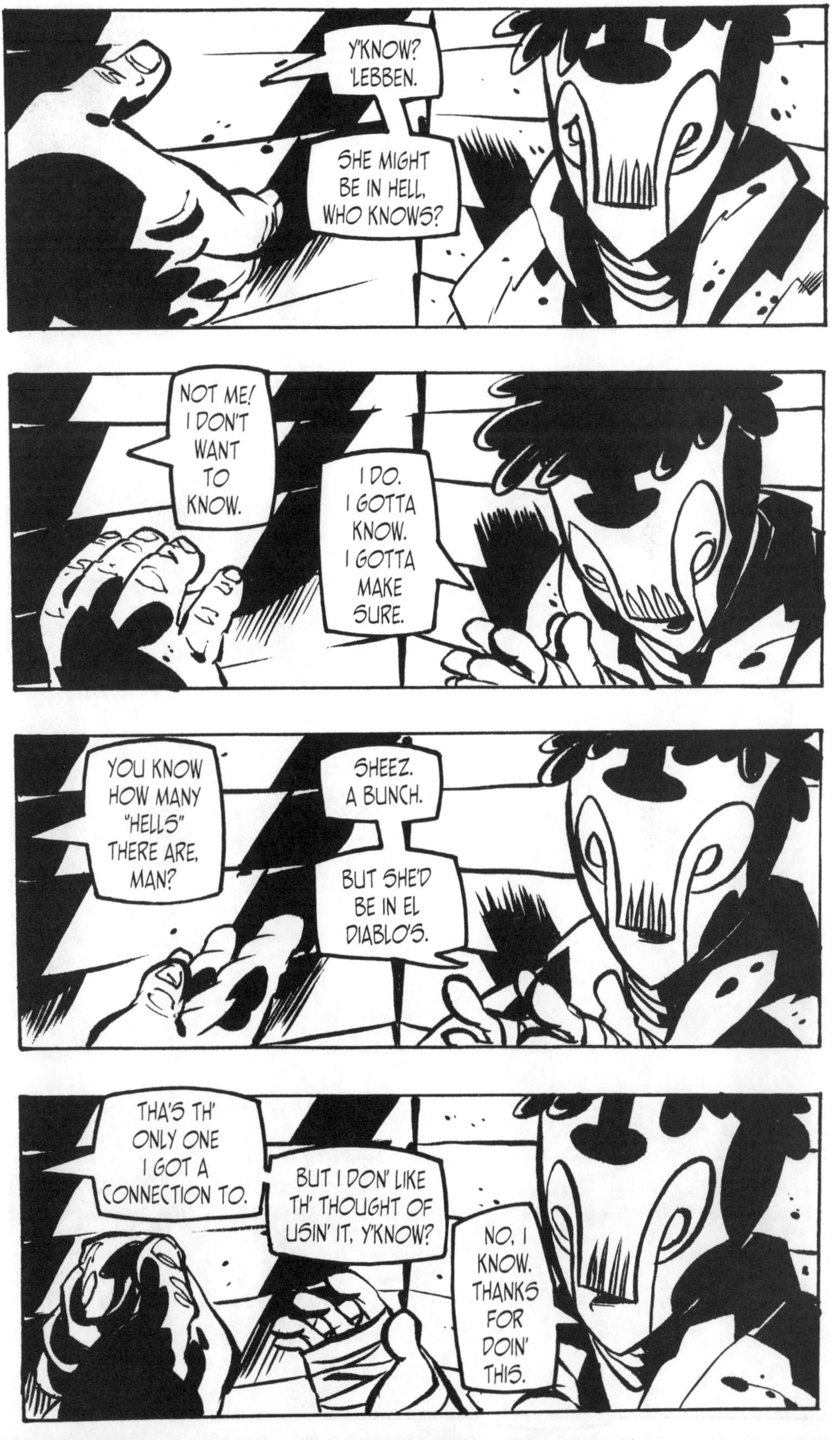
Y'KNOW? 'LEBBEN.
SHE MIGHT BE IN HELL, WHO KNOWS?
NOT ME! I DON'T WANT TO KNOW.
I DO. I GOTTA KNOW. I GOTTA MAKE SURE.
YOU KNOW HOW MANY "HELLS" THERE ARE, MAN?
SHEEZ. A BUNCH.
BUT SHE'D BE IN EL DIABLO'S.
THA'S TH' ONLY ONE I GOT A CONNECTION TO.
BUT I DON' LIKE TH' THOUGHT OF USIN' IT, Y'KNOW?
NO, I KNOW. THANKS FOR DOIN' THIS.

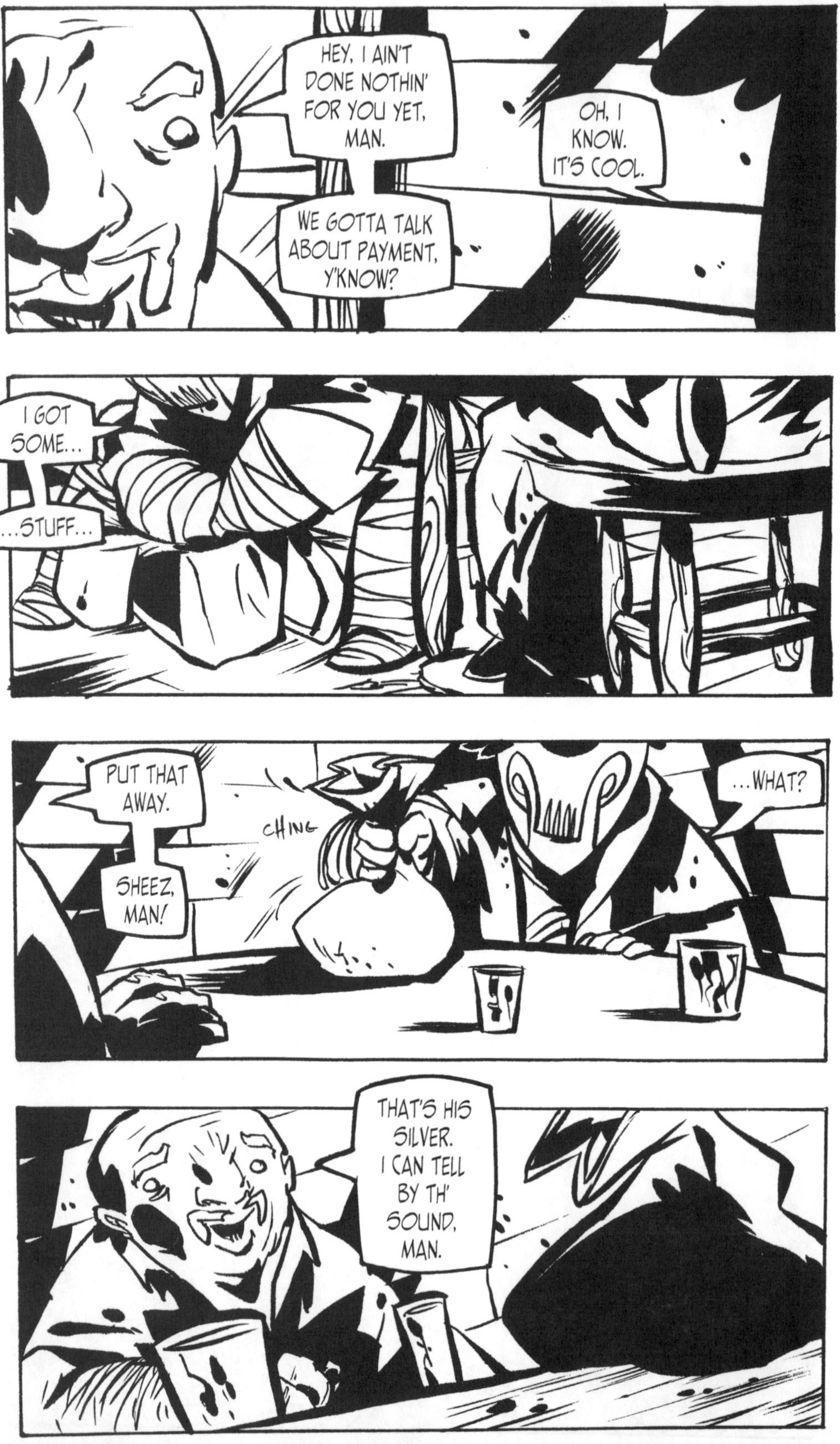
HEY, I AIN'T DONE NOTHIN' FOR YOU YET, MAN.
WE GOTTA TALK ABOUT PAYMENT, Y'KNOW?
OH, I KNOW. IT'S COOL.
I GOT SOME...
...STUFF...
PUT THAT AWAY.
SHEEZ, MAN!
CHING
...WHAT?
THAT'S HIS SILVER. I CAN TELL BY TH' SOUND, MAN.

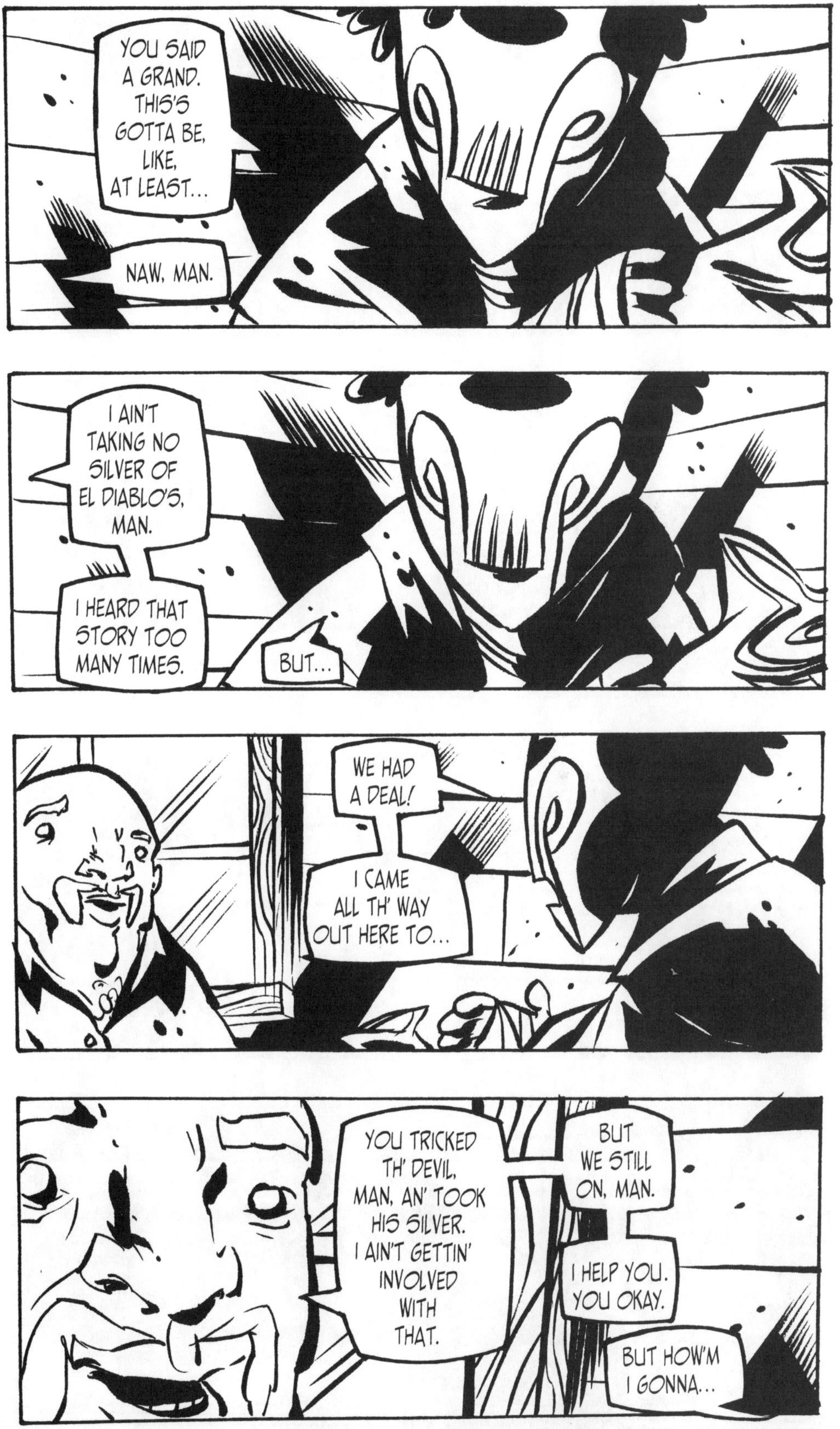
YOU SAID A GRAND. THIS'S GOTTA BE, LIKE, AT LEAST...
NAW, MAN.
I AIN'T TAKING NO SILVER OF EL DIABLO'S, MAN.
I HEARD THAT STORY TOO MANY TIMES.
BUT...
WE HAD A DEAL!
I CAME ALL TH' WAY OUT HERE TO...
YOU TRICKED TH' DEVIL, MAN, AN' TOOK HIS SILVER. I AIN'T GETTIN' INVOLVED WITH THAT.
BUT WE STILL ON, MAN.
I HELP YOU. YOU OKAY.
BUT HOW'M I GONNA...

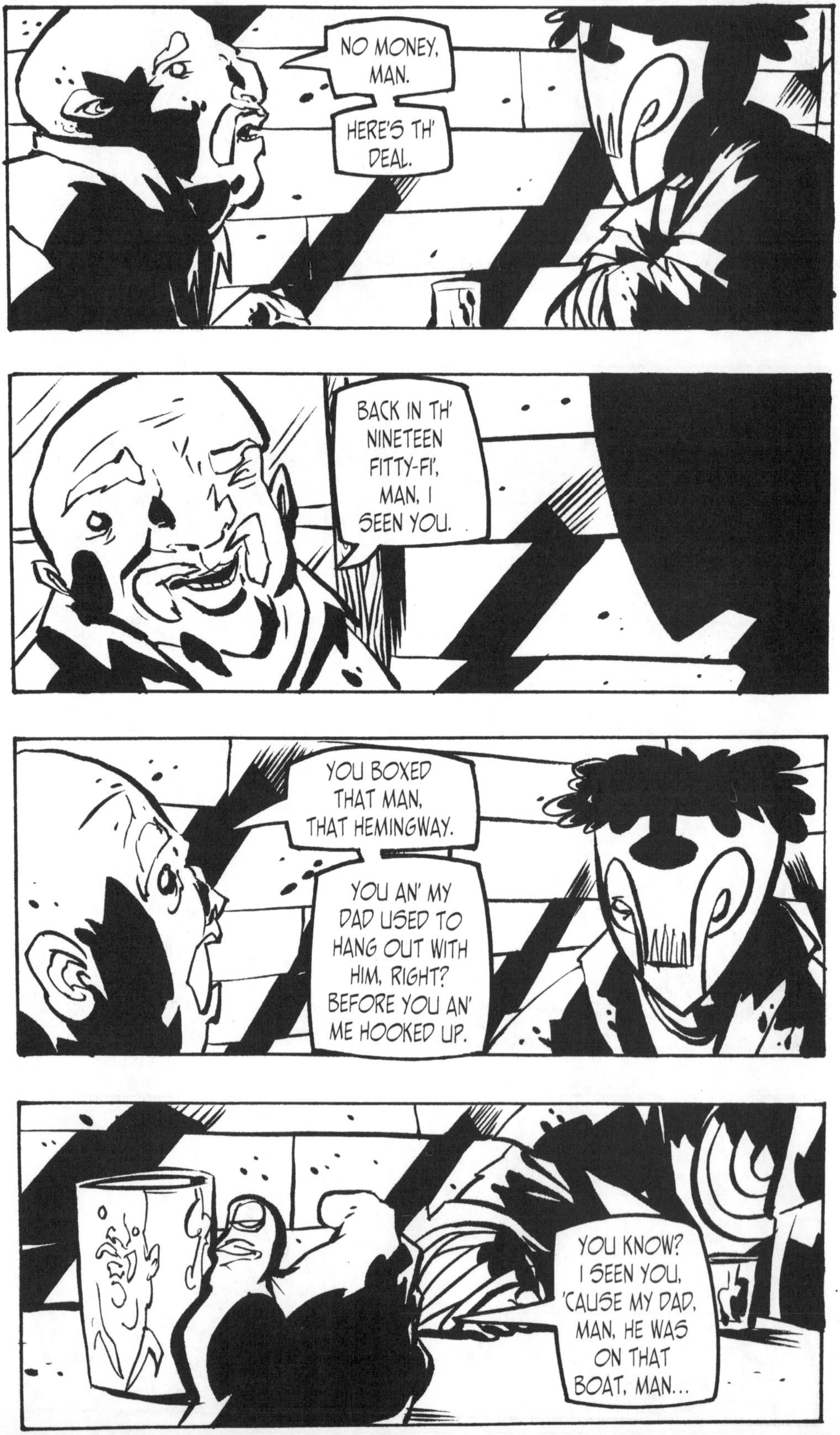

NO MONEY, MAN.
HERE'S TH' DEAL.
BACK IN TH' NINETEEN FITTY-FI', MAN, I SEEN YOU.
YOU BOXED THAT MAN, THAT HEMINGWAY.
YOU AN' MY DAD USED TO HANG OUT WITH HIM, RIGHT? BEFORE YOU AN' ME HOOKED UP.
YOU KNOW? I SEEN YOU, 'CAUSE MY DAD, MAN, HE WAS ON THAT BOAT, MAN...

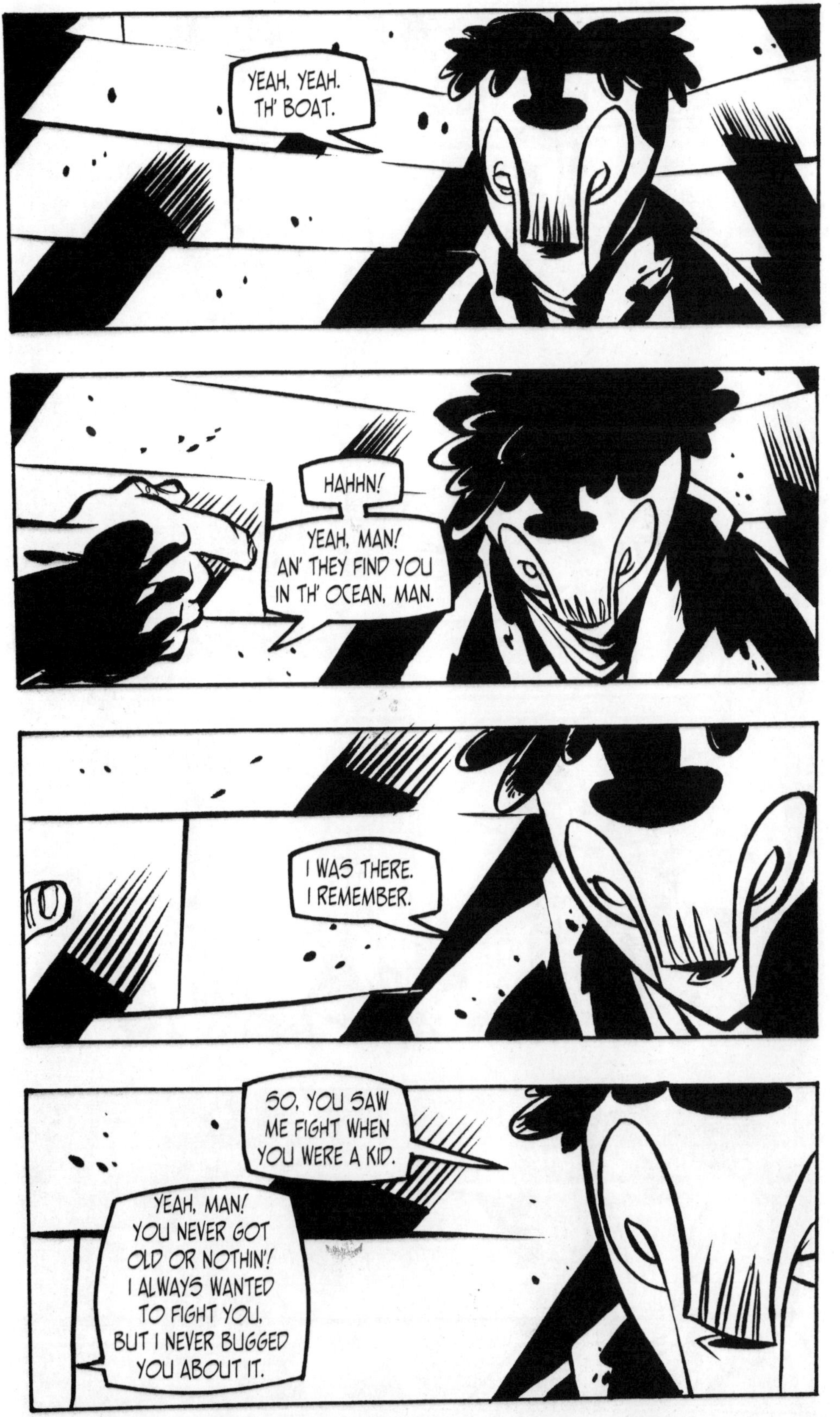
YEAH, YEAH. TH' BOAT.
HAHHN!
YEAH, MAN! AN' THEY FIND YOU IN TH' OCEAN, MAN.
I WAS THERE. I REMEMBER.
SO, YOU SAW ME FIGHT WHEN YOU WERE A KID.
YEAH, MAN! YOU NEVER GOT OLD OR NOTHIN'! I ALWAYS WANTED TO FIGHT YOU, BUT I NEVER BUGGED YOU ABOUT IT.

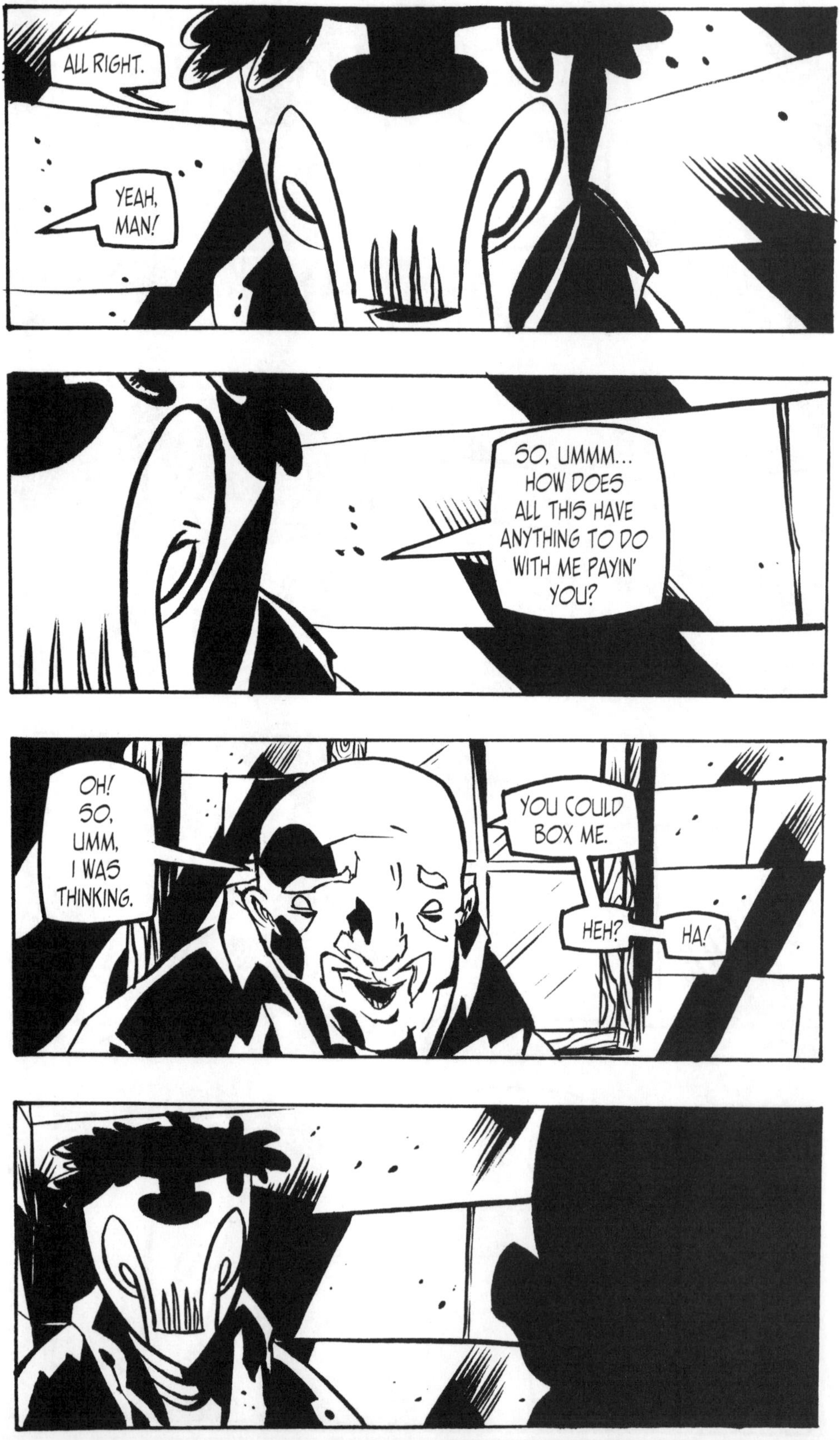
ALL RIGHT.
YEAH, MAN!
SO, UMMM... HOW DOES ALL THIS HAVE ANYTHING TO DO WITH ME PAYIN' YOU?
OH! SO, UMM, I WAS THINKING.
YOU COULD BOX ME.
HEH?
HA!

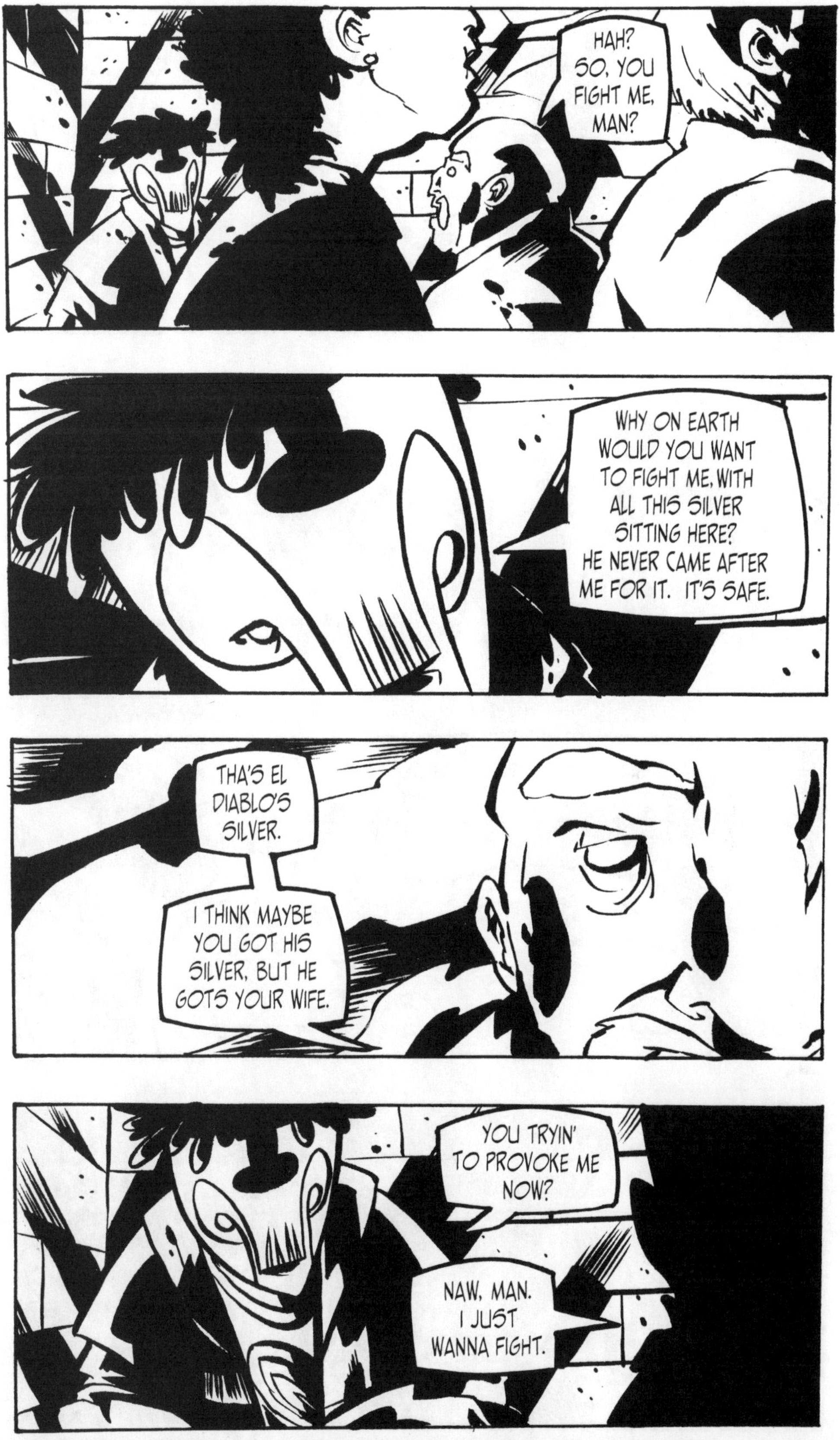
HAH? SO, YOU FIGHT ME, MAN?
WHY ON EARTH WOULD YOU WANT TO FIGHT ME, WITH ALL THIS SILVER SITTING HERE? HE NEVER CAME AFTER ME FOR IT. IT'S SAFE.
THA'S EL DIABLO'S SILVER.
I THINK MAYBE YOU GOT HIS SILVER, BUT HE GOTS YOUR WIFE.
YOU TRYIN' TO PROVOKE ME NOW?
NAW, MAN. I JUST WANNA FIGHT.

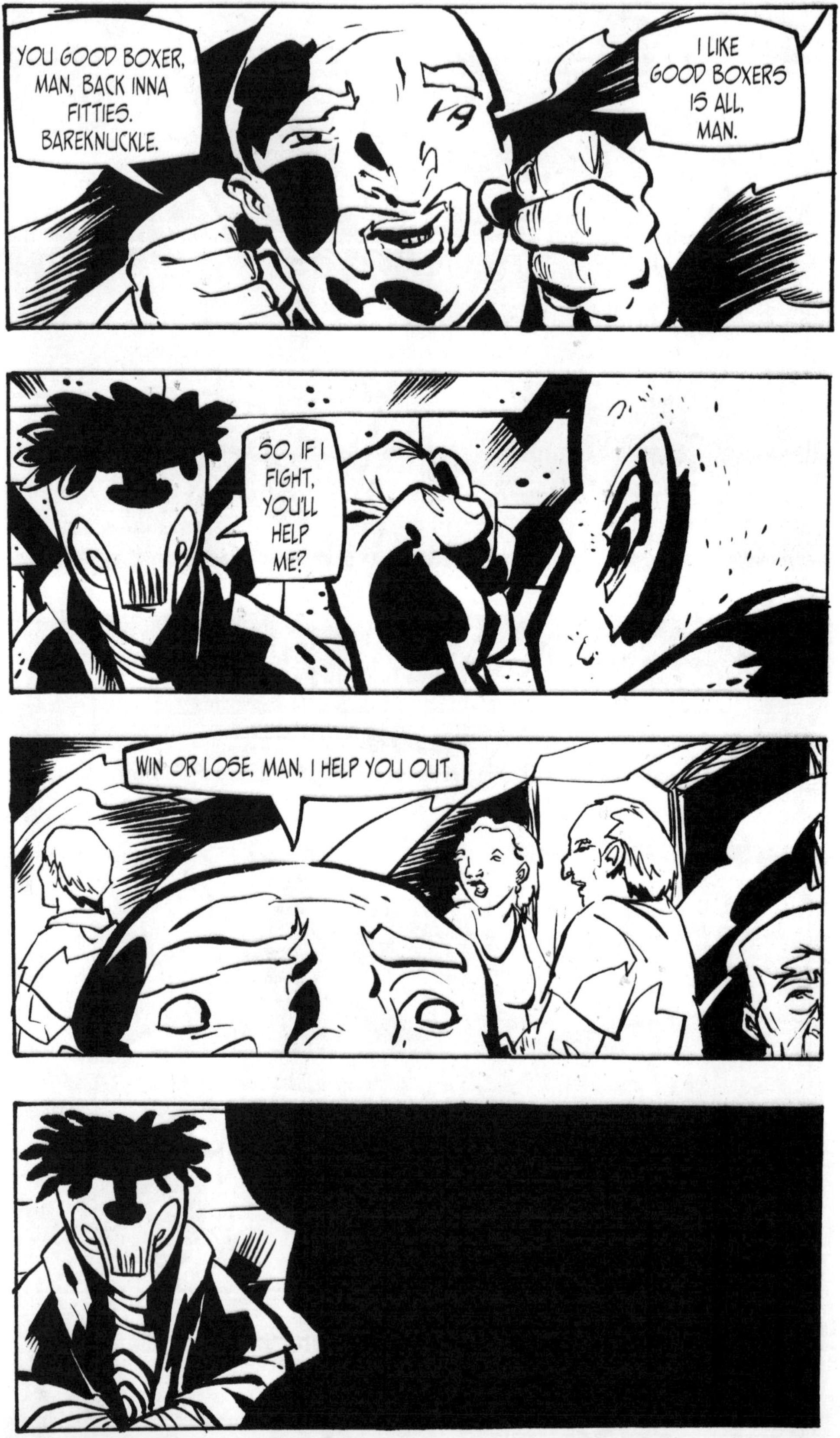
YOU GOOD BOXER, MAN, BACK INNA FITTIES. BAREKNUCKLE.
I LIKE GOOD BOXERS IS ALL, MAN.
SO, IF I FIGHT, YOU'LL HELP ME?
WIN OR LOSE, MAN, I HELP YOU OUT.

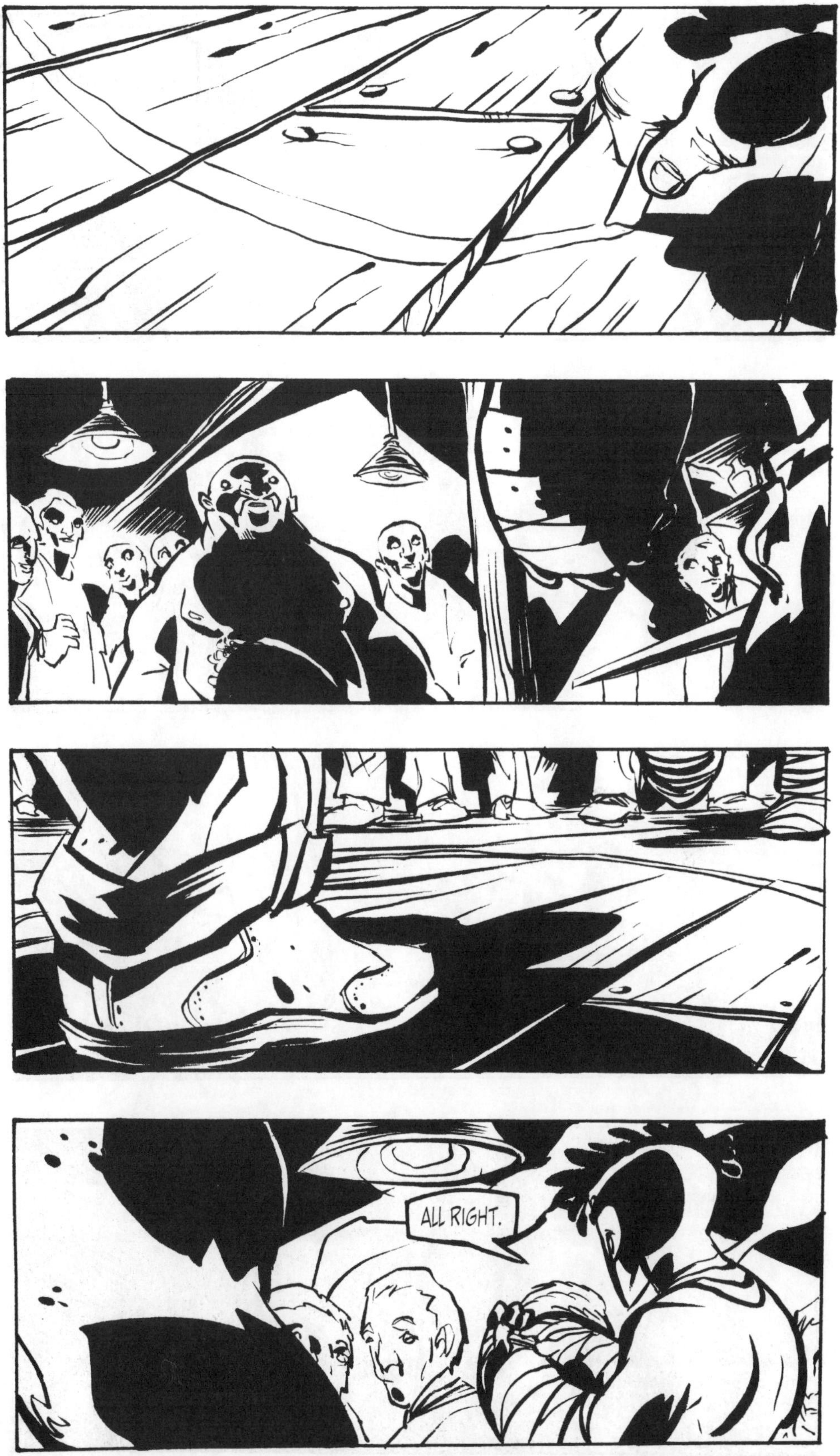
ALL RIGHT.

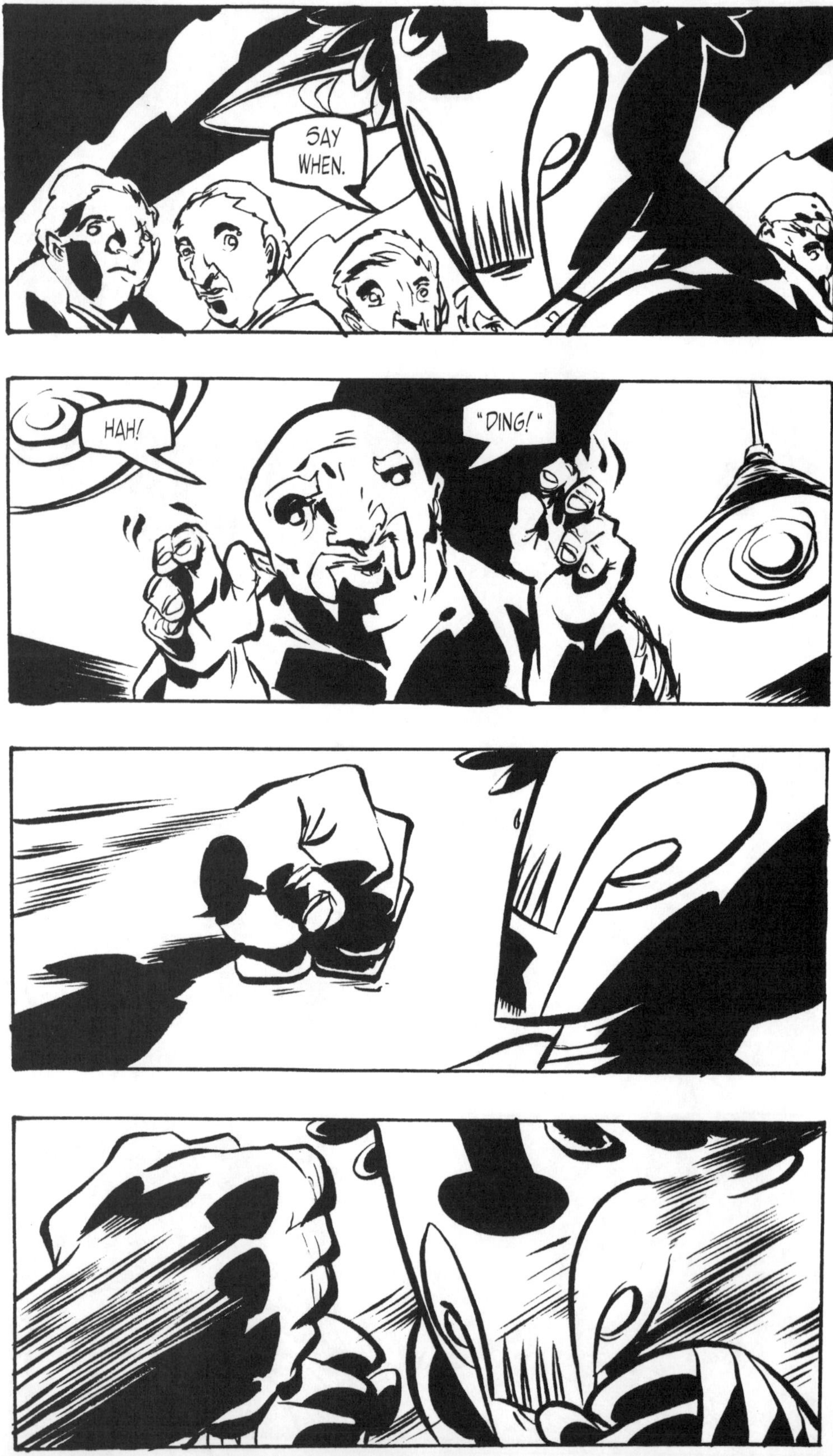
SAY WHEN.
HAH!
"DING!"

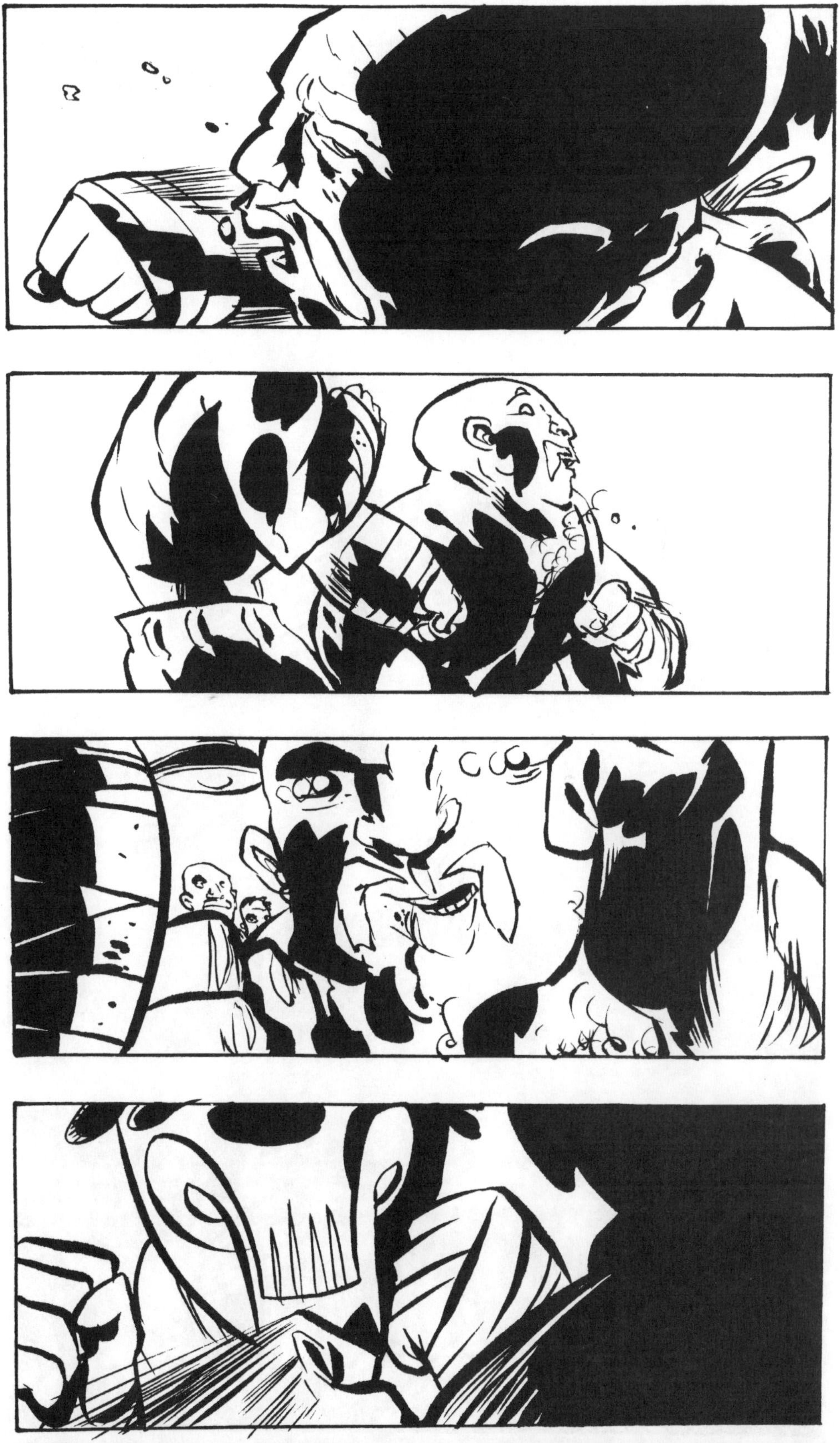

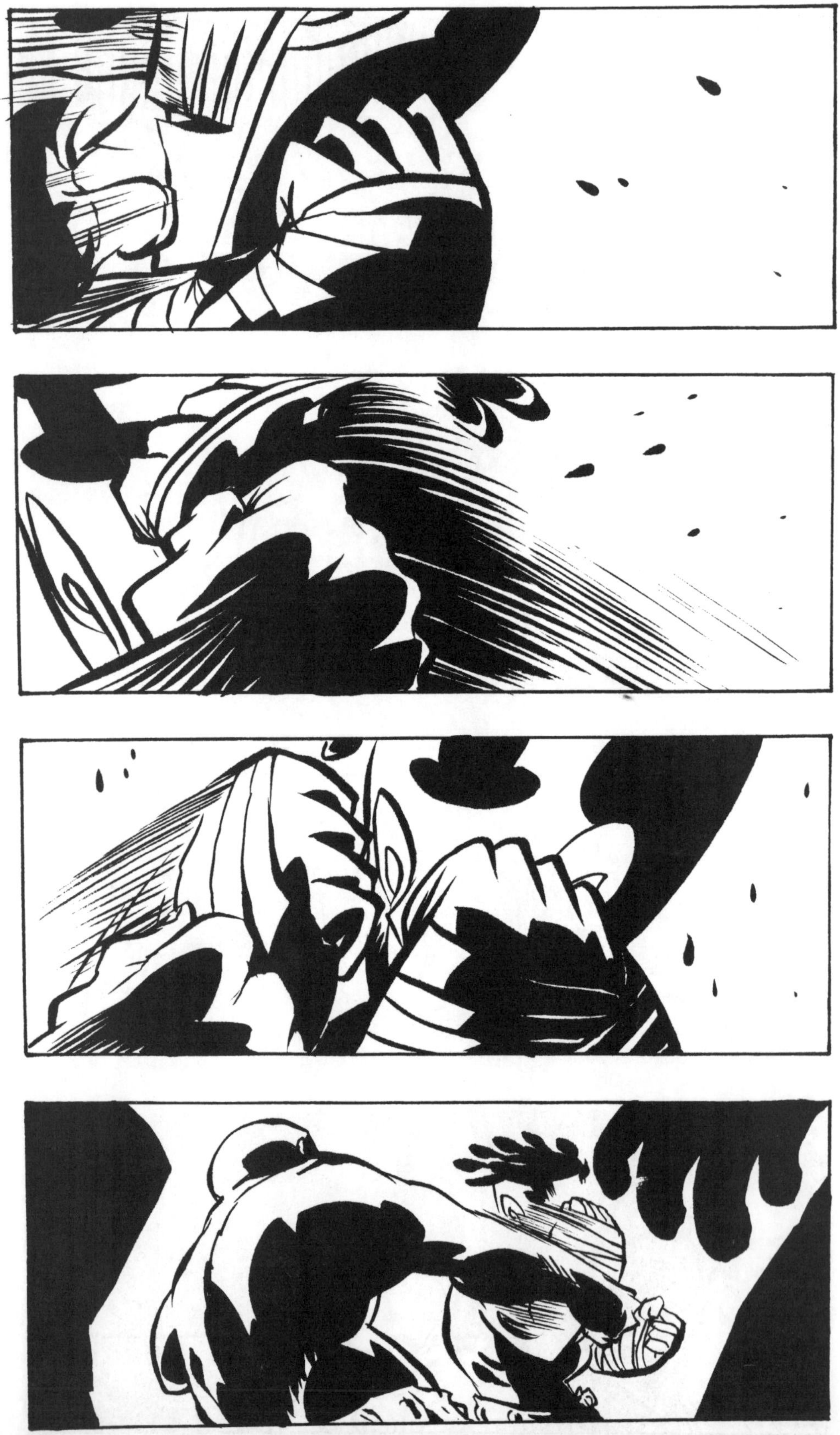

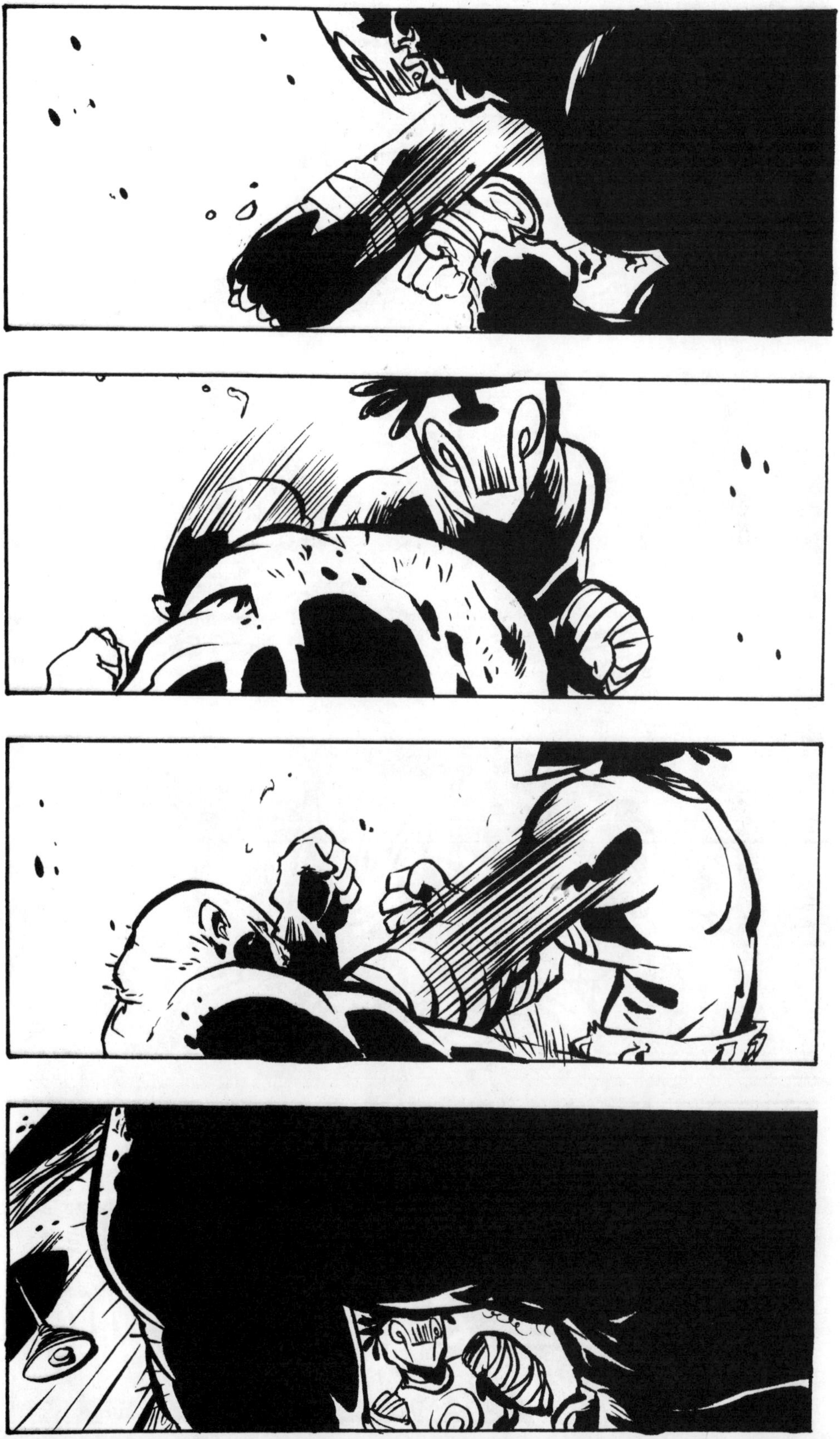

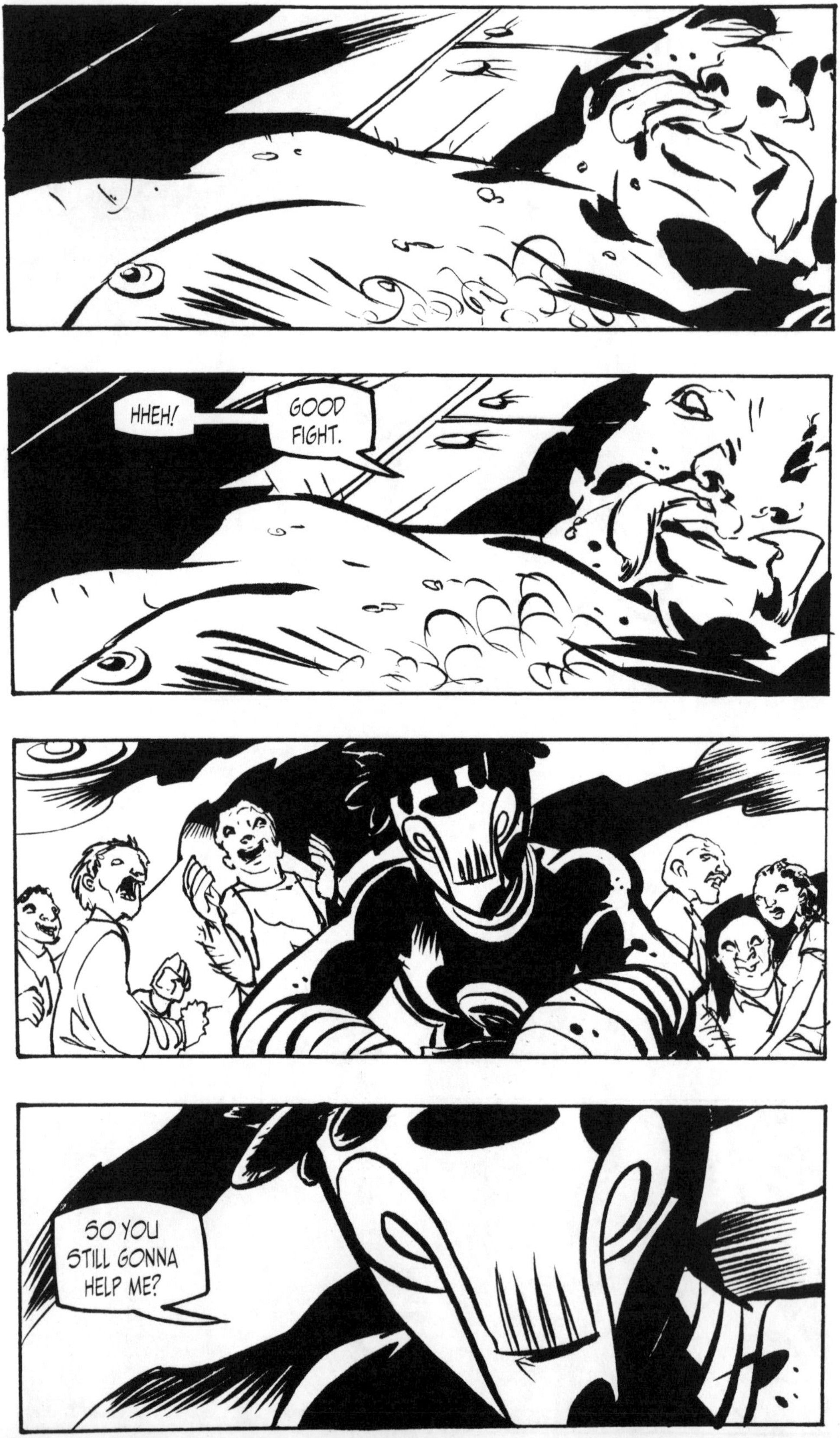
HHEH!
GOOD FIGHT.
SO YOU STILL GONNA HELP ME?

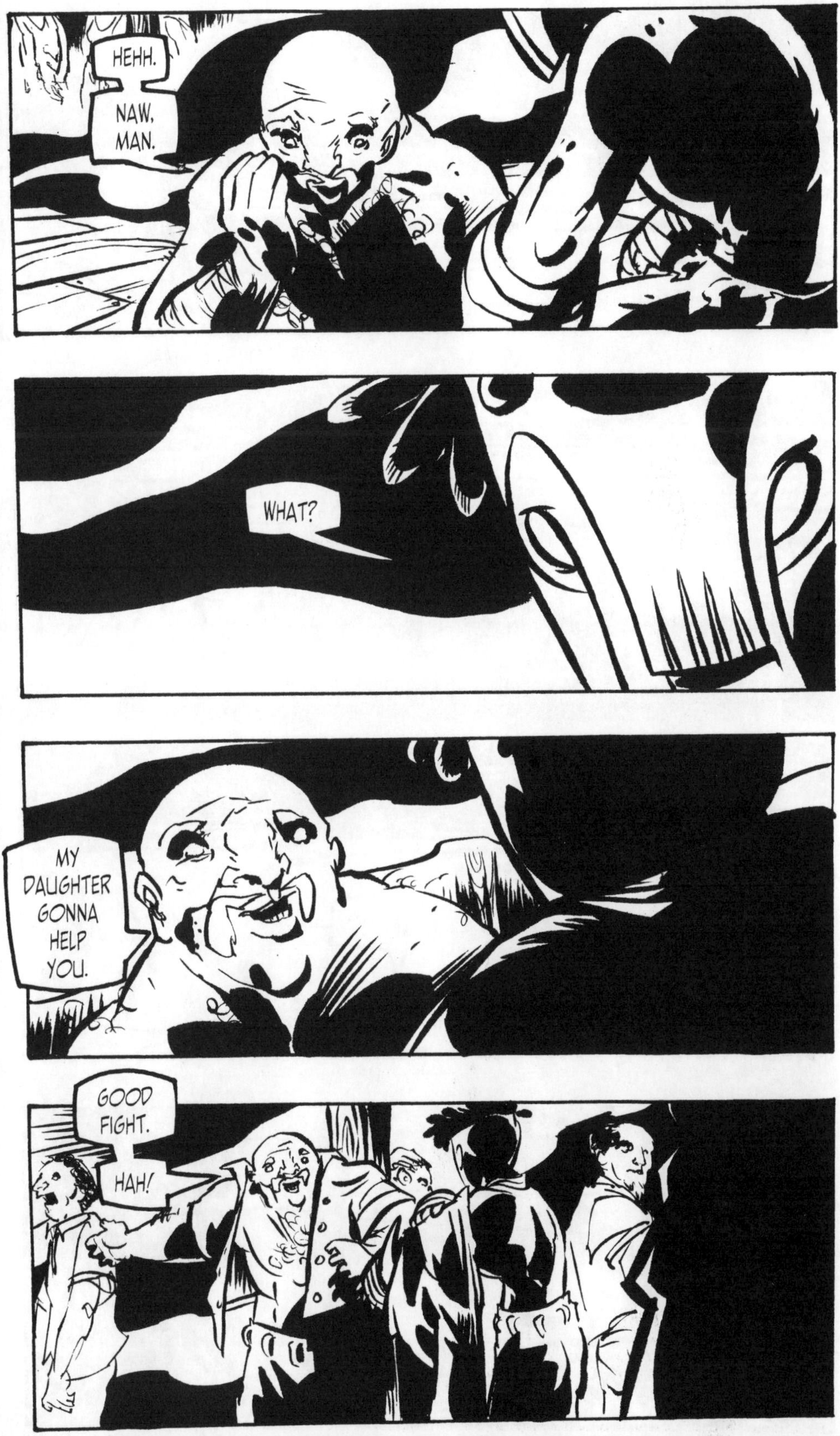
HEHH.
NAW, MAN.
WHAT?
MY DAUGHTER GONNA HELP YOU.
GOOD FIGHT.
HAH!

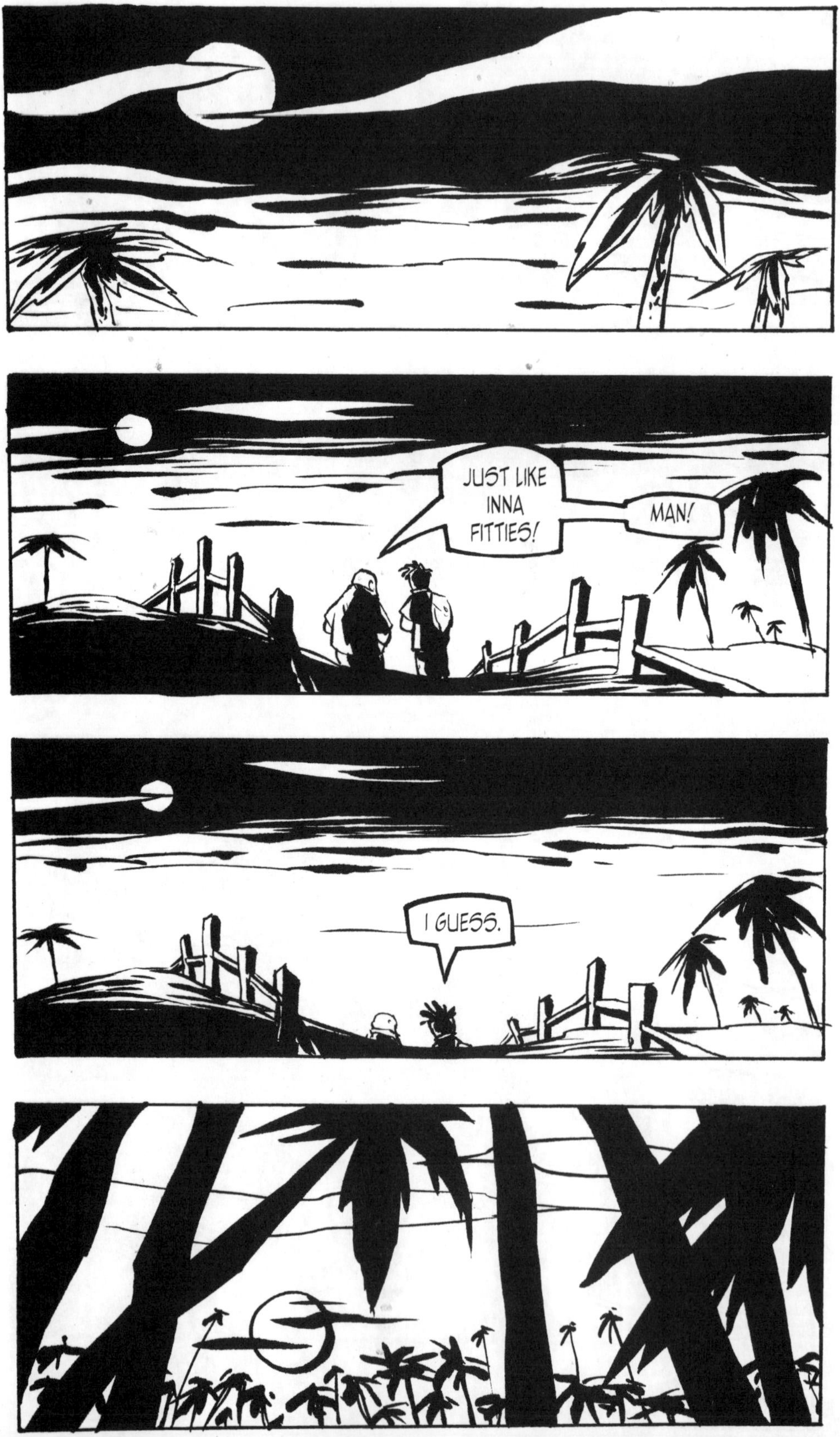
JUST LIKE INNA FITTIES!
MAN!
I GUESS.

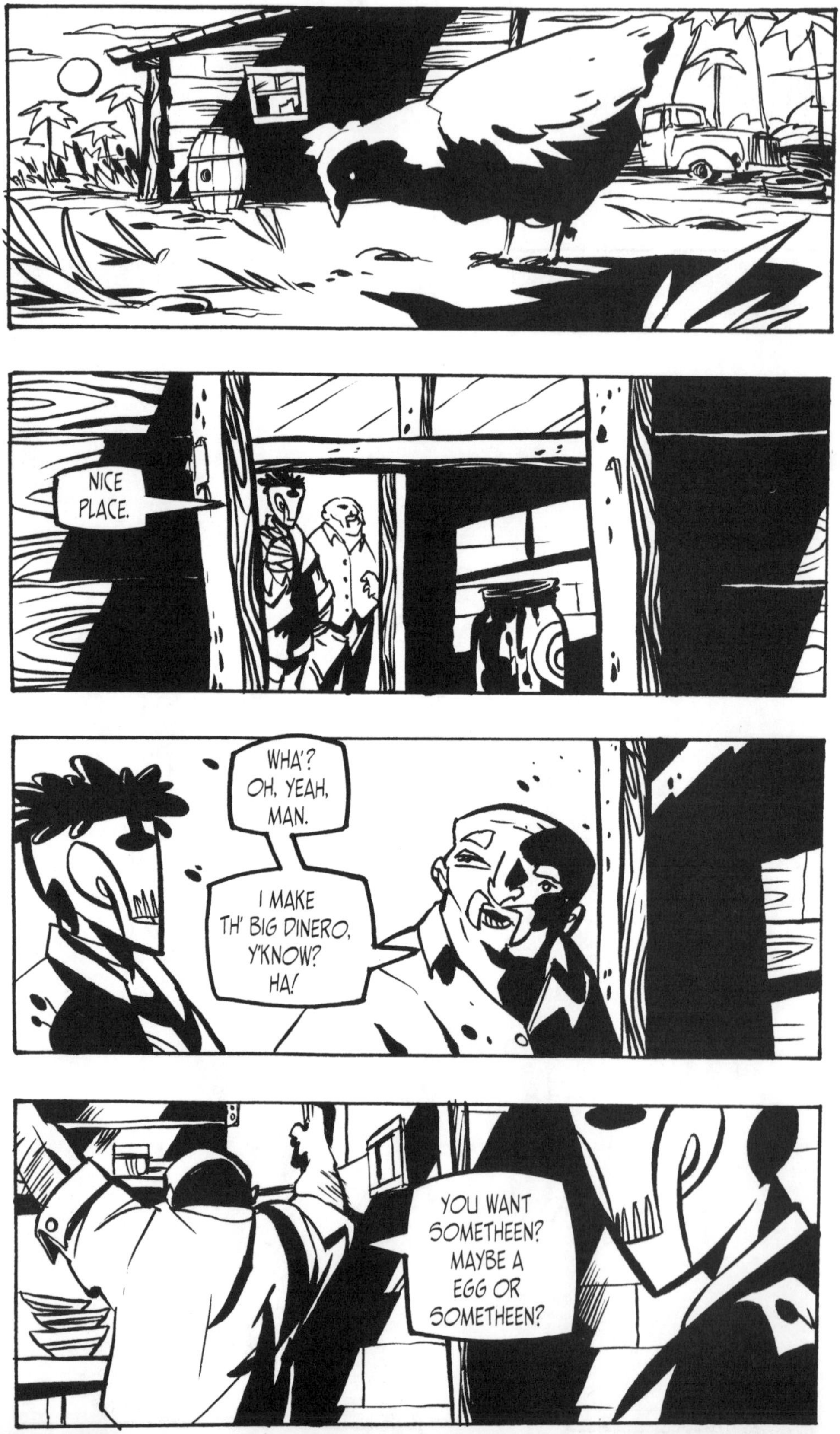
NICE PLACE.
WHA'? OH, YEAH, MAN.
I MAKE TH' BIG DINERO, Y'KNOW? HA!
YOU WANT SOMETHEEN? MAYBE A EGG OR SOMETHEEN?

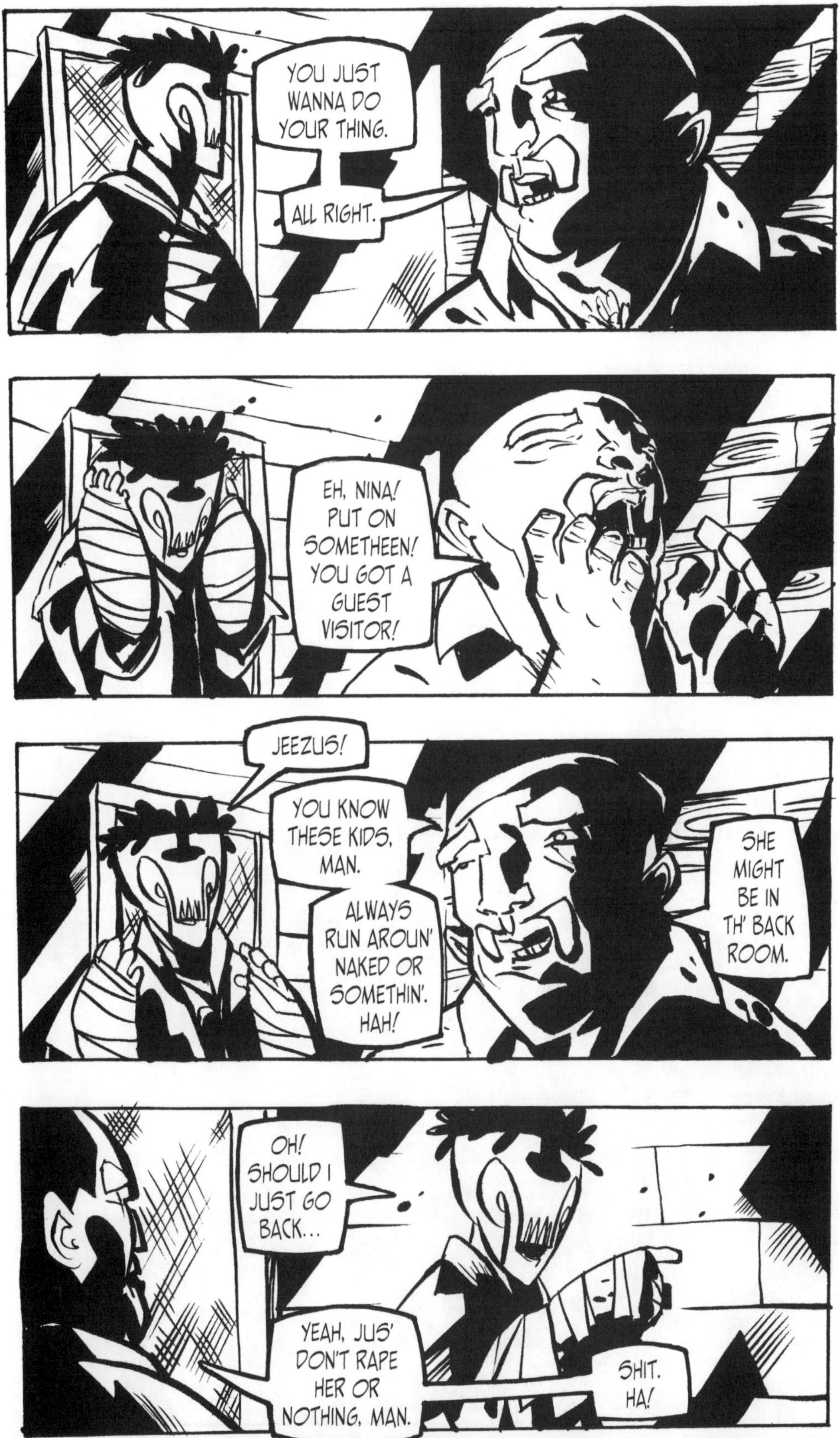
YOU JUST WANNA DO YOUR THING.
ALL RIGHT.
EH, NINA! PUT ON SOMETHEEN! YOU GOT A GUEST VISITOR!
JEEZUS!
YOU KNOW THESE KIDS, MAN.
ALWAYS RUN AROUN' NAKED OR SOMETHIN'. HAH!
SHE MIGHT BE IN TH' BACK ROOM.
OH! SHOULD I JUST GO BACK...
YEAH, JUS' DON'T RAPE HER OR NOTHING, MAN.
SHIT. HA!

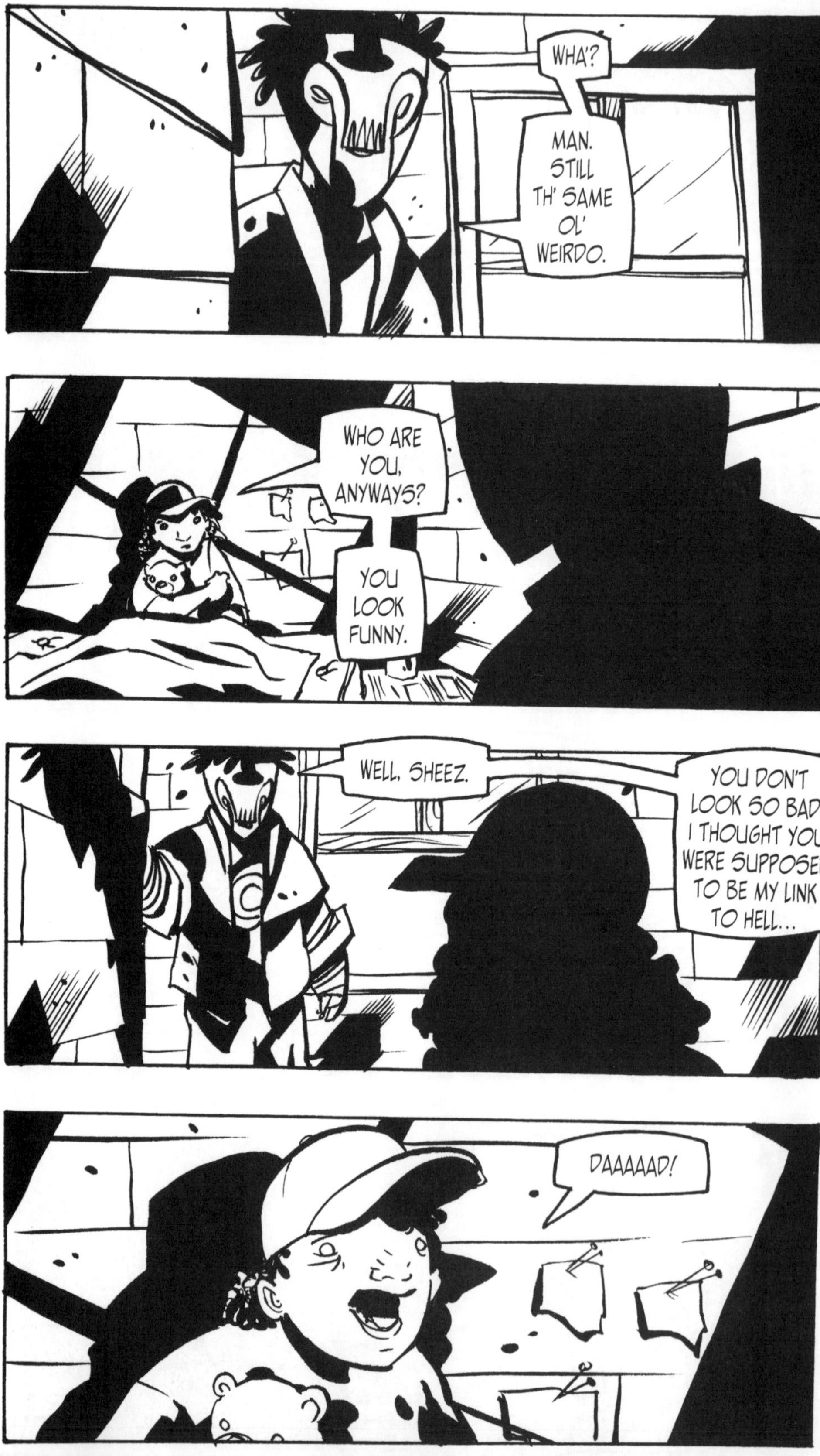
WHA'?
MAN. STILL TH' SAME OL' WEIRDO.
WHO ARE YOU, ANYWAYS?
YOU LOOK FUNNY.
WELL, SHEEZ.
YOU DON'T LOOK SO BAD. I THOUGHT YOU WERE SUPPOSED TO BE MY LINK TO HELL...
DAAAAAD!

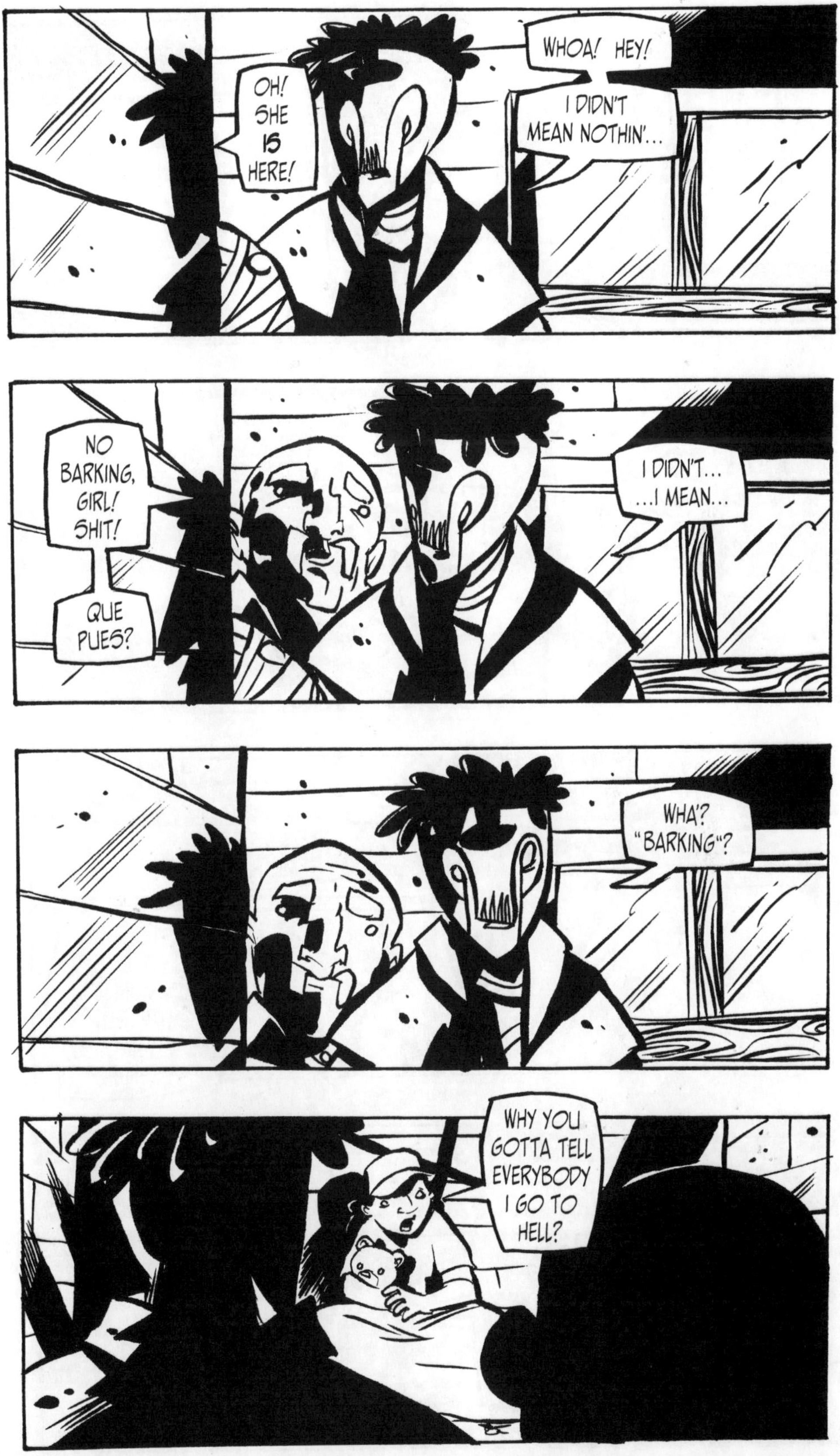
OH! SHE IS HERE!
WHOA! HEY!
I DIDN'T MEAN NOTHIN'...
NO BARKING, GIRL! SHIT!
QUE PUES?
I DIDN'T... ...I MEAN...
WHA'? "BARKING"?
WHY YOU GOTTA TELL EVERYBODY I GO TO HELL?

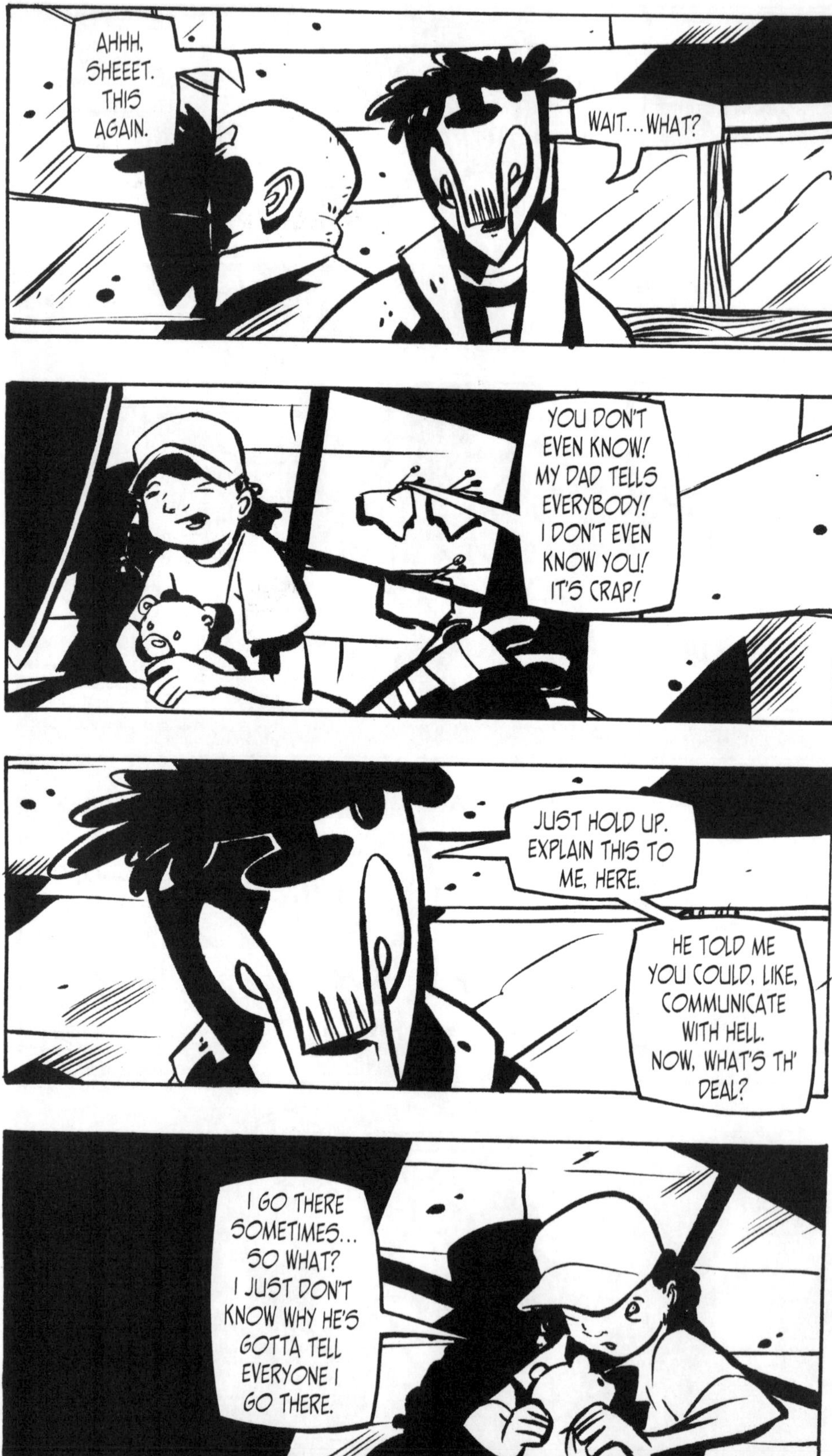
AHHH, SHEEET. THIS AGAIN.
WAIT... WHAT?
YOU DON'T EVEN KNOW! MY DAD TELLS EVERYBODY! I DON'T EVEN KNOW YOU! IT'S CRAP!
JUST HOLD UP. EXPLAIN THIS TO ME, HERE.
HE TOLD ME YOU COULD, LIKE, COMMUNICATE WITH HELL. NOW, WHAT'S TH' DEAL?
I GO THERE SOMETIMES... SO WHAT? I JUST DON'T KNOW WHY HE'S GOTTA TELL EVERYONE I GO THERE.

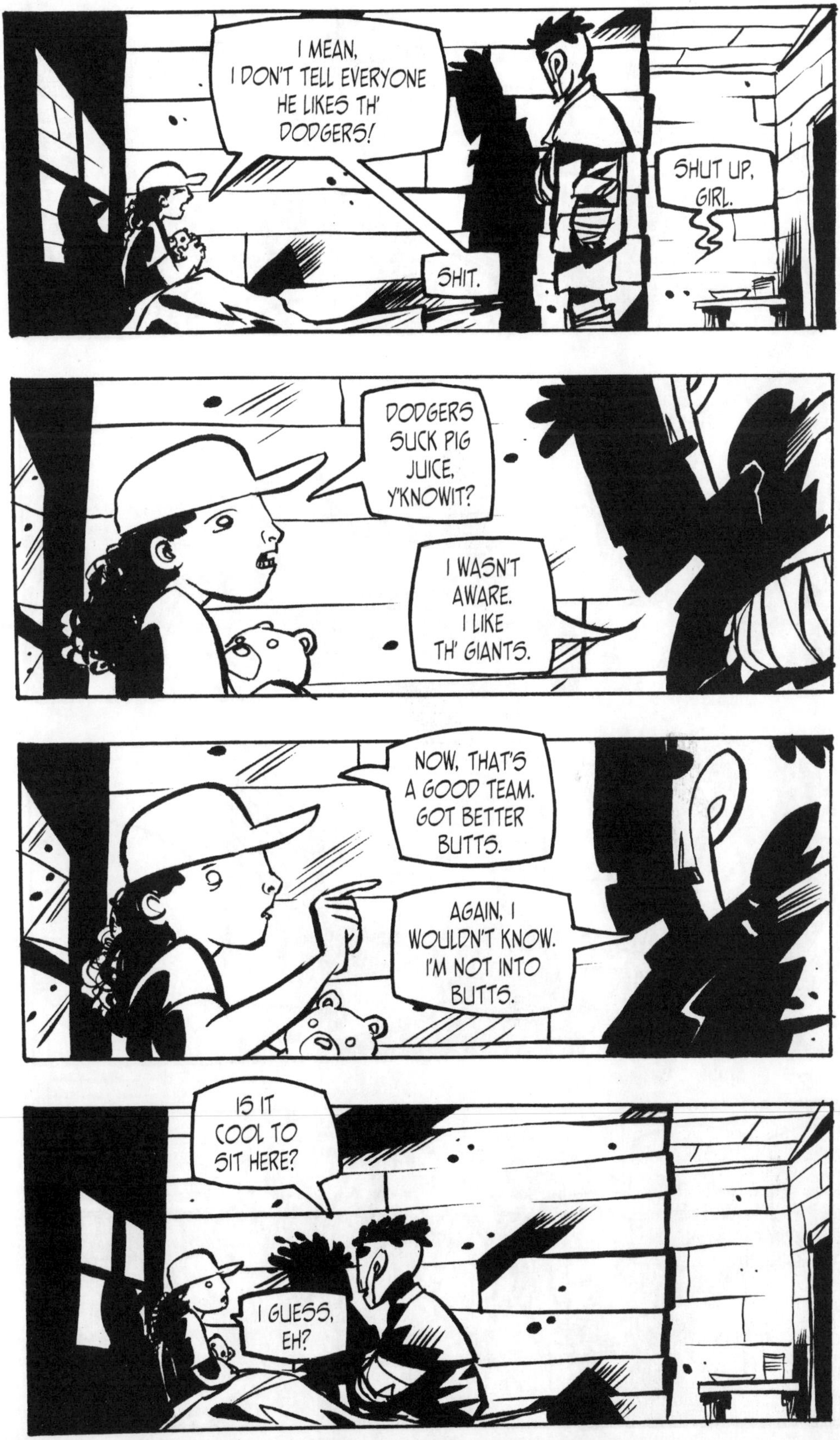
I MEAN, I DON'T TELL EVERYONE HE LIKES TH' DODGERS!
SHIT.
SHUT UP, GIRL.
DODGERS SUCK PIG JUICE, Y'KNOWIT?
I WASN'T AWARE. I LIKE TH' GIANTS.
NOW, THAT'S A GOOD TEAM. GOT BETTER BUTTS.
AGAIN, I WOULDN'T KNOW. I'M NOT INTO BUTTS.
IS IT COOL TO SIT HERE?
I GUESS, EH?

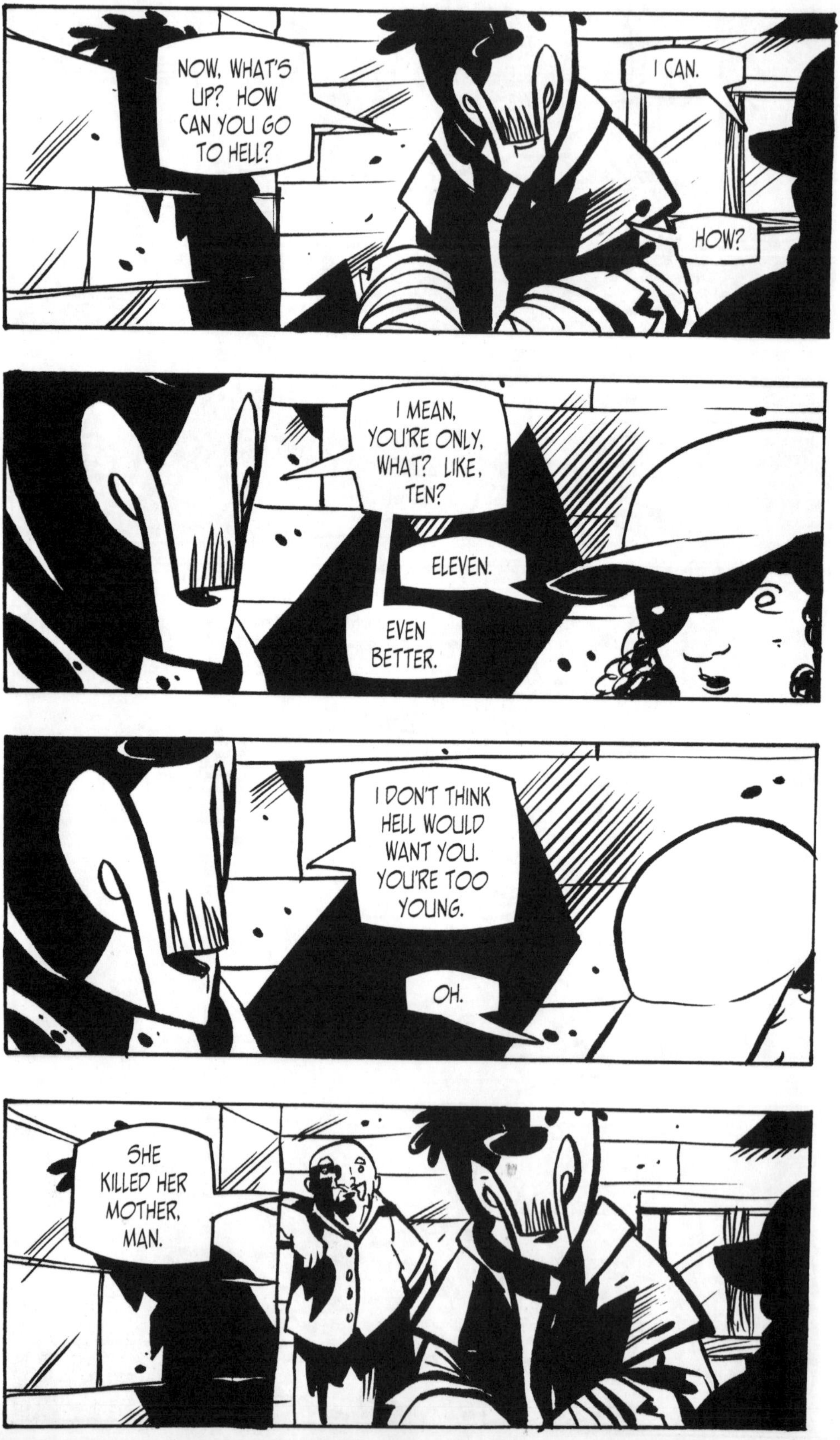
NOW, WHAT'S UP? HOW CAN YOU GO TO HELL?
I CAN.
HOW?
I MEAN, YOU'RE ONLY, WHAT? LIKE, TEN?
ELEVEN.
EVEN BETTER.
I DON'T THINK HELL WOULD WANT YOU. YOU'RE TOO YOUNG.
OH.
SHE KILLED HER MOTHER, MAN.

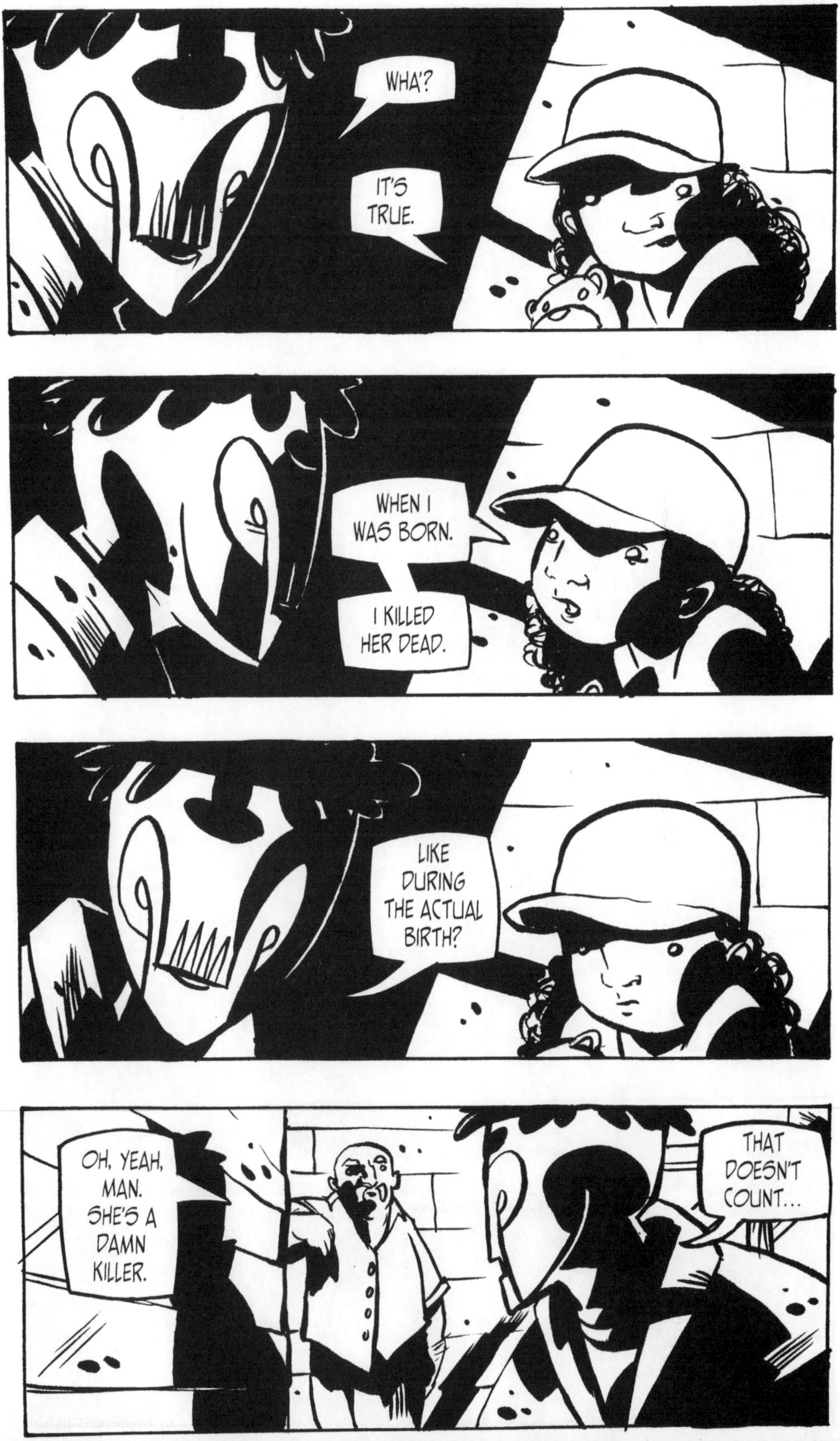
WHA'?
IT'S TRUE.
WHEN I WAS BORN.
I KILLED HER DEAD.
LIKE DURING THE ACTUAL BIRTH?
OH, YEAH, MAN. SHE'S A DAMN KILLER.
THAT DOESN'T COUNT...

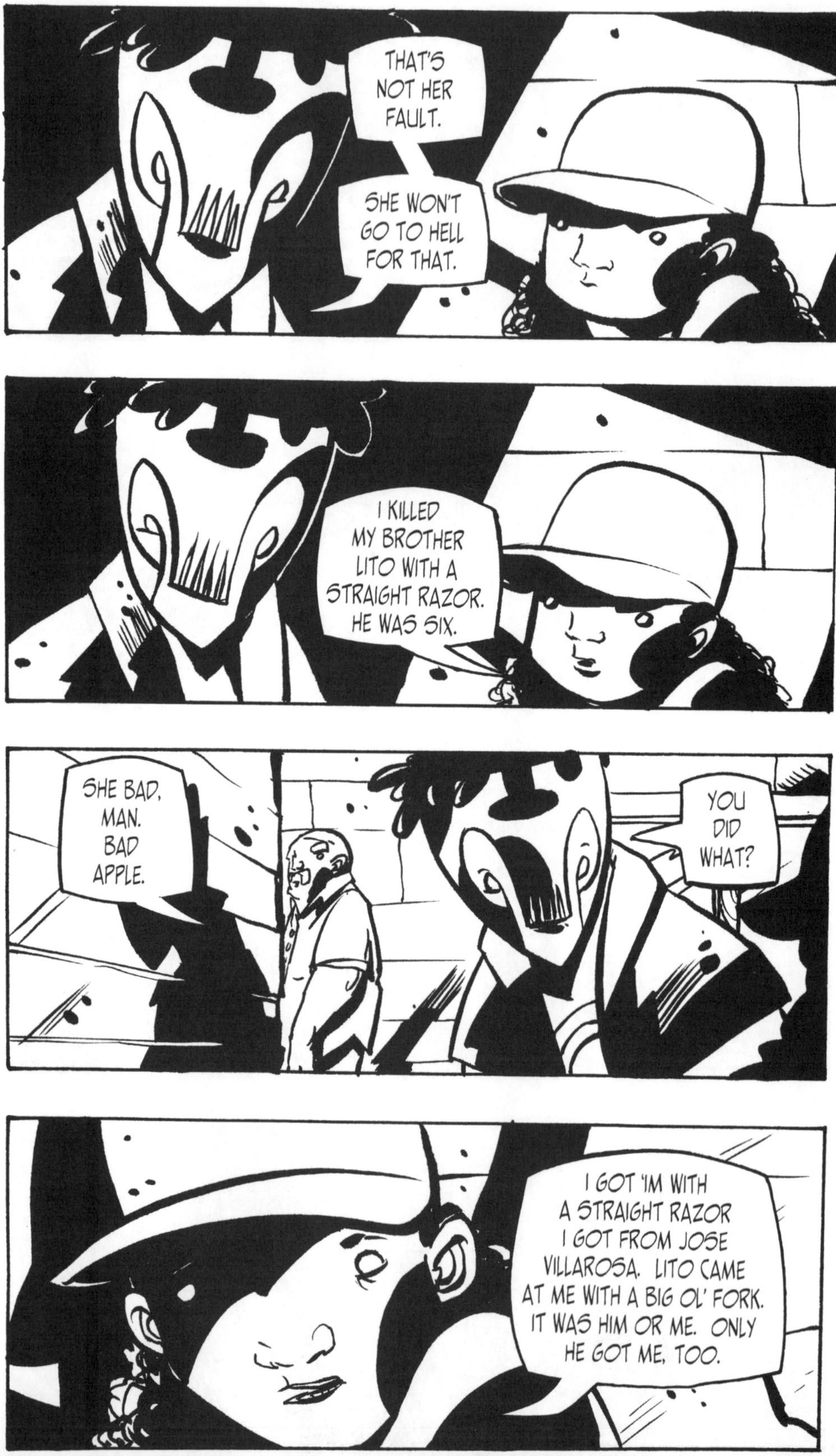
THAT'S NOT HER FAULT.
SHE WON'T GO TO HELL FOR THAT.
I KILLED MY BROTHER LITO WITH A STRAIGHT RAZOR. HE WAS SIX.
SHE BAD, MAN. BAD APPLE.
YOU DID WHAT?
I GOT 'IM WITH A STRAIGHT RAZOR I GOT FROM JOSE VILLAROSA. LITO CAME AT ME WITH A BIG OL' FORK. IT WAS HIM OR ME. ONLY HE GOT ME, TOO.

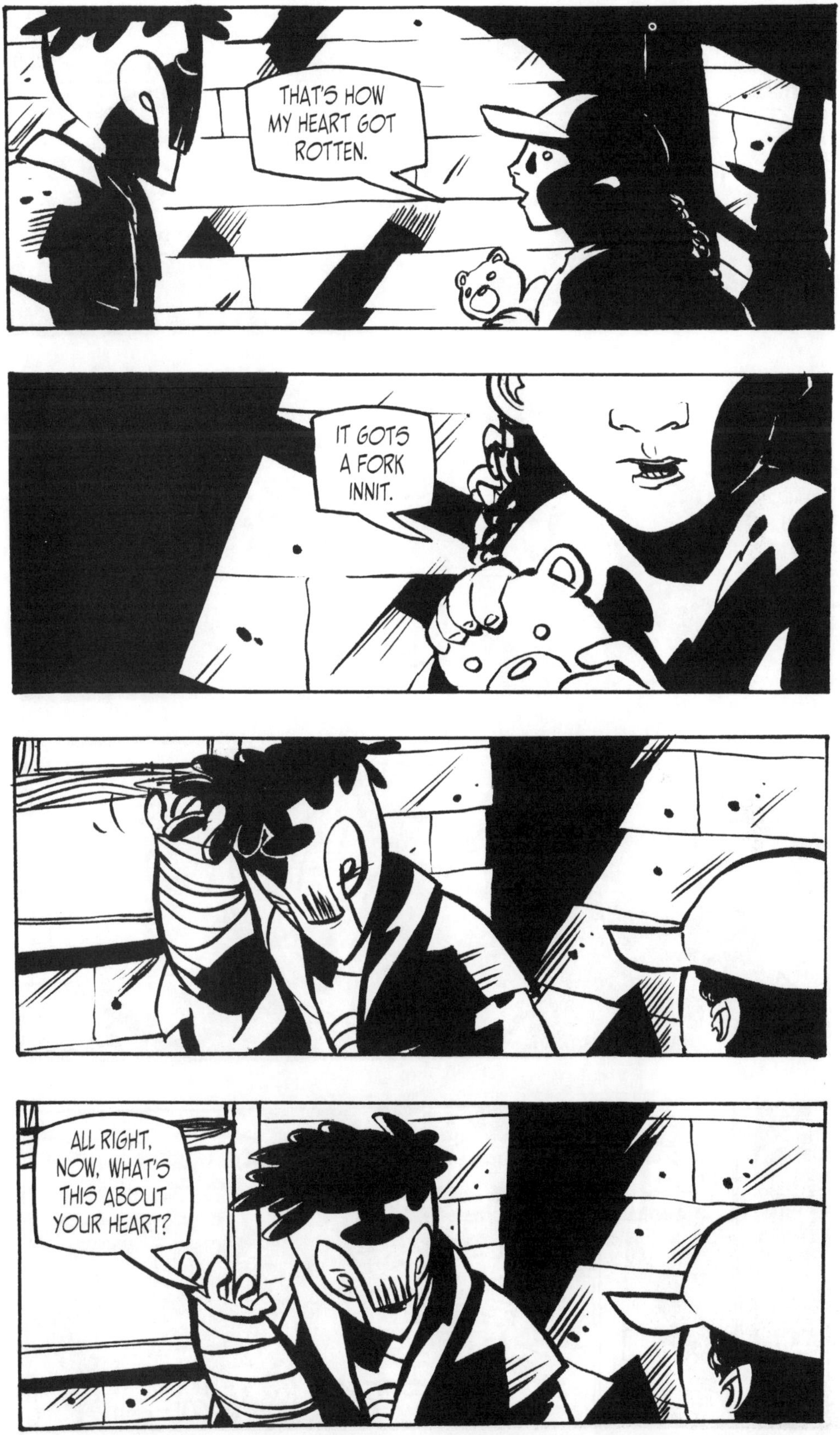
THAT'S HOW MY HEART GOT ROTTEN.
IT GOTS A FORK INNIT.
ALL RIGHT, NOW, WHAT'S THIS ABOUT YOUR HEART?

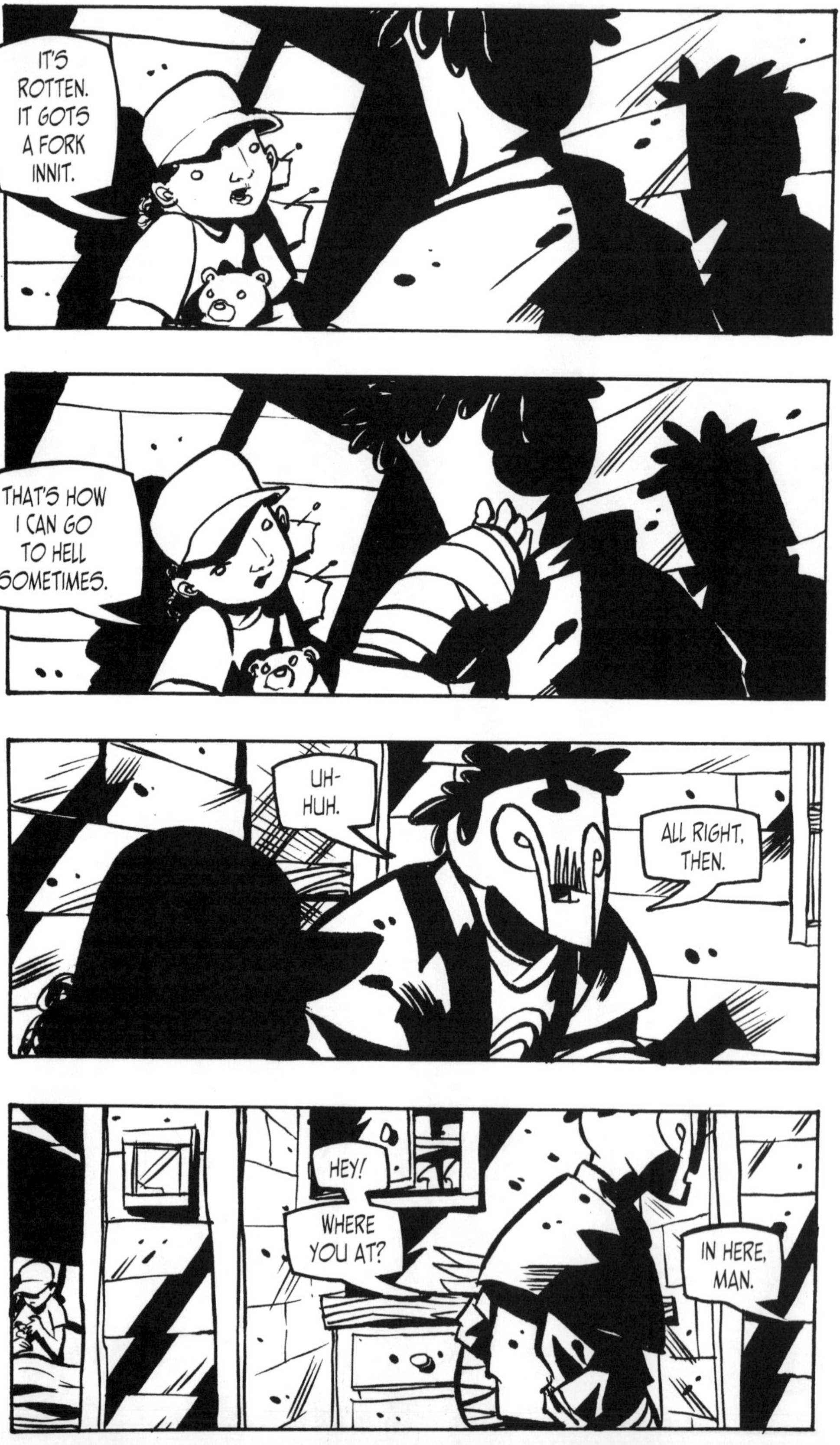
IT'S ROTTEN. IT GOTS A FORK INNIT.
THAT'S HOW I CAN GO TO HELL SOMETIMES.
UH-HUH.
ALL RIGHT, THEN.
HEY!
WHERE YOU AT?
IN HERE, MAN.

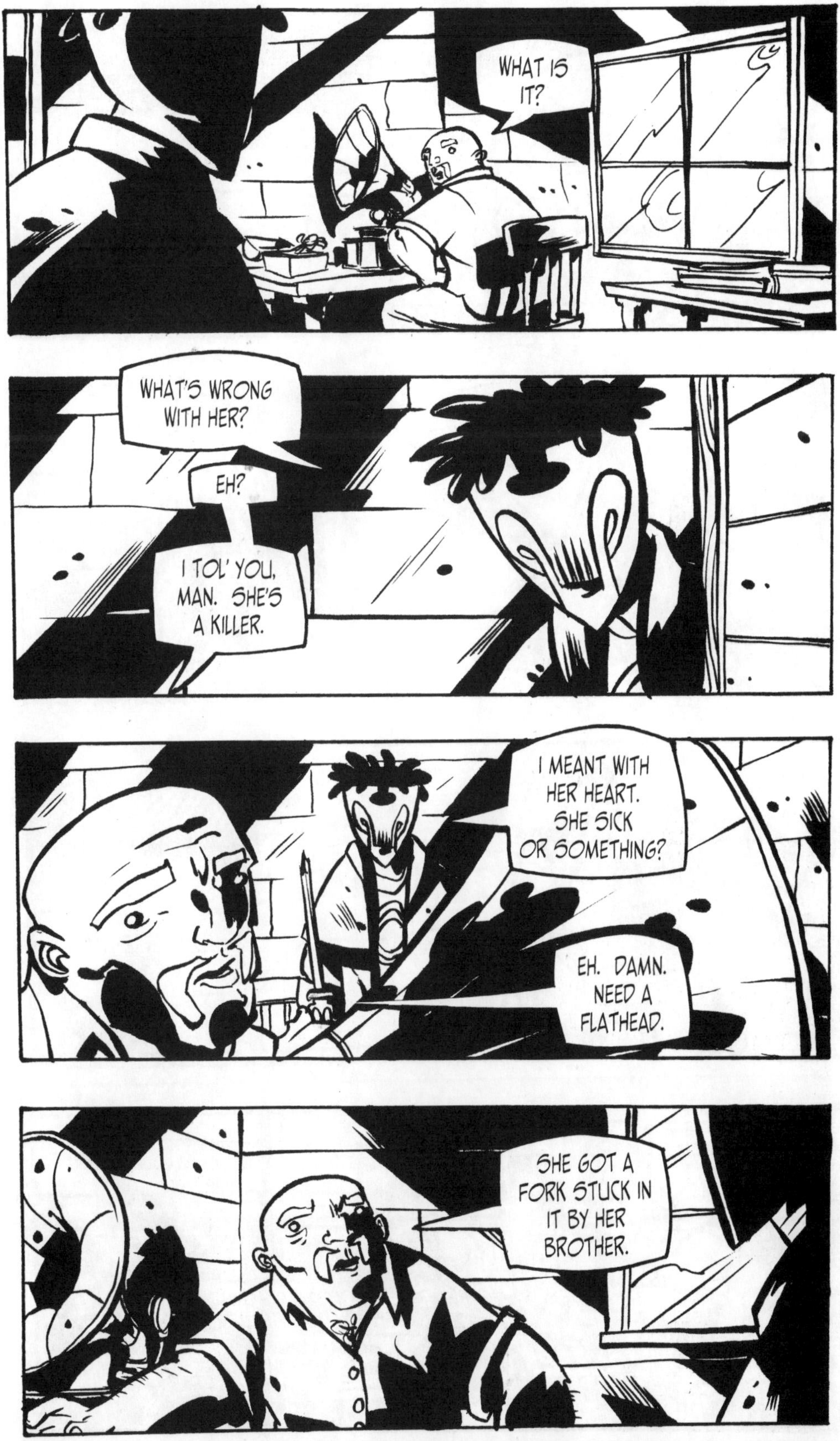
WHAT IS IT?
WHAT'S WRONG WITH HER?
EH?
I TOL' YOU, MAN. SHE'S A KILLER.
I MEANT WITH HER HEART. SHE SICK OR SOMETHING?
EH. DAMN. NEED A FLATHEAD.
SHE GOT A FORK STUCK IN IT BY HER BROTHER.

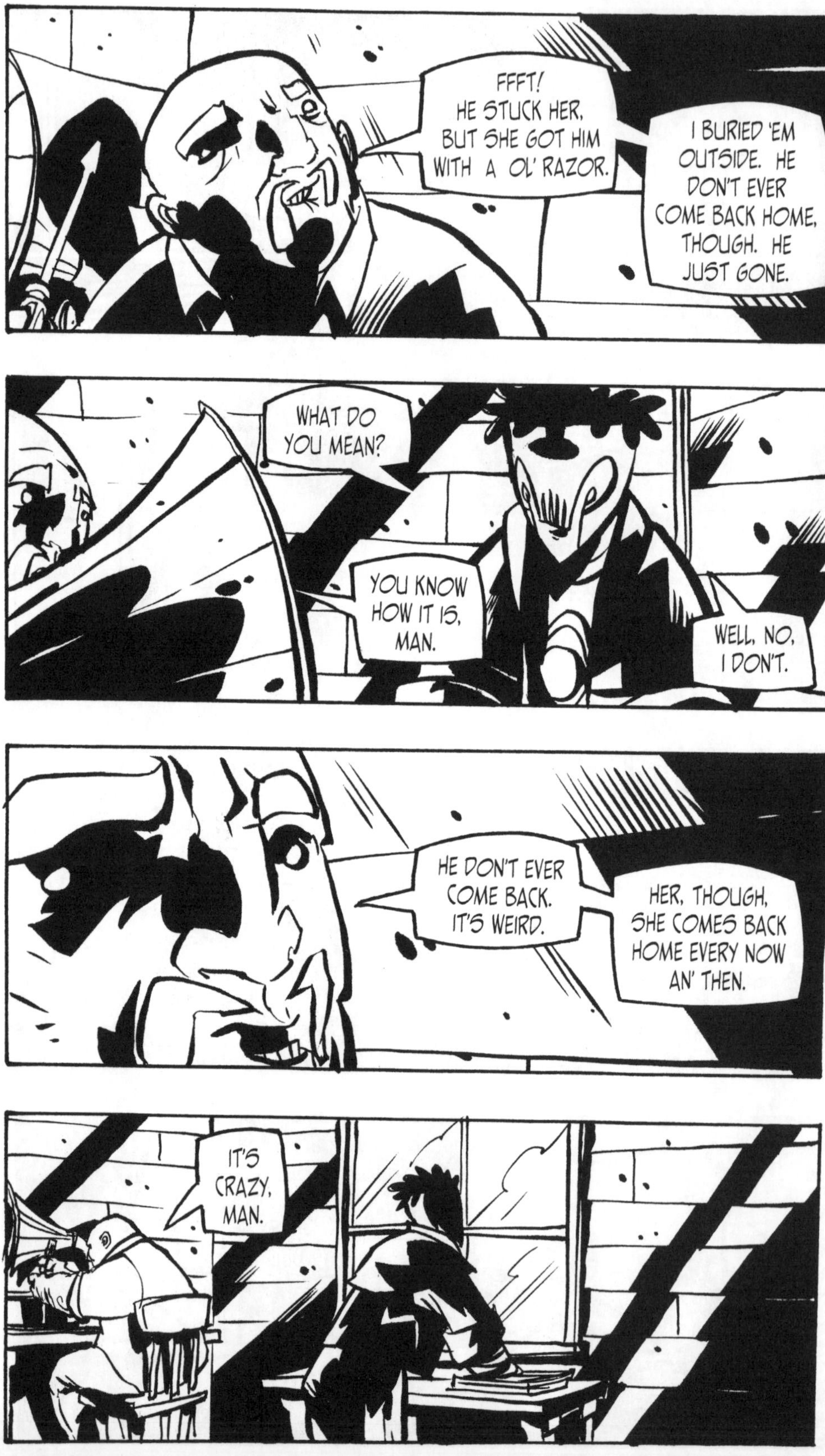
FFFT! HE STUCK HER, BUT SHE GOT HIM WITH A OL' RAZOR.
I BURIED 'EM OUTSIDE. HE DON'T EVER COME BACK HOME, THOUGH. HE JUST GONE.
WHAT DO YOU MEAN?
YOU KNOW HOW IT IS, MAN.
WELL, NO, I DON'T.
HE DON'T EVER COME BACK. IT'S WEIRD.
HER, THOUGH, SHE COMES BACK HOME EVERY NOW AN' THEN.
IT'S CRAZY, MAN.

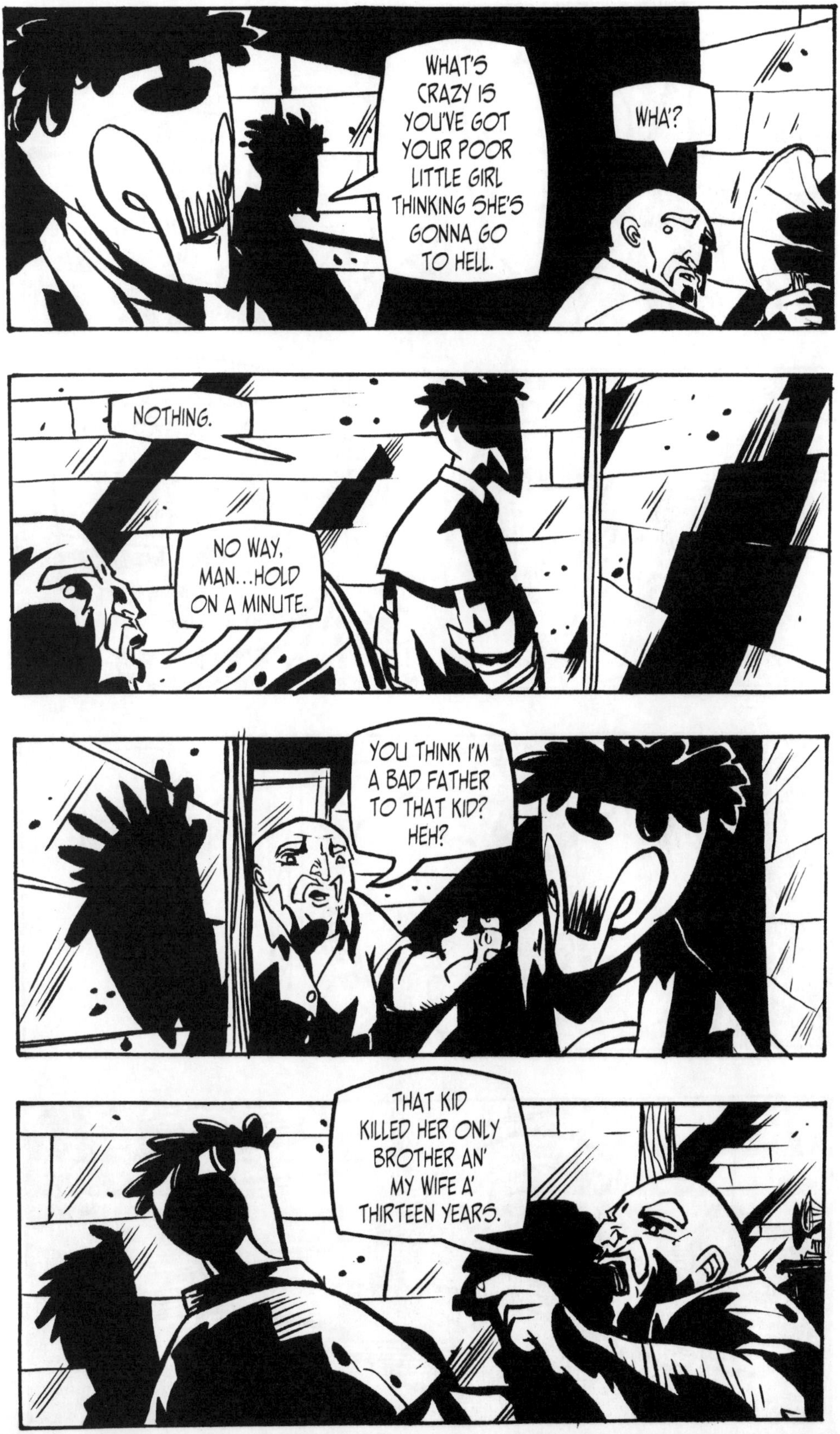
WHAT'S CRAZY IS YOU'VE GOT YOUR POOR LITTLE GIRL THINKING SHE'S GONNA GO TO HELL.
WHA'?
NOTHING.
NO WAY, MAN...HOLD ON A MINUTE.
YOU THINK I'M A BAD FATHER TO THAT KID? HEH?
THAT KID KILLED HER ONLY BROTHER AN' MY WIFE A' THIRTEEN YEARS.

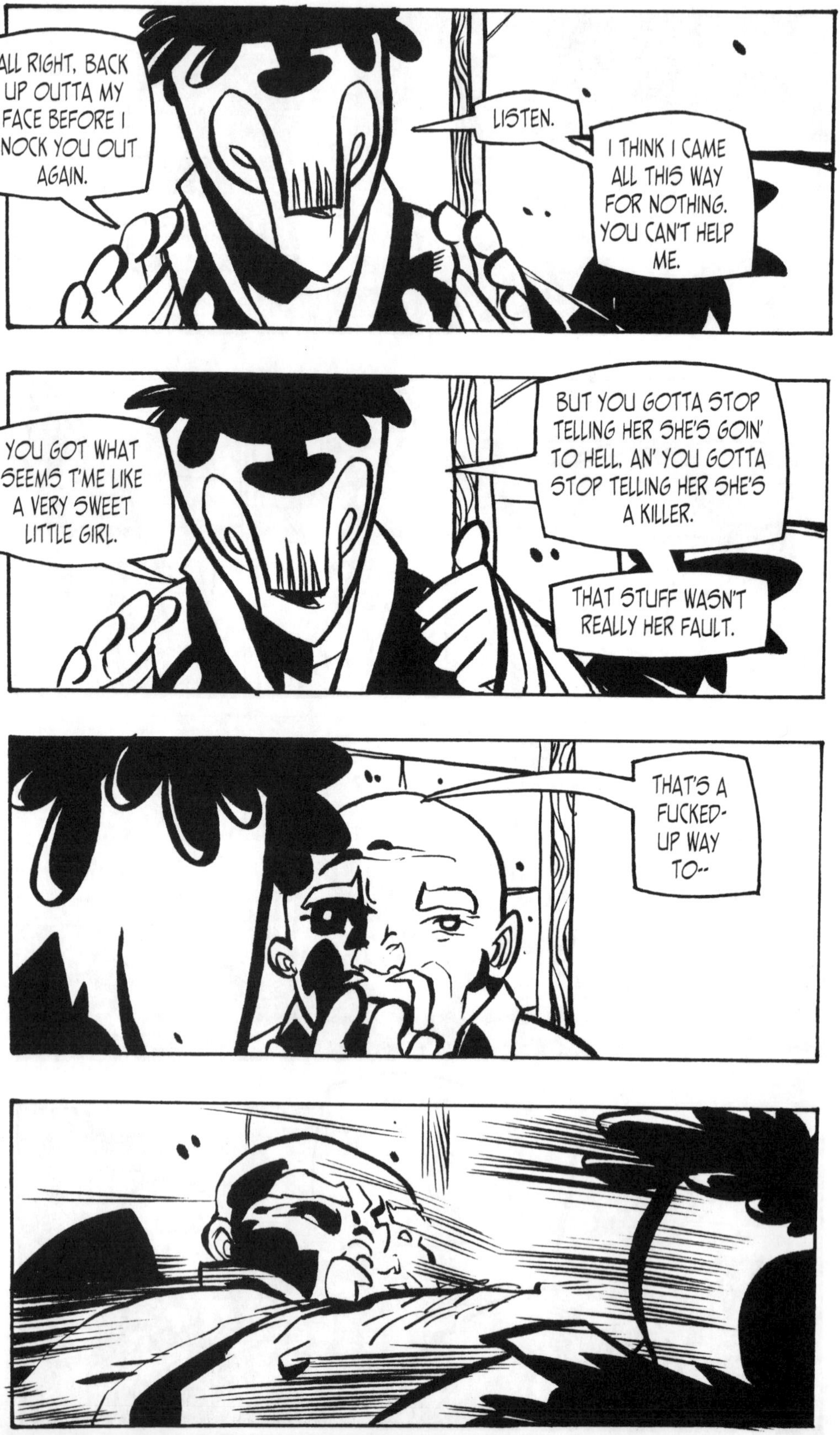
ALL RIGHT, BACK UP OUTTA MY FACE BEFORE I KNOCK YOU OUT AGAIN.
LISTEN.
I THINK I CAME ALL THIS WAY FOR NOTHING. YOU CAN'T HELP ME.
YOU GOT WHAT SEEMS T'ME LIKE A VERY SWEET LITTLE GIRL.
BUT YOU GOTTA STOP TELLING HER SHE'S GOIN' TO HELL. AN' YOU GOTTA STOP TELLING HER SHE'S A KILLER.
THAT STUFF WASN'T REALLY HER FAULT.
THAT'S A FUCKED-UP WAY TO--

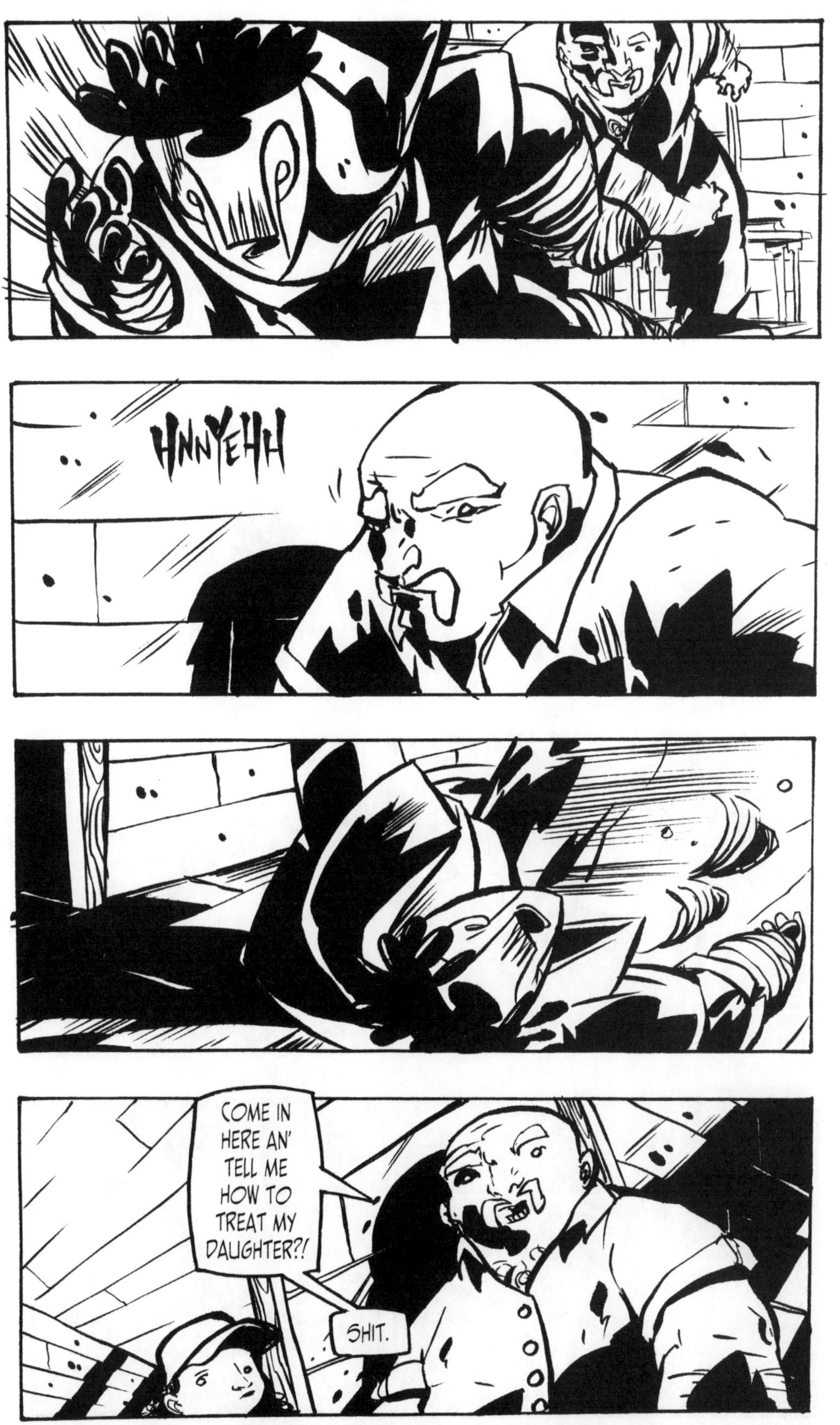
HNNYEHH
COME IN HERE AN' TELL ME HOW TO TREAT MY DAUGHTER?!
SHIT.

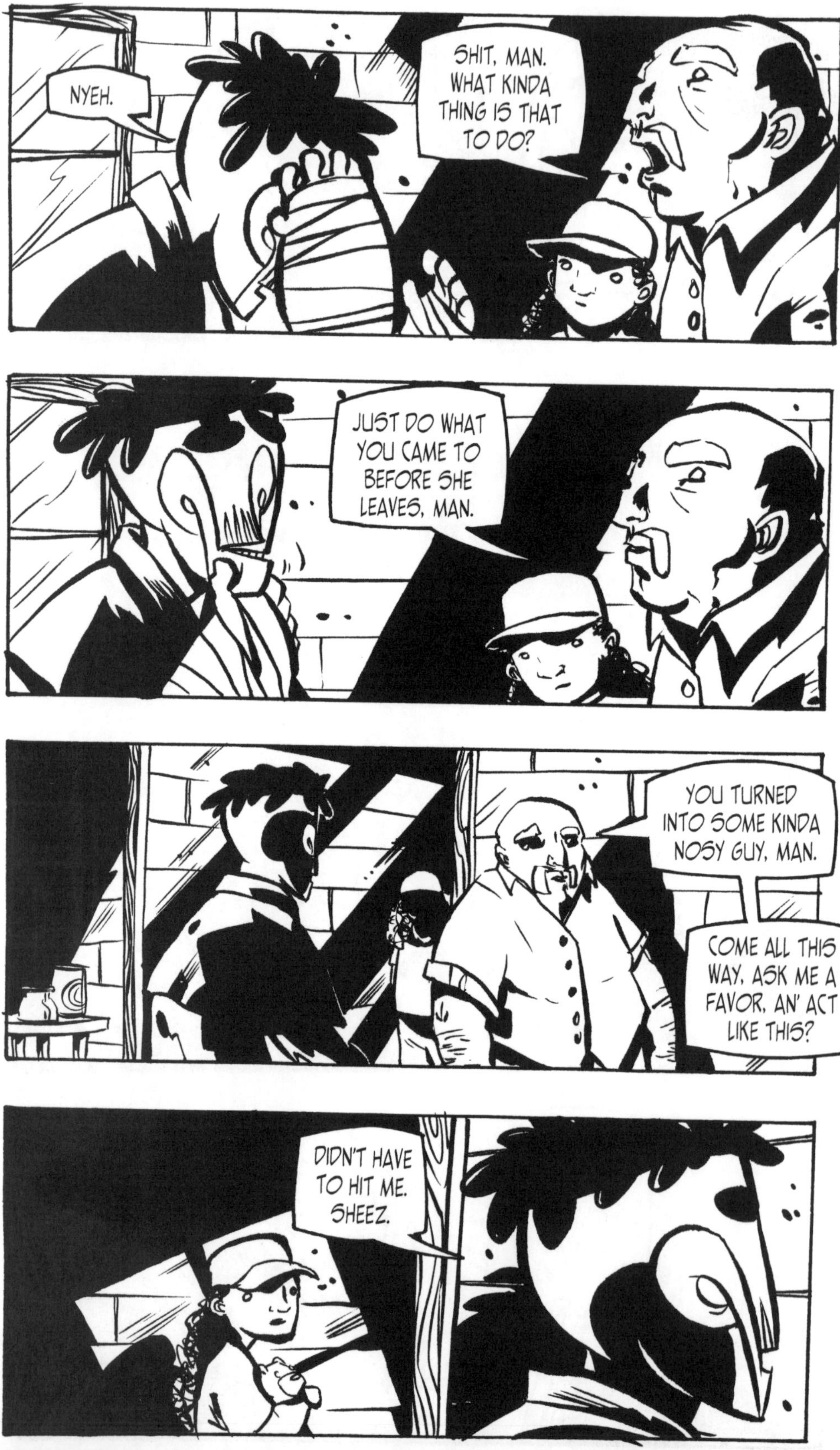
NYEH.
SHIT, MAN. WHAT KINDA THING IS THAT TO DO?
JUST DO WHAT YOU CAME TO BEFORE SHE LEAVES, MAN.
YOU TURNED INTO SOME KINDA NOSY GUY, MAN.
COME ALL THIS WAY, ASK ME A FAVOR, AN' ACT LIKE THIS?
DIDN'T HAVE TO HIT ME. SHEEZ.

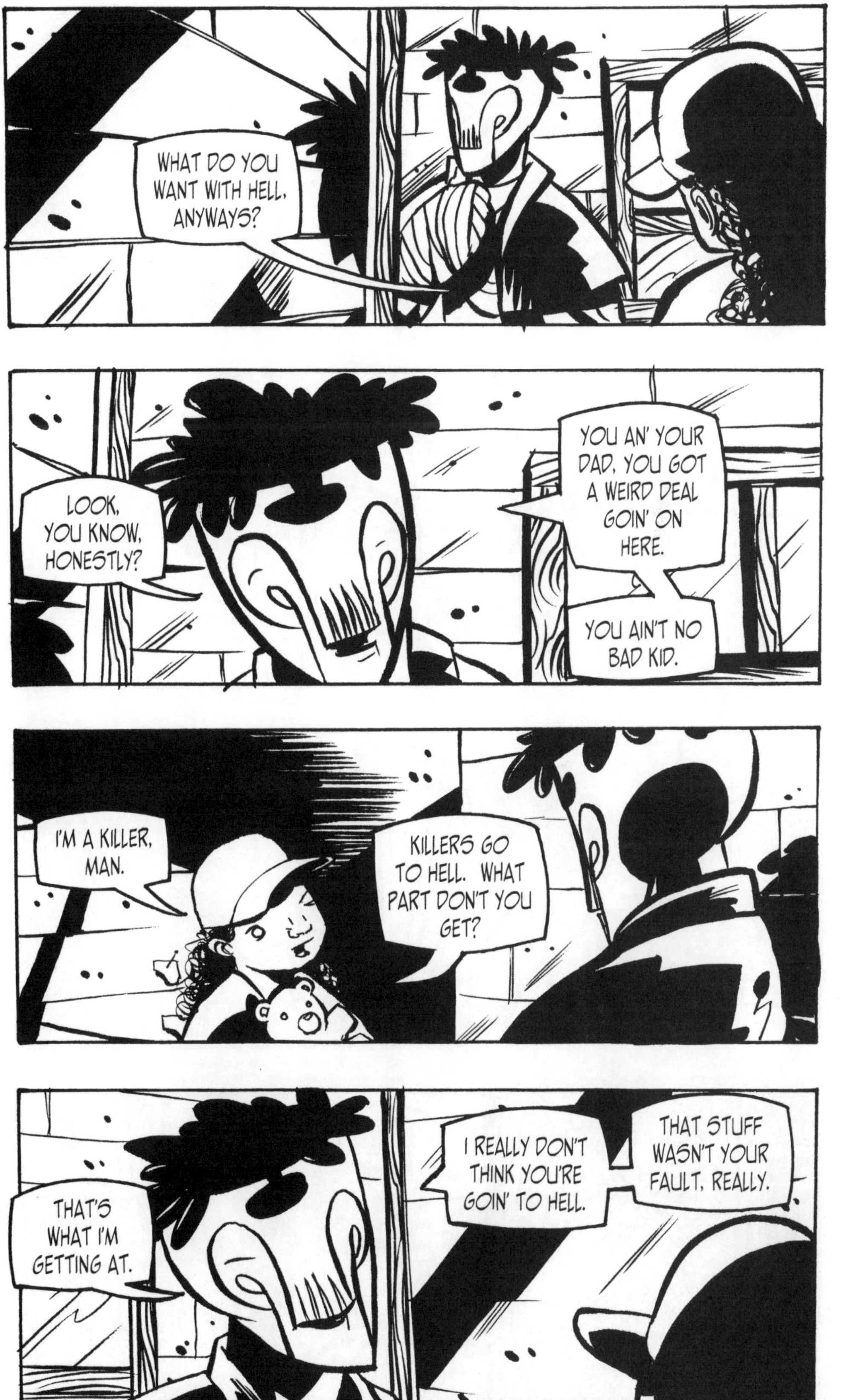
WHAT DO YOU WANT WITH HELL, ANYWAYS?
LOOK, YOU KNOW, HONESTLY?
YOU AN' YOUR DAD, YOU GOT A WEIRD DEAL GOIN' ON HERE.
YOU AIN'T NO BAD KID.
I'M A KILLER, MAN.
KILLERS GO TO HELL. WHAT PART DON'T YOU GET?
THAT'S WHAT I'M GETTING AT.
I REALLY DON'T THINK YOU'RE GOIN' TO HELL.
THAT STUFF WASN'T YOUR FAULT, REALLY.

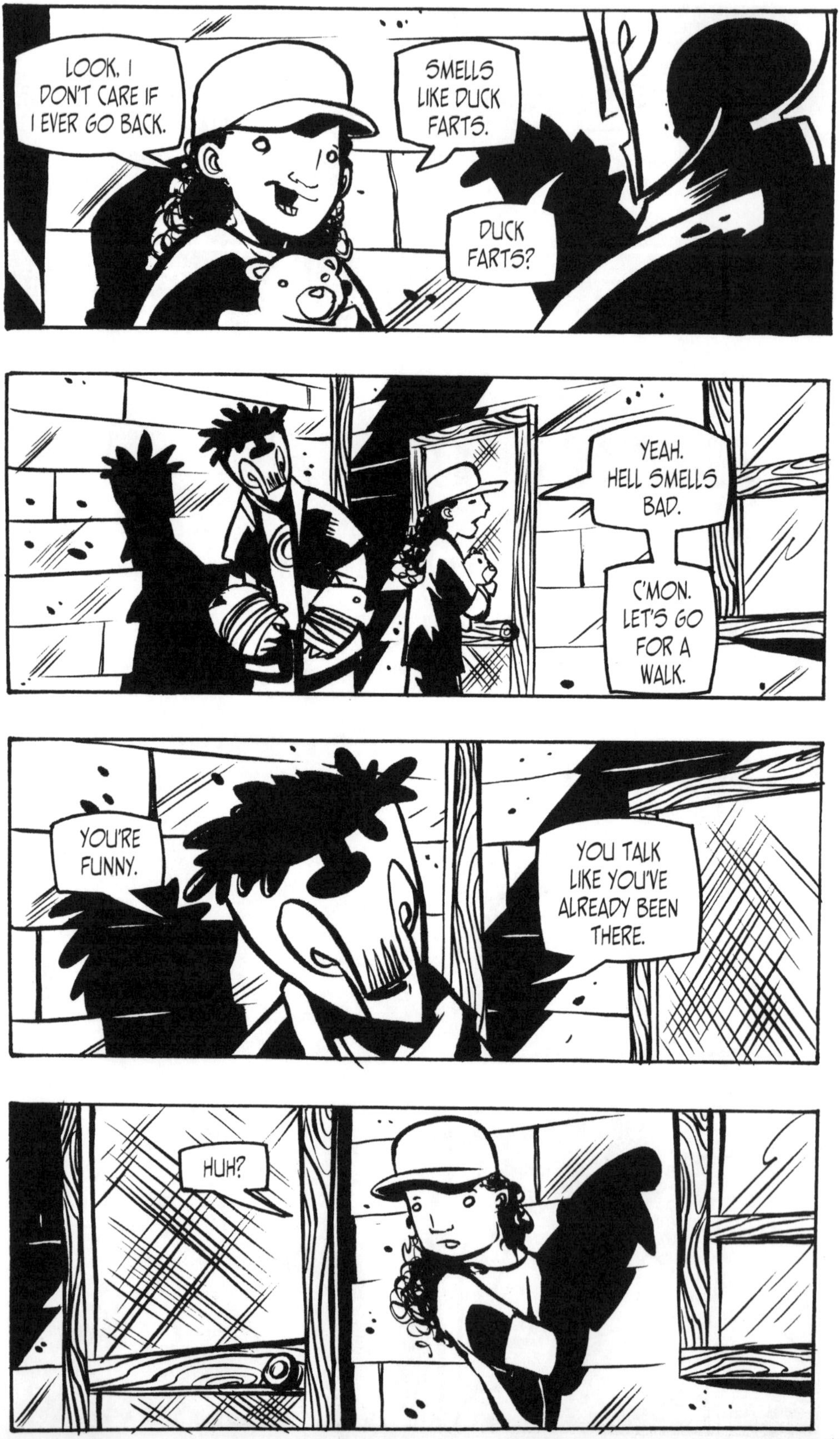
LOOK, I DON'T CARE IF I EVER GO BACK.
SMELLS LIKE DUCK FARTS.
DUCK FARTS?
YEAH. HELL SMELLS BAD.
C'MON. LET'S GO FOR A WALK.
YOU'RE FUNNY.
YOU TALK LIKE YOU'VE ALREADY BEEN THERE.
HUH?

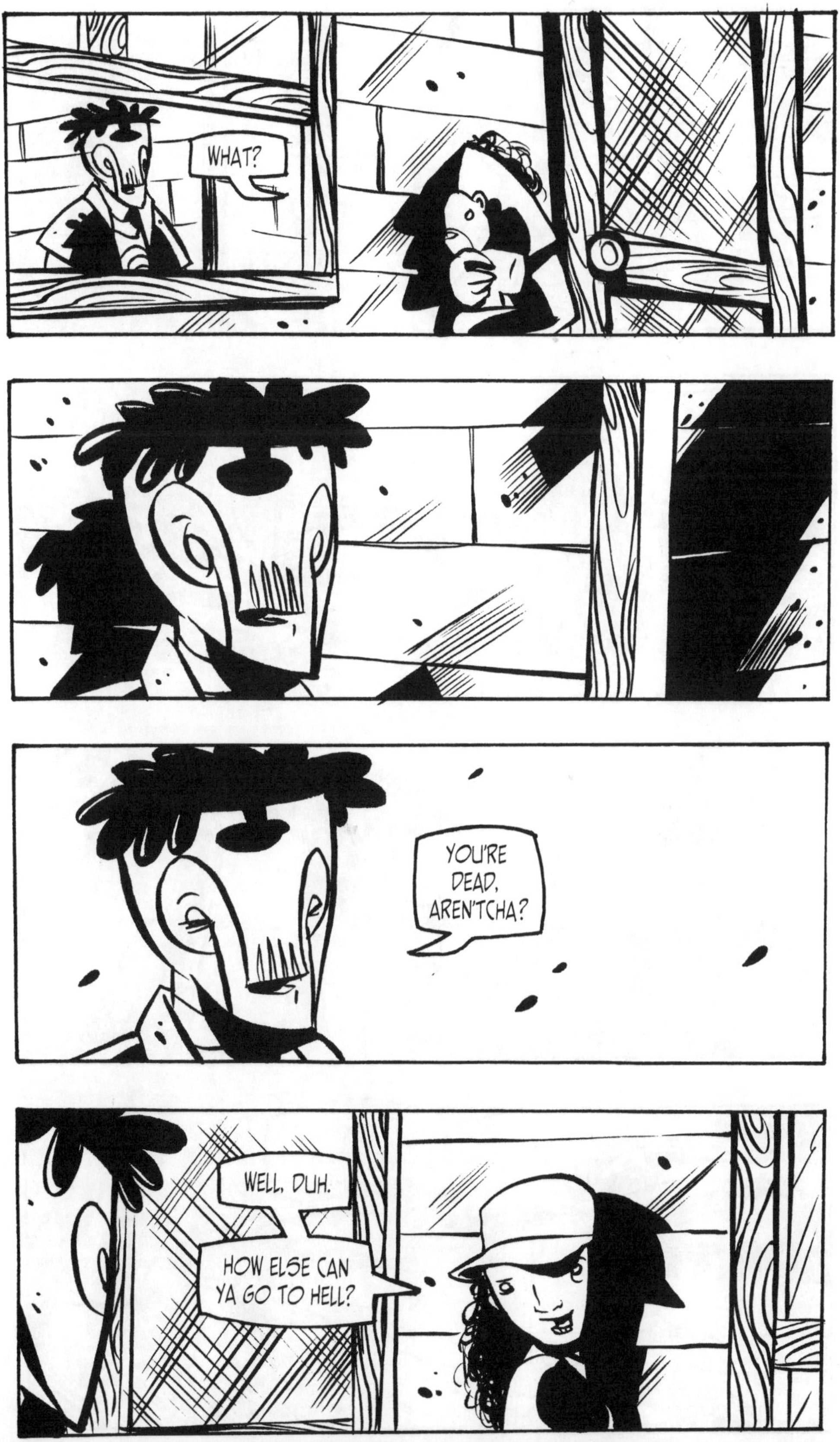
WHAT?
YOU'RE DEAD, AREN'TCHA?
WELL, DUH.
HOW ELSE CAN YA GO TO HELL?

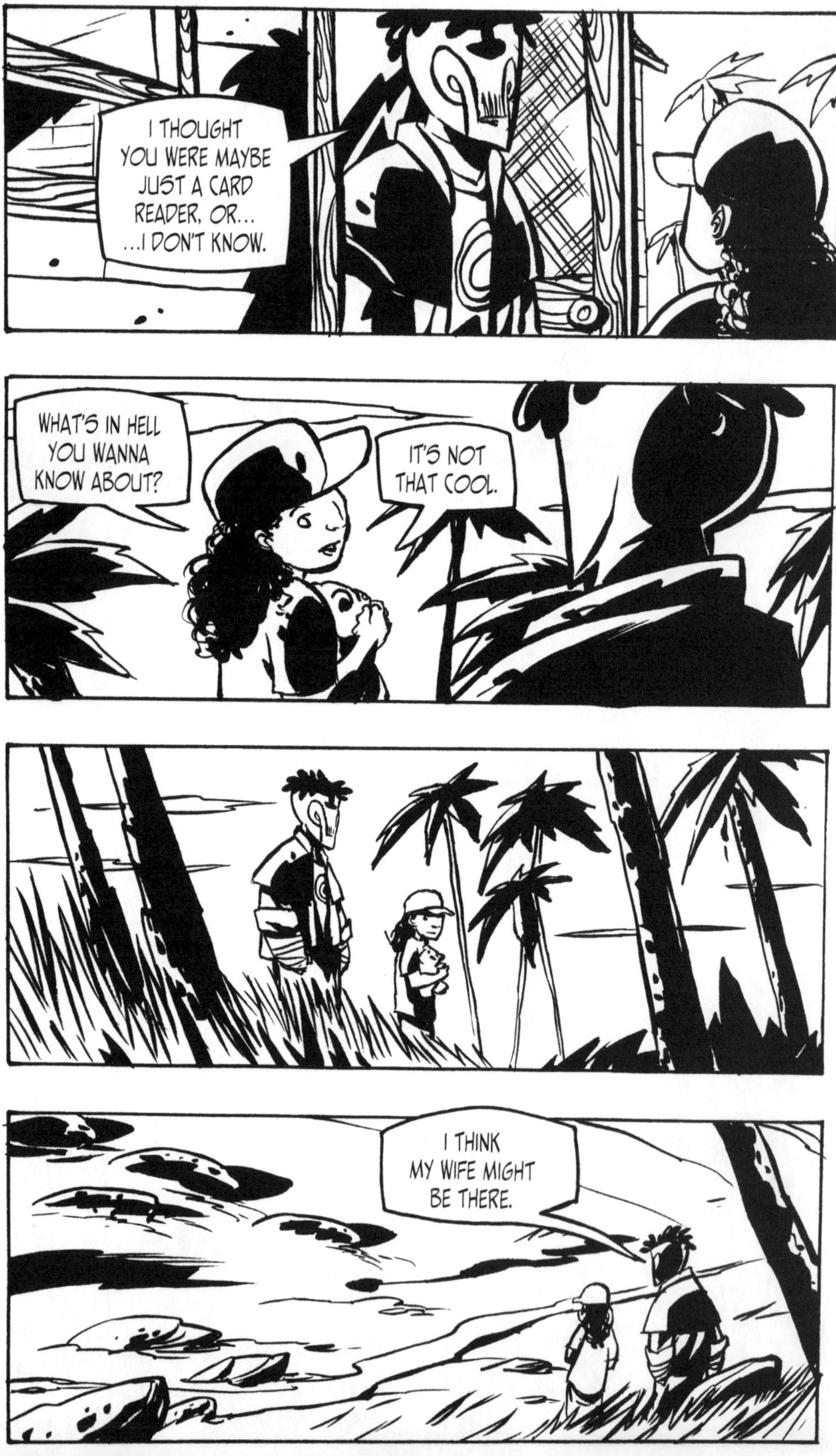
I THOUGHT YOU WERE MAYBE JUST A CARD READER, OR... ...I DON'T KNOW.
WHAT'S IN HELL YOU WANNA KNOW ABOUT?
IT'S NOT THAT COOL.
I THINK MY WIFE MIGHT BE THERE.

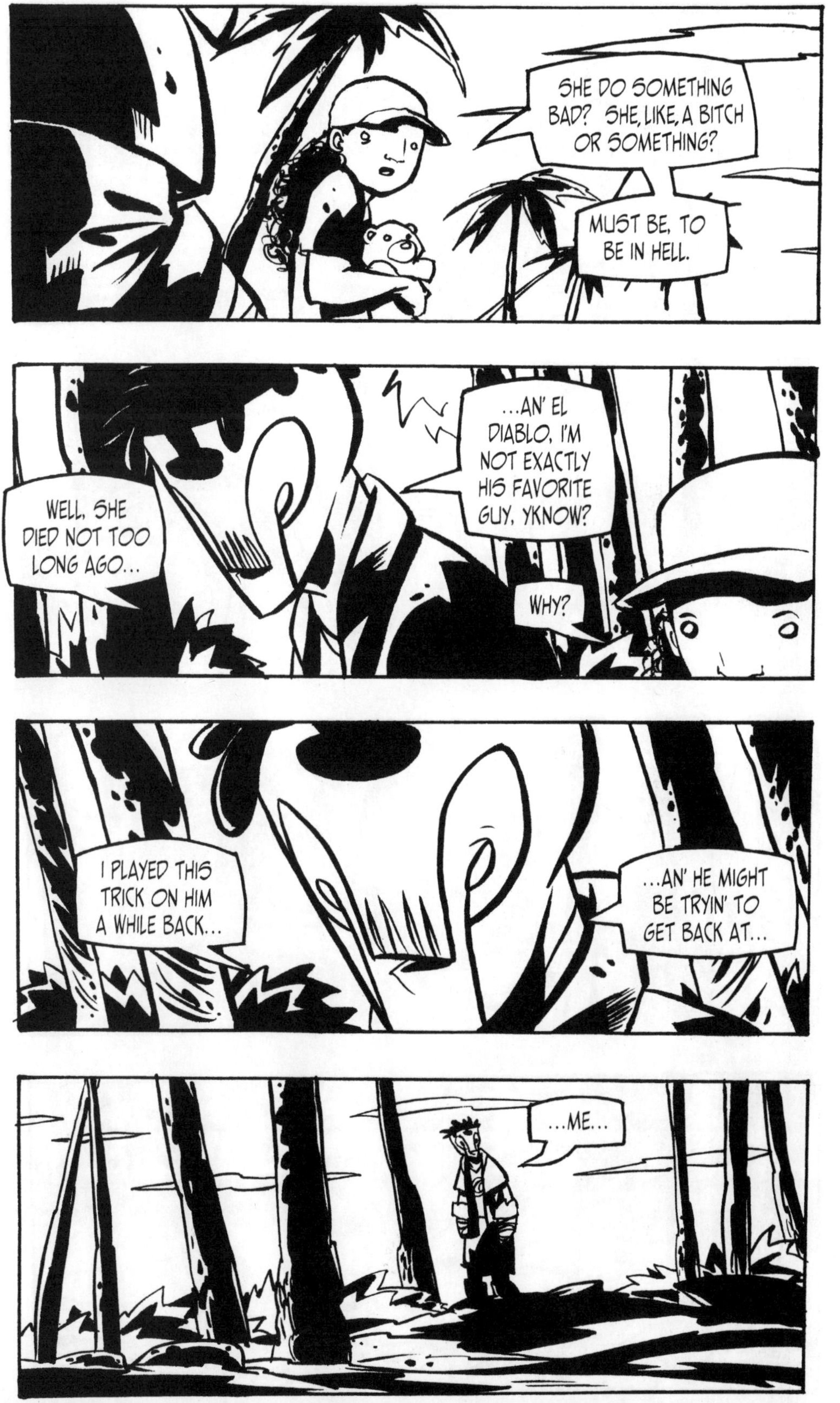
SHE DO SOMETHING BAD? SHE, LIKE, A BITCH OR SOMETHING?
MUST BE, TO BE IN HELL.
WELL, SHE DIED NOT TOO LONG AGO...
...AN' EL DIABLO, I'M NOT EXACTLY HIS FAVORITE GUY, YKNOW?
WHY?
I PLAYED THIS TRICK ON HIM A WHILE BACK...
...AN' HE MIGHT BE TRYIN' TO GET BACK AT...
...ME...

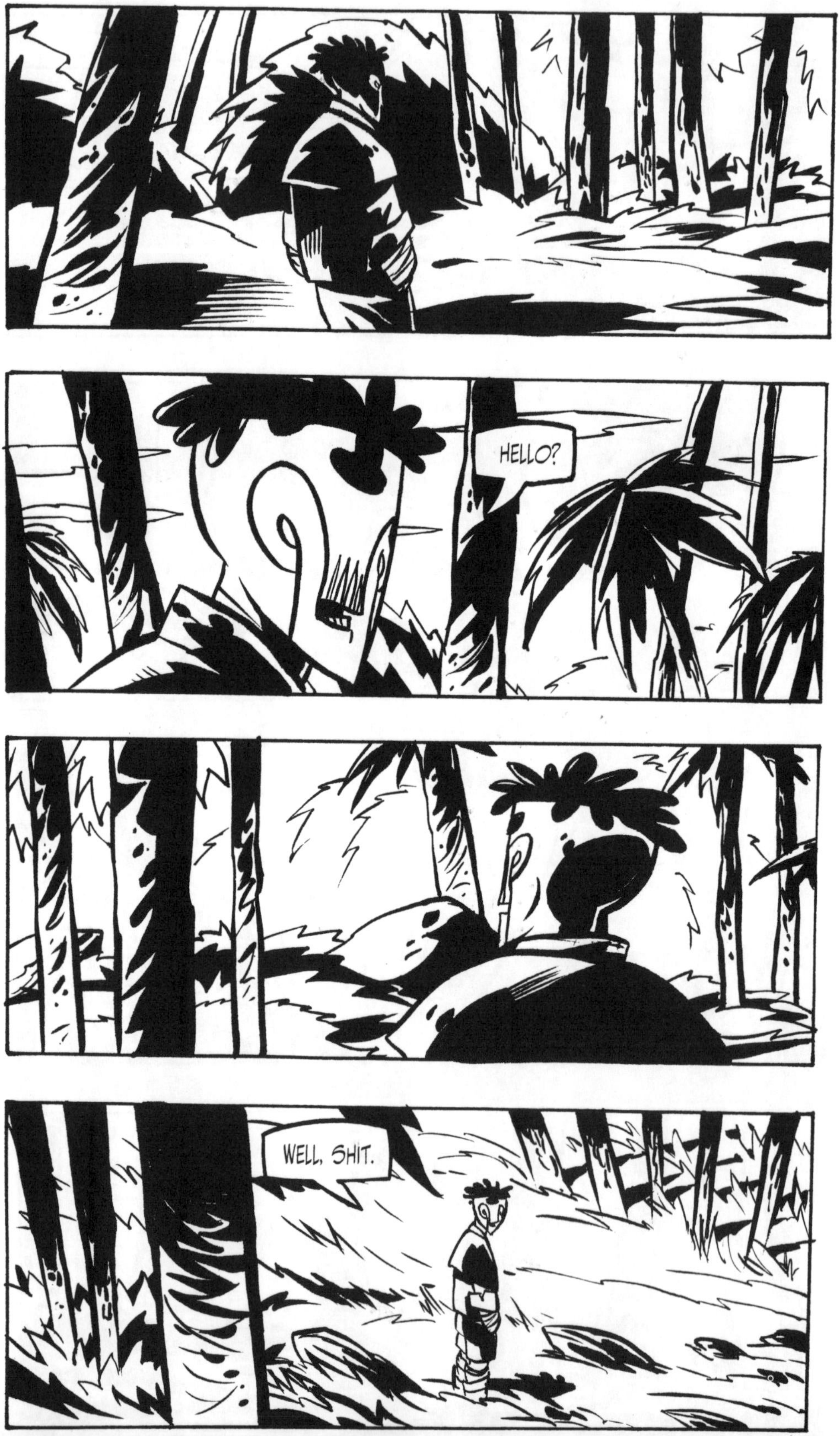
HELLO?
WELL, SHIT.

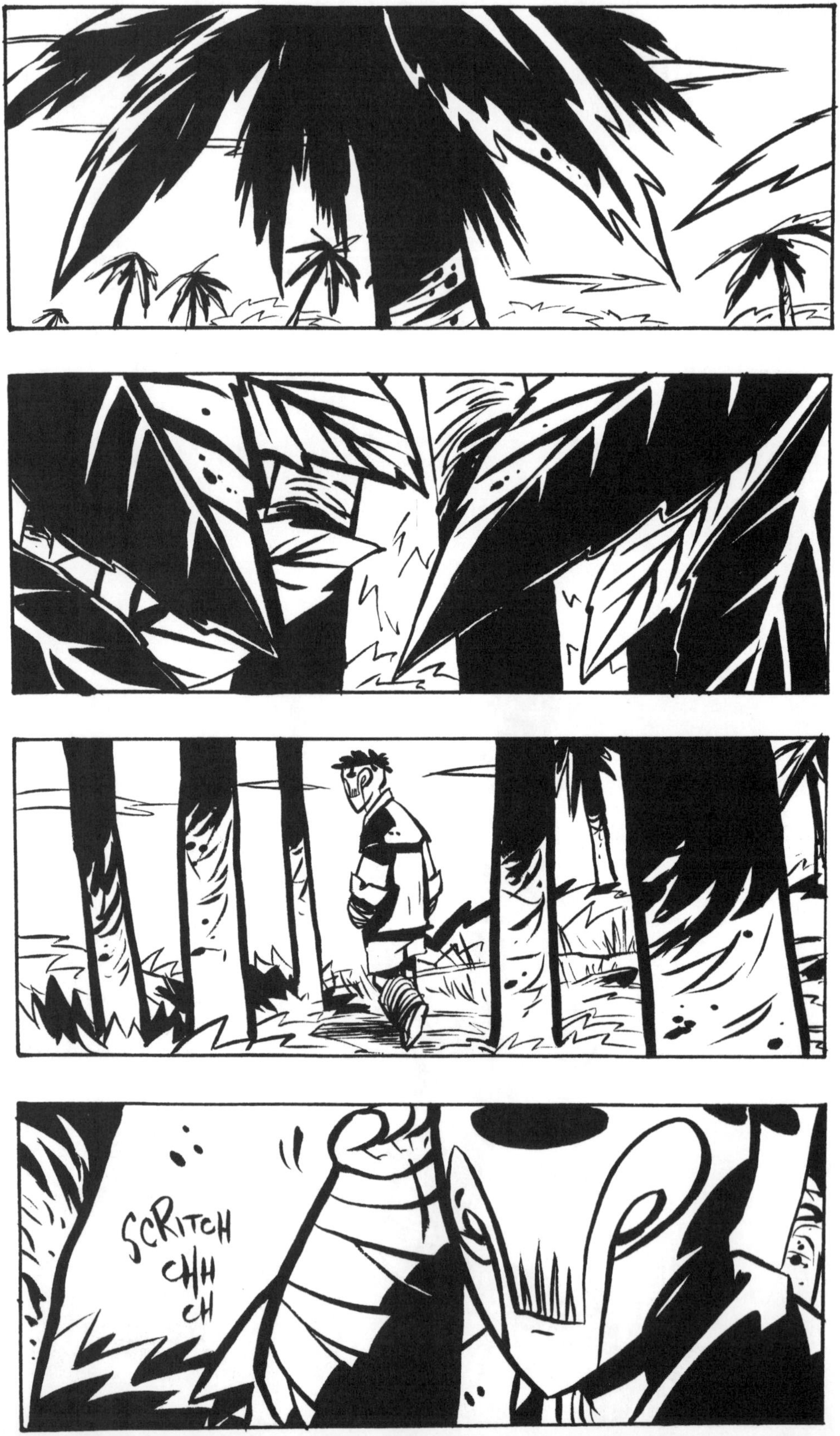
SCRITCH
CHH
CH

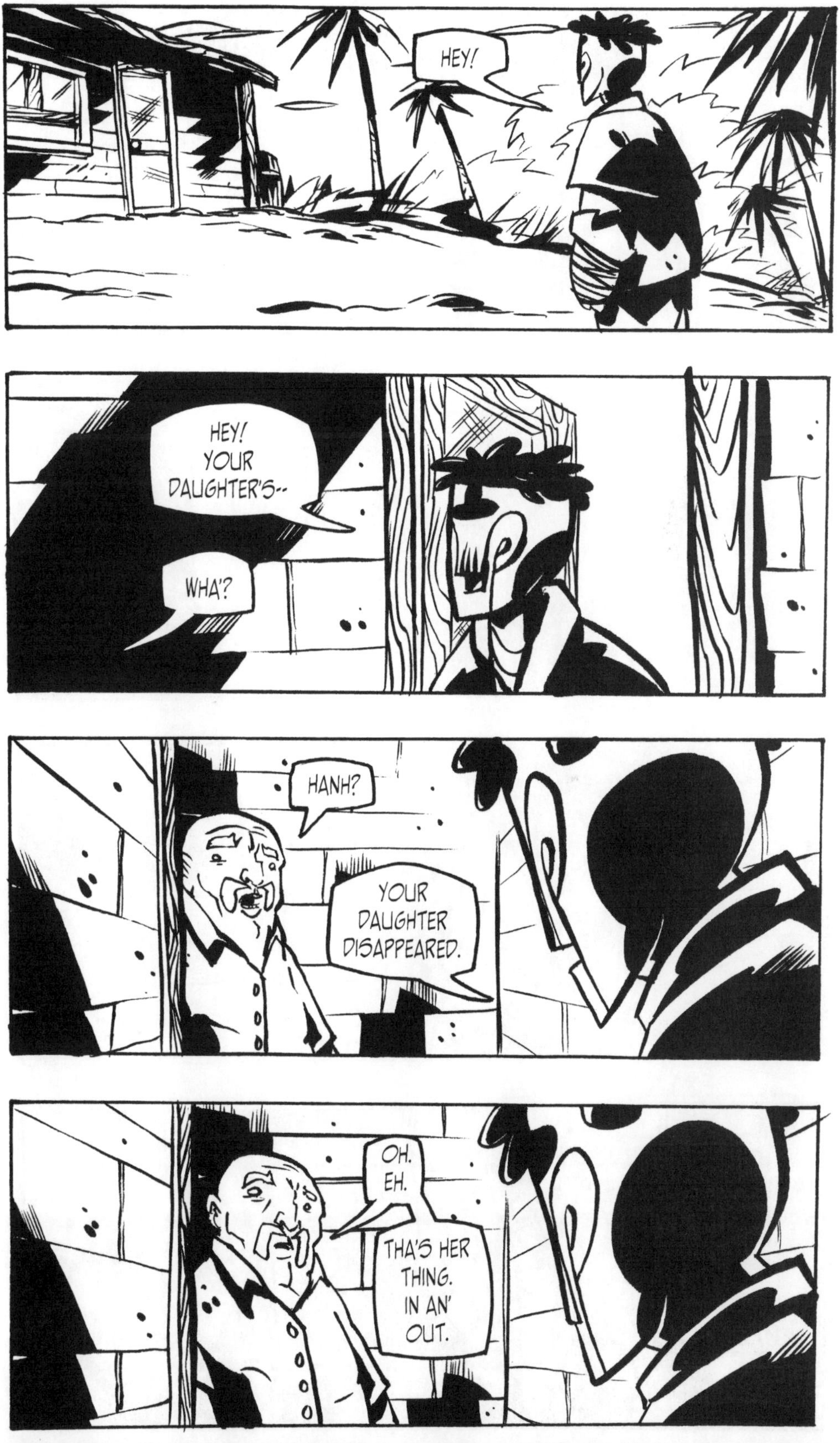
HEY!
HEY! YOUR DAUGHTER'S--
WHA'?
HANH?
YOUR DAUGHTER DISAPPEARED.
OH. EH.
THA'S HER THING. IN AN' OUT.

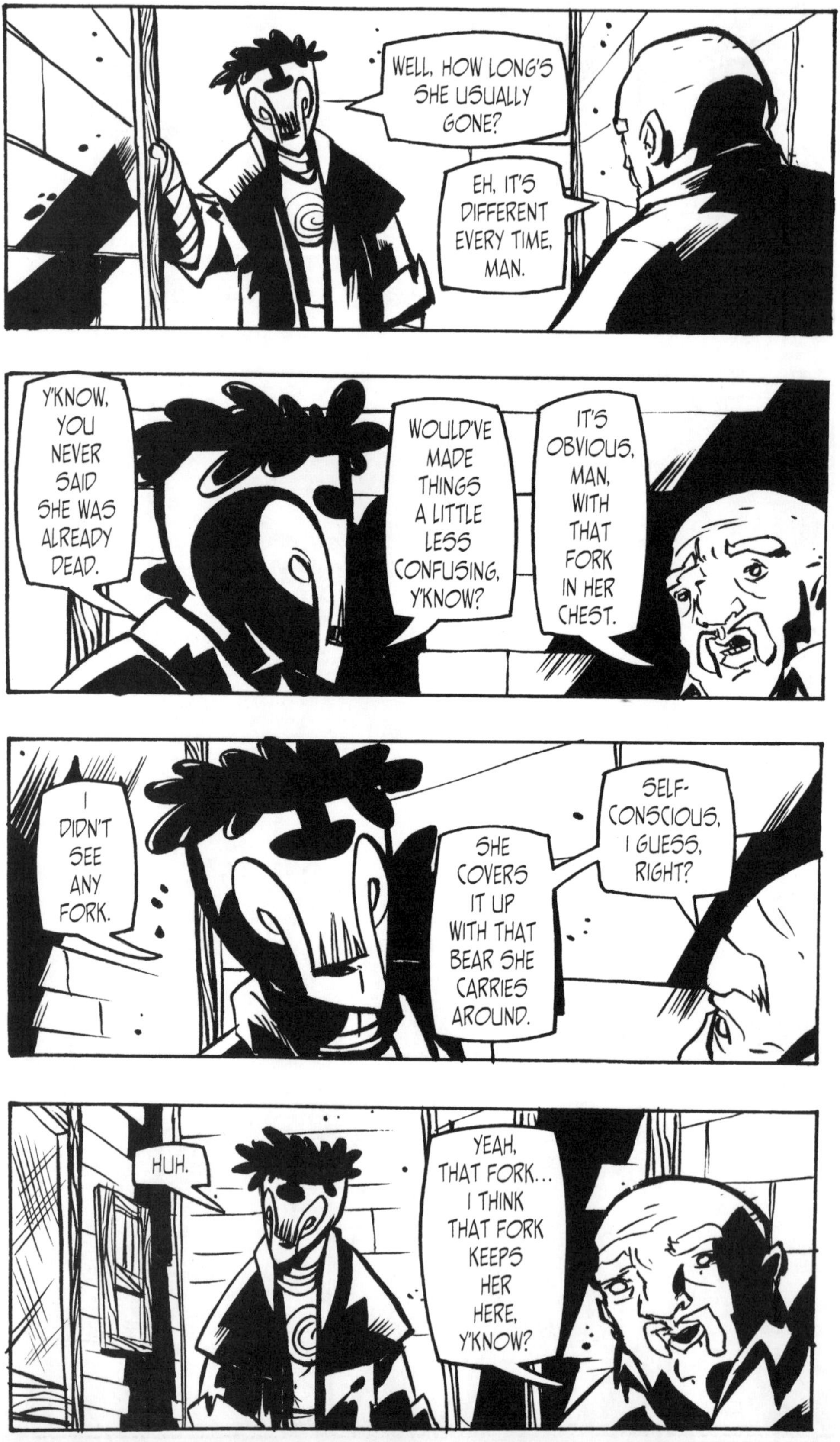
WELL, HOW LONG'S SHE USUALLY GONE?
EH, IT'S DIFFERENT EVERY TIME, MAN.
Y'KNOW, YOU NEVER SAID SHE WAS ALREADY DEAD.
WOULD'VE MADE THINGS A LITTLE LESS CONFUSING, Y'KNOW?
IT'S OBVIOUS, MAN, WITH THAT FORK IN HER CHEST.
I DIDN'T SEE ANY FORK.
SHE COVERS IT UP WITH THAT BEAR SHE CARRIES AROUND.
SELF-CONSCIOUS, I GUESS, RIGHT?
HUH.
YEAH, THAT FORK... I THINK THAT FORK KEEPS HER HERE, Y'KNOW?

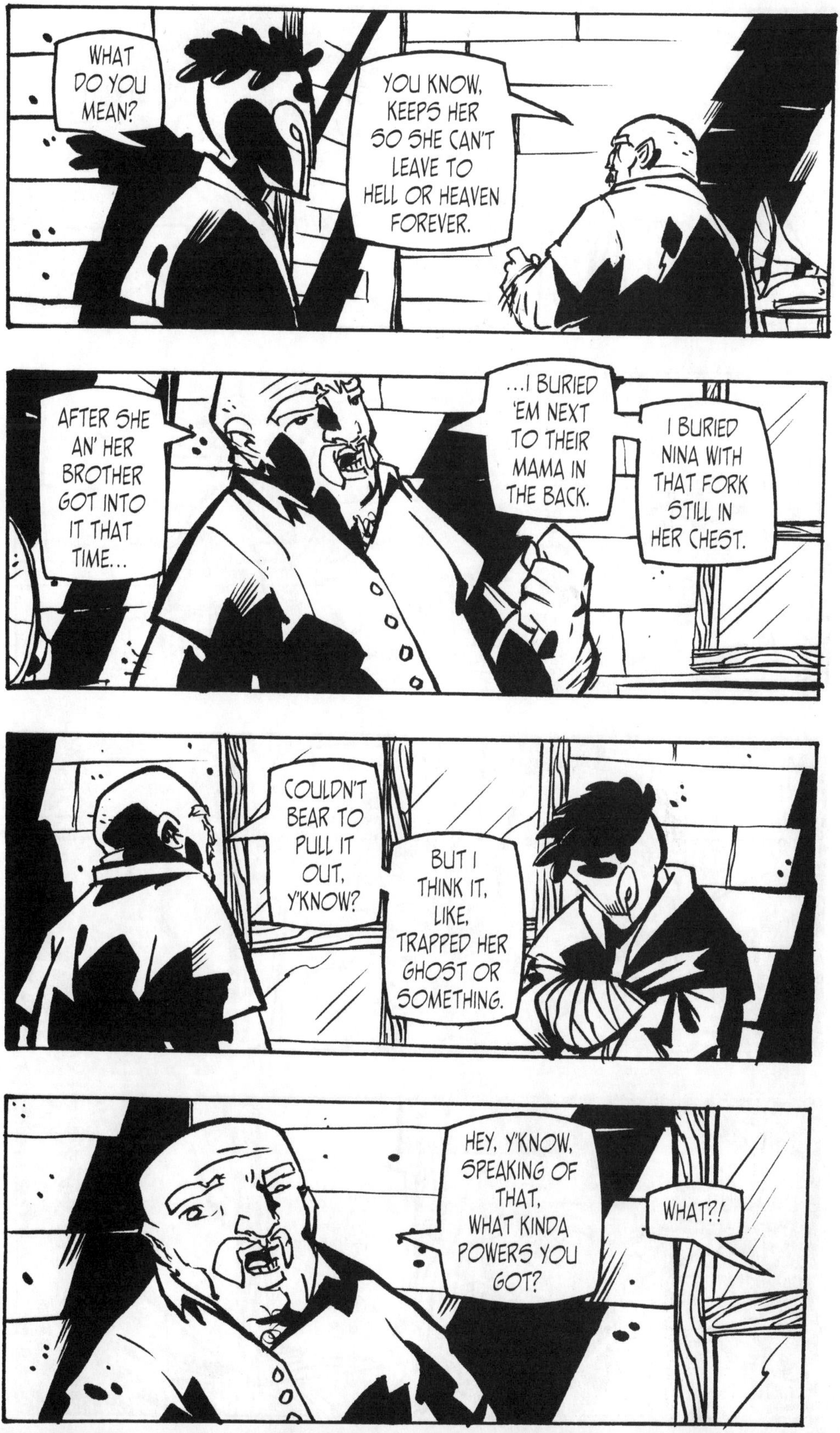
WHAT DO YOU MEAN?
YOU KNOW, KEEPS HER SO SHE CAN'T LEAVE TO HELL OR HEAVEN FOREVER.
AFTER SHE AN' HER BROTHER GOT INTO IT THAT TIME...
...I BURIED 'EM NEXT TO THEIR MAMA IN THE BACK.
I BURIED NINA WITH THAT FORK STILL IN HER CHEST.
COULDN'T BEAR TO PULL IT OUT, Y'KNOW?
BUT I THINK IT, LIKE, TRAPPED HER GHOST OR SOMETHING.
HEY, Y'KNOW, SPEAKING OF THAT, WHAT KINDA POWERS YOU GOT?
WHAT?!

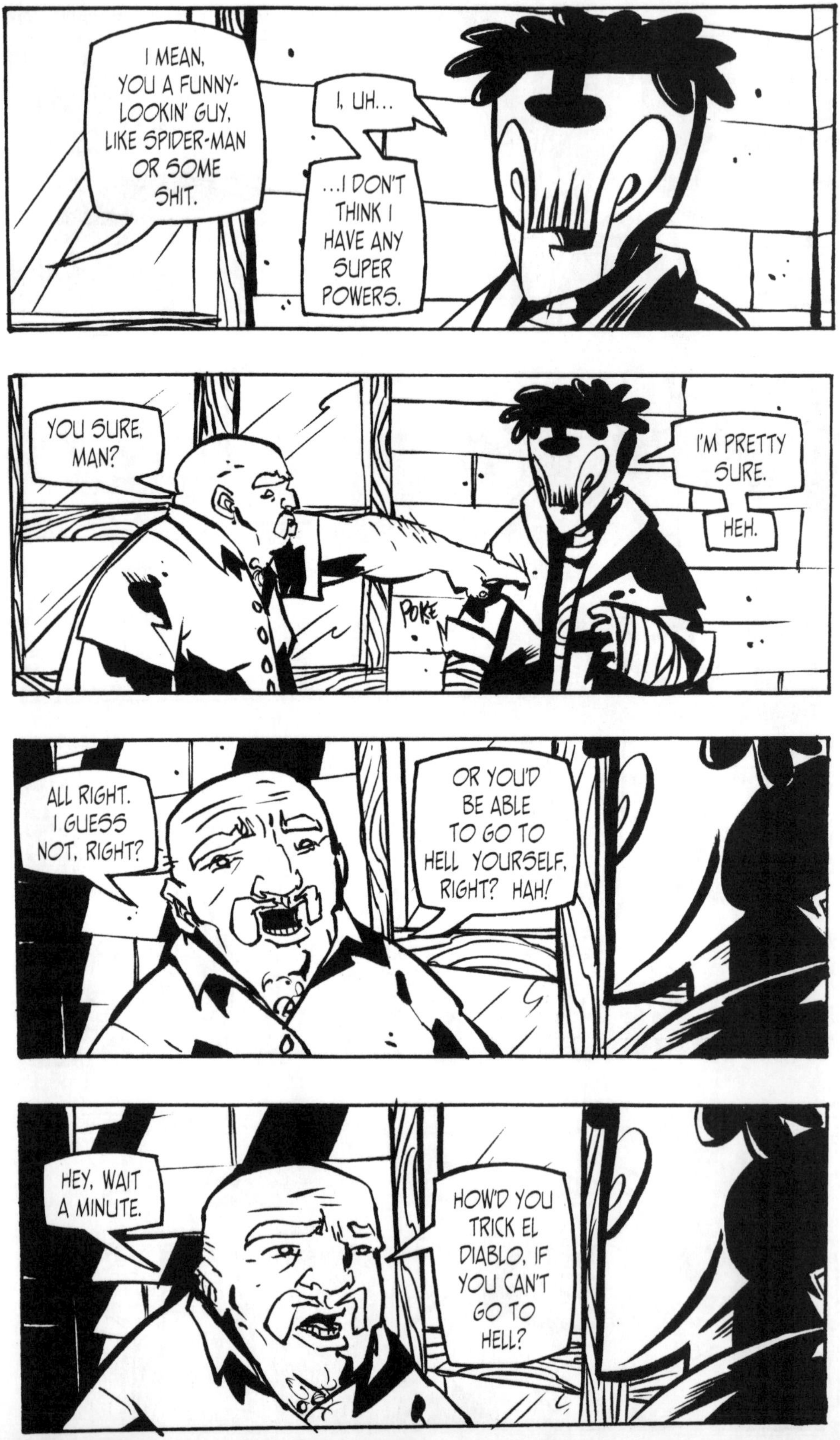
I MEAN, YOU A FUNNY-LOOKIN' GUY, LIKE SPIDER-MAN OR SOME SHIT.
I, UH...
...I DON'T THINK I HAVE ANY SUPER POWERS.
YOU SURE, MAN?
POKE
I'M PRETTY SURE.
HEH.
ALL RIGHT. I GUESS NOT, RIGHT?
OR YOU'D BE ABLE TO GO TO HELL YOURSELF, RIGHT? HAH!
HEY, WAIT A MINUTE.
HOW'D YOU TRICK EL DIABLO, IF YOU CAN'T GO TO HELL?

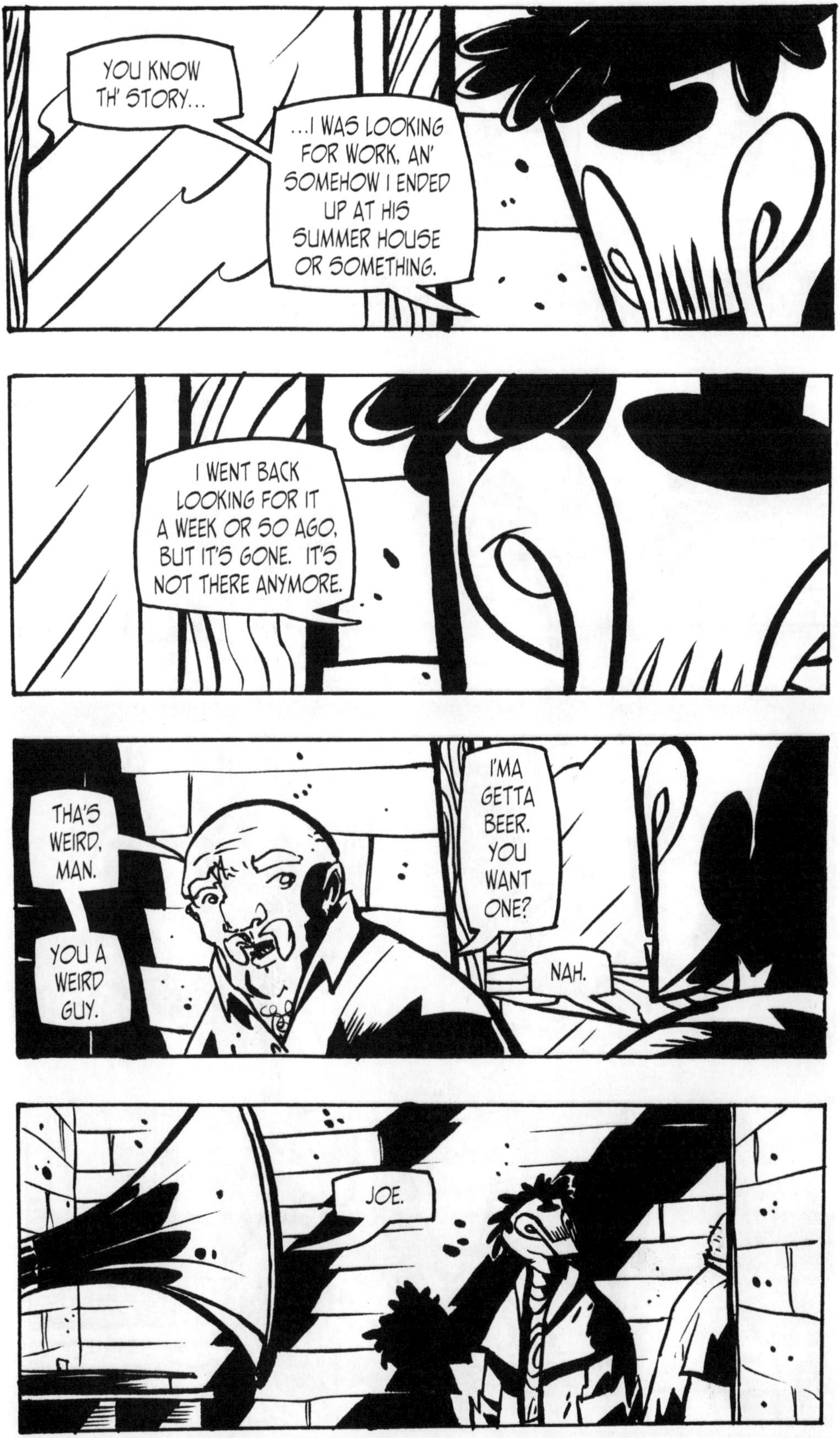
YOU KNOW TH' STORY...
...I WAS LOOKING FOR WORK, AN' SOMEHOW I ENDED UP AT HIS SUMMER HOUSE OR SOMETHING.
I WENT BACK LOOKING FOR IT A WEEK OR SO AGO, BUT IT'S GONE. IT'S NOT THERE ANYMORE.
THA'S WEIRD, MAN.
YOU A WEIRD GUY.
I'MA GETTA BEER. YOU WANT ONE?
NAH.
JOE.

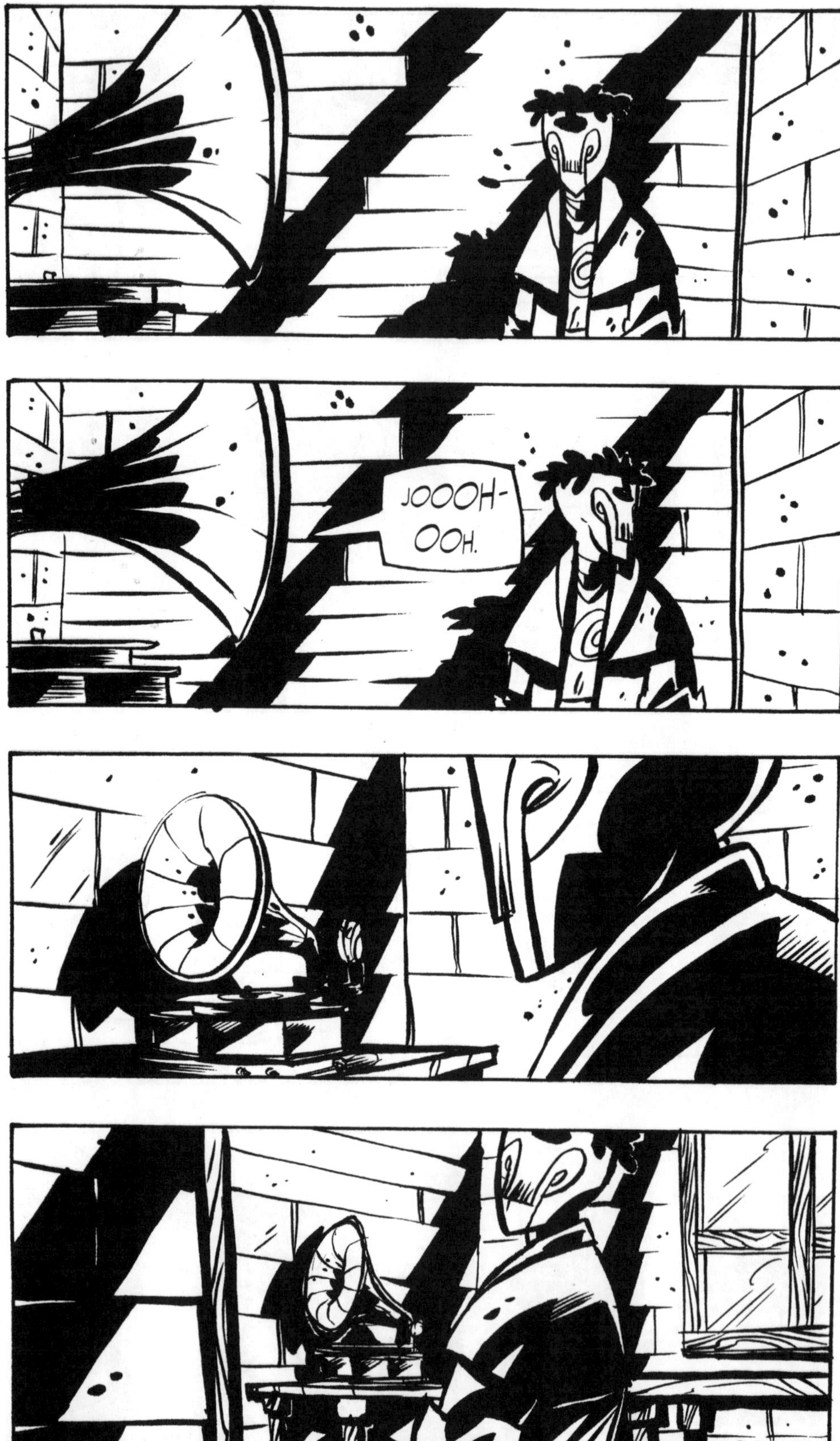
JOOOH-OOH.

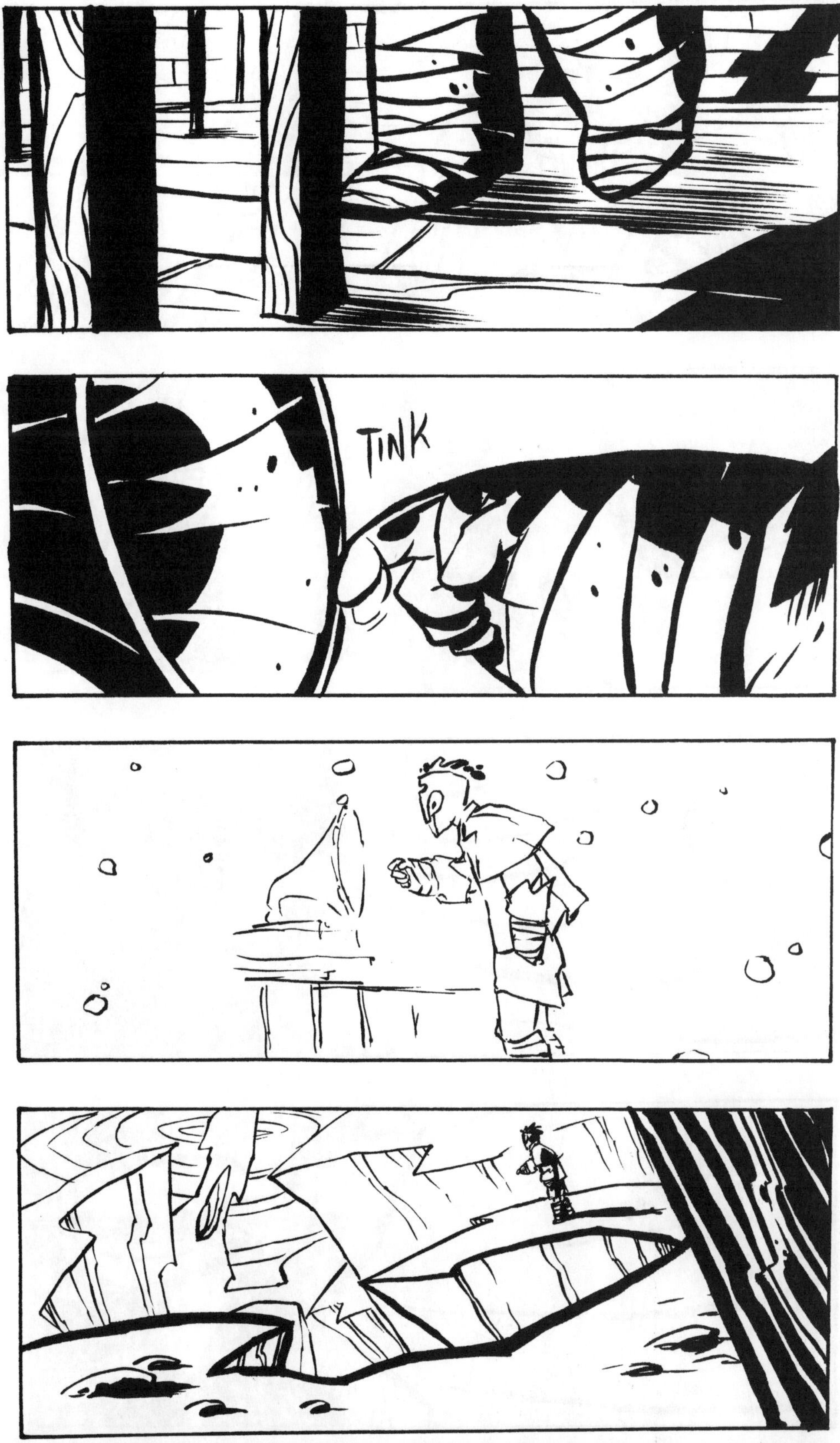
TINK

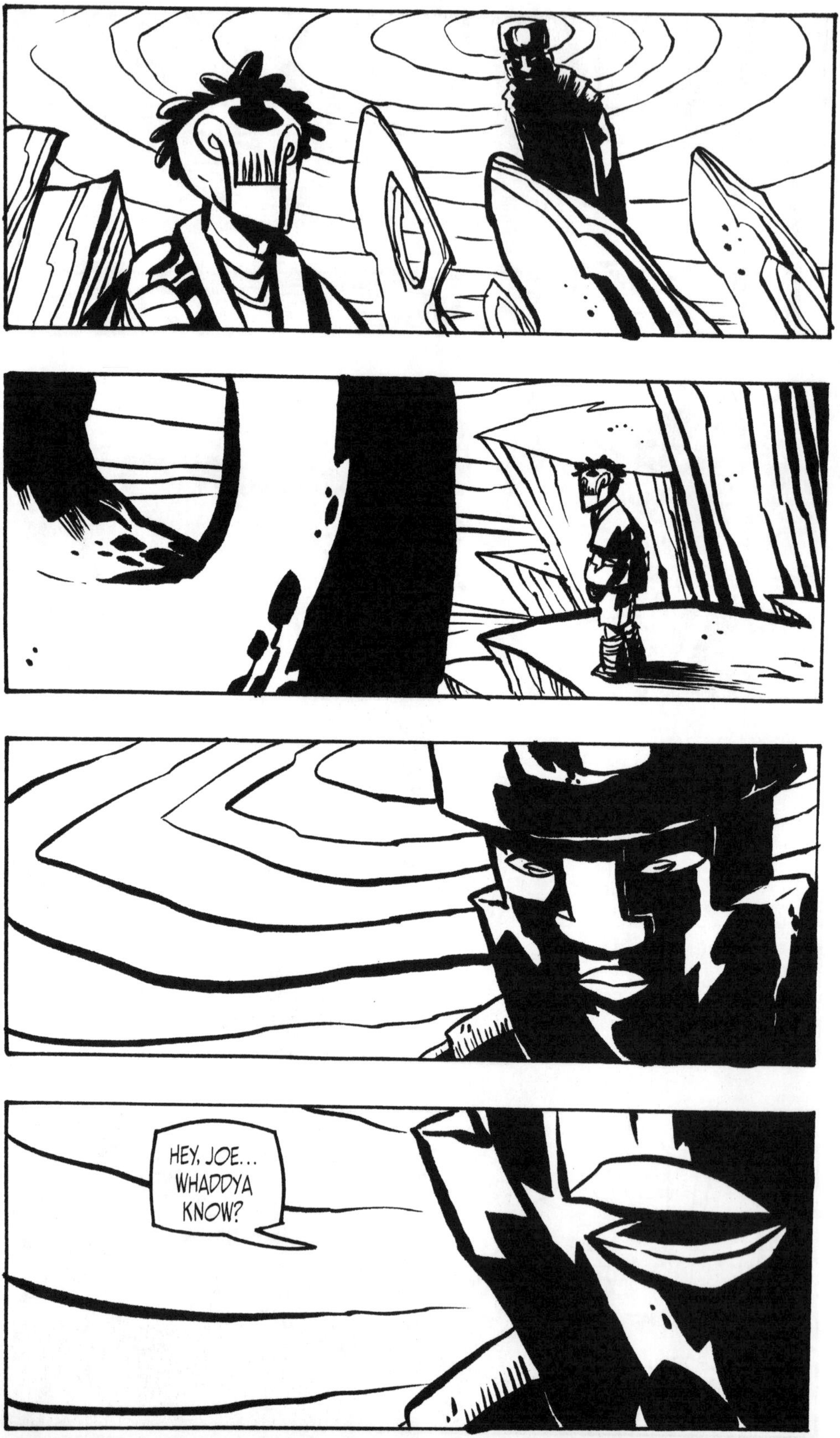
HEY, JOE... WHADDYA KNOW?

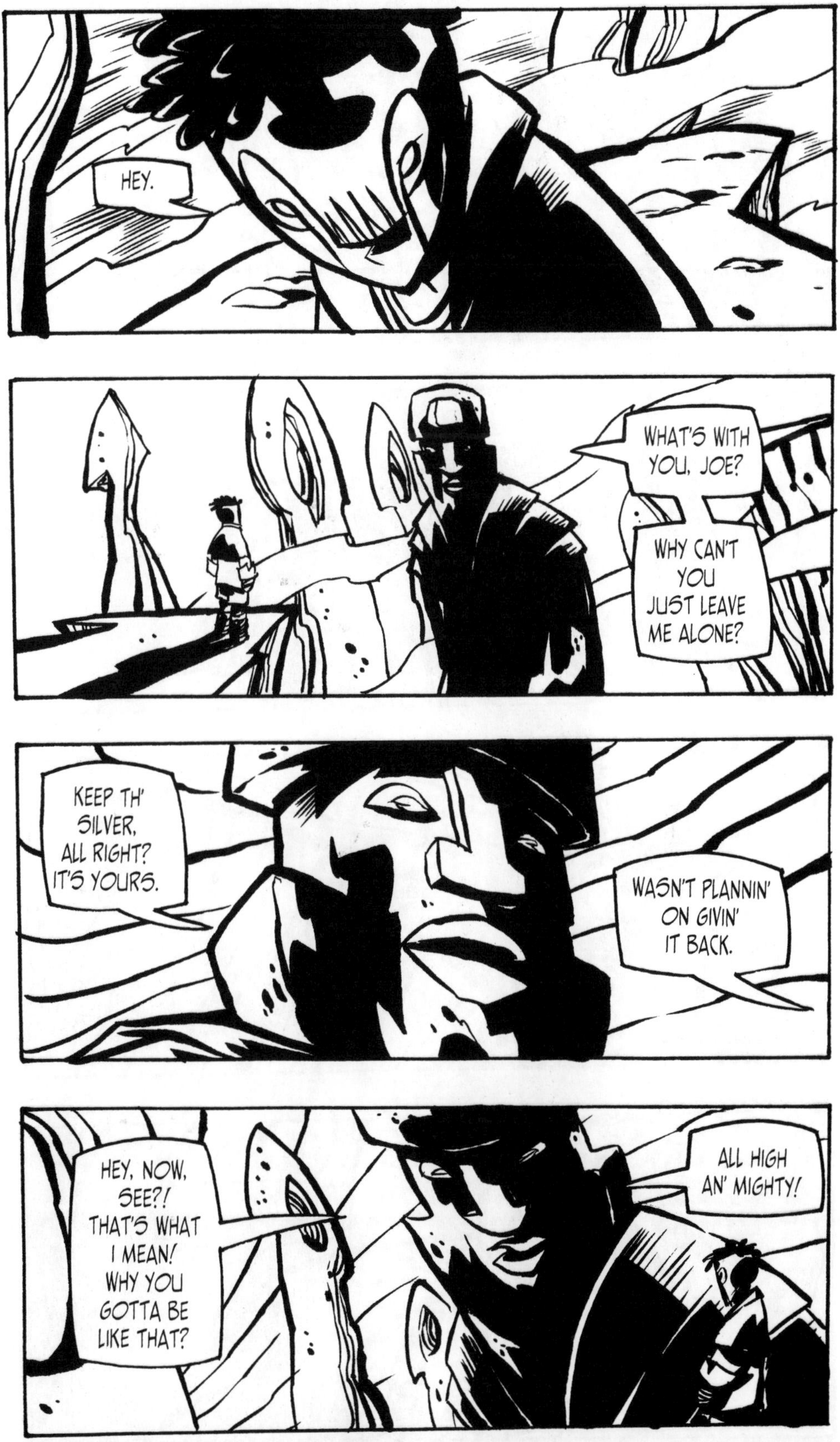
HEY.
WHAT'S WITH YOU, JOE?
WHY CAN'T YOU JUST LEAVE ME ALONE?
KEEP TH' SILVER, ALL RIGHT? IT'S YOURS.
WASN'T PLANNIN' ON GIVIN' IT BACK.
HEY, NOW, SEE?! THAT'S WHAT I MEAN! WHY YOU GOTTA BE LIKE THAT?
ALL HIGH AN' MIGHTY!

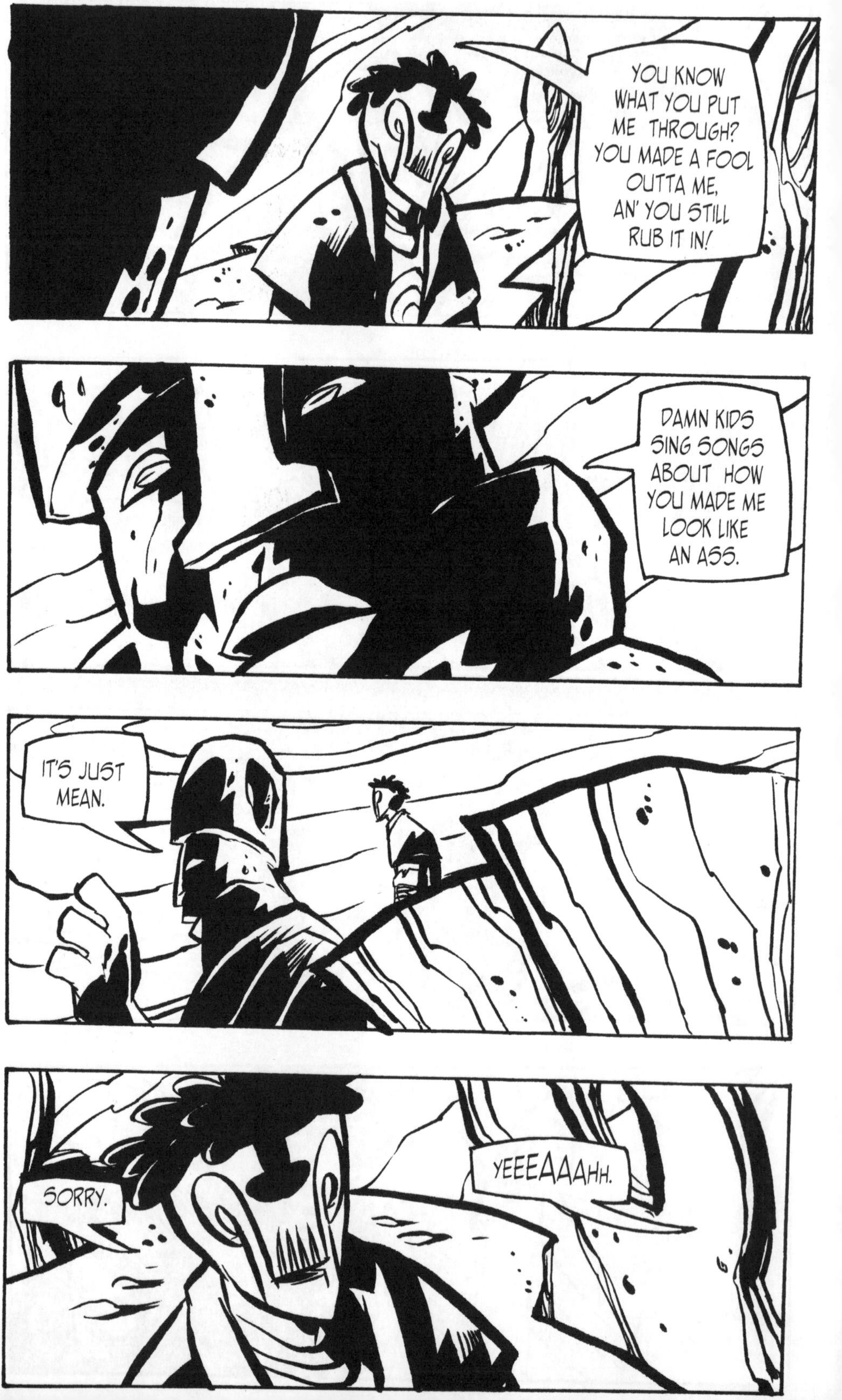
YOU KNOW WHAT YOU PUT ME THROUGH? YOU MADE A FOOL OUTTA ME, AN' YOU STILL RUB IT IN!
DAMN KIDS SING SONGS ABOUT HOW YOU MADE ME LOOK LIKE AN ASS.
IT'S JUST MEAN.
YEEEAAAHH.
SORRY.

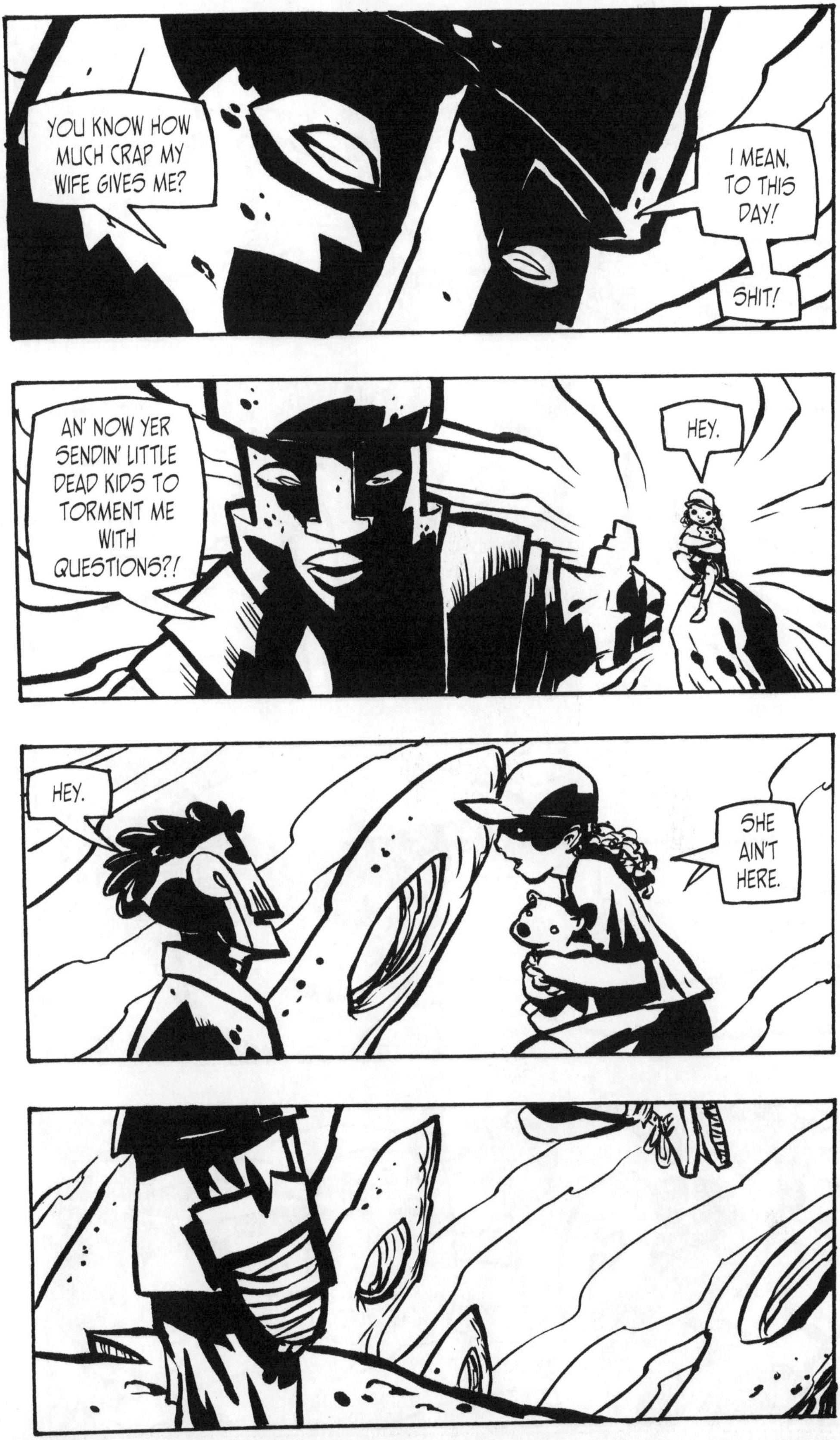
YOU KNOW HOW MUCH CRAP MY WIFE GIVES ME?
I MEAN, TO THIS DAY!
SHIT!
AN' NOW YER SENDIN' LITTLE DEAD KIDS TO TORMENT ME WITH QUESTIONS?!
HEY.
HEY.
SHE AIN'T HERE.

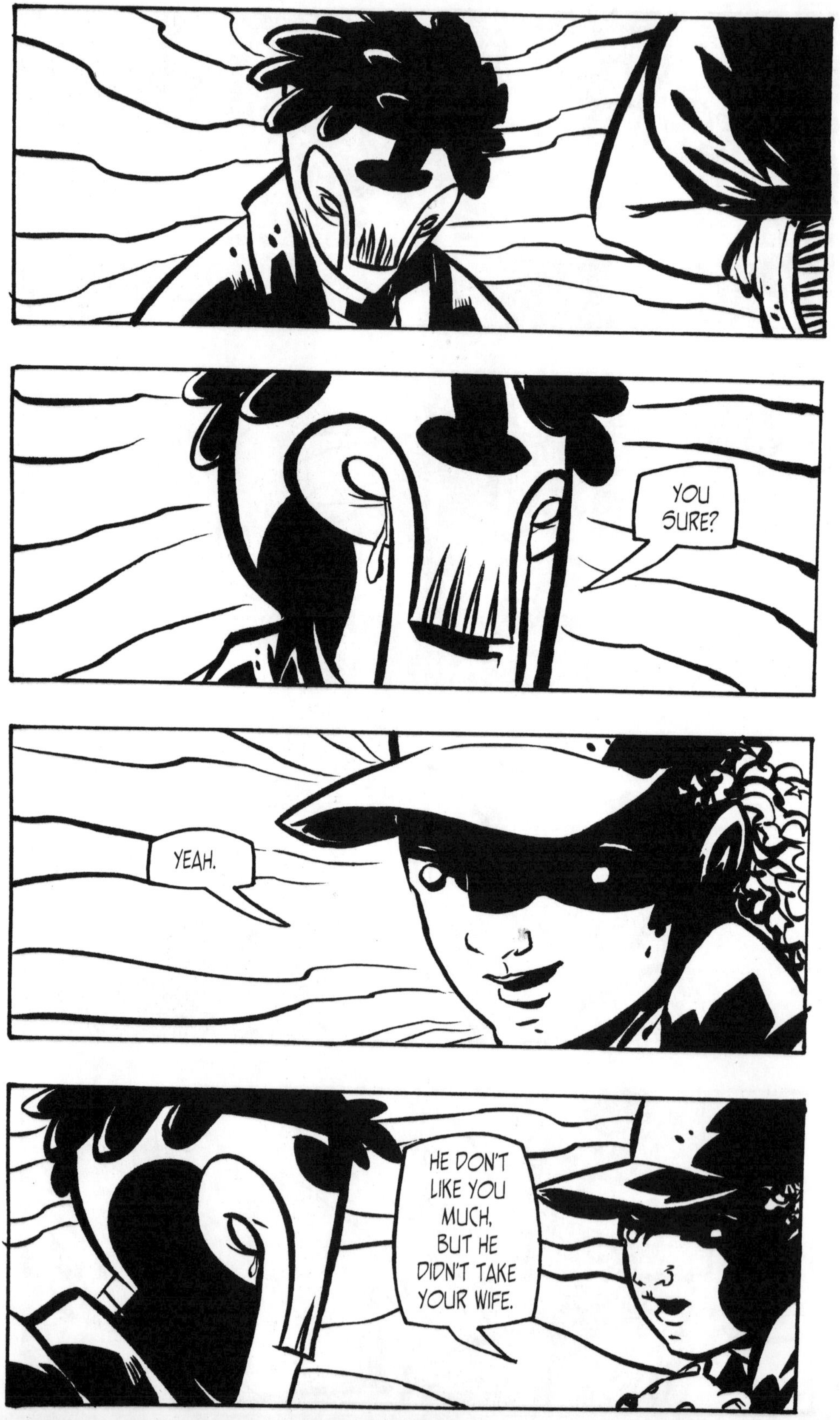
YOU SURE?
YEAH.
HE DON'T LIKE YOU MUCH, BUT HE DIDN'T TAKE YOUR WIFE.

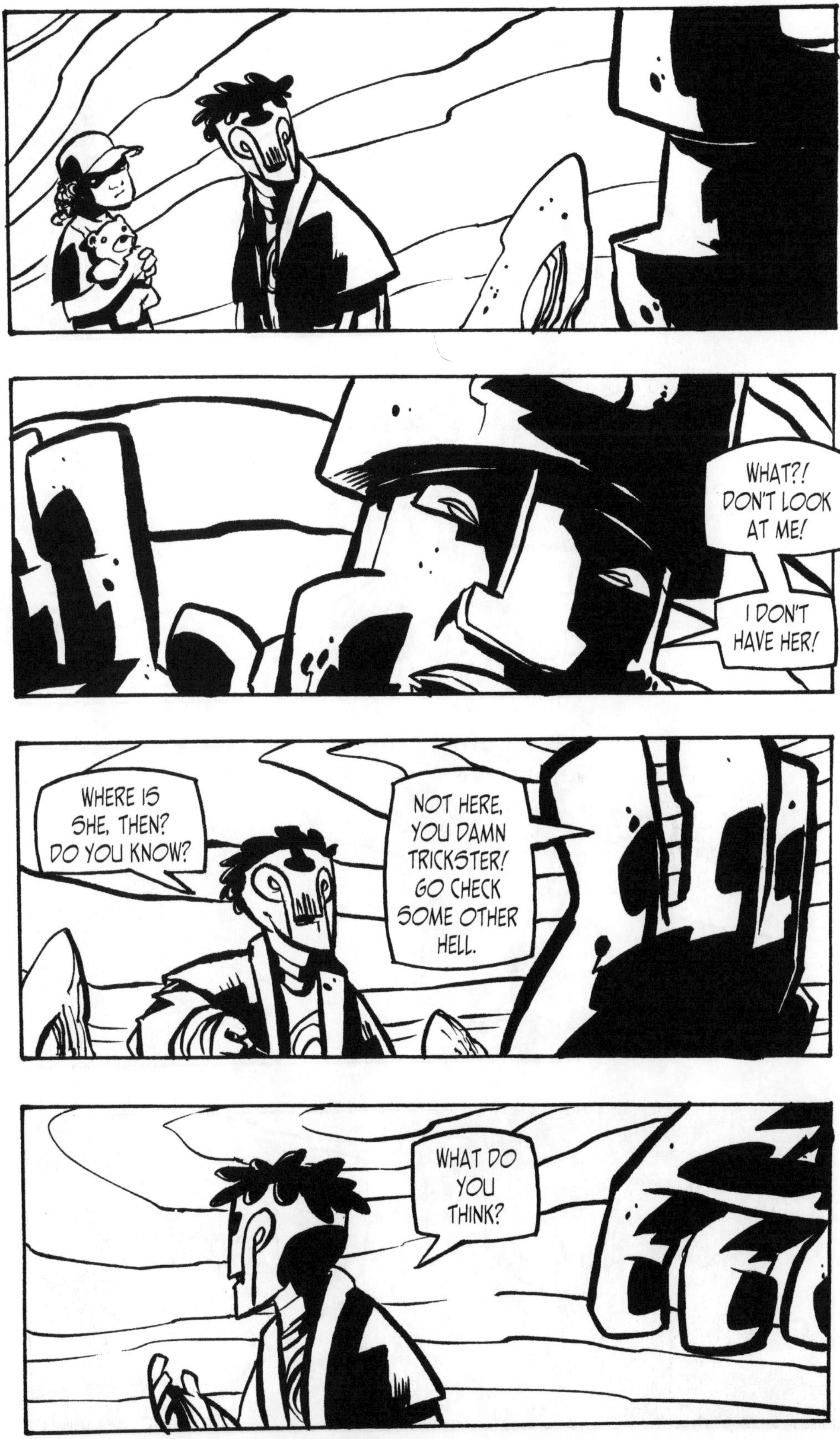

WHAT?! DON'T LOOK AT ME!
I DON'T HAVE HER!
WHERE IS SHE, THEN? DO YOU KNOW?
NOT HERE, YOU DAMN TRICKSTER! GO CHECK SOME OTHER HELL.
WHAT DO YOU THINK?

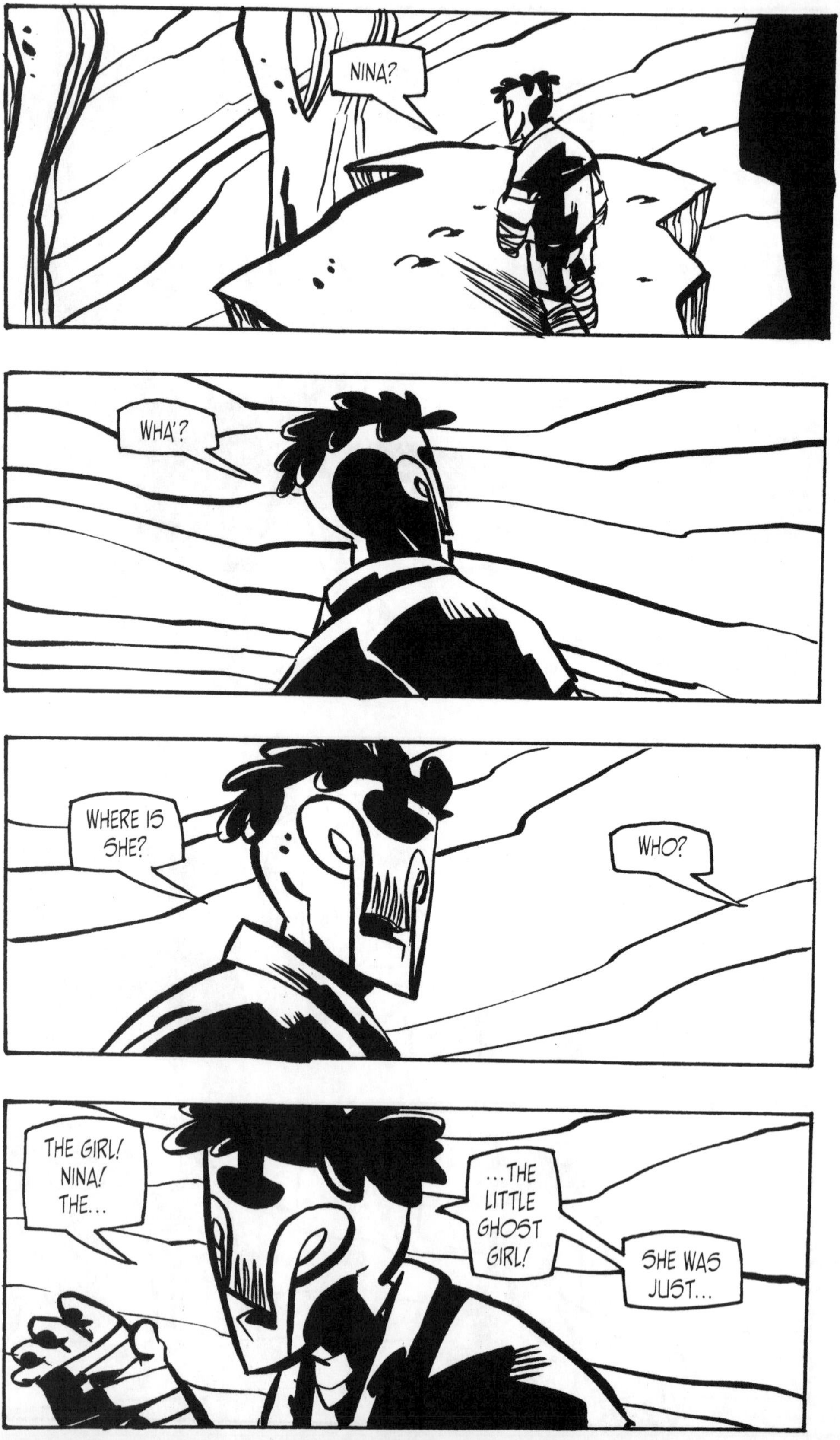
NINA?
WHA'?
WHERE IS SHE?
WHO?
THE GIRL! NINA! THE...
...THE LITTLE GHOST GIRL!
SHE WAS JUST...

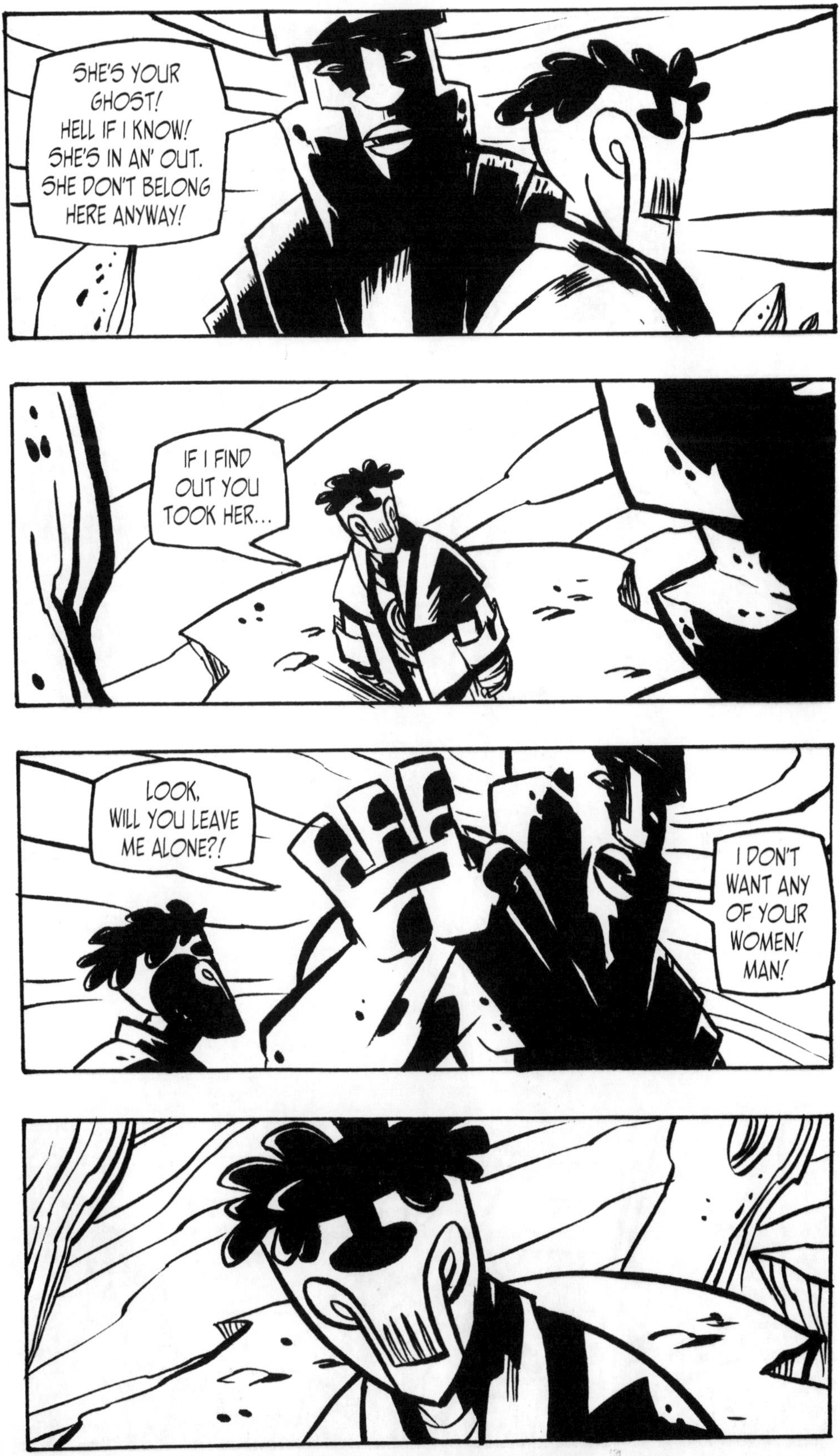
SHE'S YOUR GHOST! HELL IF I KNOW! SHE'S IN AN' OUT. SHE DON'T BELONG HERE ANYWAY!
IF I FIND OUT YOU TOOK HER...
LOOK, WILL YOU LEAVE ME ALONE?!
I DON'T WANT ANY OF YOUR WOMEN! MAN!

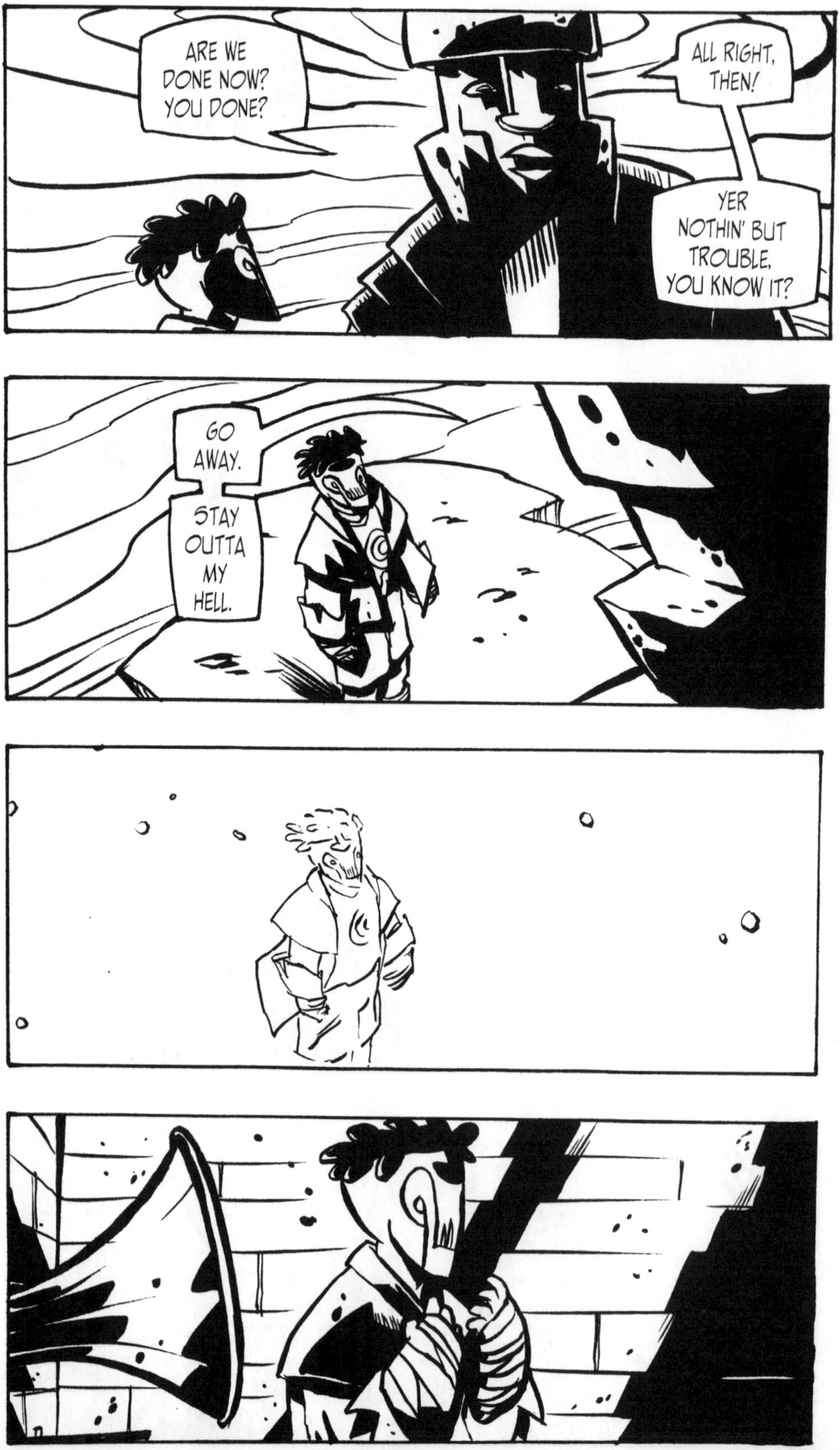
ARE WE DONE NOW? YOU DONE?
ALL RIGHT, THEN!
YER NOTHIN' BUT TROUBLE, YOU KNOW IT?
GO AWAY.
STAY OUTTA MY HELL.

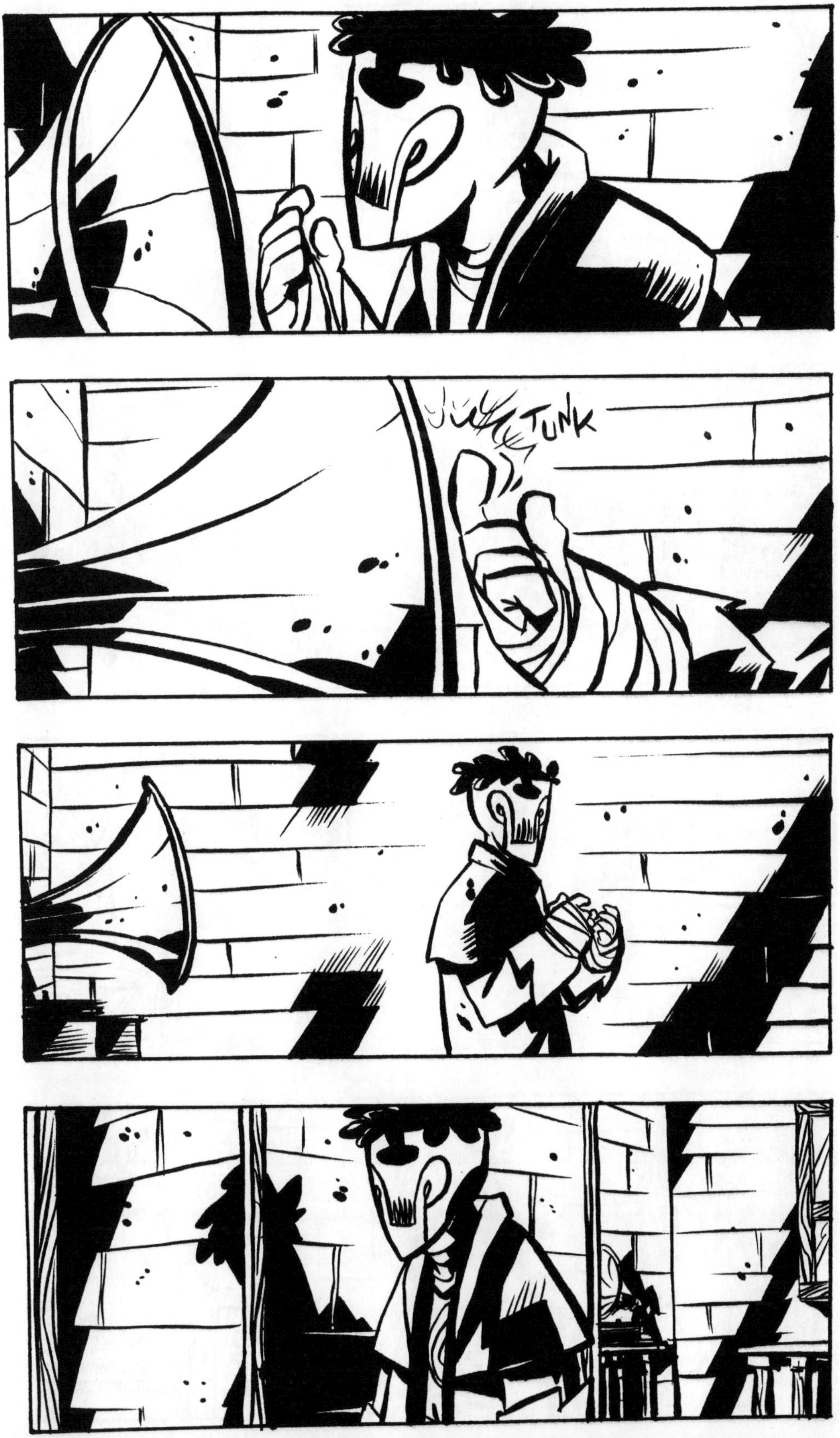
TUNK

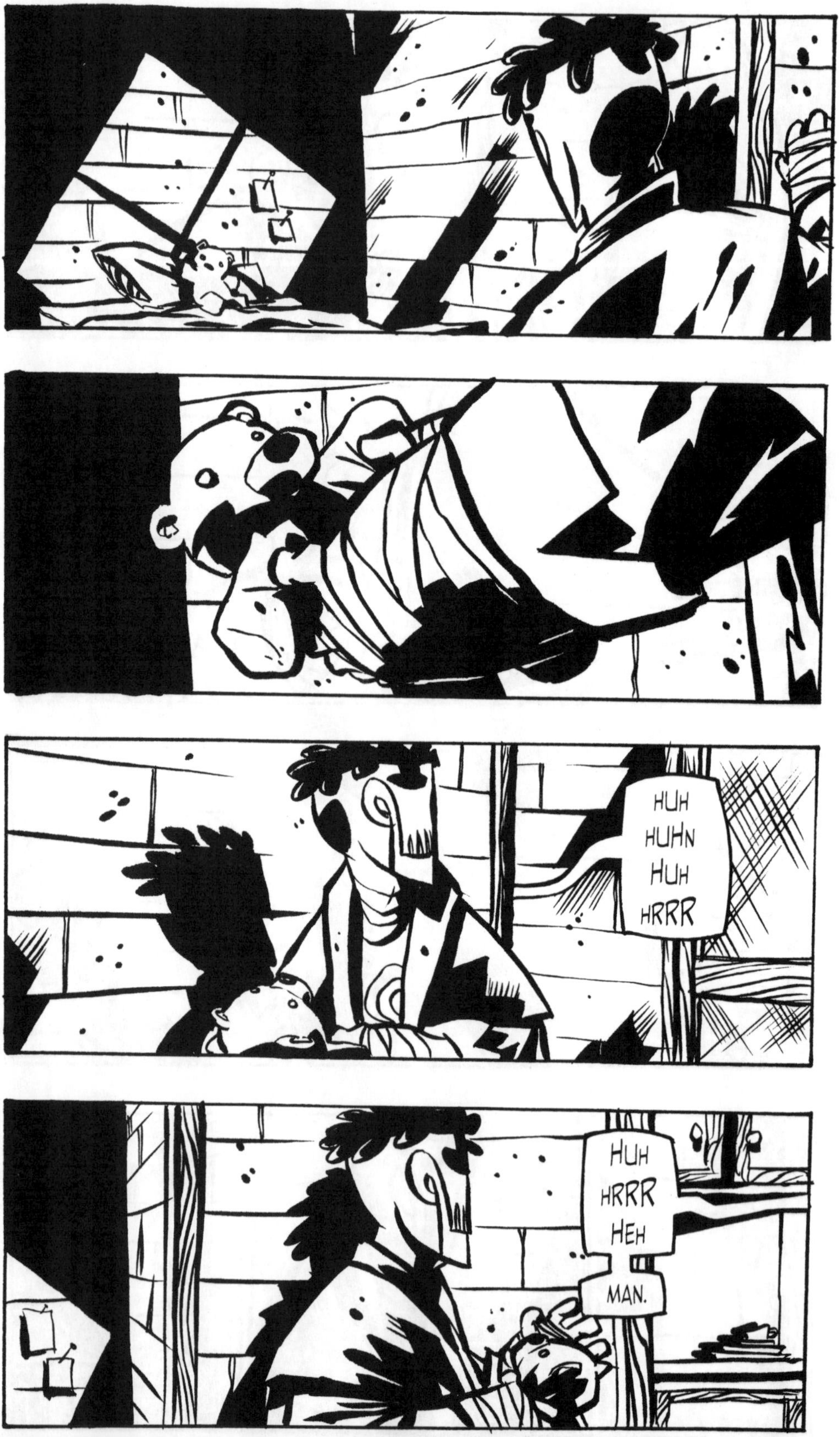
HUH HUHN HUH HRRR
HUH HRRR HEH MAN.

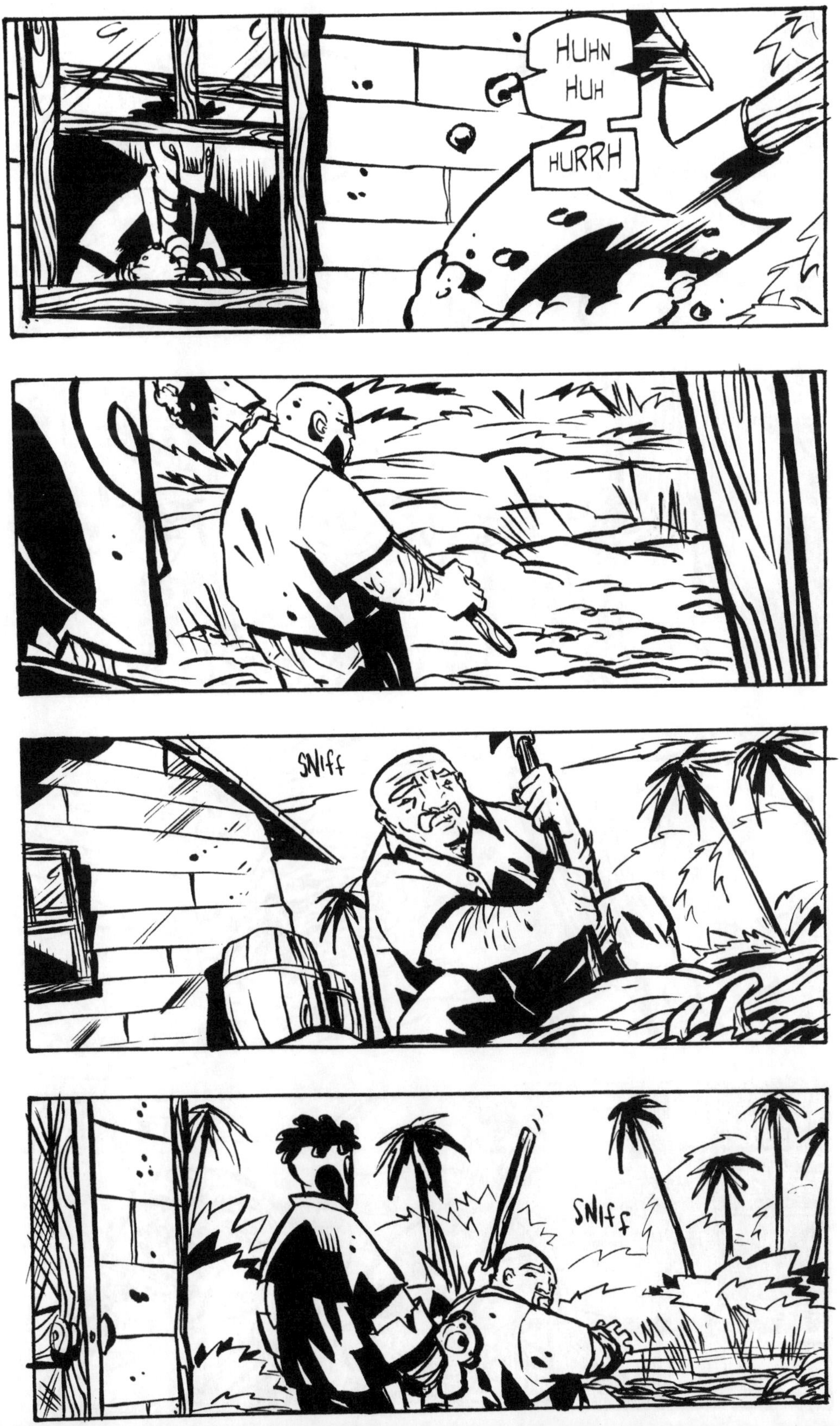
HUHN
HUH
HURRH
SNIff
SNIff

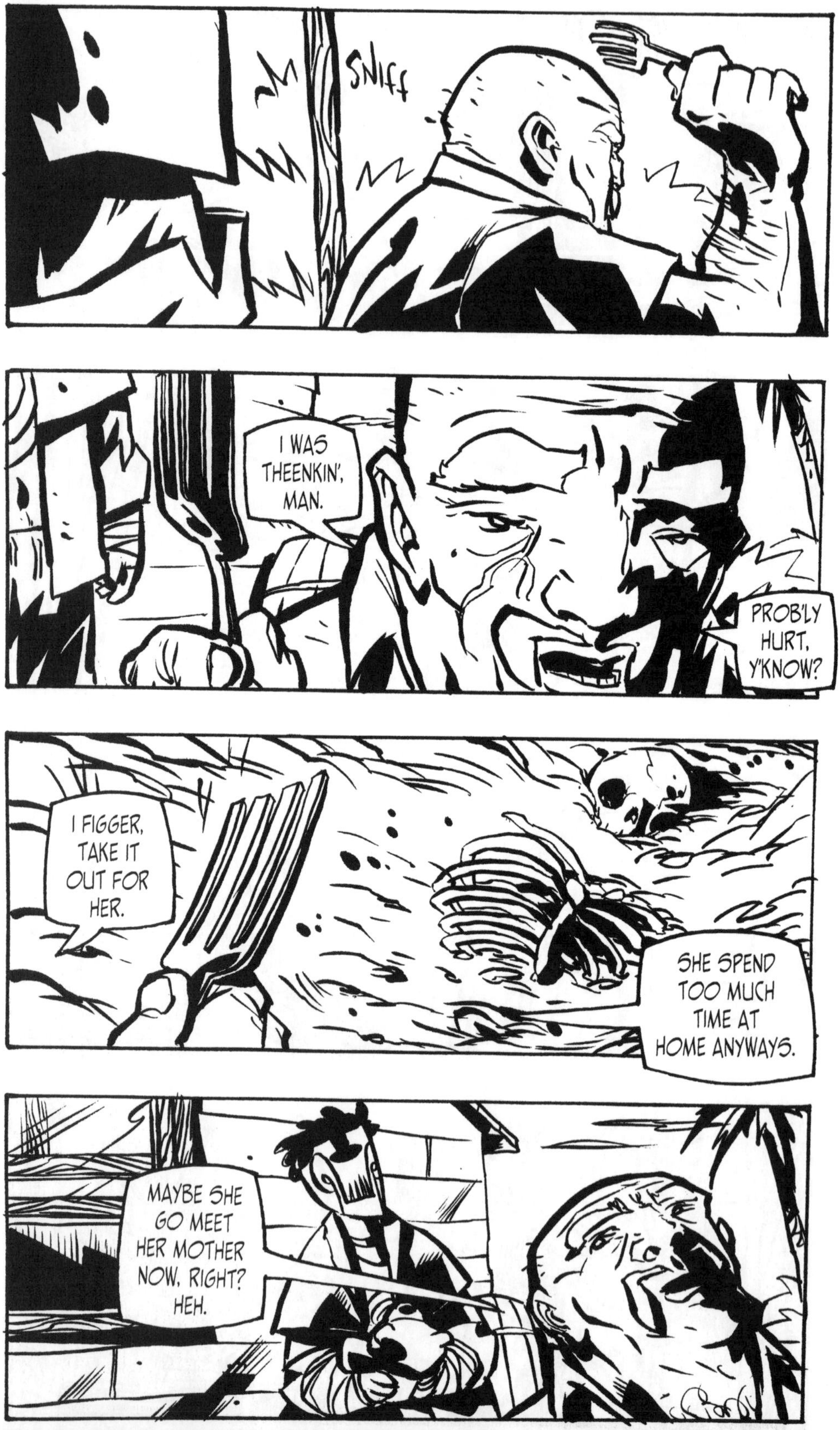
SNIFF
I WAS THEENKIN', MAN.
PROB'LY HURT, Y'KNOW?
I FIGGER, TAKE IT OUT FOR HER.
SHE SPEND TOO MUCH TIME AT HOME ANYWAYS.
MAYBE SHE GO MEET HER MOTHER NOW, RIGHT? HEH.

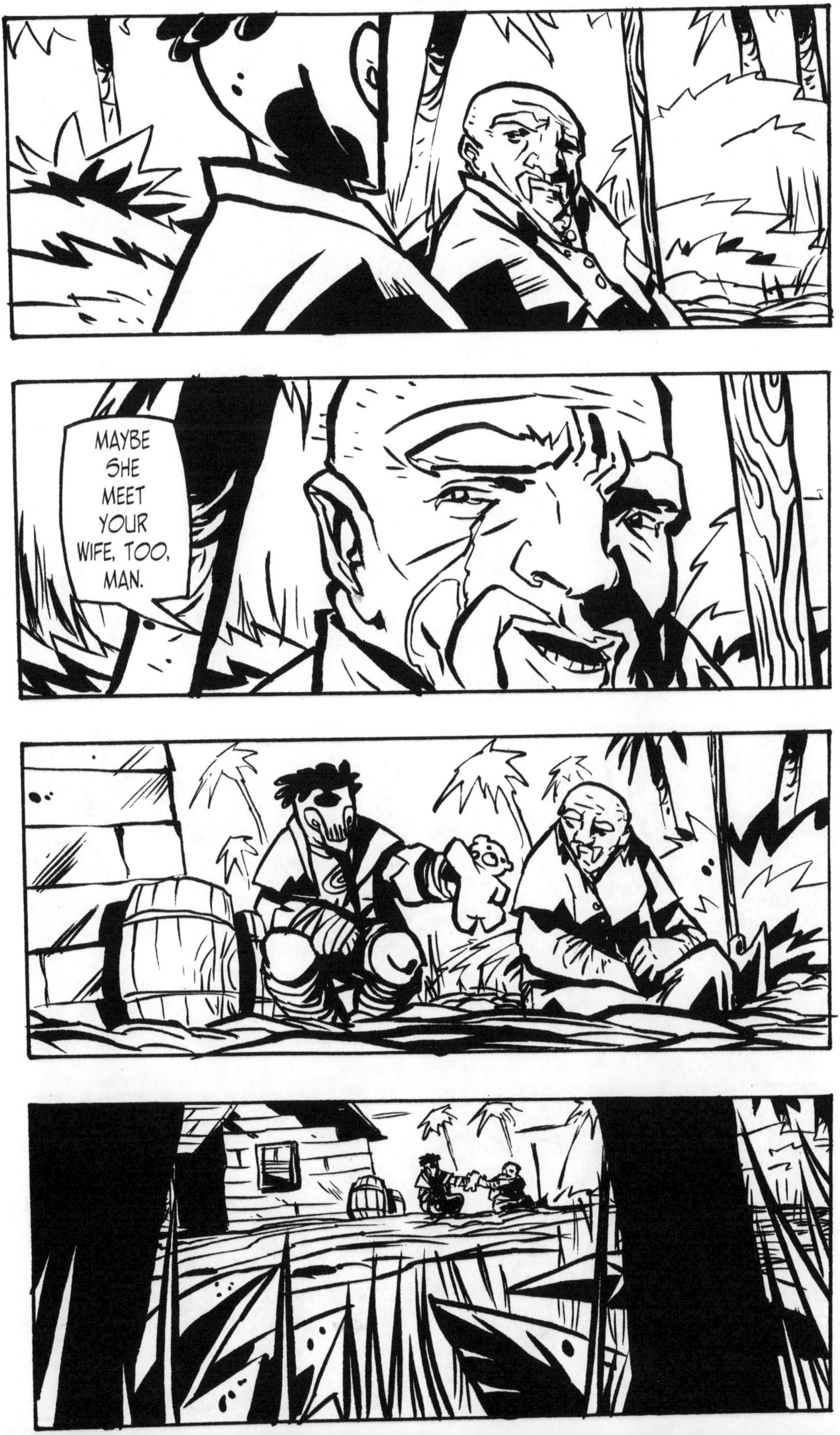
MAYBE SHE MEET YOUR WIFE, TOO, MAN.

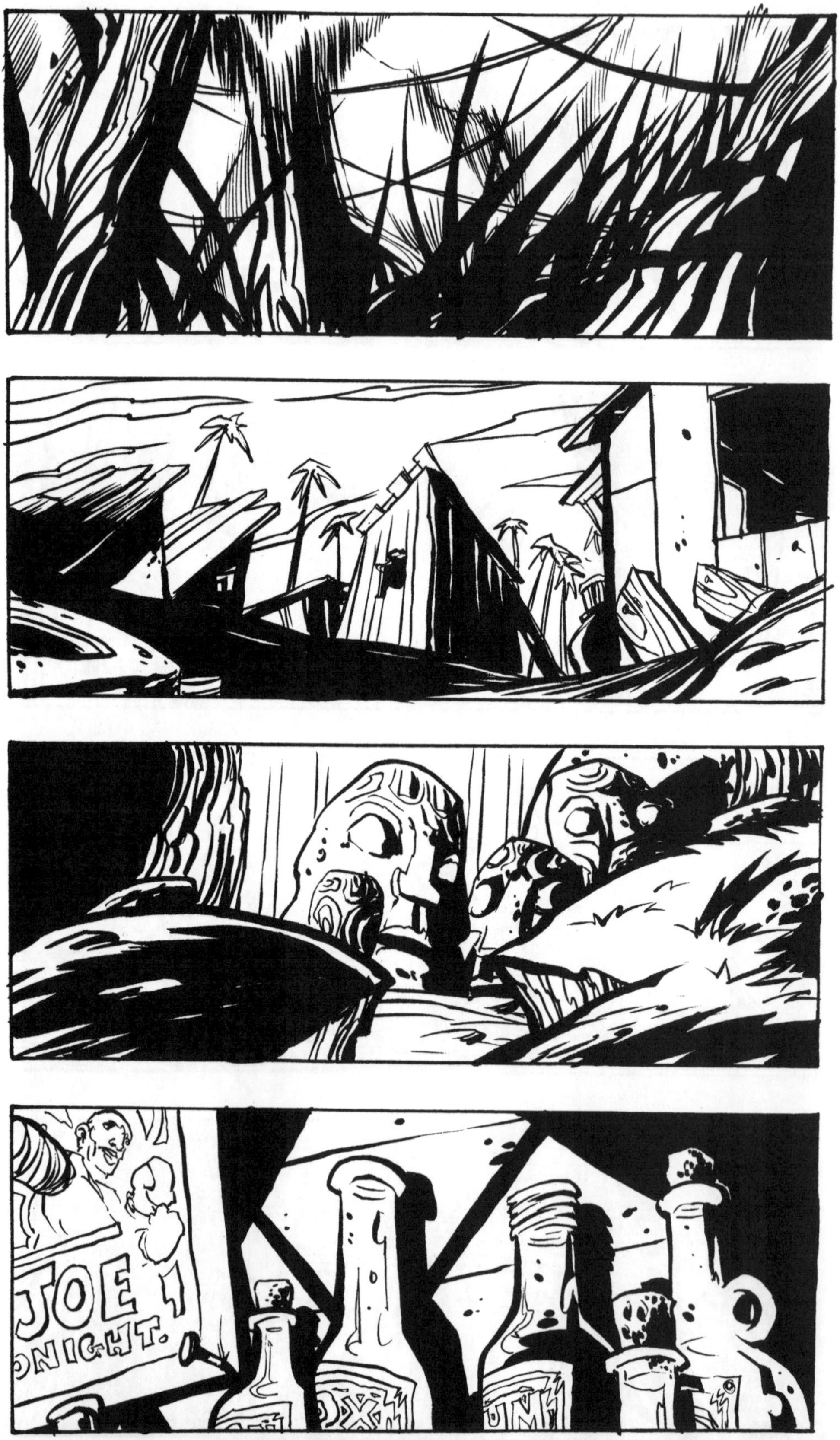
JOE
ONIGHT.

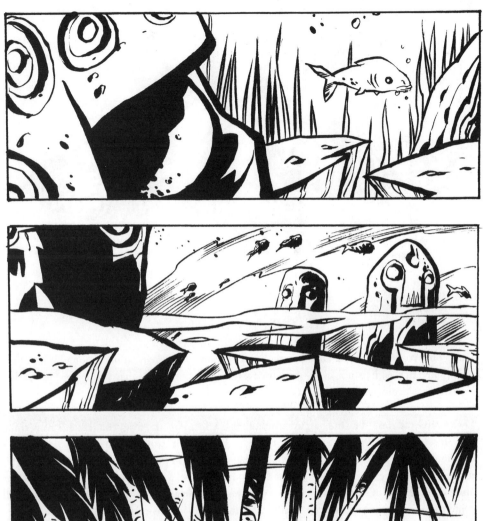

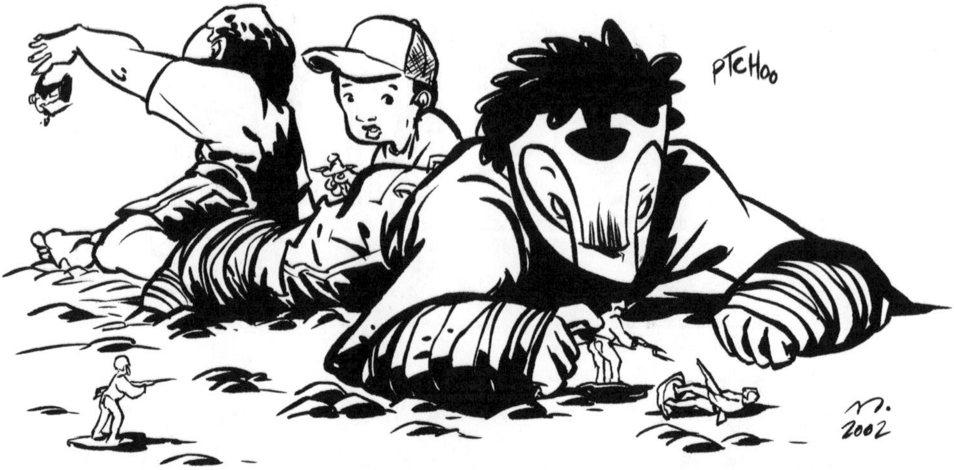
PTCHOO
M.
2002

# SOURCES

## GOD, MYTH, MAN?

Joe's going to find out what he is eventually. The journey's more than likely going to be a long one. The trick is, he's not even really interested. It's something that will evolve as another key theme is explored throughout the *Ancient Joe* mythos: Love.

Love's rarely addressed in the bastard storytelling art form of American comics. It's something that *Ancient Joe*, as a book, can't avoid, though. It's part of exploring the self, which is Joe's ongoing thing. He doesn't know who he was before a certain point in time, and, in effect, can't really know who he is. That's where the fun comes in. Joe, a social and biological enigma, has made connections of friendship and love with various human beings in his world, people we'll come to know — and know more about. It's these connections that may be the true mystery and will definitely prove to be the true journey, as Joe comes to find that, though not quite human, he may prove to be more human than many people he meets. He may prove to be *humanity*.

Joe's world seems a foreign place to him, and he's seemingly a foreigner exploring it … or is he? I wanted to set up a world that we, the audience, can believe in. The fantastic elements are drawn from cultural myths, legends, and folktales, all grounded in our world history. Joe comes from these storytelling devices, and, in essence, is more a part of our world than most of the modern, manmade things and mass media-influenced people he'll come across. It's important to me to take a moment to acknowledge the source material I'm using to build Joe's reality. It's difficult to accurately credit the origins of some of the stories and references, as some are hundreds of years old. The overall groundwork for *Ancient Joe*, it's speculated, is thousands of years old, and currently being heatedly debated by many of today's top scientists: anthropologists, geologists, archeologists, astronomers, and mathematicians. The daring among you may venture into the following books and web sites to gain insight into the world in which I'm setting *Ancient Joe* … a world that may very well be our own. And how cool would it be if it were?

— Scott Morse

# BOOKS and LITERATURE

*Funk and Wagnalls Standard Dictionary of Folklore, Mythology, and Legend*, edited by Maria Leach and Jerome Fried, HarperCollins.
ISBN 0-06-250511-4

*Favorite Folktales From Around the World*, edited by Jane Yolen, Pantheon.
ISBN 0-394-75188-4

*Hawaiian Mythology by Martha Meckwith*, University of Hawaii Press.
ISBN 0-8248-0514-3

*Heaven's Mirror: Quest for the Lost Civilization* by Graham Hancock and Santha Faiia,
Three Rivers Press.
ISBN 0-609-80477-4

*Fingerprints of the Gods* by Graham Hancock, Three Rivers Press.
ISBN 0-517-88729-0

*The Sign and the Seal* by Graham Hancock, Simon & Schuster.
ISBN 0-671-86541-2

*The Message of the Sphinx* by Graham Hancock
and Robert Bauval, Three Rivers Press.
ISBN 0-517-88852-1

*Island Ancestors: Oceanic Art from the Masco Collection*
by Allen Wardwell, University of Washington Press.
ISBN 0-295-97329-3

*The Short Stories* by Ernest Hemingway,
Simon and Schuster.
ISBN 0-684-80334-8

# WORLD WIDE WEB

*http://www.teamatlantis.com*

*http://www.bfro.net*

*http://www.giant.net.au/users/rupert/kythera/kythera3.htm*

*http://www.lauralee.com/japan.htm*

*http://www.templeofmu.com*

*http://www.bibleufo.com/ancconstjapan.htm*

*http://www.cryptozoology.com*

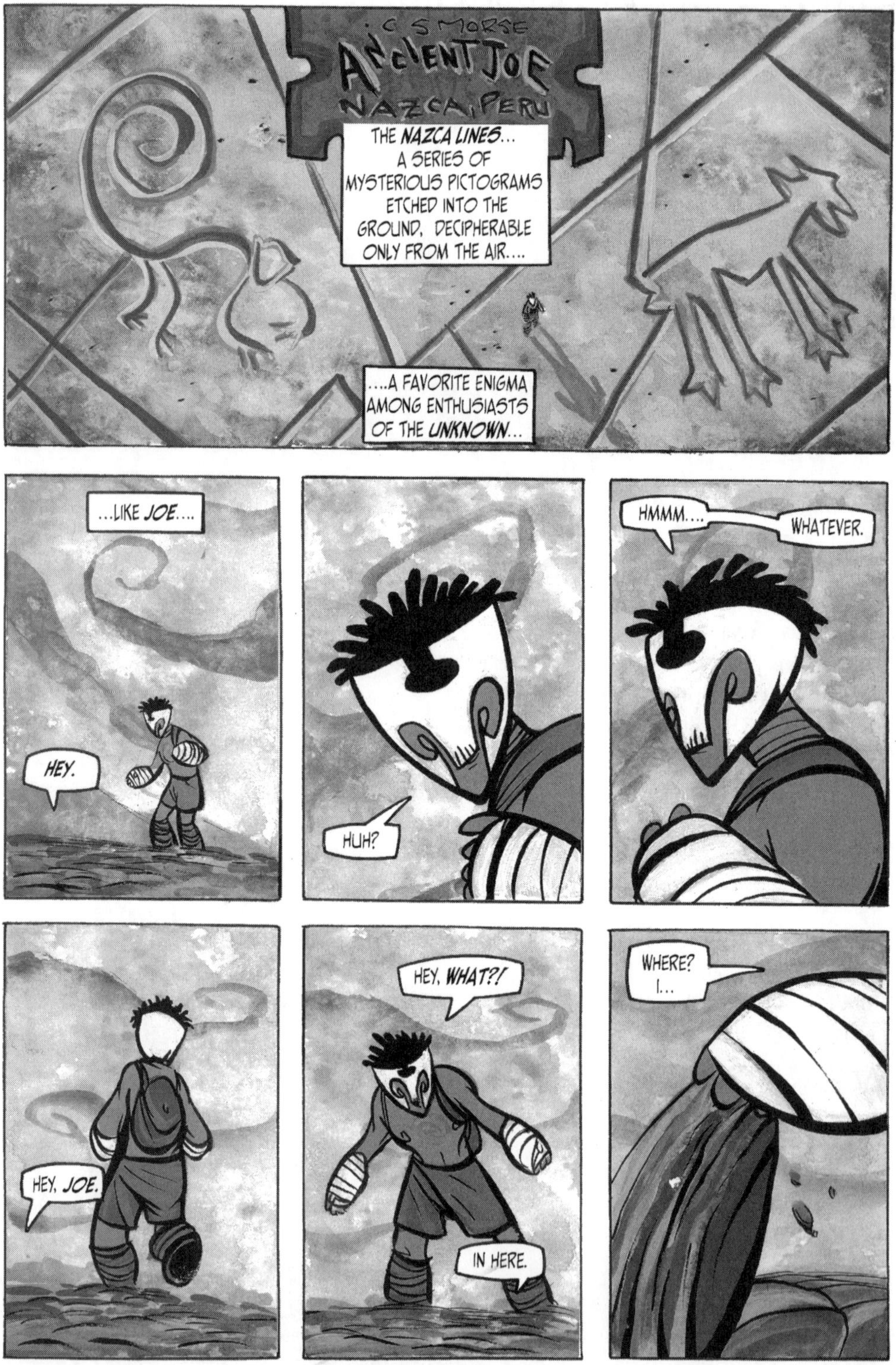
C S MORSE
ANCIENT JOE
NAZCA, PERU
THE **NAZCA LINES**... A SERIES OF MYSTERIOUS PICTOGRAMS ETCHED INTO THE GROUND, DECIPHERABLE ONLY FROM THE AIR....
....A FAVORITE ENIGMA AMONG ENTHUSIASTS OF THE ***UNKNOWN***...
...LIKE ***JOE***....
***HEY.***
HUH?
HMMM....
WHATEVER.
HEY, ***JOE.***
HEY, ***WHAT?!***
IN HERE.
WHERE? I...

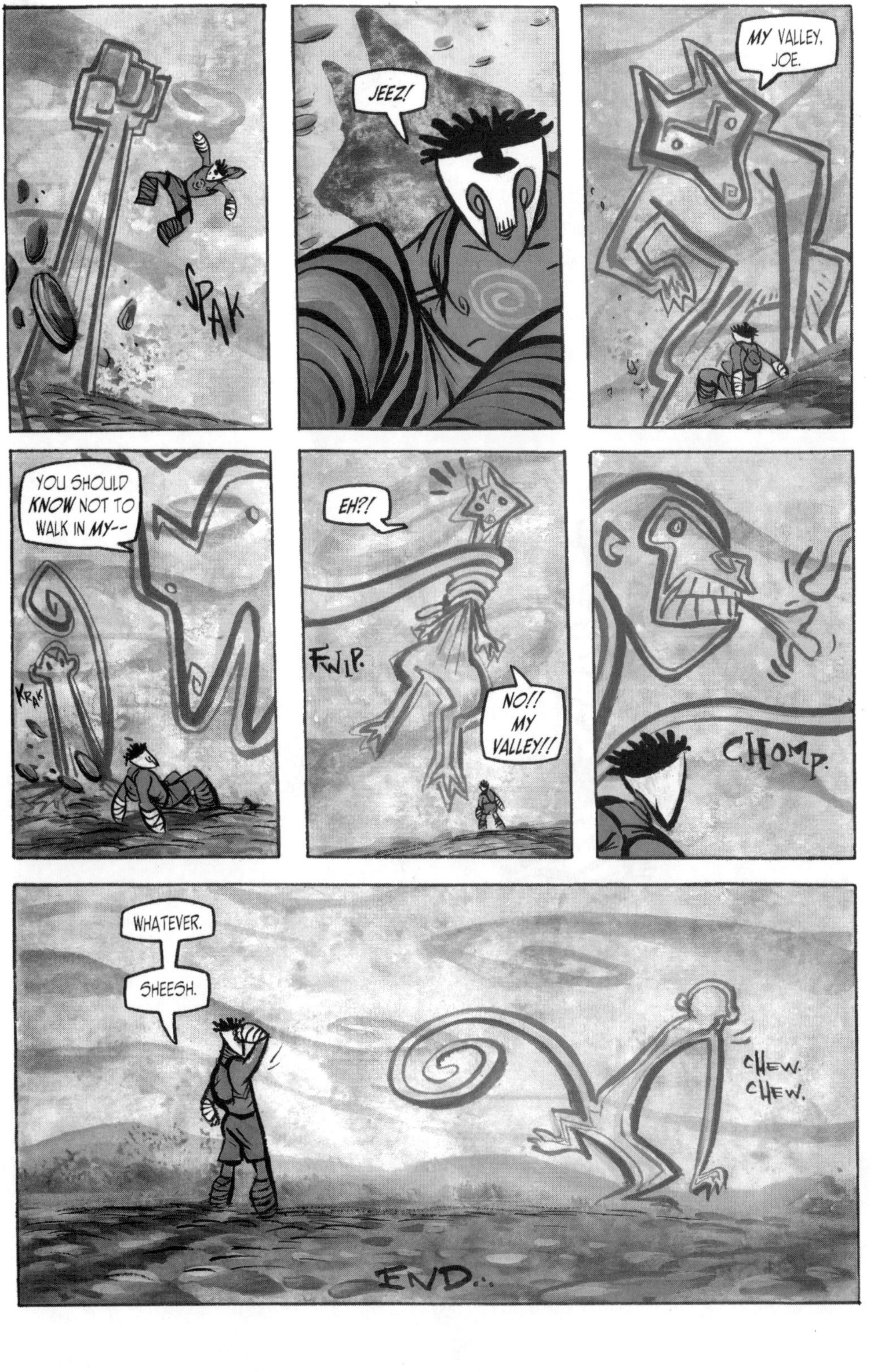
SPAK
JEEZ!
MY VALLEY, JOE.
YOU SHOULD KNOW NOT TO WALK IN MY--
KRAK
EH?!
FWIP.
NO!! MY VALLEY!!
CHOMP.
WHATEVER.
SHEESH.
CHEW. CHEW.
END...